When the Bells Tolled at Midnight

WHEN THE BELLS TOLLED AT MIDNIGHT

J.G. HAYES

When the Bells Tolled at Midnight by J.G. Hayes
© 2016 by J.G. Hayes

Cover design by Gary Ragaglia
Book design by Charles L. Ross

Printed in the United States of America.

First edition

ISBN-13: 978-1507598887
ISBN-10: 1507598882

To my "Nawshant" family:
Mike and Carol, Will and Michelle.

J. G. (Joe) Hayes is also the author of two short story collections (*This Thing Called Courage* and *Now Batting for Boston*); and the novel *A Map of the Harbor Islands*. He lives in the Boston area.

CONTENTS

CHAPTER ONE

A NEW FAMILY MEMBER

One two three four five six seven!

Blond and jug-eared, Sean Sutherland dashed down the stairs on the way to his uncle's dining room, touching every other spindle on the banister as he went. Having missed one—number 4—he froze at the bottom of the stairs and writhed.

"I don't have to go back," he said, wrestling with his old friend, his Obsessive-Compulsive Disorder (OCD). "The world will not end if I don't touch that missed spindle." But then again—he'd been doing this for years, so why start taking chances now? He danced up the few steps and slapped the banister in question.

"I don't really have OCD," he mumbled. "It's just sometimes my mind gets a little funky, and I start thinking about—" But then his attention span, never long, was again subverted.

He leaned into the elegant dining room at the bottom of the stairs. One thin eyebrow lifted in suspicion and he cracked his knuckles contemplatively: there were five places set for dinner, not the usual three. Oh, and it was the fancy Autumn Rose china— plus a fresh bouquet of purple asters and yellow goldenrod, plucked from the garden out back.

I deduce we're having company for dinner, he thought proudly.

"And who's coming *tonight*, Margaret?" Sean called behind him, toward the kitchen.

"Where am I? Why, I'm here, in back of the *Phyllostachys*, misting," housekeeper Margaret Staunton replied vaguely, emerging from the rear of a nine-foot bamboo in the far corner of the elegant dining room. One hand held a spray bottle, the other an open book.

For the large person she was, Margaret had an uncanny ability to turn up where she wasn't expected, as she roamed about the fourteen-room mansion called *Greystones* quieter than a cat.

She stuck a thumb in her book to mark her place. There were few household chores Margaret undertook without her nose in a book. Today's tome, Sean saw, was *The Origins of Tree Worship*. Sean himself could read mystery books, other mystery books, and only mystery books. A so-so student—okay, very so-so—Sean wished it was otherwise, for he had just been thinking upstairs that he'd never become anything, and go through life career-less and purposeless.

"What a strange line!" Margaret muttered. "*Since my childhood, I have had a strong aversion to the scent of wet steel.* Now, who ever heard of such a thing? No one, that's who! No one!"

She looked up at Sean as if wondering whom he might be, emerging as she was from whatever fog her book had cast her in. It was ever thus—

Sean observed further that Margaret was wearing a bright green sweater, with a red and blue plaid skirt. He almost winced. Margaret's vividness, if not her color coordination, knew no bounds when company was coming, Sean knew.

I've deduced we are definitely having company, he thought.

"Hmmm, right? That is a strange line, for sure. But who's the company?" Sean asked again, yawning and stretching after the unplanned nap he had taken upstairs while trying to study calculus. "I wanted us to have Uncle Justin all to ourselves after his trip."

"Why, exactly?" Margaret asked, regarding Sean over her half-glasses and revving back into the here and now as she closed her book. "So you could wear out the poor man's ears again? And him with only the two of them?"

"It's called conversation, Margaret," Sean sighed, plopping down into one of the velvet-upholstered high-back chairs at one end of the long table. "It's a nice ability to have—you should think about taking it up sometime. And you still haven't answered my question."

"And I won't, for that remark!" Margaret snapped, trying not to laugh as she advanced on Sean. "And take your legs off that chair, you bold thing. Ouf, spare the rod and spoil the child! I reminded your uncle of that the day you first came to us. But would he listen? Not him with his tender ways! And now you're blue-molded for want of someone's back of their hand—but that's frowned on behavior from a so-called domestic, these days. Domestic indeed! Why, I know what I'll do—I'll mist the boldness out of you! Yes, I'll mist you, I say!"

With that, the ample splotched forearm was raised, a trigger grip latched itself onto the spray bottle, and Margaret advanced, spraying as she came.

"Stop!" Sean laughed, covering his head with a linen napkin.

Margaret did stop, but not because of Sean's plea—though in truth it was a toss-up as to whom she was more devoted: Sean, or his Great Uncle Justin, botanist, professor at a local college, and Sean's legal guardian. Sean lowered his napkin and watched as Margaret froze, then lifted her elegantly-coiffed white head in the air—like an animal sniffing prey, Sean thought. She half-turned toward the three mullioned windows on the far side of the dining room. It was a full three seconds before Sean heard what Margaret already had—the scrunching of gravel along the driveway outside, signaling the arrival of someone or other.

"Uncle's home!" Sean gasped, bolting from his chair. "Margaret, if there's one word to describe your hearing, it's very large array—like those radar dishes they have in the New Mexican desert."

"How many words is that? It's three words!" Margaret responded, joining Sean in his rush to the front hall. Like every room in the Sutherland household, the entrance hall was stuffed at each window with Uncle Justin's plants, most of them peculiar, strange-smelling, and exotic. "Mind you pay more attention in English class," Margaret recommended. "And math too, so you'll learn how to count. A useful ability to have."

"Ha ha."

Margaret had the additional habit of frequently dispensing information by beginning with a question, a holdover from when she would quiz Sean on his school lessons, numbers, colors, anything at all.

She flung wide the heavy oaken door just as Professor Justin Sutherland was reaching for the knob on the other side.

"Good evening and welcome home, Professor!" she beamed, snatching at his suitcase. "Dinner's ready when you are."

"Uncle Justin!" Sean cried, bounding into his uncle and hugging hard. "What's up? How was the trip?"

"Don't be knocking the man over!" Margaret fussed.

"My my my! What a welcome!" Professor Sutherland laughed, staggering into the hall and pulling at his gray mustache. In truth he was Sean's great uncle, and closer to his seventieth birthday than his sixtieth. But his lean frame and keen eyes told of a man still bristling with vim and vigor—there were few who could keep up with him on his bird walks. "Wonderful to see you both! The trip? Fine, fine—no, actually it was marvelous! There was a most heated discussion about the cloned dualities of the lesser bromeliads, involving a team of biologists from Basel that insisted—"

"He's not with you?" Margaret interrupted.

"Errr, if you mean Professor Singleton? I expect him any moment. If you mean—uhm, if you're referring to—"

"Aye, the other one," Margaret answered tightly.

Sean felt his eyebrows bunch.

"Uhm, well…that is, actually…no! No, he's not with me at the moment. He said…what did he say? Oh yes, he said he would prefer to travel on his own. I expect him within the hour as well."

"Who?" Sean asked. "Who?"

"You haven't told Sean about him, I suppose?" the professor asked hopefully, unbuttoning the tweedy overcoat that Margaret yanked away before he could fully remove it.

"Mercy me, no!" Margaret cried, sweeping away specks of nothing from the coat with her right hand. "And wasn't I telling you before you left that I wouldn't? It's a family matter, Professor. You tell him!"

"Tell me what?" Sean asked. "Who? What?"

"I see," Uncle Justin answered Margaret, temporarily ignoring Sean. "After only twenty-five years with our family, I can understand how you'd feel you weren't quite part of it yet."

"Ouf, musha, don't try that old chestnut on me," Margaret answered. "You know what I mean! It's your duty. And it's been twenty-seven years."

"I knew it seemed longer," the Professor answered dryly.

"What story?" Sean asked, almost bursting. "Who?"

"Sean! Go follow your nose into the library and wait for your uncle," Margaret ordered. "He wants to tell you something important. Sure he'll be with you in a minute, once he gives his hands a washing and spends some time with his, uhm, darlings." (After her many years with the family, Margaret knew the occupants' habits better than they did—including Sean's little OCD ticks, which most of the time she ignored—though often Sean could see that she was bristling to say something.) Even if Uncle Justin had been out for only an hour, he must immediately examine all his plants upon his return, fussing, cooing, and measuring as he did so.

Sean entered the library off the main front hall. He breathed deeply of the academic aroma of leather-bound volumes, old parchment, and—of course—tropical plants against the far wall, where the morning sun flooded in on every fair day. Margaret, schemer that she was, had already lit a crackling blaze in the large fireplace, and turned two oxblood Queen Anne chairs toward the flaming warmth. It was only late September, but the early evening was wet and wild. The gale whipping off the nearby ocean spoke of the storm just beginning to rage outside, and already sheets of rain were lashing against the floor-to-ceiling windows. Sean wiggled his toes in pleasure—he loved a good storm.

Maps fascinated Sean, and he gazed now at some of the older ones in his uncle's collection, framed and hanging on the paneled library walls. Here in pride of place over the fireplace mantel was the fifth or, some historians said, fourth map ever made of New England, some 450 years ago; beside it was an even older map of Ancient Scotland; and beside that was the first map ever drawn of their little seaside town of Nawshant, on Massachusetts' North Shore.

As a boy, Sean, trying to be helpful and accurate, had taken down this last map with the assistance of a built-in ladder on the other side of the room, and had been just about to 'update' it with a red felt-tip pen, drawing in what the first cartographers had failed to notice: the beaches, Sea-Side Pizza, and Sean's elementary school. Margaret in her omniscience had stopped him at the last moment, explaining that Sean would have ruined a thing that was worth more than the whole house.

But this particular map was still Sean's favorite, and he mentally connected the dots on it now as he traced in his mind some of his and his uncle's favorite walks along the rocky, cliff-girt shore.

"Ah! There you are, my boy!" he heard behind him. This was always his uncle's remark when he was late for anything, as if Uncle Justin had been searching all over the house for Sean. Sean stole a quick glance at his phone and saw that fifteen minutes had elapsed since he'd first come in here. Sean figured Uncle Justin and Margaret had been comparing notes in the kitchen as to how to tell him…whatever it was his uncle was now about to tell him.

"Uncle," Sean smiled, sitting down at the older man's invitation in front of the fire.

"Ahem. Yes, that's right, let's have a little— how…how very lovely to see you, dear boy! Well, I should come right to the point, I suppose," Uncle Justin began, sitting in the chair next to Sean and fussing with his shirt collar as he crossed his legs. "Errr…but first…anything newish in your world?"

"Not much really," Sean shrugged. There was actually, but he wasn't sure he would tell his uncle. Not just yet anyway.

"Well, for example….did you…errr…win your lacrossing game Saturday? It was last Saturday, I believe?"

"Yeah we did—like I told you on the phone Saturday night. We crushed them."

"Oh yes—yes of course!" his uncle chuckled, rubbing his hands together. "I remember now! Well! I—I suppose I should tell you the big news then!"

"That would be nice," Sean said, bouncing his right knee. He'd decided that if he bounced his right knee, Uncle Justin's news would be good; the left knee, not so much—

"Well, you know…ahem! You know when you came to us, after your dear parents died—passed, passed away, passed on—I was already fifty-something then. I thought, good gracious me, I don't know the first thing about raising a biped! Errr, a child, I mean. Because you see, Sean, I had realized one day before all this—I was in the middle of a lecture, and a couple happened to walk by my classroom window just then and it hit me—'My goodness!' I remember saying to myself, 'I've totally forgotten to marry!'"

Uncle Justin tittered at his joke and straightened out his tie.

"Course I've been so buried in my work, do you see. And in a way I've had a love affair with all things that grow upon the earth. Although there was—" here Uncle Justin shuttered his eyes and sighed—"Doctor M. Louisa Peterson. Ah! I must confess I felt…quite a stirring in my breast whenever we lectured together. We even had tea, once—only once, alas—at the Raspberry Scone? Charming little cafe in Harvard Square. It was there that I hinted at my ardor for her. But she told me her heart was pledged to another."

"Oh, that's a bummer, Uncle. I'm sorry." Not a month went by without Uncle Justin referring to this sad incident of his past. But Sean always pretended he'd never heard the story before.

"Oh yes, dear boy, the only time I really felt—she was passionately in love with *Danaus plexippus*—that's the monarch butterfly, you know. Even had it as a wallpaper in her bedroom, said someone who was there. Oh, a female colleague, I hasten to add, ahem! She was an entomologist—someone who studies insects. Died when a swarm of Africanized bees had at her in the Amazon—you'd know them better by the unnecessary and somewhat sensationalistic name *killer bees*, dear boy. Dear me, I suppose I'll never get over it. But at least it forever forestalled my agony over *what to call her*, should we become more intimate: *M*? *M. Louisa*? Neither struck me as especially endearing. But at any rate...uhm, where were we?"

"When I first came to you—"

"Oh yes! Thank you, Sean. When you were first came to us, I wondered how we wouldn't make a mess of raising you. 'Get out of that,' Margaret told me. 'He's your family. All he needs is love and acceptance.' And she was right, I suppose, and it seems after all you're turning out quite splendidly, in spite of our best efforts otherwise."

Uncle Justin tittered again.

"You're the only father I've ever known, Uncle," Sean answered. "I couldn't ask for a better one. And Margaret's been like a mother."

"Really? You're so kind, dear boy," his uncle answered, rummaging for a handkerchief. He took off his wire-rimmed glasses and blew his nose. "But at any rate, Sean—well, the thing is—ahem!—have I ever mentioned the—Sutherlands of Cincinnati to you? I have, *I'm sure*."

Something about the way Uncle Justin said this made Sean feel Uncle Justin wasn't sure at all…

"Oh, I don't think so." Sean scratched his chin, checking the progress of his two-day-old goatee—which only one other person had noticed so far. "They sound like a traveling trapeze act or something."

"Ha ha ha!" Uncle Justin erupted, laughing a bit too loudly. Sean knew his uncle was stalling. "It was your brilliant mother had that keen sense of humor! That's where you get it, I'm sure of it!"

"Anyway," Sean said, extending his legs to the warming fire.

"Yes, *anyway*, right! Well, I thought I had mentioned them in passing but…well, perhaps not. At any rate—they're second cousins, twice removed on your father's side. Or third cousins, once removed from—good gracious I can't remember now. I'm much better discussing the familial connections of plants than I am of bipeds—errr, people. But regardless, we all had the same great-grandfather. I think."

"So you're as related to them as you are to me?" Sean asked.

"Exactly. Uhm, that is, at least I believe so. *Possibly*."

"But you've never mentioned them before?"

"Well, I…you see I thought I had. And we were never very close with them," Uncle Justin answered evasively, staring off at one of his plants in the corner. "And they being of course so very far away—"

"Cincinnati? And you flew down to Chile last week for that conference at the drop of a hat?"

"And there was…well, to tell the truth, there was some…*bother* over whether you'd go to them, or to me, after your dear parents died," Uncle Justin went on, ignoring Sean's comment. "Passed. Passed on."

"A family feud!" Sean gushed, sitting up straight in the chair. "Over *moi*! How cool is that? I was fought over!"

"And why shouldn't you be?" Uncle Justin asked. "But, dear boy, please! Let me offer the opinion that family feuds aren't pretty affairs. They are always to be avoided, whenever possible. Though I would hardly call what transpired a feud. It was more like…the coming of a slow, glacial epoch."

"I didn't even know we had other family."

"Well…surprise! But uhm…well, the thing is…actually—"

There was a strident knock on the library's double oak doors. Not waiting for answer of course, Margaret popped her snowy head into the room. "And did you tell him yet, Professor?" she demanded.

"Uhm, we were just getting to it," Uncle Justin answered, folding his hands on his lap. "That is…weren't we, Sean?"

"Well for heaven sakes, don't make a meal out of it," Margaret scolded. She turned to Sean. "Has he been going on about the one that was destroyed entirely by the killer bees?"

"Uhm…just a little," Sean chuckled.

"Well, when will your company be here? Soon, Professor! Very soon indeed! So please hurry it up—or you'll come to grief!" The latter expression was one of Margaret's favorites. Sean used to think as a boy that "Grief" was an actual place on the map where bad little children were taken—like Grief, Missouri or something.

"Yes yes Margaret, of course, thank you. Run along now and…finish the chapter you're reading or something."

"Humph," Margaret snorted, shutting the door in what could have almost been called a slam. Then she reopened it halfway to murmur, "Since my childhood, I have had a strong aversion to the smell of wet steel." Then she vanished once again behind the closing door.

Uncle Justin turned a quizzical face to Sean.

"A line from her book, I presume?" he asked.

"Exactly."

"How bizarre! Well, anyway dear boy—to come to the point." Uncle Justin took off his glasses and polished them with the end of his argyle sweater vest. "These Sutherlands of Cincinnati had a son, a boy about your own age. Miles? Kyle? Something. Dear me, I should remember, because I met the young man just this morning. Anyway! Apparently his was a somewhat…uhm…disciplined family, orderly if you catch my drift, and the young man has been attending a military academy in Georgia. Which all the males on his mother's side have gone to—going back almost to Thermopylae, if one understood her correctly. At any rate, the young man's father passed on three years ago, and his mother—well, we learned last month that she succumbed to a lengthy illness just at summer's end. We—Margaret and I, I mean—were rather shocked to learn two weeks ago that I had been named guardian of the young man—just as I was made guardian of you when your dear parents passed—and since he has no other relations, well, we're…going to make him part of our family. The thing is, Sean, he's…errr…ahem! Well the thing is, as I say, he's…well, I've adopted him! He's coming to live with us!"

"He is? My God, when?"

"Uhm…." Uncle Justin cleared his throat and snuck a peek at his watch. "Any moment now, actually."

For the taking of a breath, Sean was too stunned to speak. Then, "Yes!" he shouted, leaping up from his chair and pumping his fist. "A cousin—a cousin my age! And he's going to be living here? With us? That is too cool! Wait until I tell—oh my God, I always wanted a brother and—can he stay in my room? I've got the two beds and all and—"

"Oh, well, I'm sure that will be fine! Errr, as long as, don't you know, as long as he agrees to. We'll have to humor him for a bit and give him his own way in things—just until he settles in. He's not a puppy, if you understand me. But uhm…well, he may…he may be a little reticent at first, Sean—and if so you mustn't take it personally. He's coming to a houseful of strangers after all, and—"

"Reticent?"

Uncle Justin smiled as he tossed his head behind him. Off to the left of the fireplace was a heavy oaken stand, on top of which rested what must have been the largest book in the world: some kind of completely unabridged dictionary, with thin, crisp, stiff pages as large as small table-cloths. Whenever Sean made the mistake of asking what a word meant, Uncle Justin refused to tell him, referring him to the dictionary instead so he could learn it himself. It was one of only several points upon which Uncle Justin was inflexible. In fact almost every morning at the breakfast table, Uncle Justin tried to stump Sean with what he called the word of the day, a word Sean tried to guess the meaning of. Margaret was disqualified from participating, her continuous reading giving her an invincible advantage.

Sean groaned, got up, and looked up the word in question.

"You'll thank me the day of your SATs, dear boy!" Uncle Justin said, just as the library's massive grandfather clocked tolled the hour of six. "But above and beyond such unromantic, utilitarian considerations, words are power, wisdom, and magic."

Sean didn't like to remind Uncle Justin that he had already taken his SATs—with so-so results. "*Reticent*: to keep one's thoughts and words to oneself," Sean read aloud, before retaking his seat.

"Precisely," Uncle Justin concurred.

"Wait a minute," Sean asked, more seriously. "Is this Kyle or Miles or whatever his name is—is he the one you were talking about when you told Margaret he wanted to travel alone?"

"Uhm, why, yes! *Bless* your memory, dear boy!" Uncle Justin answered, shifting uncomfortably in his seat. "I did in fact stop in Georgia—or was it South Carolina?—this morning on the way home from Chile, to gather him up for the trip home. But he…well, he said that he preferred to travel—not exactly without me, you understand, but…alone. Some people do, you know. And uhm…well, to come right to the point, you should know that he isn't very happy to have been taken out of his current school and hauled all the way up here. And then of course his grief on top of it all. Besides which, the teen years can be so…volatile anyway, to which I'm sure you can attest."

Sean opened his mouth to ask what *volatile* might mean, then thought better of it—it was cozy here by the fire, and he was tired after lacrosse practice today.

"Seems ungrateful to me," Sean answered. He was still excited about a cousin he didn't even know he had coming to live with them, but anyone who was rude or ungrateful to his uncle—or Margaret for that matter—provoked Sean's disdain; but also his sympathy, for deep down he was really a compassionate soul.

"But really," Uncle Justin went on, "if I'm to be his guardian, as his late parents have entrusted me to be, I couldn't possibly do my job to satisfaction with him all the way down there. So, he's got to come up here to Nawshant, and naturally he's unhappy about it, leaving the only world he knows. Anyone would be. So we'll be extra considerate of him I'm sure, all of us, until he fits right in and becomes one of the family—eh, Sean?"

That sounded better. Sean smiled and nodded. At this same instant the front doorbell rang. Sean still had a million questions to ask about his cousin, but these he forgot as he bolted from his chair and galloped to the front door.

But Margaret, naturally, got there first. Somehow she always did, even if she was up on a ladder outside scrubbing windows, or pounding potatoes red faced in the kitchen, her voice raised in what she called song. The booming voice of the new guest told Sean it wasn't his 'new' cousin at all, but Professor Mortimer Singleton, lifelong friend of Uncle Justin and a fellow lover of Botany. While Uncle Justin was spare and lean, Professor Singleton was not; in fact, Sean had one time overheard Margaret muttering to herself out in the kitchen, after Professor Singleton's third helping of something or other, *What's the poor man built like? Why, a Kennedy half-dollar, that's what! Or a coin dollar. Like that poor Sacajawea woman! I say poor because can you imagine picking up after a passel of men over half a continent?* But on the other hand, Margaret took keen delight in Professor Singleton's vast appetite—anyone's appetite, really. In her book one couldn't eat enough of the various breads, special concoctions, and sizzling entrées she prepared so painstakingly, and she would often embellish her dishes with unusual phraseology, such as, "Would you like some more of this precisely sliced bread?" Sean wondered who could resist trying precisely sliced bread, if only for the novelty of the thing.

The two professors met in the hall and instantly fell into "shop talk," Uncle Justin beginning a lengthy account of the proceedings of the International Union of Concerned Botanists, a group formed several years earlier to raise the alarm about global warming. This year their annual conference had been in Chile, and Uncle Justin had had the opportunity to see some rare alpine plants and birds on a mountainous trek he took the last day of his trip—before stopping off in Georgia (*not* South Carolina) to try to bring Sean's cousin home.

"Now now, into the Snuggery with yez until dinner is served," Margaret commanded, herding everyone into the front parlor by opening wide her apron and kind of bluff-stampeding people into the room. It was nicknamed the Snuggery for its deeply-cushioned low sofas, subdued lighting, and vast fireplace. But really they were waiting for Sean's cousin to arrive.

"Are you sure he'll be after making it here for dinner?" Margaret muttered to Uncle Justin, as Professor Singleton spoke to Sean about the prospects of a lacrosse championship this year for Nawshant High—prospects which were no worse than usual.

"His flight landed in Boston an hour ago, and he has enough money for a taxi from the airport," Uncle Justin murmured back, glancing at his watch. "And he's got the address and our phone numbers, and he's to call if he runs into any trouble. Let's not be discourteous his first night here. Let's wait for him. I said we would."

"Well, we can't wait until we perish of the hunger, Professor," Margaret protested.

"We'll give him another hour," Uncle Justin answered. Margaret swept off and did things in the dining room before re-joining the others in the Snuggery. Uncle Justin regaled the group with an account of his trip, and of the rare plants he had seen. Sean enjoyed most his uncle's description of waking up at 20,000 feet elevation in the middle of the night—the skies had cleared, his uncle said, and he had wept at the stars—their brilliance, their proximity, their shimmer.

"I tell you, they seemed to overlap," Uncle Justin said. "Really, it's no wonder the belief systems of ancient cultures are so rich, so deep—and were and are believed in with such joyous enthusiasm. The world they knew was one of breathtaking wonder—like a strange flower unfurling, do you see, a different one every day. I say, if there are no atheists in fox-holes, there may be none atop mountains at night under clear skies."

"That's a rather broad idea, Justin," Professor Singleton remarked. He opened his mouth to say more, but as he did the front bell chimed again. Sean had positioned himself close to the entrance to the Snuggery to beat Margaret to the door.

But as he yanked open the door a moment later, the gusting wind seemed to push into the foyer a rather wide but not very tall woman of uncertain age. She was wearing a dress the color of very bright grass, a shining pink rain-slicker, and high, formidable platinum blonde hair that seemed impervious to the wind and lashing rain. In fact, Sean's odd first thought was that someone could chuck a stone at that hair, and the stone would come to grief.

The woman immediately nailed her full face into what Sean thought was an almost carnivorous, eye-vanishing smile. Then she hissed in a raspy voice, "Hi, hon! Dottie LaFrance here of Manchuso-LaFrance-and-O'Shaughnessy Realty! What's your budget?"

"What's our what?" Margaret demanded, striding through to the fore. "Who the divil are you?"

"Ah, the *Lady* of the Home! What's your budget? Dottie LaFrance here, and lemme tell you something, honey—most people have *no idea* what their homes can fetch in today's *white hot* real estate market!" the woman answered, advancing further into the hall and twirling her wet umbrella so rapidly that Sean and Margaret immediately found themselves splotched.

"Ouf! Why, you…!" Margaret cried, but before she could finish, Dottie shoved business cards at them—her picture on the cards showing the exact smiling expression that hadn't changed yet—and exclaimed,

"Look at those mullined windows! What a *classy* touch!" Advancing like a cold front, Sean thought, she broke through Sean and Margaret and proceeded directly into the Snuggery.

"Oh, hello!" Uncle Justin smiled, half-rising from the sofa. "Justin Sutherland here! And this is my dear friend and colleague Professor Mortimer Singleton. How do you do, madam?"

"Hi, Dottie LaFrance! What's your budget?" Dottie answered, snatching at a piece of hard candy from a dish on one of the end tables before pushing cards on both professors.

"I beg your pardon, my…budget, did you say?"

"We thought you were the prodigal son coming home!" Professor Singleton laughed, squinting as he tried to read Dottie's card. "A remarkable likeness," he added, looking back at Dottie.

"She's a door-to-door telemarketer, and I'd say it's high time for her to be hung up on!" Margaret interjected, bustling into the room.

But Dottie wasn't paying attention, busy as she was across the room tapping and fingering the "mullined" windows.

"Cripes, these are *real glass!*" she cried, half-turning as she rapped with meaty hands at the thick leaded panes. "I was gonna say you could get Four for this old place—but now I'm thinking Four-seven-five—maybe Five, the market's hot and, did'ja know, *the luxury market's back! It is!* Septic, or town sewer? How's your roof?"

"I say," Uncle Justin wondered aloud, retaking his seat and turning a bemused smile to Professor Singleton. "Have you any notion what she's talking about? Or whom this woman might be?"

"We're helping people in Nawshant this evening realize their American dreams by—wait for it, y'awl!—*UPGRADING!!!!!*" Dottie gushed in reply, saying the word the way Uncle Justin said *Science* and Margaret intoned *Our Lady of Sorrows*. "Oh, where's this door go to? My *GOD*, look at all this *closet space*! How many full baths you got in the place? Speaking of which, I kinda gotta use one of 'em soon haha if you don't mind too much! Any recent upgrades? What'd you say about the roof again, I missed that? Now where's the kitchen, through these doors right here?"

With that, Dottie pushed through the swinging doors leading from the Snuggery into the dining room.

"Geez Louise, a *banqueting hall!*" they heard next, echo-like, which was followed by knuckles rapping on wood, and then the surprising sounds of what seemed to be the sideboard's drawers being opened.

Instinctively everyone in the Snuggery turned to Margaret, for this was her own inviolate space Dottie was making merry with. Next the woman would surely find THE KITCHEN, Margaret's Holy of Holies. Margaret's face, Sean noticed, was an unpleasant red, and her mouth an enlarged *O*. Sean knew from experience this meant trouble for someone.

"Oh no you don't!" Margaret hissed, crossing the room at a marching pace and entering the dining room herself as she muttered, "What will I do if I find you rummaging through my things? Why, I'll break your back for you, that's what I'll do..." Of course everyone knew Margaret's bark was worse than her bite—but still, them's were fighting words—

"Oh dear," Uncle Justin commented several moments later, putting one finger to his lip, as the sounds of raised voices, ruckus, and brouhaha quickly ensued, which spread from the dining room to the kitchen. Something fell to the ground and shattered—everyone jumped—and then they heard the prodigious slamming of the back kitchen door.

"I believe Elvis has left the building," Sean observed.

Professor Singleton folded his hands across his wide stomach and leaned back into the sofa. "A most instructive interlude, Justin! A remarkable combination of aggressiveness, determination, and the insensitivity that comes with the cognitive dissonance that seems so common these days. Sadly fascinating!"

"Well I—" Uncle Justin began.

"An astonishingly humanoid *Ficus citrifolia*, one could almost say, by which I mean of course the strangler fig," Professor Singleton went on. "I wonder what degree of success she enjoys in her ventures." But further discussion was interrupted by a second rapping upon the snuggery's mullioned windows—this time from the other side of the glass. Turning, they saw Dottie's wet face—and still unblemished hair—pressed against the windowpanes, storm or no.

"Are these weedy plots out here buildable lots?" she shouted above the howling wind, once she had everyone's attention.

"I'll be calling out the guard in a minute!" Margaret threatened, bustling back into the room and making "shooing" gestures at Dottie, before she yanked the drapes across the windows. She breathlessly resumed her seat on the sofa, straightening out imaginary wrinkles on her plaid skirt and fussing with her hair.

"Did you ever see or hear tell of such a botheration?" Margaret huffed. "She's worse than Nellie Quinn on Market Day! Weedy plots, indeed!" Margaret was as proud of her vegetable, herb, and flower gardens outside the back of Greystones as she was of her immaculate kitchen floor—which was saying something.

"A remarkable specimen!" Professor Singleton repeated. "I only wish Professor Eileen Rogers—you know her, Justin, from Psychology—were here to have witnessed it. I wonder if this woman's available for study in the class room."

"Available, is it!" Margaret scoffed. "I'd say that was the understatement of the century, Professor! And her with that…seagull voice! But available or not, I agreed we'd wait an hour for the other one, *and that hour's up!* Dinner is served, gentlemen—*now.*" The silent consensus of the others in the room seemed to indicate that it would be best, under current circumstances, to comply. Everyone rose and shuffled off to the dining room—besides which of course they were famished.

"Wonderful!" Professor Singleton said, as he made his way into the dining room. He closed his eyes and breathed deeply of the steaming dishes waiting on the table. "I've no idea what we're having—oo, what's *that?*—but I can already discern that you've outdone yourself again, Margaret! Oh by the way, I have a remarkable tale to relate, at table."

Sean had the feeling the doorbell would ring just as they sat down, and he was right.

"Me, me!" he cried, jumping up before anyone else—even the still-flustered Margaret. His cousin! He couldn't get over it. A new member of the family his own age, who would live with them now! And this afternoon he didn't even know he had a cousin—how bizarre!

His heart was thumping as he reached the front hall. He took a deep breath, ran a hand through his rumpled hair, and opened the door, wondering what kind of cousin fate was sending him.

CHAPTER TWO

MY COUSIN THE JERK

On the other side of the door loomed a young man who might have been himself, Sean thought, were this person's hair not black, and his ears a bit less protruded than Sean's. Plus the stranger was at least three inches taller than Sean, and—hmmm, more filled out—that was a little alarming. In one hand he held a vast, no-nonsense black trunk with **PIEDMONT MILITARY ACADEMY, 1845** across its top in bold letters that looked like they meant business. But the thing that struck Sean most was the ramrod posture of his rain-splattered cousin: the chest puffed out, the legs pressed together as if they were holding loose change between them, and the head and eyes up—like someone had just cried, "Ten-SHUN!"

"Good evening sir, Sutherland, Kyle J. reporting to the home of Professor Justin Sutherland," he said through an unsmiling, compressed mouth. There was the hint of an accent to his speech, whether Southern or Midwestern Sean couldn't tell. His cousin's words came at Sean like bullets—he almost ducked. Kyle was dressed formally in what Sean assumed was the hunter green uniform of his military school, right down to the funny beret on his head, now rain splotched like everything else he was wearing.

Margaret would have laughed—she always said Sean was never at a loss for words—for he was speechless. Whether it was the uncanny resemblance, the martial stance, or the *sir* business—no one had called him that before—Sean stood gawking, his mouth open.

"This *is* Greystones, the house of Professor Justin Sutherland?" the young man continued, somewhat petulantly.

"Oh—oh yeah," Sean finally answered. "And ahhh....I'm your cousin Sean! Welcome home!"

Sean spread his arms wide. But his cousin, his eyes still locked onto the ceiling of the entrance hall, seemed not to notice. Instead Kyle extended his hand to shake. Sean did likewise, then grimaced at Kyle's vice-like grasp so he wouldn't squeal in pain.

"Ah! So you've made it at last! Splendid! Splendid!" Sean heard behind him, and he turned to see his uncle bustling into the hall, with Margaret in close pursuit. "Welcome, welcome!"

"Thank you, sir," Kyle said, stepping into the hall.

Sean wondered: *Was Kyle man or machine?* He sounded so...robotic.

"I am glad you arrived before the storm intensifies!" Uncle Justin continued, oblivious to the dinner napkin (tucked into the top of his shirt collar) wagging away as he spoke. "You'll have to get used to our Northeasters up here I'm afraid! Heh! And I see you've met your cousin. Sean will be happy to fill you in on all the details of your new school, which you'll be starting tomorrow. Oh yes, the bathroom's there to the right, if you want to freshen up before joining us for dinner. We've been waiting for you most expectantly! Please come in!"

"Thank you sir, but I'm not hungry," Kyle responded mechanically, after staring at Uncle Justin for a moment. "If it's just the same to you sir, I will retire to my quarters for the evening. Lights out is usually 2200 hours, but I feel a bit fatigued after the trip. No ma'am, thank you, I have this under control." This last remark was delivered to Margaret, who was trying to pry Kyle's trunky suitcase away from him.

"Under control, is it?" Margaret remarked. "Well! In this house, Mister, I'm the housekeeper, and the sooner you understand that—"

"Oh that's quite alright, Margaret," Uncle Justin said kindly. "I'm sure Miles can manage his own suitcase."

"It's Kyle, sir."

"Oh! I *am* sorry, of course it is! Well, if you're not hungry, Kyle, then Sean can show you upstairs to your room."

"Thank you sir, and good evening. Good evening ma'am."

Sean felt a little rebuffed, not getting the welcoming hug he expected from his cousin; but nevertheless he guided Kyle to the bottom of the staircase—being careful to keep Kyle in front of him as they ascended, so Sean could touch the bannister's spindles eleven times: for no particular reason it was seven on the way down and eleven on the way up. That's just the way it was, how it always had been—

But what was his surprise when Sean saw Kyle brush against the wall at the top of the stairs, and then reach out his hand to touch the other side of the wall! That same thing—if you accidentally touched one wall, you had to touch the opposite one—had been Sean's OCD 1.0 some years ago—alas, he had come so far since then—much to his own chagrin. But Kyle had "it" too? Interesting!

"It's here," Sean said, stepping in front of Kyle and leading him down the hall once they reached the second floor. Feeling a burst of empathy for Kyle, for his OCD and other reasons, Sean gushed, "This is totally the most awesome house, you'll love it, I know you will. It was actually built by our family a long time ago, like two hundred years or something—"

"In the summer and autumn of 1790," Kyle corrected.

"Ahhh…okay," Sean said, "And…then strangers bought it after World War II—but Uncle Justin got it back seventeen years ago, when he came back here from England where he was teaching. He was over there for like twenty years, that's why he still has the British accent. And that's when I came to live here after—after my parents died. So see, we have a lot in common, both orphans—you know? This room here's my uncle's bedroom—I mean, our uncle's bedroom! It seems funny to say that! And that's his study…and here's the guest bedroom—our bedroom's down at the end. Like I say it feels so weird to say our uncle after all these years—I didn't even know I had a cousin an hour ago!"

When Kyle said nothing to all this, Sean half-turned, and got some kind of grunt in response.

"Oh, and school," Sean added, somewhat encouraged. He paused halfway down the hall and turned around. "Nawshant High isn't big at all, since this isn't a big town. But everyone's friendly and cool. Oh, I play on the lacrosse team. The season started last week, but we could probably use someone else if you've played the game before—and even if not, I could teach you over the weekend, it's wicked easy to learn."

His cousin stared at him blankly. Then, "Wicked?" he repeated.

"Oh, sorry, that means *very* up in these parts," Sean answered.

His cousin stared still.

"So what do you think?" Sean prodded. "About the lacrosse?"

"I play football," Kyle answered bluntly, again after pausing for a time. It seemed his cousin couldn't answer a question without thinking about it first, and staring at the asker.

Sean felt sorry for Kyle—he sounded so miserable!—until his cousin added, "But lacrosse? That's a girl's game, no?"

For the second time in ten minutes, Sean was speechless.

He began thinking up sharp retorts, like *I know some girls at school that could probably kick your butt.* But he bit his lip, remembering his uncle's words about how badly Kyle must be feeling, at his loss and forced relocation.

"Uhm, no it isn't," Sean finally said, though he couldn't seem to avoid a touch of sarcasm. "And it was invented by Native Americans. You're thinking of field hockey, maybe."

Flustered, Sean took off his ball cap, shook it out, then put it back on. OCD style, this was a gesture that must be repeated three times whenever he did it. He performed this triple ablution quickly, a little self-conscious-ly; but his cousin wasn't even looking at him. Sean watched where Kyle's blue eyes were gazing, and turned. Kyle was seeing the ocean out the Pal-ladian window at the end of the hall. In the fading light, the sea was a blazing silver-black, and heaving in the storm.

"Ahhh…that would be the ocean," Sean said.

"The ocean," Kyle muttered, as if he were saying the words to himself. He refocused and for the first time looked Sean in the eye. There was a rusty well of sadness in Kyle's eyes—and something else behind that. Sean thought Kyle might be human after all.

"It's only about 300 yards from here," Sean explained, without sar-casm this time. They walked in silence to the end of the hall, where Kyle put his suitcase down and positioned himself at the window ledge. He smelled of rain and the fresh winds of the gale, Sean noticed.

"First time I've ever seen the ocean," Kyle mumbled. "Except…'cept a' course looking out the window on the plane here."

Once more Sean didn't know what to say—for as long as he could remember, the ocean had been playmate, companion, the soundtrack to every significant event of his life. He couldn't imagine someone going through their entire life without having seen it.

"It's awesome," Sean said quietly, now standing behind his cousin. "Always changing. You should see it up close in a storm, like tonight—bashing into the cliffs, and the waves twenty and thirty feet high. Watch—see? See? You can see them starting to rise, now that the storm's setting in. And then on a nice summer's day, we go swimming in it—and you wouldn't think it was the same place. And in the warm weather we have all the windows open, and you can hear the waves from here when the wind's from the east. Or north."

Kyle, his back to Sean, kept staring at the sea. Did he nod slightly when Sean said these words? Sean wasn't sure. They stood like this for so long, Sean began to wonder if his cousin had fallen asleep standing up. He resisted the urge to pinch him.

"There wasn't…was there ever some kind of tragedy out there?" Kyle asked eventually, in a mumble, tossing his head towards the sea, which he was still staring at through the large window.

Sean wasn't sure he had heard his cousin right.

"Ahhh….a tragedy?"

Kyle nodded once.

"Ahhh…I don't know," Sean answered vaguely. "Miss Sawyer—she's the head librarian in town—knows more about local history than I do. I think there's been a drowning or two out there, I can tell you that much. It's called Third Cliff. We live on Third Cliff."

Sean felt his eyebrows furrow as he said the words. Was Kyle morbid too, as well as unfriendly? Or just unfriendly?

"Not just a drowning," Kyle answered. "This was more like a—"

Kyle seemed to remember to whom he was speaking, and stopped. From beside his cousin Sean couldn't be sure, but he thought he could see the sides of Kyle's cheeks flush up.

"More like a what?" Sean pressed, feeling a tingle at the back of his neck. This was too weird!

"Nothing," Kyle answered immediately. This time he didn't pause before answering—or not answering—Sean's question.

"So," Sean added, after an awkward silence. Moving right along.

Kyle turned again to stare. "So what?"

"So, uhm…tell me about yourself."

Again, his cousin waited so long to answer, Sean almost thought he hadn't heard him.

"What do you want to know?" Kyle finally blurted, still looking out the window. Sean found that his mouth was open again.

"Ahhh…." Sean almost laughed at his cousin's question—talk about attitude! Sean noticed again how…well, soldierly his cousin's posture was. It was hard to believe he and Kyle were the same age, as Kyle seemed so much older, so much more serious. But he reminded himself again of Uncle Justin's words. Of course Kyle would be somber, and Sean shouldn't take any of this personally. He also wondered—since he and Kyle shared much of the same blood and all—if he himself might expect to spurt up a few more inches and become as tall as his cousin. That would be kind of cool—

"Well, ahhh….what about…like…your old school?" Sean finally attempted. "Did you ahhh…like it there and everything?" Sean didn't know much about military academies, though he presumed they were strict. All he could think of was the scene in *Oliver!* where the main character asked for more gruel, and was met with defiant outrage. Oh, and jogging at five in the morning probably, lots of pre-dawn jogging—

Again Kyle was quiet before he answered.

"It was more than just my old school," he murmured. "It was my home. My life. Everyone there was my family."

"Oh. I'm sorry," Sean said. He had the urge to hug his cousin again, but remembered how this had been denied downstairs. "But…you know, in time and everything, I think you'll come to really like it here. Nawshant High isn't all that strict and stuff, and—"

"Thing is, there can't be order without discipline," his cousin interrupted, saying the words as if he were giving a command.

Sean had to hide his laugh.

"Well, yeah, sure—but I mean…it's not like people walk around the school naked and setting stuff on fire."

"Well, this *is* Massachusetts," Kyle said—somewhat dismissively, Sean thought.

"What's that mean?" Sean asked, beginning to lose his temper.

Kyle made a scoffing sound.

"You know—liberal politics, Democrats, first gay marriage state and all that," Kyle muttered. "It's like another planet up here it's so lefty."

"Really? Well, speaking of other planets, which one did you fall from?"

Sean asked, speaking before he thought. "We like to treat everyone equal up here. That's the American Way, isn't it?" In fact Sean had debated in favor of federal gay marriage laws two years ago when he was a member of the Debate Team.

Kyle turned and eyed him.

"Maybe your America," Kyle said after a minute. But he didn't sound so dismissive this time.

"Oh. I thought there was only one," Sean answered.

They stared at each other for some time.

"Alright," Sean said finally, deciding he'd better change the subject before he said more things he'd regret. "Here's our bedroom in here." He led the way in and snapped on the light. Fortunately it was relatively clean. "That's my bed there in the corner, and yours is over there. It looks like a couch, but once you take the pillows off…once you…ahhh…"

Kyle was scowling. Sean thought such a face must come from Kyle's mother's side of the family, as it was one he himself or Uncle Justin had never made. Kyle wasn't putting his suitcase down either—

"Isn't there somewhere else I can sleep?" he blurted.

It seemed everything that came out of his cousin made Sean's mouth fall open in speechlessness.

"Why, what's wrong with it?"

"I didn't say anything was wrong with it. I just—"

"So it's the roommate you don't like?" Sean said, crossing his arms. His temper, and his hurt at this seeming rejection, were getting the better of him again.

"I didn't say that either."

"Alright, fine. Have it your way. There are more rooms upstairs, though it's colder up there. The first room is Margaret's. Way at the end of the hall just above my bedroom there's another room just like this one. We call it Aunt Sadie's Room. You can have that, I don't think Uncle will mind. I'll send Margaret up in a little while to get it ready."

"I can get it ready myself," Kyle answered. They stared at each other again. Sean could feel his cheeks flushing. He couldn't read the emotions in his cousin's eyes. This time Kyle looked away first.

"Fine, you do that," Sean answered. "Get it ready yourself. Come on, follow me."

Sean marched back down the hall, pausing near the end. "The stairway up to the third floor is through this door," he told Kyle, pointing. "Like I say, your room's way at the end."

He didn't wait for an answer, but clomped red-faced down the stairs, leaving his cousin alone. He even forgot to touch the spindles on the banisters.

Kyle stared after him, opened his mouth to say something—then shut it when it became too late. He opened the door and climbed the steep narrow stairway, sighing deeply as he did.

"Great," he mumbled. "Well that is just great."

He found his new room, but knocked anyway at the closed door just in case—that's how he'd been trained. When no one answered he entered, shutting the door immediately behind him. He was glad to see the latch on the door. He snapped it tight, then placed his suitcase on the bed. The room smelled of old wooden furniture and woolen blankets and...lavender? It was by no means an unpleasant smell—but wow, it was cold up here. What little heat came into the room passed via an old black-metal floor grate that seemed to bypass the second floor and go directly down to the first floor, for Kyle could vaguely hear muffled conversation rising up from the dining room.

Besides its chill, the room was otherwise quiet, lonely-looking, and prim into the bargain. A single iron twin bed with four posts, a bureau, a foggy, full-length standing mirror, a plain desk, and an old ladder-back chair were the only furnishings. Oddly, there was an old bird's nest someone had collected, sitting on the window sill. The wallpaper was antique silk, though it still looked in perfect shape, and depicted bunches of white lilacs, yellow jonquils, and purple crocus. It must have been imported from France, for the swirly writing said *Oo La la! Les fleurs du printemps!* here and there throughout the pattern. But Kyle thought the festive note these words struck was in sad contrast to the plainness of the room, the storm outside, and his own angst.

But certainly the room was immaculate, if a little Spartan.

Kyle opened his suitcase on the bed, then rubbed his hands against the chill. It felt like winter way up here already toward the end of September, and back at school it was still summer. If only—then he shook his head and walked over to the window facing east, and stared out again at the tumbling black sea.

"Oh no," he mumbled, after a minute or two. He stood there looking out until the ocean slurred into the darkness of the sky, and vanished. Still he stood. Someone looking at him might have almost thought he was in a trance. As if with a great effort, he finally shook his head, yanked down the shade, and pulled himself away.

He unpacked his trunk with trembling hands, then put his things away in the bureau and closet. My God, what huge closets these old houses had—a vague scent of mothballs, and a stronger one of antique lavender, wafted out to him as he stepped inside. Against the back wall was a big calendar: *Picture Yourself in a Buick!* it read—it was from 1946.

He took off his coat, shirt, and pants—part of his ex-school's uniform—and hung them up on the old wooden hangers. Before he closed the closet door he ran his right hand, reverently and softly, over the perfectly-tailored hunter green material of his jacket. Even someone in the room wouldn't have heard the name Kyle called out then, so softly did he say it. Then he put on the thickest sweatshirt and sweatpants he owned.

When he was done with that, he shut the closet door, then looked around, unsure what to do next. He was far too twitchy for sleep. He finally sat down on the edge of the bed. He buried his face in his hands. He reached behind him and grabbed at one of the pillows, then crammed it up against his face so no one would hear him.

Then, hating himself for what he perceived to be his weakness, he sobbed. The rain lashed against the windows, and the wind joined him, wailing over the roof like a grief-stricken giant.

CHAPTER THREE

HAVE YOU EVER HEARD THE BELLS?

"Musha!" Margaret huffed, when Sean returned to the dinner table and reported events. "His own room, is it? What does Mister High and Mighty think he is? Too good for the rest of us, by the sound of things! Too good for the rest of us!"

"Margaret, please," Uncle Justin urged, turning to her.

"I hate to say it, but he's a jerk!" Sean blurted.

"Now now," Uncle Justin remonstrated, "enough of that, please! That's so unkind, Sean—and so very unlike you! Is this the best you can do in this situation?"

"But he—"

"It doesn't matter. Remember what I always say—what other people do to us is their choice—and how we react is ours. You're a kind, compassionate, and welcoming person—don't let him or anyone else change you! Don't give your power away like that! I promise you, he'll come round. In the meantime, there's no harm in letting him have his privacy, is there?"

"No, but—"

"And it's perfectly normal for him to be a bit strange at first. I'll see if he's all right after dinner and have a little word with him. And perhaps tomorrow, Margaret, you could cheer up his room a bit?"

"Mary Mother of God—as if I don't have enough to do," Margaret muttered. "And my reading on top of it all."

"But didn't I warn you, Sean," Uncle Justin proceeded serenely, "that it might not be all sunshine and smiles with the poor boy?"

"Yes, Uncle," Sean sighed. His mood lightened somewhat with the idea that Kyle would, in fact, come round in time. But for three years running Sean had been voted Mister Personality for his class at Nawshant High, and he wasn't sure he'd ever met anyone that didn't get along with him—other than lacrosse referees. Oh, and Mr. Tibbins, his old math teacher freshman year. But then, no one got along with Mr. Tibbins.

Still, Uncle Justin had said not to take it personally if Kyle was less than friendly with him—and so Sean decided he would try not to. He turned his attention to the meal staring back at him from his plate, and realized he was ravenous.

"I don't know that I fancy the idea of sharing my floor with someone else, even if he is at the other end," Margaret remarked uncertainly, putting down her fork. "One t'ing and another."

"Right?" Sean quipped. "There'll be no more of those wild parties you throw up there when Uncle's away, eh?"

Professor Singleton thought this very funny, and silently laughed until his round frame shook.

"I'll give *you* a wild party if you keep that up," Margaret retorted. "Your sense of humor is a thing to be scoffed at."

"It'll all be fine," Uncle Justin said. It was his favorite remark—but somehow Sean believed it whenever he said it.

"But aren't we being the rude ones to our guest!" Margaret interjected. "Professor Singleton, you were just beginning a story. Go on with you now. You were saying?"

"Yes, my dear," Professor Singleton answered, raising his head as if he were about to deliver a lecture. His wire-rim glasses picked up the reflected candlelight on the table. He folded his hands on the white linen tablecloth and cleared his throat importantly. "Well, I was just about to relate a bit of a…well, I suppose it is a sad story, when one thinks about it. You'll judge for yourselves. But I know all of you here are familiar with Mrs. Hutchinson?"

"Sure," Sean answered. "She's the nice old lady in the huge mansion up by First Cliff. What's it called, *Linger Longer*?"

"Exactly. That is she—and it. But she's more than that, Sean," Professor Singleton answered. "But…excuse me, Margaret—would you mind? I simply must have another small taste of those *delicious* garlic mashed potatoes please. The garlic from your own garden out back, hmmm? Splendid, I knew it! Oh, and the potatoes are too, aren't you something! Thank you! A little more, please. Thank you, my dear! Yes, Sean, Mrs. Hutchinson was in fact a star of the tennis circuit in her day, back in the Year Six. Won a Wimbledon Championship I think a few years after the Second World War. Or finished second in doubles. Something. Lost her husband young—never remarried and no children. Fine old family. When your uncle and I were young lads growing up here, she traveled the world, and whenever she came back she would invite all the neighborhood children into her lovely home to give us a slide show and lecture of the places she'd been. I believe it was her photographs of the Giant Sequoia that first got your uncle and I interested in our avocations."

"Quite right," Uncle Justin agreed. "She's always been a shining example of philanthropy."

"Oh, thank goodness!" Margaret blurted, blushing. "I thought you were about to say *philandering*."

"What's that mean?" Sean asked.

"I wonder if one can read too much?" Margaret asked the ceiling.

"But she is most well remembered around here," Professor Singleton continued, ignoring Sean but eyeing Margaret curiously, "for her generous donation of one hundred acres of land that once belonged to her family. *Hutchinson Woods* is the correct name of the grant, which she gave to the Friends of Wildlife, to be set aside in perpetuity as a preserve. But most people in town refer to these woods as *the Thicket*."

"Oh sure!" Sean remarked, helping himself to more potatoes, his humor improving in direct proportion to his filling stomach. "I never knew that used to be her land. I've lost a few balls in there over the years."

"Yes, you *would*," Professor Singleton agreed. "It *is* rather impenetrable. Which is why it's such a sanctuary for our feathered friends. Why, even our spry Justin can hardly get in there, can you?"

"Just along the edges," Uncle Justin agreed. "The briars, brambles, and poison ivy are that thick. But one hears the calls coming from further in. Why, just last week I heard three separate American Bluebirds, and, *possibly*, the drumming of a Pileated Woodpecker."

"And yet you never told me?" Professor Singleton asked, laying down his fork and forgetting his meal—but only for a moment.

"There was hardly time, Professor," Uncle Justin answered. "It was the morning of my flight. But I *did* text you, I know."

"That was me instead," Margaret said. "I wondered what in God's name you were going on about."

"Oh—I *am* sorry!"

"You forgot to say, Sean, how you used to make us run by the Thicket when you were little, and we'd be walking back from Canoe Beach," Margaret added, turning to Sean. "Ouf! He was that *terrified* of those woods, especially round Halloween time. And yet he *wouldn't* let me take him the other way home either, my little lamb."

"I thought it was haunted," Sean admitted. "All the kids did."

"Well, the bats and owls do that, though really, only fools would fear them," Professor Singleton went on. "The last time I checked, we had left the Medieval Ages. But above and beyond the bats and owls, there is something rather—mysterious about the Thicket. I suspect the twisting nature of the old trees in there—*Pinus banksiana* and *Robinia pseudoacacia* in particular—that lend a rather Gothic air to the place—"

"And don't forget *Platanus occidentalis*," Uncle Justin added.

"Exactly," Professor Singleton agreed. "Or that magnificent stand of gigantic *Fagus grandifolia* on the northern edge of the Thicket, which one can only access through Mrs. Hutchinson's own grounds. "When the fog comes in it's especially…evocative.

"But to continue: I saw Mrs. Hutchinson last week when I was walking by the Thicket; speaking of rare birds. One doesn't see her as much as one used to. Well, I was out at dawn—this is when you were away, Justin, otherwise I would have phoned you—because a Snowy Owl had been spotted the day before winging around Swampscott way; and I just thought if I were a Snowy Owl, I might rest for a bit in the Thicket. Oh, have I told you," he said, turning again to Uncle Justin, "that I've rearranged my Top Ten?"

"Have you!" Uncle Justin beamed. "So have I! Do tell!"

Since the two men had been boys, they had each compiled a list of their top ten favorite birds, which they updated weekly or as necessary. Fifty years later they were still at it.

"Oh take a right, Professors, for Heaven's sakes, and get back to the story!" Margaret scolded. Another of her sayings, this request Margaret would make whenever the Professors—or Sean for that matter—rambled off into some kind of Tangent Land, as if they were driving down the road of their tale and had become hopelessly lost.

"Point taken, Margaret," Professor Singleton smiled. "Anyway—there's some extraordinary grazing in the Thicket for the birds, especially the innumerable poison ivy vines and viburnum, with their delectable—to the birds—fruits. Which is why bird fanciers of Nawshant frequently visit the Thicket—or at least its edges. So, one morning last week I was up there, when—but speaking of grazing—I'm sorry Margaret, another slice of that wonderful pie would be heaven! I've always said, one is never so full that there isn't room for blueberry pie! Thank you, my dear. Lovely! From your own bushes, the blueberries? I knew it! So, where were we?"

"At the Thicket, looking for a Snowy Owl," Sean offered.

"Oh yes, many thanks Sean. But—my God, woman, this is *perfect pie!* Mmmmm! Heaven! Might I inquire, are you saving that last slice for anyone in particular? May I then? Excellent, thank you! Well, alas, my search for the owl was fruitless. So there I was, walking home, and as I rounded the corner of Ocean Road—right where it takes the big bend at Second Cliff—there was our Mrs. Hutchinson at the edge of the street, peering out at me, squinting in the morning sun."

Here Professor Singleton lowered his fork, raised his head, and stared at each of his dinner companions in turn, squinting in imitation. Sean stifled his laugh—the professor looked like a snowy owl himself.

"*Professor, Professor!* Mrs. Hutchinson called to me, raising her cane and waving it excitedly. *I should like to have a word with you!* Course we often exchange a bit of news when we see each other, but there was something urgent about her manner that made me hurry. I thought perhaps she had seen a particularly rare specimen of bird that morning, so hurry along I did."

Sean struggled to picture this, for the Professor seemed capable of two speeds only: slow and slower.

"Indeed," the Professor said, drawing out the word dramatically, and speaking in a hush now, "she was quite agitated. More coffee? Yes Margaret, I'd love some! And it's—what do you say, shade grown, fair trade, and bird friendly? Excellent, that's our Margaret, we love the last part! But anyway, Mrs. Hutchinson's blue sweater was buttoned in a helter-skelter manner, and her gray eyes had that shifty yet—riveting quality one always associates with high drama. And overwrought nerves.

"*What is it, Mrs. Hutchinson?* I asked her. *All well?* I could see something was amiss.

"*I hope so,* she answered. *But tell me, Professor,* she went on. *Do you ever walk here at night?*

"I told her that indeed I did, at least once a week, usually just after sunset. To see of course if I could spot or hear anything unusual in the way of bird life.

"*You never come by later at night?* she asked carefully. *Shall we say, round midnight?*

"*Midnight! Good heavens, no!* I answered. *Only in the spring, when the male American Woodcock does his sky dance, and the moon is full to keep him out late. Why? What have you seen?*

"She fixed me with her eye then, and let me tell you, it was…well, fierce, frankly. She looked around, then looked back at me.

"*It isn't what I've seen, Professor,* she whispered. She lowered her voice still further. *It's what I've heard.*"

Sean found that his mouth was plopped open. Looking around, he saw that Uncle Justin and Margaret were equally entangled in Professor Singleton's story. The storm outside was intensifying. Sean now noticed the rain, thrashing the windows behind them; and the lilac bushes were scratching against the thick old panes like they wanted in.

Professor Singleton enlarged his eyes as he continued.

"*And what have you heard then?* I asked her. Again, she turned round as if someone else might be listening. Then she turned back to me. What do you think she said?"

Professor Singleton looked at the three members of his audience in turn as they digested this rhetorical question. Then he leaned closer into the table, and lowered his voice. The fact that he had blueberry pie on the edges of his grizzled beard in no way diminished his tale.

"*Bells, Professor!* she told me in a lowered voice. *Bells! Have you ever heard the bells? They only ring at night.*"

The wind rattled the windows behind them again, and Sean felt a shiver jiggle up his spine.

"*And what bells might those be?* I asked. I didn't know what to make of her question, or the urgency with which she asked it.

"Again she looked behind her, as if someone might be listening. *I don't know*, she said. *I was hoping you might have heard them. They're quite loud when they sound.*

" *Oh!* I answered. *Bells, eh? Well, surely the explanation is simple, Mrs. Hutchinson—it's people riding by on bikes, young people probably, ringing those little bells bikes have on their handlebars. To warn people they're coming, do you see?*

"She laughed at me then. *Do you think I'm daft?'* she demanded, and the old aristocrat came out in her sneer. *'These aren't bike bells—they're… church bells. Tower bells. I tell you they're deep, bonging, clanging. And they aren't sounding from the edge of the road here—they're coming from the heart of the Thicket. And it isn't a ship along the shore, or a buoy, so don't tell me that either. I've lived here all my life and I know what those other bells sound like. This is different entirely. Like big church bells, I say. From the very heart of the Thicket."*

Sean felt another chill sizzle through him. Bells tolling at night from inside the impenetrable Thicket was as ridiculous as it was riveting.

"The *poor miserable creature!*" Margaret ejaculated. "I'd say she has bats in her belfry—and bells too, apparently. What will I do tomorrow? Why, I'll run up there with a bramback. That's what."

Bramback, an old-fashioned Irish fruit bread, was one of Margaret's specialties of the house, and her cure for any and all ills.

"This is my conclusion as well," Professor Singleton announced, leaning back from the table with a Lucullan sigh. "And what a *fine* mind she had! But she is, after all, in her early-nineties—it's bound to happen to all of us I suppose, if we make it that far."

"But what if she really did hear bells?" Sean asked, unwilling to let go of the magic of the story, now that it seemed over.

Professor Singleton lowered his eyelids and smiled.

"I wouldn't think so, young man. The principle we call Occam's razor tells us that in most cases the simplest explanation among several is the correct one. So I ask you: is it more likely she's imagining the bells at her age? Or that somehow deep, gonging church bells are tolling madly from the middle of an impenetrable wood, where no one has lived since the Native Americans, and there's hardly a path to be found?"

"I guess I see what you mean," Sean admitted.

"Ouf!" Margaret laughed, "I know what Sean's after! He's thinking of the *Mystery of the Hidden Voices*, and anxious for another case to solve—aren't you, love?"

"I'm afraid I don't know that one," Professor Singleton said, sipping his coffee.

"Well," Margaret explained, "Old Earl Stafford up Second Cliff way insisted he heard voices at night, coming from the bushes just outside his bedroom window. Which was odd—he's deaf as a stone, as anyone can tell you. Almost every night he'd call the police and report that there were people outside his bedroom window, talking and laughing and whispering. So, the police come out, they come out again, once or twice more and sniff around they did, each time without sight nor light of anyone. But wasn't it that spring our Sean trimmed Earl's hedges, and Earl told Sean all about the voices. Sean believed the poor old soul, went inside, and found a radio under Earl's bed that Earl had left on two months earlier, God help us! Old Earl only heard it when he shut his bedroom television off, right before he went to sleep. He was pleased as seven lords, and told Sean he was a better detective than the entire Nawshant Police Department put together. He gave you a bit of a remembrancer for that, didn't he Sean?"

"A hundred dollars," Sean admitted.

"Did he?" Uncle Justin beamed. "I'd forgotten. That was kind!"

"And so Sean's been on the lookout for another mystery to solve since then," Margaret added with a laugh. "My little lamb!"

"I'm afraid there isn't much of a mystery here, young man," Professor Singleton said, snatching at his dessert plate to get the last of the crumbs as Margaret tried to clear. "Just a dementia of some kind, sad to say." And then he and Uncle Justin fell into indecipherable conversation about various forms of mental loss, and whether the lesser carnivora were subject to this as well.

Sean rose absent-mindedly from the table and helped Margaret heft the dirty dishes out to the kitchen. He was silent as he rinsed the plates, handing them to Margaret, thinking not only about the bells, but his cousin upstairs, and how sad it was Kyle had missed out on such a sweet dinner, and such a strange story.

"Anyone game for a stroll?" Uncle Justin asked a minute later, popping his head through the swinging kitchen door. "I'm walking Professor Singleton home, and it's a lovely and wild night!"

"In this storm?" Margaret asked. "Mercy me! Have you the sense God gave a goat? And where's your hat?"

"Oh, somewhere, I'm sure," Uncle Justin replied vaguely. "Sean, are you interested? The sky and sea are up to something!"

It was always a treat to be out with Uncle Justin in a storm, for he made the whole thing come alive. "Sure!" he said.

"You'll do no such thing!" Margaret said, putting an arm across the doorway to bar Sean's way. "He's forgetting the calculating test he has in the morning, or whatever you call the dang thing."

"Calculus," Sean sighed, remembering, his whole demeanor changing. "Right. Sorry Uncle Justin."

"No problem, dear boy," Uncle Justin answered. "Duty before pleasure and all that. See you all soon."

"Be careful!" Margaret warned. "And don't go too near any of those cliffs, or you'll come to grief!"

"Margaret, you outdid yourself, and my gratitude knows no bounds," Professor Singleton said, sticking his head through the door and buttoning up his overcoat tightly. "Goodnight all!"

After a bit more small talk with Margaret, Sean drifted upstairs to his room to study for a bit. It seemed odd, to have his room empty, lonely, and his cousin just above him, alone too. Funny, his room had never felt empty or lonely before tonight. He had half an ear cocked upward as he studied, thinking he might hear his cousin above him—but all was silent. Perhaps he'd gone to bed already. Oh well, hopefully Uncle Justin was right—maybe Kyle just needed time.

It was around tennish when Sean heard Uncle Justin come back home. A minute later Sean heard him treading upstairs to the third floor, to say goodnight to Kyle. Shortly after he lightly rapped on Sean's door.

"What did he say?" Sean murmured, opening the door.

"What did who say?" his uncle asked, running a towel over his rain-splotched head.

With anyone else, Sean would have responded *Duh!*

"Kyle."

"Oh." His uncle closed his eyes and made no sound at all. "That's what he said. He's asleep, I imagine."

"Oh, okay. Goodnight Uncle."

"Goodnight, dear boy. Sleep well. And thank you for being so welcoming to your cousin. He'll come round, don't you worry."

"Thanks, Uncle Justin. Goodnight."

Sean came back into his room, closing the door behind him.

One of the things Sean loved best about these four walls was how his bedroom became drenched with the sweetest smell imaginable for the last two weeks in May. An ancient wisteria vine, climbing up from the shrubbery beds two stories below, nearly smothered the exterior of this side of the house, going all the way up to the story above, and then beyond that to the Widow's Walk at the apex of the attic roof. When the wisteria's pale purple blossoms exploded into bloom in late-spring, Sean's bedroom was steeped in the sweet fragrance he loved best, an odor unlike any other. It really got to him, this smell.

He often thought he was so partial to its heady aroma because he had come here when he was one year old, in May; and perhaps the smell reminded his subconscious of warmth, security, and a new home with people who loved him, after the tragedy of losing both his parents. Uncle Justin had been teaching at Oxford University in England then; but he had grown up here in Nawshant, and had always planned on returning—being named Sean's guardian gave him the perfect excuse and, as he had just won the Benninger Prize in Botany, he was able to purchase Greystones, the old mini-mansion where he had cut the grass when he was a boy. Greystones had originally been built by a Sutherland about two hundred years ago—no, 226, as Kyle had corrected him—and now it was back in the family.

When he was twelve, Sean discovered another new and exciting feature about the wisteria vine: its ankle-thick, woody branches were strong enough to support him all the way down to the ground outside. It was a perfect way to exit and re-enter his bedroom when secrecy was called for. At first the experience had been a little harrowing, climbing out the bedroom window and clinging onto the thick woody vines—but by now he'd had five years of practice. He felt he could descend the plant blindfolded if he had to.

For some reason, Sean had always kept this a secret—from everyone, even his best friends Matt White, and twins Timmy and Regina Quinn. Somehow the pleasure was more delicious when it was secret. Sometimes—on a dazzling full-moon night in May, a crisp autumn evening, or during a Northeaster snow storm in January—he'd climb down just for the secret thrill of being outside, at one with the beautiful world of nature around him. It seemed he had the whole world to himself then, and no one knew.

He thought about this now as he closed his math book, certain that if he wouldn't ace his calculus test tomorrow morning, neither would he flunk it. He had been exhausted after lacrosse practice—but now he wasn't tired at all. Between the excitement—and then the disappointment—occasioned by the arrival of Kyle, and the idea of ghostly bells peeling madly from the Thicket—which Sean still thought might be a little possible—his mind was too restless for sleep.

The heavy tolling of the massive grandfather clock down in the library, bonging eleven, seemed like a sign. At any rate Sean didn't need any further convincing: he would sneak out and hike up to the Thicket and do a little investigating on his own. Tonight, *right now*. It certainly wouldn't do any harm to just look. And if by chance he should hear the bells—

He peeked out the curtains and saw that the rain had given up the ghost as the storm roared off to the northeastward. Though the wind was still howling, it had shifted from the northeast to the northwest, and clearing would soon begin. This storm had been a fast mover. That would mean a serious intensifying as it raced explosively up the coast—Maine, and the Maritime Provinces of Canada, would be in for it later.

He was already wearing black jeans and a sweatshirt, and to this Sean added his navy blue rain parka, hood up. If he was going to be snooping about, he wanted to make sure no one would see him, hence the dark clothes; he didn't want to be mistaken for a prowler. Mrs. Elizabeth Campbell, the retired principal of Nawshant Middle School, had shot at Uncle Justin five years ago when he was out and about in the middle of a March night, listening for the first peepers of the season. While it's true she had missed, Sean didn't want to take any chances.

He slipped on his sneakers, tiptoed to the bedroom door, opened it carefully, then peeked out into the hall, listening like a thief.

Nothing. All was quiet except for the normal, funky sounds any 226-year-old house would make on a windy night. He shut the door, then stalked over to the window on the left of his bed. He drew back the heavy maroon drapes, and lifted the window carefully: it was old and inclined to tell tales, squeaking and rattling when it was shoved up too quickly. He was surprised to see the storm windows down already—summer really was over. Apparently Margaret had done this during the week, because last weekend the screens had still been up. She would never allow the heat to be turned on until the storm windows were all down. This made things a little trickier, as the screen was easier to get down behind him than the storm window—but no big deal, no one would notice unless they came into his room—and if they did that, they'd know he was gone anyway by the empty bed. He wouldn't leave pillows under the covers to imitate his own sleeping body—he wasn't that devious.

Once both windows were open, he climbed out backwards, feeling blindly with his right foot for the thick 'V' just below the window where two main branches met—he couldn't have designed a better stepping-out place himself. With his left hand he latched onto another part of the thick plant. A blast of cool air—the first really cool weather of the autumn season—struck him in the face and he breathed deeply.

Thus secured, he reached up with his right hand and pulled down the window—slowly, gingerly. Then he climbed down the wisteria's thick trunk, passing just to the left of the mullioned windows of the Snuggery. He landed on the slippery wet ground among and behind the huge rhododendrons and yews that lined this side of the house.

He waited a moment, as he always did, his heart pounding with the illicitness of what he was doing. It would have been easier to leave Greystones through the more conventional way—just quietly sneaking down the main stairs and out the front door, as Uncle Justin was quite the sound sleeper. But Margaret, even though she was up on the third floor, had hearing that Sean didn't want to put to the test. And he knew from experience that the fifth, sixth, and seventh steps on the front stairway creaked something awful. He had casually mentioned this to Margaret more than once over the years, but she only eyed him suspiciously, and never had them fixed—probably just for that reason.

He counted sixty as he always did, looking up at Uncle Justin's window, and then beyond that to Margaret's. All well, all dark. At first he forgot to look at his cousin's window—then he remembered. That was black too, and shadowed by the upper branches of the wisteria.

Keeping within the edges of the huge shrubbery bed, Sean snaked around to the back of the house, walking beside the vegetable, herb, and flower gardens. Then he vanished into the large grove of hemlock trees that separated Greystones from the three houses behind it. He emerged from the hemlocks at a line of arborvitae shrubs that served as the border between the McNichols and the Quinns, two of the houses to the rear, and he crept along the shadows of these. Someone was up watching TV in the Quinn's house—he kept going half-crouched until he made it out onto Crow's Nest Road.

It was only fifty yards from here to Ocean Road, but these he knew were the most dangerous, as anyone looking out their front windows might see him and report to Uncle Justin or, worse, Margaret: living in a small town had its disadvantages as well as its good points.

He put his hands in his pockets and adopted what he thought was a casual stroll, just in case. He couldn't wait until he was eighteen and then he wouldn't have to bother with all this nonsense…eighteen! Just a few more months and then he would be a man, and could come and go as he pleased! Of course he was a man now, but somehow the world wouldn't acknowledge this until an arbitrary date on the calendar.

He rubbed at his downy goatee to remind himself of the fact.

He reached Ocean Road and let out a gush of relief-breath. This was the circuitous road that wound crazily around the high, cliffy perimeter of north and east Nawshant, following the rocky heights along the shore as it did so. While there were homes on the landward side of the road, houses on the ocean side were few and far between, mostly because it was too rocky to build there. But those that were on that side had views that snatched breath away. Since the high road was so old—and had been built almost 400 years ago on an ancient Native American trail that was of course older—towering trees lined both sides of it, though the ones on the ocean side were twisted, gnarled, and bent from the ravages of such a close encounter with the sea and its storms. Sean looked through the limbs of one of these patriarchs now—a massive, brooding white pine—and saw a glimmer of moonlight on a distant part of the ocean, as the skies cleared. He looked up—there was no moon here yet, but the clouds above him were higher and thinner now, and they were streaming and tearing like rags in the wild northwest wind, occasionally leaking glimmers of moon-glow—but no moon could he see here yet. It was a wildly dramatic sky. It was a perfect night to do a little snooping. Almost a little *too* perfect.

He thought about Margaret's words as he moved closer to the beginnings of the Thicket—*he's just looking for another mystery to solve.* Was that true? He was glad to have helped the voices-hearing Mr. Stafford out last year—people were beginning to say the poor guy was cray-cray—but above and beyond that, Sean really had been thrilled no end with the idea of people hiding in the bushes in front of Mr. Stafford's house, talking and whispering. The absurdity of it enchanted him. Why would people do that? What were they talking about? Where did they go by day? Certainly Sean had an insatiable curiosity about people, their conversations and their actions—Margaret could vouch for that. And he had watched every episode of old *X-Files* reruns so many times he could recite the dialogue word for word, to his friends' amazement. And while he was certainly no scholar, a whole corner of the library downstairs was devoted to Sean's mystery books—the only reading he truly enjoyed.

But could one make a career out of solving mysteries? Maybe. He was happy with his current job, as founder, CEO, owner, and full-time employee (the only one, although friend Timmy helped now and then) of *Mow-Town Landscaping*—but he wasn't sure he wanted to do that for the rest of his life. He hated that he seemed to have to make some kind of decision now—*What do you want to do, where do you want to do it? What will you be studying in college?* He was sick of the questions already and had lately thought of replying *insect veterinarian* or *maybe graffiti artist* just to get people to shut up.

The truth of it was he didn't have a clue. Because of this he had begged Uncle Justin to let him take a year off before applying to any colleges. His grades were okay, nothing better—nor did he have the intellectual discipline or interest to stay locked in a library all day pursuing knowledge, as Uncle Justin did. That gene had apparently skipped him. If it was anybody else, Sean might have suspected he had disappointed Uncle Justin—and Margaret too for that matter—by his utter... averageness. But from day one, he felt there was nothing he could do that would make either of them love him any less than they so obviously did. In an uncertain world, that was one thing he could count on.

What *would* he do? What did he want to do? He had no idea, which is why he wanted to take the next year off from school.

The road twisted again and there in the distance lay the beginning (or end) of the Thicket. Sean knew it by its blackness. He stopped and regarded it seventy yards away.

He thought the night—any night, really—was only blackness. But as he studied the Thicket he realized this was not the case. He saw then—and would remember from this time on—that the night was varying shades of darkness, leading to but not quite reaching utter blackness. Utter blackness was the Thicket. The night on the other hand was deep navy, smudged with shifting degrees of gray and purple and blue where the moon shone behind the shredding clouds; or rather, the ghosts of gray, purple, and blue. He looked back at the Thicket. Yes, an utter darkness the night could never equal, as if the Thicket were a black hole sucking all the light of the universe into it, where the light would wander for a moment before dying.

Sean took a few baby steps forward. A fresh flood of storm-clearing wind poured in from the west and his rain parka wasn't up to the challenge. He could hear the gale roaring through the Thicket, could hear the centuries-old trees swaying and creaking—it sounded like the cussing of old people and the hissing of cats—could hear the curtains and tangles of briars and thorns lift, rise, then fall again into places that barred advance and offered concealment to—to whatever might be in there. All this he could hear clearly—but he could see none of it. He walked closer. He was just across the street from these wild woods that might or might not contain some kind of weird presence that for reasons unknown was tolling deep bells in the middle of the night, where no bells should be. Now that he was here, a part of him seemed less eager to investigate.

"C'mon," he whispered to himself, "there's nothing to be afraid of. They're only woods. C'mon, this is what you came for."

He took a deep breath and crossed the street. He was now right at the Thicket. It was like looking into an anvil. He reached out his hand. It snagged on a thorn and he withdrew it quickly with a tiny *ahh!* of pain. He drew his hand to his mouth and licked the trickle of blood away.

As if on cue the grisliest scenes from every horror movie Sean knew, and their accompanying staccato soundtracks, came back to his mind now to—well, haunt him. Maybe this wasn't such a good idea. A barred owl hooted only several yards away—*who who who cooks for you? Who who who cooks for you all?* This was a sound he usually relished, but tonight it gave him a sudden and nasty brain freeze.

The moon smeared out just then. It lit up the world around him in its odd, color-stealing throb, but stopped short of the Thicket as if a wall was here. The moonlight illuminated the first several trunks, a tangled curtain of thorns or two—and then dimmed, and vanished not more than ten feet in.

But the hooded figure lurking just inside the Thicket, with its back to Sean, was only seven feet away, which is why Sean saw it.

CHAPTER FOUR

MORE MYSTERIES, AND THE LADY IN BLACK

The gasp that came out of Sean then only increased his wide-eyed terror, because he didn't at first understand that his gasp was a sound of his own making. A thing that felt like cold electricity shot up his spine. Immobilized by fear, he couldn't move, couldn't look away, could hardly breathe—and the hooded figure, whoever it was, seemed more terrifying because of its utter motionlessness. Again and again Sean's disbelieving brain ordered his eyes up and down the figure's hulking dimensions—and still the figure remained. The racing pulse of Sean's heart sounded in his ear, and its cadence was like booted soldiers, marching. He noticed, even in his panic, that the number 17 was stenciled on the back of the figure's dark hooded sweatshirt in golden characters.

He couldn't move. He willed himself to take a step backwards—carefully, quietly—and at the same time he saw the head of the person turn slightly, and look up, in a peering kind of way. Whoever it was still hadn't seen or heard Sean, and that was his only hope now.

Sean took a step back with his right foot. Then another, with his left. It seemed he could manage what should have been instinctual flight only by ordering his wigged-out brain to do each little thing necessary in its own order. *Lean back. Lift your right foot up. Pull your right leg backwards…my*

God, it was like the Hokey-Pokey—

When he was halfway across the street, he turned and bolted, the roaring wind (hopefully) erasing the sound of his flight.

As he fled he refereed a quick, decisive battle between his fear, and his curiosity. Not surprisingly curiosity won out. He ducked behind the massive trunk of a Silver Maple on the other side of the shadowed road. The tree's solidity, the deep fissures of the gnarled bark that his fingers explored now, reassured Sean somehow, almost back to a state resembling normalcy. He waited for his breath to return, and for the thumping in his ears to recede.

Someone was in the Thicket. It was close to midnight on a Thursday night in the quiet seaside town of Nawshant, where nothing ever happened—and a large, hooded figure was standing inside the Thicket at midnight.

As absurd as all this seemed, it was true. *Pay no attention to surmise and suggestion, but judge everything on the evidence!* The words he had heard Uncle Justin say a thousand times when Sean would confront his uncle with rumors, urban myths, or something outrageous someone had said at school, came back to him now. Well, he had seen the person himself. It wasn't the shadows, it wasn't the moonlight, and it wasn't the play between these two messing with his head. Someone was in the Thicket at midnight and if they meant well, as Margaret would say, then her name was Nosey Parker.

He slowly leaned his head to the left. A little more, a little more. He peered across the street. He squinted. The wind buffeted his face.

The figure was gone.

How Sean knew this he couldn't exactly say, for the velvety-blue shadows and creamy moonlight were still running in and out of each other along the margins of the Thicket. But he knew it as well as he knew his name—the figure was gone. The same instinct that reports when one is not alone in a dark room was at play here, and Sean's instincts had never served him wrong. The person was gone. There was a total absence of the strangling dread he had felt just moments ago.

He crossed the street again to be sure. The moon burst out brightly as if to accommodate him—though it still failed after penetrating no more than ten feet into the black tangle of the Thicket. He carefully approached the exact spot where he had stood just five minutes earlier.

There was nothing there. He remembered the stark whiteness of one particular birch tree, how it had played such contrast to the darkness of the hulking figure beside it. Nothing. Plus he felt it. That, somehow, was even stronger than seeing it. Or not seeing it. Next to the birch was an old twisted Juniper, or Eastern Red Cedar as its common name was, and it was uncanny how this evergreen, from this angle, looked exactly like a figure in a robe and turban, arms outraised and palms up, delivering a public proclamation of some urgency. He hadn't seen this optical illusion before, because the figure had been blocking it.

"Interesting," Sean mumbled, as he let go a vast breath. He felt his jigged body slacken a bit. Yes, the person in the hoodie was gone.

A thousand questions jostled to the front of Sean's brain—*what were they doing here, who were they, want did they want, where did they come from, did this have anything to do with the bells? If so, how?*

Or…Sean paused, bent halfway over, and got all peery…could it have been a—ghost?

He shouldn't wonder. He'd heard all kinds of talk of ghosts before, his whole life really, in this old seaside town, and he loved every startling word of these tales, no matter how much they might keep him awake, later. There were any number of storytellers in Nawshant, and the more "professional" (sometimes self-styled) of these would perform at Town Day, and the Holly Folly, and the Fourth of July picnic; and occasionally they were hired out for private parties. Mrs. Little Bo Peep (or Big Bo Beep, as she was known beyond her own presence, aka Nancy Gleason Patterson, once an unsuccessful candidate for the Nawshant School

Committee) was a favorite among mothers, if not always their children. Donning frilly skirts, petticoats, woolen leggings, a pink bonnet, and a shepherd's staff, she spun into various birthday parties and civic events with her Mother Goose stories spilling from her lips. Her long-suffering Labrador Retriever Rex brought up a reluctant rear, perhaps because of his sheepskin costume—a car-seat-covering just lately snatched from the front seat of Nancy's Range Rover, fastened around Rex with safety pins and bungee cords.

Nursery rhymes were her forte but even these she often would bungle when she performed after sunset or on weekends, for at those times she would suggestively call out to any adults present, *My! Isn't this thirsty work! Mrs. Bo Peep could certainly use a glass of wine!* The result of this imbibing was that children were told of Little Bo Beep who went up the hill and then jumped over the moon, and other novel interpretations of old classics. And then she would get into politics, alas. A certain childless, adult element in town was suspected of hiring her for her 'camp' factor, her unintentional hilarity. Nancy guessed these folks were laughing not with her but at her—but a gig was a gig, the money didn't hurt (despite her seemingly-inexhaustible trust fund) and besides, she was born, she felt, to bask in the limelight that is public performance. How people received her was really very much beside the point.

Storyteller Miss Sarah Sawyer (she absolutely refused to be called Ms.) was another thing entirely. A force to be reckoned with, she was President of the Nawshant Horticultural Club (NHC), Head Librarian of the Nawshant Public Library, and a gardening columnist for the weekly *Nawshant Tides* newspaper, which every Thursday ran her *Tip-Toe Through the Tulips with Miss Sarah Sawyer* column. Sean cut her massive lawn weekly from late March until mid-November; each session proved an adventure. She was acknowledged (especially by herself) as *New England's Rare Rhododendron Expert.* Her grandfather and eleven forefathers before had been sea captains, and, when in the right mood (a foul one) she would change the subject abruptly from what fertilizer worked best on Lady Abbot Tea Roses, or whatever, and launch into allegedly-true tales of the sea—involving shocking accounts of piracy, mutiny, murder, tragedy, cannibalism, ghosts, shipwrecks, and disasters; stories that would curl people's hair and make them scurry to the door with their children in tow, if they had any with them. *I shouldn't be telling this story now—not with young children here, I mean,* she would always announce out of the corner of her fuchsia-lipsticked mouth when she was about to change tack, *but just this once...did you never hear of the Screeching Lady of Marblehead? No? She is said NOT be one of the friendliest ghosts. She was...violated, you know. Yes, violated, I say, and then murdered by pirates, right up the way near Fort Sewell, when she refused to give up the diamond ring she was wearing. Oh my yes, they say you can still hear her on certain nights, begging for mercy, and then screeching—screeching something horrible! What happened was...*

If you approached Miss Sawyer and demanded one of these stories she clammed up and refused. Sean—who was addicted to her gory tales for several reasons—had found the best way to pry a story out of the ancient sea-chest of Miss Sawyer's memory was to find her in her home garden, doing an unpleasant, even miserable, chore: she had to be in ill-humor to tell one of the really bad (that is, good) stories. If the day was sunny, and the chores done, and Miss Sawyer was sipping mint tea in her garden's gazebo, by herself or with other ladies from the NHC, you'd get a smilingly-delivered forty-five minute discourse on what grew best in a sea-side garden; or the proper way to uproot and divide perennials; or the only way to assemble watercress-and-cucumber sandwiches when one was "putting together" a Garden Party—especially if you were an aspiring landscaper, as Sean was.

Though Sean semi-appreciated these golden horticultural nuggets, what he really longed for was the kind of story that made him swallow his gum in alarm, and never mind the garden parties.

One of the good sea yarns would be forthcoming *only* if you caught Miss Sawyer in a nasty mood. Put her in a viciously thorny rose bed yanking weeds on a scorching July afternoon; casually walk by her garden gate; then innocently announce what a lovely day it was—and if you could ignore her telling you to go to—well, the devil, the next thing you knew you were hearing about *Captain Finn's Atrocious Harpoon Rampage* or perhaps *When Sailors Must Eat Other Sailors*.

It was from Miss Sawyer that Sean had heard the alarming account of *The Lady in Black*, and, his mind as tangential as ever, he thought of that ghostly personage now as he stood facing the Thicket, wondering whom—or what—he had just seen. Could it have been the Lady in Black?

He really had played it just perfectly, and this is how the telling of that ghostly tale had come about, only a month and a half ago: an otherwise slow Tuesday afternoon just this past August became slightly more exciting (not too much happened in Nawshant) when a rumble of a twelve-wheeler was heard as Sean was cutting the Quinns' lawn. Racing to the front yard, Sean saw a vast, smoke-belching truck turn the corner of Ocean Road and shimmy up the hill. Scrawled on the back end of the truck in white drippy spray paint were the words *Purcell's Pig Farm*. This could mean but one thing: Miss Sawyer's garden was about to receive its annual load of pig manure fertilizer.

I DO apologize! Miss Sawyer would smilingly say to adjacent—"acute" would be a better word—neighbors for the next two weeks, *but really there is nothing better for my darlings!* The stench was beyond bearing, and most of those within smelling distance scheduled their late-summer vacations accordingly—and who could blame them? The truck would beep-beep-back-up into Miss Sawyer's side yard, deposit its wares, and then instantly decamp in a cloud of black diesel stink—the driver couldn't stand the smell either. For the next week Miss Sawyer would trudge about her grounds, shovel in hand, flinging this "black gold" here and there on her "darlings."

During this time she was a veritable barometer of the local weather: if it was cool, and the wind blew freshly from the west, she did this chore upwind with silent resignation; but if it was hot and sticky...

The particular afternoon Sean was recalling now was stiflingly warm, insect-ridden too, and Sean knew the warmer the day, the richer the smell, and the richer the smell, the fouler Miss Sawyer's mood would be. He had waited a knowing hour, then snatched at a sprig of mint from Mr. Quinn's herb garden and raced up to *Lily Vale*, Miss Sawyer's lovely Shingle-style Victorian estate near Second Cliff.

"May I...ahhh...be of some assistance, Miss Sawyer?" Sean asked, tipping his ball-cap as he confronted the red-faced, spade-wielding, rubber-booted septuagenarian flinging shovelfuls of piggy poop hither and thither, with cusses Sean pretended not to hear. A small mint leaf, placed at the end of each of Sean's nostrils, gave some relief from a stink so bad Sean could almost see it, shimmering through the hot air.

"*No!!!!!*" Miss Sawyer bawled, her usually elegant gray coif tangled now and Medusa-like. The flies had arrived and couldn't seem to decide which was more delectable, the manure, or Miss Sawyer herself.

"But can't I help you shovel some of this sh—stuff around?" Sean asked innocently.

"No. For the simple reason that you wouldn't know how much each plant should receive," she explained, somewhat less testily.

"Oh I see. Wow, this stuff must really be good for the plants, huh?" he further ventured.

"It's the best!" she replied briskly. "I would use nothing else. Manure of a porcine nature is loaded with..." Miss Sawyer stopped. She flung down her spade with resolution. "Just hand me that damn hose Sean, will you? I need a break!"

Sean opened the Beaux-Arts wooden garden gate with its charming tinkly bells and complied. He watched and heard, for the first time, someone over seventy gulping water from the end of a green garden hose with all the abandonment, and slurpy audio, of a five year old.

"Ahhhhh, that's better!" the old woman gushed, smacking her lips. She flung the hose down and ambled over to one of the red metal garden chairs against the house wall, beneath an arbor draped with a breaking wave of crimson roses. She commanded Sean to turn off the spigot, then waved him into the chair next to hers with a gesture as imperial as it was irrefutable. She scowled and brooded for a while, in a kind of throbbing, red-faced silence. Sean said nothing, knowing that if he spoke now the jig would be up. Finally she turned to him and whispered,

"As long as I'm here and you're here, Sean, and you being somewhat ignorant, let's have a story then, shall we? Have you never heard of *The Lady in Black*?"

"Huh…gee, no, I don't think so," Sean answered, stifling a fake yawn. But *Bingo!* was what he was thinking.

"She *walks*, you know!" Miss Sawyer dramatically pronounced, leaning herself and her somewhat unpleasant odor toward Sean and wagging a soiled finger at him.

It took Sean a moment to realize Miss Sawyer meant that the Lady in Black was a ghost, and had actually been seen here and there walking around. His arms tingled, even with the heat.

"Well stay in your chair, Sean, and for the love of Heaven don't interrupt me and…oh, for God's sakes, Sean, stop *fidgeting*. Want some water, dear? No? Alright, well, it seems that…"

Thus it was that Sean, by conniving, first heard of *The Lady in Black*. The flies flew unnoticed and the pig poop went unshoveled for the next hour as Miss Sawyer, somewhat aggressively, told of how, during the Civil War, captured officers from the Confederate Army were held as prisoners of war at Fort Warren on George's Island, just a mile or so off Nawshant's southeast shore. Now it seemed one particular captured Confederate officer from South Carolina came from a wealthy rice planting family.

"He was young, and had just married six months earlier, two weeks before he 'joined up,'" Miss Sawyer explained. "Though the prisoners were sometimes let out by day for the fresh air, he was kept in a part of the fort known as the 'Corridor of Dungeons.' Has quite the...ominous ring to it, eh Sean?"

"I'll say."

"*No interruptions!* Now, his wife was no *clinging violet*, no no...*hothouse flower!*" Miss Sawyer pronounced, glaring at Sean as if he doubted every word. "She was a bold thing as my grandmother would say, and since most of the prisoner of war camps were pest houses—between small pox and typhoid and 100 other things they didn't even have names for then—why, three out of four men who went into prison camps then *never came out alive!* So this officer's new bride, when she learned that her husband had been captured, and where he was being held, decided she wouldn't take a chance on losing him. She came up with a bold plan. She was a bold thing with a bold plan, get it?"

"Got it," Sean said, not knowing the question was rhetorical.

"I *said* no interruptions!" Miss Sawyer eyes expanded.

"Sorry," Sean mumbled.

"There's another! Two strikes! One more and you're out!"

Sean just nodded in understanding this time.

"Anyway—where was I?"

Sean—naturally—didn't answer.

"I say, where was I?" Miss Sawyer repeated, with feeling. When Sean said nothing still, thinking this might be a trick, Miss Sawyer brayed, "The raconteuse gives permission for a quick, explicit answer!"

"She was a bold thing with a bold plan," Sean blurted.

"Ah yes—thank you, dear. Permission to speak revoked starting now. So, our enterprising young lady made a journey from the wilds of South Carolina *all the way up to Boston! Behind enemy lines*, you understand! You have no idea what travel for a lady was like then." Miss Sawyer eyed Sean as if this was his fault.

"The stage coaches getting bogged down in muddy sink-holes, the ruffians, brigands, and blackguards on the road, the train tracks bombed out by the enemy—and you have no idea how *hostile* people up north here were to Southerners then—why, we were at war with them! There was even a part of the Underground Railroad right here in Nawshant! It's lucky she wasn't roundly—well, *bitch-slapped*, I believe, is the course, vulgar, and disgusting expression you young people use."

Sean had never used this expression in his life, but filed it away for future use, if and when it might prove useful.

"Aha, you admit it!" Miss Sawyer accused. "Revolting! Why, if I were still teaching…! But anyway, come up she did, came all the way up, just the same—to rescue her husband, as I say—and she reached Hull, just to the south of us. Look, that's it over there, across the Bay. See it? And there's the end of George's Island right there, even closer, where Fort Warren was. Now," Miss Sawyer continued, lowering her voice to a whisper, "do you know what she *bought* in Hull, Sean? Three things. Do you know what?"

Sean knew better this time than to open his mouth. It almost looked like Miss Sawyer was disappointed he hadn't.

"Number One, a pick. Number Two, a sack to carry her things in, which included an old gun she had brought with her. And Number Three, a magnificent black velvet gown," she told him, fluttering her hands downward. "An elegant, full-length piece of *art*, as clothing used to be. You see, she had written to her husband, and made a plan—she would come up and rescue him! She would row out to George's Island and steal him away! You see Sean, security wasn't really lax at Fort Warren, but the captured Confederate officers had a bit more freedom than is usually the case because, after all, they were on an island—it was too far to swim anywhere, so where could the prisoners escape to? And how would they get there? See?"

Sean pointed to his right eye in reply. This elicited half a glare from

Miss Sawyer.

"Well, anyway—once she had these items, she found lodging with an ex-Southerner who was living in Hull, and every night she would watch, with a telescope, Fort Warren on George's Island, where her husband was imprisoned, until she knew the layout of the place. On a dark night of driving rain, the Southerner she was staying with rowed her over to George's Island. By this time she had cut her hair short, and dressed herself in men's clothing.

"After avoiding two sentries on patrol, she came to the outside of the Corridor of Dungeons. She began whistling a tune she and her husband loved, and eventually she and her bundle were lifted up, and pulled through one of the narrow windows in the Fort's walls, for she was very slight of build. She found herself reunited with her astonished husband. And now, with the pick she had brought, they had a way of digging out of the fort. But instead of that, they came up with a bold plan. They, along with the other 600 or so Confederate prisoners, decided they wouldn't tunnel *out* of the fort, but tunnel *in*, toward the center of the Fort, where there was a large grassy field used as a parading ground. Once above ground, they planned to take over the Fort by subduing the 80 or so Union soldiers stationed there, then mount the parapets and turn the 248 guns of the fort onto *the city of Boston,* and reduce it to rubble! They would change the course of the war, and assure victory for the South.

"The men succeeded in tunneling almost all the way out to the parade ground. But then a sentry heard the sound of the pick, told the commanding officer, and an immediate search of the Corridor of Dungeons was ordered—and the tunnel was discovered. Everyone was ordered out. The woman stayed behind, planning on surprising the guards with her gun once all the men were outside. *Put your hands up!* she cried, jumping out of the tunnel once all the other prisoners had been out for some time. *I've a gun and I know how to use it!* Colonel Dimmock, the Union commander of the Fort, thought quickly. He raised his hands in surrender, then began slowly walking toward the woman, his soldiers behind him. Soon they formed a circle around her. The Colonel made a quick lunge for the gun, hitting its barrel, just as the woman fired. But the gun was old and rusty. It misfired, exploding in the process, and a fragment of metal pierced the head of her husband—he was killed instantly! Two days later he was buried in the Fort's graveyard. A few days after that the woman was sentenced to hang.

"They asked her if she had a final request. *Why yes*, she answered, *I'm tired of wearing men's clothes. I'd like to put on my gown once more before I die.* Her magnificent gown was fetched, and they hanged her in it.

"Well, that was the tragic end of Mr. and Mrs. Rebel Rice Planter of South Carolina—*or so it appeared.*"

Another shiver jiggled up Sean's spine.

"Just seven weeks after her death, a certain Yankee soldier, Private Richard Cassidy—I know the story well!—was patrolling in the middle of the night near the area where the execution had taken place. Suddenly he felt icy fingers go round his neck and begin choking him. Struggling madly, he turned and twisted until he was able to see his assailant: the Lady in Black! Summoning all his strength, he broke free and didn't stop running until he reached the guard house. The men laughed at first, thinking this was some kind of joke, but they stopped laughing when it took over an hour to calm the frantic Cassidy down. Just the same he was given 30 days in the guardhouse for deserting his post. Eventually the war ended, and the years passed. Fort Warren was closed after the Spanish-American War, then reactivated again during the First, and then the Second, World Wars. Now, would you believe it?"

Miss Sawyer—who frequently stood to tell her tales, the better to accommodate her vigorous body language—did so now. Then she leaned into Sean's face. "People stationed on the island began seeing her! These were military men now—no civilians were allowed on the island and certainly no women were there—mark that! It's not like we're talking about pot-smoking hippies or New Agey, past-life channelers! These were military men! And if you know military men as well as I do—" here Miss Sawyer cleared her throat—"which of course you couldn't, you'll realize I'm not exaggerating when I say they are a fairly prosy lot. As I say, mark that well! Now—there was the Saturday night poker game, when suddenly every man there felt this icy chill blow into the room, even though the door was shut—and then a few moments later, an empty chair was dragged across the floor! Then dragged back! *Those men signed affidavits certifying this!*

"Later a guard was making his nightly rounds of the fort when he opened a storeroom door. The room was entirely empty. Immediately a woman's voice roared, "Don't you come in here!" Needless to say, he didn't. There are many other sworn statements made by the men stationed out there that they have seen her. Another man was court-martialed for deserting his post one midnight—he said he'd been chased away by the Lady in Black, her black gown billowing in the breeze as she floated after him! Many other men have seen her, standing on the parapet on a full-moon night, a blacker shadow against the black sea and sky, moaning and weeping and sobbing! Look, it's just across the water right there! Surely she might visit Nawshant once in a while! Would *you* go out there some midnight, Sean Sutherland?"

That was always how Miss Sawyer ended one of her terror tales, by asking the audience if they would go to such-and-such a place to see so-and-so. Oh, Sean knew you could also get her in a foul mood by beating her at chess; but Sean had never accomplished this, though he and Miss Sawyer played a dozen times a summer or so, on the lazy afternoons when he'd finish cutting her enormous lawn and she'd entice him over with Lavender-Lemon Balm iced tea. In fact it was she who had taught Sean this old and noble game. Miss Sawyer had a gorgeous chess set, each figure almost a foot high, hand carved and Medieval in design. He'd almost beat her once or twice; but then she'd rally, mount a comeback, and rub her hands together and snicker as she mumbled, "Resistance is *feu-dal*." Sean didn't get the joke the first few times.

That had been six weeks ago, when Sean had half-tricked Miss Sawyer into this tale. He blinked his eyes and brought himself back to the present. It was with a great deal of relief that he remembered that this person he had seen in the Thicket ten minutes ago may have been draped, as Miss Sawyer would say—but this…presence definitely was not wearing a gown. No, whoever it was, it wasn't *The Lady in Black*, as he doubted a Civil War ghost with a fondness for fancy clothes would have a big honkin' number 17 on the back of her gown. He'd have to check with Miss Sawyer next time he saw her—next time he saw her and she was in ill humor, that is—to see if there were any other disembodied spirits floating around the town—especially around the Thicket. Plus he needed to interview Mrs. Hutchinson herself, to get the story of the bells from the horse's mouth, as it were. But the main thing was—if someone was hanging around the Thicket at midnight, perhaps Mrs. Hutchinson *really* was hearing bells—

Sean lingered five more minutes, listening to the wind roar through the Thicket. Creakings and moanings he heard—but no bells. He turned and began trotting home, keeping his head down—just in case *The Lady in Black* was out and about tonight. He breathed easier the closer he got to Greystones.

But as he snuck along the shadowed shrubbery between the Quinns and the McNichols, something in the sky caught his eye—some kind of beam of light. He took it at first to be the moon, or shafts of moonlight leaking out from the tearing clouds—but then he turned and saw the moon *behind* him. *What the…?*

It wasn't a plane flying low, for there was no sound of one. There it was again! A flash of long, silver light! Then it was gone—then here it was again!

He instinctively lowered his body into a creep, and inched forward, beyond the bushes. Greystones lay before him on its own little rise of land. The beam of light seemed to be coming from—it almost seemed to be coming from the other side of his house!

He dashed across the back gardens. Panting, he threw his back flat against the stone walls when he reached the rear of Greystones. He inched down to the next corner, then slowly pushed his head around.

He looked up.

His cousin Kyle's third-floor window was thrown open, as was his shade; and his cousin, holding a very long flashlight, was standing shirtless at his window, signaling up to the sky.

Sean didn't know much Morse code, but the *dot dot dot, flash flash flash* message was plain enough for anyone living in a seaside community to read: SOS, the distress signal, the call for help.

CHAPTER FIVE

MATT, TIMMY, REGINA, AND A HOTTIE

What did it mean? What could it mean? For the second time in an hour, Sean doubted his senses. He closed his eyes, shook his head, then looked again—and as he did, he saw the window in his cousin's room slide down. For a second the bare-chested figure behind the glass, illuminated by the now-thunderous moonlight, lingered—then Kyle vanished in a swirl of darkness as the shade was yanked down.

Sean didn't move, leaning against the mossy corner of Greystones' foundation. Yes, there could be no doubt: his "new" cousin Kyle had just been signaling the international call of distress through his open bedroom window. But why? And to whom? Who up in the sky did Kyle think would see his signal?

Sean waited for something else to happen. And he learned what might have been the first lesson of true detecting: when one watched for something to happen, most times nothing did. Such was the case now.

He looked up at the window again and, seeing nothing, grabbed onto the wisteria and climbed up. The smooth wet wood was slippery. He approached his own window carefully, half expecting the hooded figure he'd seen in the Thicket to leap out at him.

But no. He slipped inside, carefully lowered the windows, then pulled his shade down against the brilliance of the moonlight—but only half-way; a mess of moon spilling into his bedroom was not an unpleasant thing. He undressed and got into bed, listening for any sounds from directly above him—but all was still. If it were anyone else upstairs, Sean would have gone up to see what was troubling Kyle.

He now felt more tired than ever before—and yet, try as he might, too much had happened tonight, and he cast about this way and that for a while before falling into uneasy sleep. When he finally did go off, he dreamed, and it was of himself at the Thicket, staring at the strange hooded figure. The figure turned and became-—the Lady in Black. And then his cousin. And then Mrs. Hutchinson herself. And then that odd real estate lady, Dottie LaFrance, with the head of a seagull. Sean must have had this dream fifty times, and each time the hooded figure with the #17 became someone else—even a chuckling Professor Singleton, demanding more blueberry pie.

His last dream of the night involved himself walking toward the window at the end of the second-floor hall. Kyle was at the window, but half-turned around, and staring back at Sean, beckoning him—silently and ominously—to come closer, and gaze out at the ocean. Sean peered out to where Kyle was pointing. He couldn't see anything, but there was a ghastly moaning and crying, a wave of acute human distress, rising up from the rocky shore.

He woke with a bolt. The moaning became his alarm clock.

Oh, no—seven o'clock already! Sean wondered how he could feel so wide awake and sleepless at one in the morning—and then, after six hours of sleep, wake up more exhausted than he could remember.

"Math and science should study useful problems like this, not calculus," he mumbled, clomping from his warm bedroom into the chilly bathroom, where he showered and got ready for school. Halfway through his shower he remembered the events of the night before, and exactly why he felt so tired this morning. And then he was wide awake again. A mystery to solve! *Two* mysteries to solve! No, make that three: the Bells ringing in the thicket, the person hanging out in the Thicket at midnight, and why his cousin might have sent out the SOS signal.

He emerged from the bathroom in a puff of steam. The morning September sun was slanting across his bedroom floor like warm honey. He dried off in its embrace—heaven. He lifted up the three windows in his room, and opened the storms: naturally Margaret would blast him later for this, saying, *What happens when you leave the windows open? Why, all manner of creepy-crawly creatures get into the house, that's what! And birds! And what would happen if a bird flew into my hair? All HELL would break loose, that's what, and you'd all come to grief!*

It was just sublime this morning—as usual after a storm. A few lazy clouds were sunning themselves in the cobalt sky, slowing as they drifted, as if they wanted a last look at land before casting off across the North Atlantic. The wind had eased up, and was now a fragrant puff, rather than a worrying shriek. The trees and bushes just outside were drippy-drenched with bird calls, and Sean picked out the liquid trills of cardinals, tufted titmice, and robins. There was a refreshing slap to the late-September air, but the day would warm—maybe enough for swimming after school. If he had time. He had lacrosse practice, and also he needed to speak with Mrs. Hutchinson, and get the story directly from its source. And of course, he greatly desired to see his friend Matt after practice—just to see if anything else would happen, after the astonishing events of yesterday after practice.

About which Sean had told no one yet.

It was seven-thirty when Sean came downstairs, his usual time. He swept into the sun-dappled dining room and found Kyle, Uncle Justin, and Margaret already breakfasting. No one really waited for anyone in the morning as a rule, as they were all on different schedules—much to Margaret's chagrin.

"Ah! His Highness joins us at last!" Margaret said. "Forgive me for not standing and singing *Deutschland Uber Alles.*" One never knew what

Margaret would say in the morning—or any other time. It all depended on what she was reading.

"As long as it doesn't happen again," Sean answered, though it was all Greek to him, and he looked askance at Uncle Justin.

"Some of our forebears came from Germany 400 years ago," he muttered by way of explanation. It looked like he was trying not to laugh. "That's a sort of…uhmm…anthem."

This morning's fare was oatmeal and wheat germ cereal, with wild raspberries fresh from the garden, just-squeezed orange juice, and Irish soda bread that Margaret had made that morning. *Eat like a king in the morning, a prince at noon, and a beggar in the evening,* Margaret was always saying in the morning, and certainly her breakfasts were royal. But she never trotted out this epigram at lunchtime or dinner—meals that were equally imperial. Sean's food was already waiting for him, and Uncle Justin and Margaret had been chuckling about something. Kyle, sitting up in his chair as if his life depended on the rectitude of his posture, was eating mechanically and silently, keeping his eyes on his bowl.

Kyle's presence appeared to be strictly ornamental. He was dressed in the dark green dress pants he had worn the night before, and a white long-sleeve button-down shirt—far too slick an outfit, Sean thought, for a typical school day at Nawshant High. Sean himself was in a tie-dye T-shirt and navy blue board shorts. But maybe Kyle had nothing else to wear?

"Hey everybody, good morning," Sean called, plunking down. Margaret had put Kyle beside Sean, while she and Uncle Justin were at the respective heads of the table, as they usually were. A fresh bouquet of goldenrod and asters, still wet with this morning's dew, glowed from the center of the table.

"And uhmm….how did everyone sleep through the storm last night?" Uncle Justin asked brightly. Sometimes he corrected papers while at breakfast, or went over the notes of his upcoming lectures; but this morning he was doing neither, perhaps for Kyle's sake.

"Fine," Sean answered, feeling himself color a little. His cousin said nothing.

"There were all kinds of things going bump in the night last night!" Margaret ejaculated. "I was almost thinking that one of you might have snuck—"

"Oh sorry, pardon me, Margaret!" Sean blurted loudly, not meaning to be rude but only wishing to change the subject instantly.

Several moments of shocked silence greeted his query.

"Yeeeeesssssssss?" Margaret answered warningly, scandalized that Sean had interrupted her. Uncle Justin and Kyle looked over at him.

"Uhm...oh! There's this...ahhh...juniper tree! Up the street, right? And ahhh...it looks *exactly* like a figure in a robe and a turban, about to give a public proclamation!"

Even Kyle made a face of bemusement at the strangeness of Sean's statement; Sean would have done the same, and he wondered why he had thought of that funny looking bush, of all things—but he was desperate to change the subject—

"It's true!" he went on, committed now to the topic. "You know, like the arms outraised and the palms up, like he's...ahhh...beseeching people to...to...do *something*. Or come over to his way of thinking about some...ahhh...important issue, like. And uhm...I was just wondering, what would each of you say to the world, if you had the chance—I mean, if you suddenly found yourself up on a rooftop, like, with a massive crowd gathered at your feet? What would you...uhm...proclaim?"

There was an awkward silence—

"What a *fascinating* question!" Uncle Justin beamed at last.

"Mary Mother of God, is it *drugs* you're on this morning?" Margaret fretted, at about the same time.

"Now Margaret, don't be absurd!" Uncle Justin intervened. "What kind of encouragement is that for Sean, when it's such a philosophically *vital* topic? What truths *would* we proclaim, having the chance? What truths do we stand for? Do we even know?"

Margaret made answer, being Margaret, about exactly what her truths were, and the first of these was that young people should never interrupt their elders. Soon she and Uncle Justin were embroiled in their own little tête-à-tête. Sean took the opportunity to turn to Kyle.

"Hey uhm, people usually don't get all dressed up for school, Kyle," Sean advised, lowering his voice. "Casual is kind'a the rule. If you want, maybe we can go shopping this weekend, if you need some new clothes." Sean felt bad for Kyle—after all, he had sent out distress signals for heaven's sake from his window the night before—and Sean was trying to be helpful at the same time. *No one* dressed up for school in Nawshant!

Kyle kept his head down. Sean thought he looked like he was going to bawl.

"I prefer to dress for school," he mumbled, after a minute.

"Good man yourself!" Margaret heartily opined. Of course just because she had been speaking with Uncle Justin, this in no way meant Margaret would miss any other conversation at the breakfast table.

That ended that attempt to draw Kyle into talk. But at least it had changed Margaret's topic about people sneaking out—

"Ahhh…hey, my friends Matt, Timmy, and Regina will be picking me up soon, if you want to ride to school with us," Sean added, unwilling to give up so easily.

"I'm all set," Kyle mumbled. He didn't bother looking up.

Sean rolled his eyes. *Attitude!* He caught Uncle Justin staring at him and the latter shrugged his shoulders as if to say, *Keep trying, Sean, he WILL come round.*

"And why wouldn't he want to walk?" Margaret demanded, setting down her cup of steaming tea. Her index finger raised itself and began jabbing the air—speaking of proclamations. "The laziest blackguard on earth would want to walk this morning! 'Tis a day so glorious 'twould make the angels weep!' And what better way for Kyle to see his new hometown? Now, some others I know could walk as well—but *no*—not them! They must be *chauffeured*, if you please. And 'tis only a mile each way, God help us! When *I* was a wee slip of a lass, didn't we walk five Irish miles to school, each way, and—"

"It was uphill both ways?" Sean teased.

"May I be excused, sir?" Kyle murmured, looking over at Uncle Justin. He had already finished his breakfast.

"Oh, yes, why ahhh, certainly, Kyle, certainly! We'll uhm…see you at dinner this evening."

"And what time might that be, sir?"

"Oh, ahhh, usually, well, if no one has an appointment—and if company isn't coming and all—"

"Seven sharp, and not a moment after," Margaret muttered without looking up, wiping the corner of her mouth with her napkin. "By the way, I read last week that George Washington was such a stickler for punctuality, he would wait outside the room in which he had a meeting, and sweep in just as the clock was tolling the hour, the very soul of punctuality." She looked meaningfully at Sean as she said this.

"Very good. See you at 1900 hours," Kyle answered.

"Enjoy your first day at Nawshant High!" Uncle Justin smiled.

"Thank you sir, I shall try," Kyle answered, picking up a slim navy-blue backpack that was leaning on the wall behind him. "I wish a fine day for you as well, sir. Ma'am, Sean." He tipped his head, then strode out into the hall. A second later they heard the front hall door close quietly.

"Well! The poor soul won't wear out anyone's ear, that's for sure," Margaret commented, rising to clear the table. "Unlike some others we know, who could talk to a crack in the wall. God help us! The poor miserable orphaned creature! And the fine looking lad he is too! Well, handsome is as handsome does, I always say, and I suppose he really doesn't…" The rest of Margaret's commentary wandered off with her into the kitchen.

"At least he said goodbye to you, Sean," Uncle Justin commented, sipping the last of his coffee and rising from the table. "And he will come round. I commend you for your efforts to lure him into conversation, as well as into your coterie of companions. Keep it up! Remember, he's family, and we're all he has now. And I shall ponder your earlier question throughout the day, regarding what I might say from the rooftops! Oh, today's word! I was almost forgetting! How about…let me see now… *taciturn*."

Sean didn't answer immediately. Very often the Word of the Day had something to do with what had transpired at the breakfast table.

"Ahhh…quiet?" Sean ventured.

"Excellent!" Uncle Justin called behind him, dashing into the hall and grabbing at his jacket just as Margaret rushed out to get it for him. "That's it exactly. *Habitually un-talkative*, one might add. Have a lovely day, Sean, and the very best of luck on your calculus exam! Goodbye Margaret, see you this evening."

"You're forgetting your briefcase, Professor."

"Oh! Am I? I am! Thank you! Where *would* we be without you?"

"Ouf! Get out of that!" Margaret pooh-poohed, but she was smiling as she said it.

A moment later Sean heard the beeping of the Volkswagen Bug outside in the driveway, signaling that his friends had come.

"Uh-oh," he mumbled, glancing at his phone, then dashing upstairs to brush his teeth—not forgetting to touch the respective number of banisters along his frantic OCD way.

"He's not ready yet again!" he heard Margaret bellow outside the hall door, and this elicited a chorus of *What else is new?* from Timmy, Regina, and Matt waiting in the car. "And yet you still touch those banisters, God help us, late or not!" Margaret called out after Sean.

"Can't help it!" Sean cried two minutes later, flying down the stairs and out the front door, Margaret in hot pursuit with his backpack.

"You never forget the touchies, but here's your backpack, you *ama-*

dán!" Margaret panted, shoving the backpack at Sean. "Who is he like? Just like his uncle! Between the two of them they run me ragged. But do I get any thinner? No, not I! Not one ounce! Perhaps it's because I've never sniffed the smell of wet steel!"

"My turn for the front," Sean panted to Timmy, who was sitting in the front passenger seat. It was Regina and Timmy Quinn's car—Regina drove to school and Timmy drove home, so Sean, and Matt White, and Timmy Quinn took turns "riding shotgun" in the mornings. Positions were reversed on the way home, with Timmy driving, but this was where the system got complicated, as very often after-school activities made one or more of the group miss their afternoon rides. Still, everyone knew the system and the schedule, but that didn't stop anyone from trying to get away with an extra ride in the front should somebody else forget.

"Damn, I was hoping you'd disremember," Timmy mumbled, hopping out and squeezing into the back beside Matt, giving Sean a high-five in greeting as he did.

"That's not a word," Regina accused. "Disremember."

"Sure it is, cuz I just said it," Timmy answered.

Regina and Timmy Quinn were red-headed twins. Looking at them, one never forgot either fact. "Regina's the long-haired one," everyone had said growing up, trying to tell them apart, for until their teens they were almost indistinguishable. Now that they were seventeen, there were of course many other obvious differences, although they were still the same height. They seldom quarreled but frequently snipped, were almost always together, and usually shared the same opinion about things, which saved time during heated discussions about what to do and when to do it. They had been best friends with Sean since he had wandered into their backyard—directly behind the back gardens at Greystones—when he was four while Margaret was hanging out sheets.

The Twins were amazing (Sean thought) artists who had already been accepted to Massachusetts College of Art in Boston for next September.

The one issue between them now was whether to move to Boston next fall, or commute. Regina longed, desperately, to live in the city; Timmy wanted to commute because almost all of the paintings he created were abstract seascapes depicting Nawshant's rocky shores, grottoes, and beaches—the ocean was his muse. Regina's point was that they had been in Nawshant all their lives, and ought to take a chance and live in an exciting, bustling city. Nawshant and its inhabitants were beautiful and it and they would always be "home," Regina felt; but it was getting a bit old—it was time for a change. *There's the good OLD ocean again*, she'd say dryly, seeing that familiar landmark, or, *Oh, there are all our good OLD friends...again*, trying to change Timmy's mind.

Look how beautiful the sunset on the water is tonight! Timmy would counter, or, *aren't we lucky to go swimming in the ocean after school almost every day in September, and half of October?* They had to apply for dormitory space by November 15 if they wanted it, so the disagreement was coming up more often. Lately Timmy had been saying that if they took dorm space without really needing it, they would be depriving two out-of-state students from attending. *Those poor, gifted artists in Kansas!* he'd murmur, and Sean and Matt would laugh. But Regina countered that there were plenty of apartments for rent around what would be their new college, and therefore Timmy's argument didn't signify. She also waxed lyrical about all the new young women Timmy would meet—he had had about ten girlfriends already over the past few years, the relationships (obviously) never lasting very long.

"What can I say, artists get bored quickly," he said in defense.

"He's just afraid of commitment," Regina always answered.

"Commitment?" Timmy would counter. "When you're seventeen? Eighteen? Are you crazy?"

"What was Margaret talking about, *the smell of wet steel?*" Timmy asked Sean, as they put on their seat belts. "What's that about?"

"Oh, something...something. It was a line she read in a book yesterday, about someone always disliking the smell of wet steel. She thought it was such a weird line she's been repeating it ever since."

"I love how the only allusions Margaret ever makes are to her own quotes," said Matt from the rear.

Matt White, with shaggy dark hair and hazel eyes, lived on the other side of town, just after the end of the Causeway that linked Nawshant with the mainland. He played on the football team. Sean and Timmy played lacrosse and were always encouraging Matt to quit football and play lacrosse with them. But Matt could seldom be moved on things.

Matt's mother was a single mom who ran the *Sea Witch Fortune Telling Parlor and Day Spa* a few towns up in Marblehead—an amazingly lucrative business she had built from the ground up. Women—and now, for the past three years, men, too—could go in for a haircut, massage, facial, whatever, and also get their fortunes told at the same time. In addition to great word-of-mouth referrals, her shop had been featured on some Hollywood-esque television show two years earlier, and since then people had to book their appointments a month in advance, as her place was enjoying a national vogue. Mrs. White drove a motorcycle and was deemed *uber* cool among many of the teachers and most of the students at Nawshant High. But Matt had said more than once growing up that he wished his mother was more "normal," though most kids couldn't believe it. Sean himself thought Mrs. White was nice, although perhaps a bit *grand*, as Margaret would have called it, and certainly faddy. She called Matt *Matty Darling*. Before Matt got his license, she'd forget more often than not to pick him up when arrangements had been made. Often she excused herself by saying she was trying a new diet. "It's not a lack of *love*, Matty darling," Sean had heard her explain on one occasion, "it's a lack of *carbs*." If Matt had ever had a father living with them, he must have left the family early, as there was never any mention of one.

Like most of the kids at NHS, Matt listened to rap, but his favorite music was old Motown soul songs. That was why Matt had suggested to

Sean the name for Sean's lawn-cutting business: *Mow-Town*.

During the annual Parent-Student-Teacher Night ten years earlier, in the second grade, Uncle Justin had got talking to a colleague from his university, and that was when eight-year-old Sean had seen Matt sitting alone at the back of the room, keeping one dreary eye on the door and the other on the clock. Sean had rushed over to him immediately.

"Where's your parents?" Sean had asked sympathetically, wondering if he had found another orphan like himself.

"I don't have a *stupid* father, and my mother probably forgot," the boy blurted, kicking out one leg. "She's always working. I *told* her it started at seven!"

"Oh," Sean answered. "You're lucky. I have an awesome uncle, and Margaret too—she's our housekeeper? But I don't have a mother or a father. They both died in a car accident."

It seemed natural that they should be best friends since that night, and they had been. Two other things Sean and Matt had bonded over was their love for skateboarding, and for maps. In fact frequently they made their own maps, with invented names for countries and rivers and cities. Last year in World History, Matt had passed Sean a map depicting the topic they were covering that day (the conflict-ridden Middle East) and Matt had labeled the whole area *Hotmessapotamia*. But just a week or two ago Matt had passed Sean a map during Math class, when Matt was in one of his darker moods, depicting a country called *Despondia*, the "saddest country in the world." "My native country," Matt had written on the map. The thing was, Matt had a semi-large purple pucker of a scar or birthmark on the left side of his face, under his left eye. No one knew how he got it because no friends ever asked—and if rude people or strangers made inquiries, Matt glowered at them, and they didn't ask again. The scar hadn't seemed to bother Matt much when they were younger, but Sean had noticed lately how Matt was becoming increasingly self-conscious about it, staying away from parties, standing in the shadows during dances at the high school, and always sitting in the last row in all his classes, so that only the windows would be on the "scar side" of his face. He declined dates even when girls did the asking.

Sometimes Matt got into his mother's cache of alcohol and drank, becoming even moodier. Some kids at school drank whenever they could, but when Sean was twelve he had given his solemn word to Margaret, whose brother had died of alcoholism, that he wouldn't drink alcohol until he was twenty. He was curious about it, because everyone said it made you feel awesome—but the evidence seemed to the contrary as far as Matt was concerned, who only got angrier and more depressed when he drank. Plus there was the dreaded "hangover" the next day that everyone talked about, and lots of times Sean had seen kids vomiting after a dance or party—and Sean hated that more than anything in the world. Plus drunk people always seemed a bit ridiculous.

In truth and in private, Sean thought Matt's scar made him look even more handsome than he was—dashing, like a pirate or something—though of course he had never said this to Matt, and felt guilty about feeling this way, because he suspected it was "patronizing" of him. *Patronizing* had been Uncle Justin's Word of the Day one morning two years ago. Once Uncle Justin had defined it, Sean had thought about his feelings regarding Matt's scar. It was easy for Sean to feel the scar was cool and mysterious, because he himself wasn't the one who had to walk around with it for the rest of his life. That's why he felt guilty.

"My mother makes people beautiful for a living, but she can't do jack about this," Matt had said just two weeks ago, when he had been drinking a little. "I look like it's Halloween, year-round."

Sean had felt terrible when Matt said these words. He had wanted to say something, many things—but was so afraid of insulting Matt by saying the wrong thing that he ended up saying nothing—which was probably worst of all. He had decided he would say something though—which is why he had said what he'd said yesterday, after lacrosse and football practice were over and he and Matt were alone on the fields behind the high school.

This was the thing he hadn't told anyone about yet.

As Regina put the Bug into gear, Sean and Matt nodded to each other, nothing more—Sean wondered if Matt felt as awkward as Sean did, after what had happened the day before. Not wanting to show this, Sean instantly launched into conversation, his cure for all awkward social moments. But he was interrupted by the sound of a pert *toot-toot*—

"Hi'ya kids! Wanna make a *thousand bucks*?" a voice rasped beside them. Turning, they saw a woman in a late-model luxury sedan pulling up right alongside their car.

"Good grief!" Sean half-laughed under his breath. It was that pushy real estate woman Dottie LaFrance again. Today she was wearing big round black sunglasses, though her facial expression remained the same as it had been last night: almost painfully cloying.

"Huh?" Matt called from the back seat.

"That's right!" Dottie gushed. "Anyone gettin' me a lead for a house sale or buildable lot gets a check for one *thousand* dollars!" She then began shoving business cards at them.

"Legitimately?" Timmy asked from the back.

"It's all on the up and up!" Dottie went on. "Gimme a call if you know *anyone* selling their house or buildable lot! I got *dozens* of clients just bustin' to come out this way! Make sure you ask for Dottie LaFrance! That's ME!"

"We have to go now," Regina blurted, driving off. "What a weirdo," she added a moment later, looking in her rear view.

"She's been all over town for a while now," Matt said from the back. "I've seen her car around." Matt was really into cars.

"We literally had to throw her out of the house last night," Sean said. He paused. "But there's something funny about her."

"How do you mean?" Timmy asked.

"I don't know, I can't really put my finger on it. I mean for one thing—well, she's got corporate breath."

"*Corporate breath*?" Regina and Timmy asked in unison. Matt made a face of bewilderment.

"I mean," Sean explained, "you know how I get with smells, right? Like super-sensory and everything? And my chemical sensitivity? She doesn't...she just doesn't *smell* like a real estate agent."

"Oh, right," Timmy said after a minute. "And ahhh....what does the average real estate person smell like again?"

"Dude, it's no joke! Well for one thing, they ahhh...well, usually they douse themselves in perfume—or cologne if they're a guy, I've noticed that—and the women usually wear a ton of make-up and stuff—"

"Get back to the corporate breath," Timmy said. "You're inspiring me, dude! I think my next painting will be *Nude Descending a Staircase with Corporate Breath*."

"Okay, fine, make fun. But seriously, I noticed last night when she... invaded our house, she has a different smell to her—like...spreadsheets. She smells like spreadsheets and...calculators kept at a chilly temperature. I don't know, it's hard to explain. But I don't think she's who she says she is."

"She's not Dotty LaFrance, she's Peggy LaFrance," Matt joked.

"Chilly calculators, hmmm," Regina commented gently. "And this isn't your overactive imagination? Or having watched too many *X-Files*?"

"Alright, well...forget about her for a minute," Sean said, "though she's up to something. Dudes, *why* didn't you answer my texts last night? Or call me back? I tried to reach you all like 400 times. You are not going to believe what happened last night. Check this out!"

Sean related the astonishing existence, then arrival, of his cousin Kyle, leaving out the fact that Kyle's attitude needed major adjustment. "I had *no* idea I even had any other family!" Sean finished. He refrained, too, from mentioning Kyle's OCD, another link they shared.

"Oh my God, really? A lost cousin?" Regina gushed, as they turned onto Ocean Road. They always took the scenic, dawdling way to school, as long as they weren't running too late, for they had discussed this, and had all agreed that this, too, would be their way of living life, the unhurried way. "How cool is that? Does he resemble the word *hottie*?"

"Does he want to play on our lacrosse team?" Timmy asked.

"Does he have opposable thumbs?' Matt wondered.

Sean thought this last remark so funny he snorted.

"So how come he's not with you now, if he's going to Nawshant High?" Matt asked further. Matt always got to the heart of matters.

Sean answered the last question first.

"His mother died like a month ago," he said. He opened his mouth to say more, then thought better—or worse—of it. It wouldn't be right to say more, and it would be disloyal to talk about his cousin's…well, jerkiness. That might turn his friends against his cousin before Kyle even had a chance with them. "I think he's still dealing with it and he just…wants to be alone, like."

"That stinks," Regina and Timmy said, simultaneously.

"He seems to be the quiet type, but at night he lip-syncs to Beyoncé records in front of the mirror, dancing around with an orange wig," Matt said. Matt had a keen (if different) sense of humor. Sean had to laugh just at the thought of this.

"Don't be cruel, Matt White," Regina scolded. "So, is he a cutie?"

"*Is he going to play lacrosse?*" Timmy repeated.

"Well, you can all draw your own conclusions," Sean answered, "and ask him yourselves—that's him right up ahead."

Such was the case. They all turned, and there was Sutherland, Kyle J., marching along the verge of Ocean Road as if he were part of a North Korean military parade. In one of his swinging hands he held what clearly was a map. But as he walked along Kyle kept gazing out at the ocean, ruffled and blue as a peacock's feather this morning. Sean was about to say he had only been kidding, as he was sure Kyle didn't want to be bothered right now; but before he could, Regina gave a friendly tap on the car horn and pulled over.

"Hi, you must be Kyle!" she called. "Sean was just telling us about you. Hop on in!" Then she beamed her great disarming smile.

"Kyle, this is Regina, her brother Timmy, and Matt," Sean said. He noticed that his cousin's eyes—the quick flash that he saw of them—were red-edged—as if he'd been crying? Or was it just hay fever?

"How do you do," Kyle said, rising to his full height and nodding at each of them in turn, but keeping his eyes downward. "And thank you, Miss, for the offer, but really I'm all set."

Sean turned to Regina to see what her response might be—especially after being called *Miss*. But he wasn't sure he had seen this look on her face before—the green eyes wide and shining, the smiling mouth open. She half waved and drove off with the car in third gear, and it shuddered and bucked until Timmy yelled *Clutch, Sis!*

"*What* a cutie-patootie!" Regina sighed, quickly turning the wheel to avoid going off the road, but still keeping one eye on the rear-view mirror. "Oh my *God*, Sean! *Whoa!*" She turned to Sean, her radiant green eyes speaking volumes.

The rest of the car went silent—shocked at Regina's reaction. While Regina had done some dating the last three years, she had announced that this year, senior year, she wouldn't be dating at all: she was thinking about her future "next year in Boston," she said, and didn't want to get "bogged down" dating someone from Nawshant. She also had said once or twice that her experience with the eligible males of Nawshant High had led her to believe that many of the good-looking guys seemed to be not the brightest bulbs in the circuit, the smart guys were somewhat geeky, and the really nice ones were taken. "I know that sounds so stereotypical and lame," she had explained, "but if the shoe fits..." She was looking for intelligence, she explained, intelligence, kindness, and nice looks, a good person—qualities she thought she could find only in a larger, more cosmopolitan, locale—like Boston, for example.

"Sweet mystery of life, I have found you at last!" Matt sang-teased from the back seat.

"Shut up," Regina snapped as she half-turned to Sean. "Tell me *every single thing* about him, Sean!"

"Uhmm....really? Well, I don't know much," Sean answered, adjusting his green Boston Red Sox baseball cap in the visor mirror and checking out his now three-day old goatee. "He's been going to a military academy down in Georgia all his life. Apparently his—"

"Georgia?" Regina interrupted. "Oh my God! I thought I heard one of those awesome Southern accents! He has one, right Sean?"

"Uhm, a little, I think," Sean answered. "He ahhh…hasn't said much so far, so it's hard to tell. He just came up last night. Uncle Justin's his guardian now because, like I say, his mother just passed away last month, and I guess his father died a few years ago. I think—I think Uncle Justin said he was a little unhappy about having to leave school and come up here because—"

"Well *of course he is!*" Regina gushed. "Who wouldn't be? Oh, the poor thing, with no friends and all." She fell silent, and everyone could tell plans of a rescuing-and-romantic nature were forming in her head.

"No wonder he looked a little like he was crying," Timmy said.

"Oh, *was he?*" Regina asked, and Sean had never heard her voice so full of concern applied to anything other than a wounded animal by the side of the road.

Just then they rounded another serpentine bend on Ocean Road, and there before them lay the beginnings of the Thicket. Sean opened his mouth to report the details of this adventure as well—but something held him back. Though the Thicket looked infinitely more benign with morning's first kiss of sunshine adorning it, Sean shuddered when he recalled whom—or possibly *what*—he had seen here last night. But his heart skipped a beat when he saw someone else moving around its outer edge—

"Stop the car!" he shouted.

"What, what?" Regina cried, jumping at Sean's words. Everyone peered out the windows to see what had startled Sean so—

"You scared her—she's got Georgia on her mind," Matt teased.

"Oh, that's just what's-her-name," Timmy called. "Mrs. Hutchinson there."

"I know it, but pull over anyway," Sean instructed. "I need to—I want to ask her something."

"You gonna ask her to the Halloween Dance?" Timmy asked.

"No, it has to do with…something Professor Singleton told me." Sean hopped out of the car when Regina stopped, then put his head back in the window. "You guys go on."

"You'll be late for our calculus test," Timmy sang in a warning tone, wasting no time in hopping into the vacant front seat.

"No I won't, I'll run," Sean told his friends. "Go ahead, go, I'll see you soon. If I miss Home Room tell them I'm coming soon."

He waved his friends off, then crossed the street. Mrs. Hutchinson, seeing Sean, was already making her way toward him.

"Funny seeing you, Sean Sutherland," she called as she approached him. "I was going to call you today. Come here, please! I'd like to speak with you about something quite strange!"

CHAPTER SIX

SEAN ON THE CASE

"Oh, sure, Mrs. Hutchinson, what a beautiful day!" Bird song was falling like rain, and the morning sun brightened both body and spirit.

"What?" the old woman asked sharply. She looked up and around. "Oh yes—yes, I suppose it is, but I have no time for—Sean, listen, I want to ask you something. As I say, I was planning on calling you this afternoon." She was wearing a blue sweater and a white tennis hat.

"Oh. Sure thing, Mrs. Hutchinson." Sean thought perhaps Mrs. Hutchinson wanted to hire him out for some landscaping work.

"Do you remember," she began briskly, "when poor Earl Stafford heard those voices coming from his front bushes? What am I saying, of course you remember, you solved it!"

"Uhm, sure. I just…I just sensed he was telling the truth."

Mrs. Hutchinson was eying him keenly. "Exactly!" she said, tapping her cane squarely on the edge of the road. "You knew he was telling the truth." She didn't seem at all to be suffering from some kind of dementia, as Professor Singleton had theorized. In fact quite the contrary; she seemed as sharp as—well, a razor, though perhaps not Occam's.

Just then Kyle swung up the road, striding along in his odd short-stepped martial way, like someone somewhere was playing Souza. Sean waved to him. Kyle looked over with a puzzled expression and nodded curtly, never missing a beat.

"Now who's that young man?" Mrs. Hutchinson asked, squinting. "I don't think I've seen him before. But you young people grow so quickly."

Sean filled Mrs. Hutchinson in on the events that had brought Kyle up to Nawshant and Greystones.

"Hmmm. Imagine that. Well, he's come to the right place, that's certain. I'm sure he'll be happy in time, though he seems reticent now."

"Reticent," Sean smiled. "Exactly. Reticent and taciturn. Well, you were saying, Mrs. Hutchinson?"

"Well, Sean, what I want to ask you is this." She cleared her throat and fixed him again with her eye. "Would you believe me," she said in a lowered voice, "if I told you that—well, frankly, bells, large, clanging bells, were ringing from somewhere inside here—" she half turned and waved her cane vaguely at the Thicket, "at night? Quite late at night?" Her watery gray eyes, larger behind her glasses, lost their fierceness, and took on a pleading look.

Sean recalled Professor Singleton's words about Occam's razor, and whether it was more likely Mrs. Hutchinson was imagining things, or that someone was ringing big honkin' cathedral bells inside an impenetrable wilderness of tangled trees, vines, and brambles. His head sided with Professor Singleton—the idea was absurd—but his heart, his instincts, whatever one might call a sixth sense, told him that Mrs. Hutchinson had been hearing bells—real bells. On top of this, his inclination became a certainty when he remembered the strange, hulking figure he had seen right here last night. Clearly something funny was going on in the Thicket—

Sean looked Mrs. Hutchinson squarely in the eye.

"I do believe you, Mrs. Hutchinson," he said firmly. "I do."

Her thin white eyebrows lifted up, while her eyes softened.

"Bless you, Sean," she said quietly, grasping his forearm. "Bless you. I know there are some in town who wouldn't and won't believe me—*she's gone off her rocker, at her age*—but let me just say that I can still do the *Times* crossword puzzle faster than anyone I know—even Sarah Sawyer, though she'd die before she admitted it. When that ceases to be the case, only then will I doubt my own senses. Oh, I am glad you believe me, Sean. Can you guess why?"

"Uhm, well, I'd think anyone would want–"

"Above and beyond the obvious human yearning for sympathy," Mrs. Hutchinson interrupted. "I can't expect you to know this, Sean, but when I announced to my seventh grade class a hundred years ago that I would win a tennis championship someday, they laughed. So I've become used to living without sympathy, although it is nice of course when one gets it. But it's important that you believe me for another reason."

"Oh?"

"Yes—because I want to *hire* you to solve this mystery for me."

Sean's surprise at Mrs. Hutchinson's words was exceeded only by his elation. Hadn't he been wondering only last night if he could ever make a life out of solving mysteries? Maybe the Universe was signaling to him that the answer to that was a resounding *Yes*.

"I won't let you down, Mrs. Hutchison," Sean vowed.

"Well, you helped old Earl out, and I think you can help me out too. Certainly you have more energy than I do. You have an innate curiosity too, I've noticed. And it goes without saying you're a lot spryer than I am, and can get inside the Thicket and see what this is all about."

"Okay," Sean answered. He had to restrain himself from busting into a break-dance. He slipped his back-pack off, then went hunting for a note-book. "Okay, why don't we start by getting all the facts down."

Mrs. Hutchinson chuckled. "You sound like someone in a detective movie," she said. "But that's good! I agree."

"Oh, and Mrs. Hutchinson," Sean added. "I have a bit of information for you, too, regarding this case."

"Oh?"

Sean loved the way the wealthy old woman drew the word out into three syllables—

"I do. Okay, well, to tell the truth…uhm…Uncle Justin had Professor Singleton to dinner last night, and he—"

"Ah, I see! Say no more! And Professor Singleton told all of you the story of my hearing the bells, and my questions to him last week."

"Uhm, well—yeah. And—"

"Good old Nawshant! People say sailing is our favorite occupation—but we all know better! And I *know* he didn't believe me. But I can't say I blame him, exactly. We want our learned people to be somewhat skeptical, I suppose, until they see hard evidence. But that's why I'm hiring *you*, Sean, and not him. Anyway, go on."

"Well, I couldn't sleep last night, I was so fascinated by the story. And uhm…well, just between you and me—"

"*Sub rosa?*" Mrs. Hutchinson asked. "Oh. I can see you don't know what that means. What are they teaching you in that school of yours? I always said when Latin was no longer mandatory—but, well, you don't want to hear my old-fashioned notions. It means 'under the rose,' referring to an ancient practice of hanging a rose above a clandestine meeting, to signal secrecy."

"Hmm, the DL. Yeah, *sub rosa* then. I like that! Well anyway, I wouldn't want Uncle Justin—and especially Margaret—to know this, but sometimes I…well, occasionally over the years I've…well, snuck out."

Mrs. Hutchinson laughed. "Don't all young people? My sister Abby and I did the same thing when we were young—we'd play tennis at midnight, when the moon would light the court out back like daylight. But what in the world does *DL* mean?"

"Cool!" Sean said. It startled him, though only for a moment, to think that Mrs. Hutchinson had once been his own age. "Oh, *DL* is *Down Low*. Like, don't go flapping your gums about something. So anyway, I couldn't sleep last night, thinking about the bells ringing and all—"

"I knew I hired the right man for the case!" Mrs. Hutchinson interjected.

"And I think it was sometime after eleven when I decided I couldn't stand it anymore, and I had to come up here and take a look myself. I came up Ocean Road from Crows' Nest Lane, then came across the street to this spot right here." Sean slowed down, approaching the point with relish. "Well, I was standing like just *here*, when the moon came out and I saw—someone in the Thicket. Like seven feet in, right by that white birch tree."

"Then that explains *this*!" Mrs. Hutchinson said, grabbing Sean by the forearm and leading him several feet down the side of the road. "Look!" she added, pointing her cane at a clear set of large boot-tracks heading into the Thicket.

"You know what?" Sean answered excitedly, "you'll laugh maybe, Mrs. Hutchinson, but now I know how you felt when I said I believed you, about the bells. Since last night a part of me has been wondering if I just *imagined* seeing someone here last night, with the moon in and out of the clouds and all. Now I *know* I saw someone."

"What did they look like?" Mrs. Hutchinson hissed. "What were they doing?"

"Well, they were big, for one thing. He—I'm sure it was a he—was wearing a hooded sweatshirt, hood up, with the number 17 on the back of it. He was looking around a little and…I don't know, maybe like he was almost waiting for someone. Or something. And…well, that's really all I can tell you, because it freaked me out something fierce to see someone here at midnight and I…well I—"

"Bolted?" Mrs. Hutchinson suggested.

"Yeah," Sean admitted with a laugh. The encounter didn't seem quite so sinister now, on this beautiful late-September morning.

"He who retreats today, lives to fight another day, Sean. Or as your Margaret puts it rather pithily, *a good run is better than a bad stand.*"

"Let me see if I can see how far the tracks go in," Sean said. He pushed his way into the edge of the Thicket. Not ten feet in he snagged his right hand on a thorny briar, drawing blood, as he had done the night before; then on the way out he put a small rip in his shorts. He fought the OCDish urge to put a small rip on the *other* leg of his pants, for balance.

"You'll have to come back later, Sean, when you're more appropriately dressed for bush-whacking."

"Well," Sean said, retreating back to the side of the road where Mrs. Hutchinson awaited him, "whoever it was went in further than ten feet anyway. The tracks go off a ways in that direction…." Sean started walking farther up the side of the Thicket, "and come out here. Look!" It was true. The same large footprints were clearly visible twenty feet farther up, because of the rains the night before.

"Hmmm."

"I'll come back this afternoon," Sean said, "and see how far they go in, if I can get in a little more. In the meantime maybe you could tell me what's happened so far." Sean took his notebook out.

"I've written it all down, Sean," Mrs. Hutchinson said, rummaging in the large pocket of her sweater. "Dates and times when I've heard the bells ringing." She pulled out a small green notebook with lined, age-yellowed pages, wrapped with a rubber band. She undid the book, wet her thumb, turned to a page in the middle, and began reciting while Sean made notes.

"Okay, let me see now…August 17. Listen what I've written. *I had the oddest dream last night—the moon was just past the full and it was rather warm in the room. I woke up and could have sworn, just as I was falling asleep again, that I heard bells tolling from away out back, towards the Thicket, but I must have been dreaming.* Alright Sean, that's the first time then, August 17."

"More than six weeks ago," Sean noted.

"Right. Very well then, four nights later, August 21:

"*I'm positive that I hear bells tolling from the middle of the Thicket!*

And now I'm sure that wasn't a dream the other night, when I thought I heard them. It's just after midnight and I'm sitting on the balcony outside my bedroom and the sound of them awakened me five minutes ago. Okay, they've just stopped now, but they were deep, clanging—a church tower's bells, but not at all like the bells in either of the two churches in town—and much closer.

"Okay, then we have…wait a minute…" Mrs. Hutchinson turned a few pages. "Okay, I see that we have nothing for a week—and I was half listening for them by this time—then two nights in a row on the 28th and 29th, at 11:45 the first night and 1:17 the second. Then nothing for four days, then three nights in a row on the 3rd, 4th, and 5th."

"And the times on those nights?" Sean asked.

"Wait a while…oh, 2:15, 11:30, and 1:05. On the third night in that stretch, I got dressed and went out to the back orchard, which is always the direction from where they seem to be coming. But by the time I got there, they had stopped. They only seem to go for a minute or two."

"Do they ever ring more than once in a night?"

"No. At least not that I've heard."

"Hmmm," Sean said, looking at the dates and times. "No real…pattern. Except they never seem to come earlier than 11 o'clock."

Mrs. Hutchinson was silent for a moment.

"Well, then again, Sean," she said, "I don't go to bed earlier than 11. Before that I'm usually in the sitting room, listening to music while I read. Or looking at television. The sitting room is way at the other end of the house. I'm not sure I'd hear them from there. I just thought of that."

"Humph, that's interesting. Maybe some night we should try to see if they come earlier."

"The past two weeks have been about the same. Three or four nights in a row, a few nights off, and always after 11. So…any ideas?"

"Well, of course I'd like to hear them myself!" Sean laughed. "It's… fascinating, isn't it?"

"Well…it is that, I suppose—but troubling too. How could bells be in there? And who's ringing them? And why?"

"Right."

"Well, you'd have to hack your way into the Thicket to get anywhere, Sean, and I'm not sure the *Friends of Wildlife* that I gave this land to would approve of that. And even if they did, I'm not sure how far you'd get. Look at this place, it's so thick. But I give you permission to stake out my grounds whenever you need to—and if you do need to hack a bit here and there to advance—well, it'll be our little secret. There's a trail or two leading from the back of my orchard into the Thicket—or at least there used to be, though it may all be overgrown now. It's on the west and south sides of the house that one hears the bells from. But do be careful. What else?"

"Well, I think I'll run these dates and times through my computer and see if I can find any kind of pattern, even though it seems random. Uh-oh! Numbers!" Sean looked at his phone. He had missed homeroom, and had seven minutes to get to math class. Not so good!

"I'll give you an update in a day or two, Mrs. Hutchinson," he called, breaking into a run. "And thanks for the opportunity! We'll get to the bottom of this!"

"I hope so, Sean," Mrs. Hutchinson waved. "I hope so."

She turned back and looked again at the huge boot-prints in the muck, and a shiver went through her. She wondered if she should tell Sean the rest of the story.

No, she thought. *Not quite yet. It's probably not them at all.*

CHAPTER SEVEN

WHAT HAPPENED AFTER PRACTICE

Sean had been right in his prediction for his calculus test: he didn't ace the thing, nor did he flunk it. He knew he could have done better if he'd studied more—nothing new there—but there was no way he'd been able to resist the delicious temptation to check out the Thicket the night before. And he was glad he had. But that was the story of his life, he thought—he seemed stuck in a glob of mediocrity—mostly because of his own choices.

Since Nawshant High was a small school—less than two-hundred students, in a Beaux Arts two-story rosy brick building a century old—one saw the same faces throughout the day. So it was no surprise that Kyle was in four of Sean's six classes. It soon became apparent that Kyle's "attitude" wasn't limited to Sean alone.

Of course Kyle was the talk of the school, being such a novelty. Nawshant was a friendly place, so tons of kids went up to him in welcome. Kyle returned the greetings, but stiffly, and said nothing more. It was almost as if he had made a decision not to make any new friends here. Still, Sean felt obliged to sit next to his cousin in every class they shared, even though Kyle had told him—somewhat brusquely—that he didn't have to. "I don't need no escort," he had drawled at one point. Whatever!

It also became apparent (not that there had been much doubt) that Regina was making attempts to "get to know Kyle better."

"I would say the *I'm going to wait until next year when I'm in Boston before I date again because no one here is good enough* phase is definitely over," Timmy observed at noontime, watching Regina and her lunch tray sit down across from Kyle, who was at a table by himself. But from what Sean saw, Regina didn't seem to be having much luck either—unless one considered monosyllabic answers and curt head-nods getting lucky. Nor was she the only one: by the end of the lunch period, five other girls and one boy had stopped at their table, ostensibly to talk with Regina, before they asked with glaring smiles, "So! Who's your friend?" and waited—rather predatorily, Sean thought—for introductions.

It was after school when Sean, heading down to the basement locker room with Matt and Timmy to get ready for practice, saw Kyle up ahead, going into the office of Coach Cotter, who ran the football team.

"Huh. He must be trying out for football then," Matt observed. "God knows we need all the help we can get." After three games the team was still looking for its first win—to go with its one win of last season. Matt was a wide receiver and wildly fast—uncatchable really—but none of the quarterbacks on the team seemed able to get the ball to him.

Sean just nodded, for a tingle of excitement, mixed with a little nervous fear, was running through him. He wondered, after what had happened yesterday, what might happen after practice today. Would Matt wait for him again after his own practice was over? And if he did…

This was the thing he had hesitated in reporting to Uncle Justin—or anyone else. Even with the astonishing arrival of a new cousin he never knew he had, and the bells, and the figure in the Thicket, and getting hired by Mrs. Hutchinson—*yes!*—this had been the first thing on his mind today.

Funny, that. What had happened the day before was this:

Sean was putting away the goal post nets after practice. Again. Not that he minded—Uncle Justin had said years ago that one of the best ways to start the day was to ask, *How may I be of service today?* Sean had tried to live by this (when he remembered) and after every lacrosse game, Coach Carson asked for a volunteer to put the goalie nets away. If no one else volunteered, Sean always did, and many times Timmy would stick around to help him. But yesterday Timmy and Regina had to rush off for dental appointments, so Sean had been left alone with this task. As it so happened, football practice finished at the same time, and Matt had wandered over from the other end of the field, to help Sean out with his responsibilities, meager as they were. Soon they were the only two people left on the field, for every town-born child could tell a storm was imminent.

The color of the thick lush grass was of the emerald vibrancy it only attained in mid-May and mid-September. Beyond the fields, homes of various shapes and sizes, rising up to the cliffs at the edge of the sea, marked the neighborhoods. Many of the trees around them were already streaked in red, yellow, orange, and purple, a hint of the glorious explosion that would climax one month later. These patches seemed to glow the brighter against the deep green of the fields, and were slow to fade as the mist, fog, and darkness swirled in from the ocean. The brilliant trees reminded Sean of Christmas light bulbs, the big, old-fashioned kind.

The string of one's life, Uncle Justin had once told Sean, was made up of beads of moments, many of which, maybe most of which, flew through one's hands unnoticed and un-reflected upon, as one rushed on to The Next Thing To Be Done. *So enjoy each moment, dear boy*, he had advised Sean. *Take time to reflect, and decide on how you want to engage life. You'll be my age before you know it. I can't urge you in strong enough terms to stay awake and present to the beauty of the now.*

Sean had always remembered this, for he felt it to be true. But something about this early evening—everything about this early evening, the color of the trees, the brilliance of the grass, the feel of the moist wind running along his bare arms and legs, the rich echoes of his and Matt's voices ringing around the field, the silky softness of the grass upon his naked feet—they had both chucked off their cleats and socks—began to rise up before Sean's attention like a lovely unnamable fragrance. There was a bliss in just being, and breathing, and noticing. Remember all this, Sean told himself. And yet it was nothing, really—just a typical after-school afternoon on the practice fields, with one of his best friends.

Or was it?

They were heading down to the far end of the field to retrieve the last of the goal-nets. On a whim Matt blurted, "Gonna beat your butt!" and then had burst off at a ferocious gallop. While Matt was undoubtedly the fastest player on the football team, Sean was the swiftest on the lacrosse squad, and over the years it had never been determined who was fastest between the two best friends.

Sean tore off after Matt. At first it seemed Matt's head start was too much to overcome; but Sean bore down, and finally saw himself making progress. When he ran like this, something else took over his body— some kind of wild, vibrant electricity—and he closed his eyes as he felt every nerve, socket and fiber pushed to its seamless limit.

Lately Matt had won the impromptu races between them: but he hadn't yesterday. Sean hurtled past Matt just as they reached the goal-net. Matt dove for him with a chortle of surprise, but Sean snapped back, avoiding Matt's lurch. They both flopped down on their backs, snatching at breath, a smile at nothing in particular and everything in general on their faces, and an occasional laugh-for-no-reason escaping the bubble of their mouths.

"Arrgh!" Matt panted.

"Better luck next time," Sean sang. "Need a bigger head start?"

That strange but intensely wonderful feeling, the sense of being connected and present to each plopping second, every single thing around him, flushed back over Sean. While just that morning in math he had been down for no reason, *black and blue* as he liked to call it, now he found himself elated: after all, how good it was to be alive, and how beautiful was the world, as long as one was lucky enough to have the basics. How lovely just to lie here against the earth, his pulse humming through him like an engine; the wind running up his legs; the clouds lowering and expanding dramatically as the storm approached; and one of his best friends beside him. He often thought that if enjoying the gift of life was a skill, this would be one he would excel at. Purposeless as he may have been when it came to what he wanted to do in life, he nevertheless was more often than not a very happy camper.

He turned his head to see Matt looking at him. "Dude, it's good to be alive," Sean said, speaking his thoughts.

Matt's dark eyebrows lowered for an instant, then rose.

"You're right there," he mumbled back. This had all been yesterday. "Sometimes. Like when someone gets to Lubec, Maine."

"Mmmm," Sean sighed in agreement. For a couple of years now they had been planning a skateboard trip to Lubec, Maine—as ridiculous as that might have sounded. Lubec had been chosen for no particular reason, for its distance, its name, which they thought exotic, and for the fact that it was the easternmost point in the continental USA. Matt loved the idea of just up and leaving, via skateboard, saying the notion had appealed to him ever since he heard a lyric in a Joni Mitchell song, something about wishing one had a river to skate away on.

"You still want to go sometime, then?" Matt asked—dubiously.

"Oh, I do dude," Sean answered immediately.

"You sure? Why, though? Not for my escapist reasons, I bet."

Sean thought for a moment. "No, not that."

"You got nothing you need to escape from," Matt answered, flopping back down on the grass. He was right. Sean wondered what Matt wanted to escape from.

"It would be so cool," Sean answered. "That's why. And I bet the stars would be strange there, no?" Sean had learned the constellations from Uncle Justin, on all their late-night walks.

"Maybe. But I think you have to go south for that. I like how that sounds though, *where the stars are strange.* So, when? We missed it this summer, somehow."

"Yeah but we finished our map of the route. And, well, Margaret *did* catch me heading down the driveway on my board, with a tent in my backpack," Sean commented. "At midnight. You remember. All hell broke loose."

"I was there, hiding in the bushes," Matt said.

"Once I'm 18…"

Matt grunted like he didn't believe it.

Sean bolted upright. "Matt, *we're going to do this.*"

Matt jumped. And then Sean started reciting the name of every town—there were dozens and dozens of them—they would pass through on the almost 600 mile journey. "Lynn, Swampscott, Marblehead, Salem, Beverly, Manchester-by-the-Sea…"

Now Matt sat up, when Sean was about halfway through. "Okay, okay, I get it!" he laughed. Matt's face lit up, changing his whole demeanor like Sean hadn't seen it change in ages. But it was clear now to Matt that Sean had been dead serious about this dream of theirs.

Sean smiled back at his friend, and threw some grass at him. Matt covered his face and fell back against the emerald lawn.

Sean felt a strange catch in his throat—it seemed to him…it was funny, but it seemed to him that Matt had never looked more beautiful—not so much from a point of physical attractiveness, but in an objective manner, as another manifestation of creation on this beautiful evening. Flat against the earth, one knee raised up, his arms spread out behind him, a pluck of grass in his mouth—Matt, Sean thought, was as beautiful as the scarlet maples, the flame-colored oaks, the green grass. Actually more so—

It occurred to Sean that this was the time to say something to Matt, to reassure his friend that his scar was the least of him, that he was more beautiful than words could say—

But before he could, Matt murmured, "Sean—you know what I like most about you?"

The question surprised because—well, they were guys, and there were rules it seemed, and they seldom if ever talked like this. It was a moment before Sean could answer. Their eyes were still locked.

"Ahhh...what then?"

"You...all the years we've been friends, you never once asked me how I got—my scar."

Sean didn't answer at first. The statement startled.

"Well I...I figured it was none of my business," Sean finally answered. "I figured...I figured you'd tell me, if you ever wanted me to know." He shrugged. "And then...I don't know, I stopped seeing it after a while. I don't see it at all anymore, dude—never. I just see...you."

Sean wasn't sure he had ever seen such a smile on his friend's often clouded face.

"Tell me something," Matt answered, his voice a dreamy murmur. He looked up at the lowering clouds, then back at Sean, letting go a deep sigh. "Tell me something you never told anyone else."

"Like...like what?" Sean half-laughed. He found that he was plucking at the grass beside him again.

"I dunno. Something...no one else knows about you, like."

"Ahhh, well...okay," Sean answered, dithering a little. "Ahhh, okay, well, you might think this weird—"

"That's what I want to know. Something no one else knows. Don't be afraid. You...can tell me anything." Matt was still smiling—but there was something else at the back of his unreadable hazel eyes.

"Okay, well—" Sean took a deep breath, "ever since I was a little kid, every time I ride or walk by First Cliff, and the McWilliams' house up there—you know the McWilliams' house?"

"Yeah, sure."

"Well, every time I go by there, I get this weird feeling. It's like…it's like a flashback from a previous life or something. I can see myself stepping out of a horse-drawn carriage and it's like 135 years ago—like 1878, 1880, something like that. I'm a man in this vision, and I'm wearing a long tweed dress coat, and a tall black hat—like an Abraham Lincoln hat, you know them? And a bright red scarf. It's snowing lightly and it's Christmas Eve, just getting dark, and I have a bag of presents under my arms—for my wife and little girl. They're inside waiting for me and I live in the Mc-Williams' house. My little girl is sick. But not wicked sick, just like a cold or something. I've just come home from work. I work near South Station in Boston." Sean sat up, so serious was he.

"That's all," he shrugged. "I guess it's déjà vu or—I don't know, maybe I had a dream one time. But my God, it's so real. I don't know what to make of it. Like I say, it seems like a previous life or something."

Matt nodded his head slowly. "Trippy," he pronounced.

"Yeah, well—the trippiest part is about a year ago Uncle Justin told me that my great great grandfather lived in that house way back then."

"Huh. Even trippier."

Sean decided it was time to say what he wanted to say to Matt.

"Matt, look," he mumbled, dangling his own bare foot back and forth through the lush grass, and looking still at his friend. He half raised himself up on his elbow and cleared his throat. The funny mood he was in shut off whatever filtering process his mouth usually labored under. The funny mood he was in—it would be wrong to say less than the truth now.

"Matt, I've been meaning to tell you…ahhh…about what you said. About your scar? A few weeks ago? I think…you shouldn't worry so much about your scar like you do, because…ahhh…you're…I mean … you're—beautiful. I think you're so beautiful."

Sean gulped. There, he'd said it. *I should've said handsome instead of so beautiful,* Sean immediately self-criticized. *So beautiful sounds kind of…*

kind of—

But he had meant it. They were still looking at each other. Once again, Matt's eyebrows lowered, then lifted. He gulped. He looked away, then looked back. His dark eyes expanded. His mouth tightened as his smile grew.

They kept staring. The world seemed to contract, and contain nothing but the two of them now. Nothing but the two of them, yet this was the whole universe. The ticking seconds slowed, then stopped. The longer they stared, the more they knew it meant—something. Sean hadn't cared about saying what he'd said because at that moment, these words had seemed to contain all the truth in the universe—but now he was thinking what else they might imply. He became aware of a thudding noise in his ears.

"Now, you tell me something," Sean said, just to break the electric silence.

Matt held his eyes a bit longer; then he half-mumbled/half-sang, "If I were your woman, and you were my man, you'd have no other woman, you'd be weak as a lamb."

Sean waited for Matt to say more, or to explain this cryptic message. But no, that was it. He was still staring at Sean. They both seemed to be holding their breath.

Sean didn't realize at first that this was a song, one of Matt's Motown oldies, and Matt was singing it to him. But what did he mean?

But that was forgotten when Matt half-sat up, reached out his hand, and, still keeping his eyes on Sean, ran his forefinger, slowly and tenderly, down the side of Sean's face.

"Sean," he mumbled. It wasn't a question.

Something like an expanding meadow of delight unfurled inside Sean—while at the same time a fire of panic seemed to be scorching that meadow. He was still keeping his eyes on Matt's, but Matt's eyes were darting up and down between Sean's eyes, and his mouth. Matt sat up straighter and leaned toward Sean. So wildly frantic had Sean become, he totally forgot to ask Matt to touch the other side of the face, as his OCD ordinarily would have demanded. The entire known world seemed to be slipping away—

Holy Crap! Sean thought. *He's going to kiss me!* The thudding in his ears doubled. He panicked and jumped up.

"I'll beat you back too!" Sean cried, taking off at a wild sprint for the other end of the field.

But after half a minute he half-turned, and became aware that Matt wasn't anywhere near him. Just the same, Sean kept running until he reached the opposite side of the field. He turned around.

Matt was gone. The field was empty. Terribly so.

Sean caught his breath. He replayed the wild events that had just transpired. *My God.*

Full of bewilderment, Sean walked around to the front of the school, which sat on a little hill of its own. When he reached the top of the high front stairs, he could see Matt, just about to vanish around a bend in the street way down Nawshant Road. Matt was slowly jogging, his head down and his hands jammed into the pockets of his hoodie.

"Oh no," Sean mumbled, putting a hand on the top of his head.

Right then, and for the first time in his life really, he became aware that he was in love with someone. Undoubtedly. It was Matt.

Sean's walk home was slow, thoughtful, even as the clouds opened and grey rain poured down in sheets. But he was oblivious—he felt nothing but the warmth of what had just happened, as well as confusion. These were a balmy cocoon around him. He had to sit down three times on his walk home—under trees, against a mailbox—not from fatigue, or to escape the rain—but from the power of what he was feeling.

This was so unexpected it troubled him. Did this mean he was gay? Was Matt gay? Or was it just one of those weird things?

He wished he hadn't panicked and raced off like that. He had a sudden curiosity to know if Matt had really meant to kiss him—and what that would have felt like. He could feel his face turning red-hot—

"Oh God," he whispered, covering his face with his hands.

Sean really didn't have a huge problem with being gay, if that was his fate—it just wasn't what he had planned. When he was thirteen he had had a huge crush on Regina. Whenever she walked into a class room he forgot all else, and could do nothing but stare. In fact the crush was requited, and they had "gone out" for a while (two months) and had kissed and even talked about getting married someday, at which time they would join Greystones with the Quinn's smaller property out back.

But it fizzled. One day after school, Sean had seen Regina walking home while holding hands with Paul Spano, another kid in their class; and a minute after he realized he didn't care, and that had been that. Since then he had had a few dates with girls, had kissed some of them, nothing more, but nothing seemed to come of it. He told himself that he, like Regina, just hadn't found "the right one." And now this.

"It is what it is," he finally said to himself, when at last he reached the long winding drive leading to Greystones. Whether he was gay, or straight, or something in between—this was a question only time would answer. He ran the rest of the way to the front door, got a benign tongue-lashing from Margaret for being out in the rain, then went upstairs and showered and put on clean clothes

Afterwards he lay on his bed and tried to study for the calculus test the next day.

But every now and then his mind wandered back to that moment on the field—and a wide, involuntary smile would arch across his face when he did, displacing numbers and theorems into a foggy background.

Then he had fallen asleep, and Matt was waiting there.

This had all been yesterday. Sean had been paying attention all day to

Matt and his mannerisms to see if anything might be different—and Matt did seem a little more—intense? Distant? Nervous? Sean wanted to do something or say something to reassure his friend, but he couldn't think of what.

Despite being hired by Mrs. Hutchinson to solve the Mystery of the Bells, and despite the arrival of his cousin Kyle the night before, Sean had been thinking more about Matt than the other two matters—and he had been thinking about the other two matters a lot. Would Matt come over to the lacrosse field again after practice today? Would anything happen if he did? If yes, what? Did Sean *want* something to happen? And if so, what? Should he start something, or wait for Matt?

His head was spinning. Nothing ever happened in Nawshant and now everything was happening, all at the same time.

Practice, though intense, wasn't very long because they had a game the next morning, a Saturday, at 10:00. The football team was at the other side of the field, and Sean could see that his cousin appeared to be working out with the team—*as quarterback*. Kyle seemed to be throwing the ball to Matt a lot. Oh yeah, it was Matt—no one could run and move like that. A funny feeling squiggled through Sean's stomach.

Finally his own coach called it quits and everyone on the lacrosse team gathered in the middle of the field for the brief team meeting, which was more like a pep talk. They were playing Danvers tomorrow—they were 3-0 and one of the best lacrosse teams in the state. The Nawshant team was 2-1.

"But I know you can play with them. And what's more, I know you can beat them!" Coach kept saying, to louder and louder applause.

We get the point, Sean was thinking. He really liked Coach, and he himself had fine team spirit, but enough was enough and Sean was anxious to see what might happen after practice, with Matt. His hands were sweating. Coach finally dismissed them, with instructions to get a good night's sleep.

"You want me to wait around and help?" Timmy asked Sean, for once again no one else had volunteered to put away the goal nets.

"Naw, I'm good," Sean answered. It was gorgeous and he never minded walking home from school alone—it gave him a chance to unwind after the day—but he refused the ride for another reason.

"Dude, you sure?"

"Yeah, no biggie. I'll call you later." Sean was going to add, "I've lots to tell you," meaning the mystery of the ringing bells, and being hired by Mrs. Hutchinson. But Timmy had no patience for delayed disclosures and would have pestered Sean mercilessly until the beans were spilled.

"Okay, later."

The members of the lacrosse team drifted away in twos and threes, while Sean began gathering the equipment. He was taking his time—while football practice had come to an end as well, the team was still having its after-practice meeting, everyone standing in a circle. The lacrosse team always sat on the ground during their after-practice meetings, but not the football team. They stood up, leaning into the center, hands on their hips. Sean could hear Coach Cotter's booming voice ricocheting around the field. Sean found it annoying right now.

Wasn't it weird, Sean thought—all these life-changing events (the arrival of his cousin, the mystery of the bells, being hired as a detective)—and yet none of these things could compete with a finger draped tenderly down the left side of his face, and a lingering look between himself and someone he had known nearly all his life. Or the singing of a song. He had downloaded the song last night and there could be no doubt—it was definitely a love song.

"While it's certainly an improvement over the rapping, must we hear that tune again?" Margaret had yelled up the stairs before dinner.

Sean put the first goal net away, and still the football meeting dragged on. Finally it broke up, just as Sean was dragging the last net across the field. He tried to be nonchalant as he kept one eye on where he was going and the other on the drifts of players shuffling away. But where was Matt? And Kyle? Finally he saw them both, with Coach Cotter, who apparently wasn't done with them yet.

Sean dragged the last net inside the locker room. When he came out, Coach was working with Matt and Kyle alone, practicing various plays. It seemed Matt finally had found a quarterback who could catch up with his blazing speed, for more than once Sean saw Matt dive for a bomb. He caught every pass Kyle threw to him.

Sean stood alone in the middle of the lacrosse field, watching them practice, filled with a strange sadness.

Matt never once looked over. Nor did his cousin.

More disappointed than he could understand, and a little hurt—didn't Matt see him over here, waiting for him?—Sean left the field and trudged home. He'd been walking on eggshells the last 24 hours, waiting for something to happen—and now this void, this…nothing.

"This stinks," he murmured.

To lift himself out of these doldrums, he yanked his mind back to the amazing fact that he had actually been hired—*hired!*—to solve the mystery of the bells. His spirits lightened. Well, he would take this responsibility seriously—he would go up to the Thicket again, and perhaps Mrs. Hutchinson's grounds too, and dive into the case.

This very night.

Little did he know what was waiting up there for him.

CHAPTER EIGHT

MORE BELLS;
MISS SAWYER SPINS ANOTHER TALE

Sean began to walk faster with this new determination. Okay, so maybe his love life—if that's what you could call it—might be a weird hot mess right now—and maybe his new cousin had been a massive bust in the friendship department so far—

But didn't Sean have the chance he'd always been dying for? The chance to prove his worth as a detective? As a *paid* detective?

Indeed he did. Sean almost broke into a jig, so excited did he become. *Focus on the positive*, Uncle Justin was always saying, and Sean could see now the benefit of this philosophy. The early evening sun oozed down in fat golden shafts between the ancestral limbs of the ancient roadside trees; the birds chirped deliciously; the ocean and sky were a fresh-rinsed, robin's egg blue—he could have sung in sudden joy.

As he rounded one of the innumerable bends along Ocean Road, a blaring toot sounded behind him. Turning, he leapt out of the way of a 1962 Coup de Ville convertible, wanton scarlet in color and picked out with more shining chrome than an orthodontist's office. Of course there was only one such car in Nawshant, if not in New England, and its proud owner was Miss Sarah Sawyer, Head Librarian, *Mow-Town Landscaping* client, and garden columnist for the *Nawshant Tides* paper.

It occurred to Sean that this was just the person he wanted to see. He had something vital to ask her, involving the case: *Were there any ghosts in the Thicket?* If anyone knew, it would be her. Miss Sawyer was accompanied by one of her friends from the gardening club, riding shotgun (as the saying went) beside her—Ms. Lydia "Dolly" Worthington, who had recently retired as professor of English from the same university Uncle Justin taught at.

"Wait up, Miss Sawyer!" Sean called, giving frantic chase. But stop she didn't, apparently not hearing him: classical music was blaring from her car's surprisingly loud speakers, and both of the older women's ears were rakishly covered with long flowery scarves, wound round their heads and fluttering dramatically behind them in the breeze.

But fortunately Ocean Road was especially twisty right here, and Miss Sawyer was always particularly careful when she took *Princess Margaret*—her pet name for the antique car—out for a jaunt. When the weather was bogus or the roads slick, she got around in her other vehicle, an ancient Jeep, and she drove at those times *like the divil himself,* in the scandalized words of Margaret.

After a minute of hard puffy running, Sean caught up.

"Good afternoon," he panted, "Miss Sawyer, Ms. Worthington."

"Why, good afternoon, Sean," Ms. Worthington smiled.

"Oh, hello, Sean, there you are!" Miss Sawyer shouted over the music, pulling over and swiping off her large mirrored sunglasses. "Did you come running after us to tell me when you'll be cutting my grass? It's getting long you know after last night's deluge."

"Excuse me?" Sean asked, cocking his head forward.

"Turn the music lower, Sarah!" Ms. Worthington cried, tugging at Miss Sawyer's sleeve.

"Oh, pardon me!" Miss Sawyer laughed, turning down the volume. "We were just trying out my new sound system—seeing what she can do, as the proverbial expression goes. Vivaldi, you know. *The Four Seasons.*

This is *Autumn*, of course—isn't it divine?"

"Lovely," Sean answered. When in Rome…

"And how *utterly* perfect for a halcyon afternoon such as this! Dolly and I were just planning a weekend trip up to the White Mountains, so inspired did we become by the weather and the numinous change of seasons. And Dolly was just giving us a perfectly apropos poem—weren't you, darling? Take it from the top, and let Sean feast on the edification of the gloriously polished word!"

"Well, it isn't Eliot or Yates, and some might call it doggerel," Ms. Worthington temporized, "but it *is* just the thing for today. As a matter of fact, I've often noticed that some of the keenest pleasures can be found in the lowest places—"

"Dolly, darling, you can skip all that," Miss Sawyer gently interrupted. "Sean's too….uhmm, young, to be a sour fountain of critical thought, as many of your academics are. Say on!"

"Well…alright, then."

Ms. Worthington cleared her throat, smiled bashfully, leaned forward solemnly, closed her eyes behind her sunglasses, and intoned:

There is something in the autumn that is native to my blood-
Touch of manner, hint of mood;
And my heart is like a rhyme,
With the yellow and the purple and the crimson keeping time.
The scarlet of the maples can shake me like a cry
Of bugles going by.
And my lonely spirit thrills
To see the frosty asters like a smoke upon the hills.
There is something in October sets the gypsy blood astir;
We must rise and follow her,
When from every hill of flame
She calls and calls each vagabond by name.

"Brava! Oh, Brava!" Ms. Sawyer cried, clapping her white-gloved hands. "You read so well, dear! Doesn't she, Sean? You could slice a hair on her enunciation!"

"Awesome," Sean agreed. "I like that. Calling each vagabond by name." He made a mental note to look up *vagabond* when he got home.

"So you see, we're *infected* with the spirit of the day!" Miss Sawyer gushed. "Poetry, Vivaldi, the open air, the beckoning road—autumn—heaven! This is our *seventh* time around!"

"Uhm...eighth," Ms. Worthington corrected.

"It's just too nice to go back home," Miss Sawyer continued, "so we've been boulevardiering with *Princess Margaret*, round and round Ocean Road."

"I'm not sure one can use that word when one is not walking, Sarah," Ms. Worthington suggested. She took her words seriously, having been a professor of English for forty years. "I should put it that we were *motoring*."

Miss Sawyer rolled her eyes at Sean, a gesture Ms. Worthington couldn't see.

"What-ever," Miss Sawyer said carelessly, throwing up her hand. "Bless me, Dolly, you're such the *word police*. Oh but Sean, you should see my grounds today. Some of the ladies from the club and I lunched *al fresco* this afternoon out on the south lawn, and everyone agreed my garden had never looked better. The asters, the mums, the Japanese anemones, one and all just *exploding* into bloom. Glorious! Sublime!"

"I'm sure it's beautiful," Sean said, trying to hide his disappointment. It appeared Miss Sawyer was in a *splendiferous* mood, as she herself would name it; and since Sean wanted to call upon the woman's ghostly storytelling skills, he knew he'd get nothing out of her if she wasn't in ill humor. "And uhm...I can come by tomorrow afternoon to cut the lawn, after our lacrosse game. Like one o'clock?"

"Splendid, splendid!" Miss Sawyer beamed. "I'm having guests over tomorrow evening for dinner, and so you see the mowed lawn will be the perfect finishing touch to the gardens' beauty."

"To say nothing of the heady scent of fresh-cut grass," Ms. Worthington added, inhaling deeply through her Roman nose, "to which I hope none of your diners are allergic."

"If they were," Miss Sawyer said archly, after a pause, turning to her friend, "they would never be friends of mine. I've always thought allergic reactions to any part of Mother Nature's world are the result of subconscious antipathies to the environment."

"Nonsense!" Ms. Worthington brayed.

"Nonsense, is it? Nothing of the sort! Why, I can give you a thousand examples…"

While the ladies discussed this rather abstruse point, a sudden plan took root in Sean's mind. An ancient hemlock on Miss Sawyer's property had recently become infected with a virus carried by the Wooly Adelgid, a non-native, sap-sucking insect that attacked hemlocks. Miss Sawyer had told Sean two years ago to be on the look-out for any telltale signs of infection on this particular tree, as, without treatment, the disease was fatal. Sad to say, he had seen the first signs of infestation just last week, on two of the tree's lower branches. Just to be on the safe side, he had taken a section of branch to a certified arborist two towns over, a friend of Uncle Justin's, who had made the final unhappy determination. Sean had been wondering since then how to break the news to Miss Sawyer, for the tree was one of her favorites, having been planted by her great-grandfather when *Lily Vale*, her ancestral home, was first built. Sean knew she would go ballistic. She would be crushed; she would be disappointed; she would be…well, pissed-off—in short, *just* the sort of foul mood he needed her to be in to tell him what he needed to know.

"Ahhh, Miss Sawyer, excuse me," Sean began, rocking nervously from one foot to the other. Miss Sawyer snapped her head around. "I ahhh… hate to bring this up just now, but uhm…well, I have a bit of bad news. It's about….it's about your garden."

"Oh?" Miss Sawyer wondered, drawing out the word. Her smile

smeared into a pout and one eyebrow arched dangerously.

"Yeah, well...I was going to tell you tomorrow when I cut your grass, but...well, on second thought, maybe I should just wait until Sunday, after your dinner party tomorrow night."

"You tell me *now*!" Miss Sawyer demanded. Her grip on the steering well intensified.

"Well, I...I noticed some funny white stuff on...on the hemlock the other day? The big old one you love so much? And so I—I—"

"Oh *no!* Well, go on! Don't *stumble* over the words! Speak up!"

"Well, I took a sample branch to an arborist friend of Uncle Justin's, and—"

"Tell me the worst! Do it quick and do it now!" Miss Sawyer blared. Ms. Worthington sat up straighter in her seat and began to look alarmed at her friend's devolving behavior.

"I'm afraid— I'm afraid it's got the Wooly Adelgid disease."

Miss Sawyer held Sean's eyes even as her own narrowed ominously. She swallowed. She punched off the stereo with a quick whack of her fist.

Sean braced himself.

Overhead the birds were still singing blissfully; the gentle breeze was still stirring the flame-colored leaves; and Sean could plainly hear the ocean dreaming and lapping fifty yards away. But in the immediate vicinity of the car, a death-like silence had settled: no more Vivaldi; no more poetry; no more gushy, rapturous happy-talk from Miss Sawyer.

"*B******S!*" she suddenly ejaculated, so loudly and unexpectedly that several birds instantly decamped from the trees overhead, cawing in alarm as they went. Apparently Ms. Worthington knew what was coming, for she delicately unlocked her door and placed one gloved hand on the door handle.

Miss Sawyer slammed both fists on the padded center of the steering wheel.

"*B******S!*" she repeated. "*B******S! B******S!*"

"Call me later, dear," Ms. Worthington said with a weak little wave, slipping out of the car and walking off as if for a wager. *At least she didn't live too far away*, Sean thought.

"Get in the car," Miss Sawyer growled, jerking her head at Sean. "I'll take you back to my place and you can point the miserable *B******S* out to me."

Sean complied, of course; this was all part of the plan. He felt a tad guilty…

…but then again, everything he had said was true, and he knew (of course) that he had to break the nasty news to her sooner or later.

Remarkable to say, Miss Sawyer actually laid rubber as she put *Princess Margaret* in gear and took off, before Sean could even reach around to put his seat belt on—but alas, there were no seat belts in these older models. So instead he made a desperate lunge for the handle above and beside him—what Timmy always referred to as *the holy s**t handle*—and closed his eyes as they took the many twists and turns of Ocean Road at a Hollywood car-chase pace. But there was no handle! Poor *Princess Margaret!*

Sean was further surprised when Miss Sawyer left the road and *drove across her own grounds* to reach the ancestral hemlock in question, smack in the middle of the large south lawn that rolled down to the road, spinning up clods of previously-manicured lawn in her wigged-out wake. *Well*, Sean thought, *here was one rather large strip of lawn that wouldn't want cutting tomorrow.* Red-faced, heaving, panting, Miss Sawyer swung out of her car, slammed the door, and, shoulders rocking back and forth, marched to the tree in question as if she were heading to a street brawl.

"Ah-HA!" she roared, spying the pesky little critters herself on two or three of the lowest branches. "THERE you are!" She raised her gloved fist, then thought better of it and bustled back to the car, as Sean was getting out.

"Got a cigarette lighter on you?" she heaved.

"Ahhh…no, actually I don't, since I never—"

"Ugh! *Young people today!*"

She grabbed her voluminous pocketbook instead, from the rear seat, then headed back to the tree, chuckling demoniacally.

Sean wondered if this was the same woman who, in just yesterday's edition of *The Nawshant Tides*, had repeatedly urged her *gentle readers* to make sure one always sliced off the crusts of the watercress-and-cucumber sandwiches during said gentle readers' next garden party. *The little delicacies,* she had further penned, a*re of the utmost importance in setting the right tone of utter refinement. As Woman of the Manor, you really need to be charming graciousness itself, a smiling, one-would-almost say retiring, Lady Bountiful, ready to anticipate all the needs of your guests. After all gentle readers, you don't marinate yourselves in your eau de parfum—well, most of you don't anyway, thank God— so, please, slice off those crusts, and feed them to our feathered friends...*

Sean wasn't sure what the connection was between perfume and swanky sandwiches, but he knew the wearing of too much perfume was one of Miss Sawyer's (many) pet peeves, especially for outdoor occasions when said aromas would interfere with one's olfactory appreciation of the garden. While Sean waited for what would happen next, he recalled the story Miss Sawyer once told of attending a posh garden party some years back, and how she had followed her nose, sniffing here there and everywhere, wondering aloud what that *malodorous stink* was—until she landed on the overly-*parfumed* neck of her hostess.

"And yet," Miss Sawyer had quietly told Sean that day, "despite the ensuing unpleasantness, I didn't apologize—why should I have?"

Why indeed, nor did Sean expect her to apologize later for her behavior now. She repeatedly jumped up and off the ground, swatting her pocketbook at the offending buggy creatures, crying out epithets Sean pretended not to hear as a vermilion sunset spangled the grounds. Sean further recalled Uncle Justin's words, when the latter was describing a fertility rite he had witnessed in Borneo, involving frenzied dancing and exotic costume: "Most primitive cultures recognize that, in order to keep one's sanity, one must occasionally go a little crazy." Perhaps it was these intermittent squalls of distemper that allowed Miss Sawyer to be, ordinarily, the most genteel, refined person in Nawshant.

"Take THAT! And THAT! And THAT!" she cried, jumping and swatting, jumping and swatting, using her pocketbook to full advantage.

By and by Miss Sawyer blew herself out, as it were, like a summer storm. She lowered her pocketbook, then circled the tree trunk several times, surveying her work and catching her breath; then she came back to the car, still heaving and panting.

"Call that arborist friend of Justin's and have him come over first thing tomorrow and start spraying," she muttered to Sean, yanking up some kind of undergarment through her pink dress.

"Certainly, Miss Sawyer," Sean answered, pretending to come back to the here and now with a shake of his head. "First thing, sure. I'm sorry, I'm a bit preoccupied."

"Oh?" Miss Sawyer panted, sounding only slightly ominous.

"Yeah, I was just thinking about someone…uhm…someone at school today, who was saying that there's a ghost that haunts the Thicket. I told them what a crock that was—because if there were, I definitely would have seen it when I was younger, because I was always messing around the edges of the Thicket, looking for balls I'd lost in there."

There, Sean thought—*that should get her tale-telling tongue wagging.* While Sean wasn't sure ghosts could leave boot prints, he didn't want to take any chances when he went up to the Thicket again tonight. If anyone would know about ghostly presences in the Thicket, it would be Miss Sawyer; and now her mood was appropriately sour.

Her eyes narrowed. Sean crossed his fingers behind his back.

"Ghosts in the Thicket, eh? Humph. I've only heard tell of one, and that was very many years ago," she said. She dabbed at her sweaty neck with her handkerchief. "But even if she's still around, *you* of all people wouldn't have to worry about her."

"Ahhh…really?" Sean asked. "Huh! And ahhh…why is that?"

"Oh, well, for the simple reason that the ghost is your Great Great Great Aunt Sadie. But of course, *you know all about that.*"

Miss Sawyer got back in her car and fired it up. Sean hopped into the passenger seat.

A shiver ran down his spine. He had no idea what Miss Sawyer was referring to—but if he played his cards right, he shortly would.

"Right!" he chuckled. "Right! I was forgetting about that! But ahhh… it's been so long since…I heard the story, it's all kind of forgotten."

"Your own family's history? And you've forgotten?" Miss Sawyer demanded, with outraged incredulity. She put the car in reverse and, turning around and throwing a meaty arm over the back of Sean's seat, carefully followed her tracks, retracing the car's path back to the road.

Sean played his trump. "Well my parents died before I was old enough to hear about—"

"Oh yes yes yes yes yes," Miss Sawyer answered. "Of course, God rest them." She was silent for a moment as she chewed at the side of her cheek. Sean knew this was the pivotal moment—demand something of her now and she would clam up. Remain silent and—

"Well, how much do you recall?" Miss Sawyer asked as they pulled into her garage. *Bingo!*

"Ahhh…not too much."

They got out of the car and Sean followed Miss Sawyer over to the patio, paved with ancient, lichen-encrusted fieldstones.

"Ouf! Appalling! Well, see that you always remember what I'm about to tell you then. Sit down, in that chair right there. Oh, stop fidgeting Sean—and remember—*no interruptions!*"

"Okay!" *Yes!*

"There's one!" Miss Sawyer glowered, as she took her own seat.

Sean made no answer.

"Well, as you no doubt know, your Great Great Great Aunt Sadie

Sutherland was Justin's great grandfather's maiden sister. She was strikingly beautiful, and the few portraits done of her vouch for that fact. I'm sure you have at least one at Greystones. Oh, and the large oil painting in the Children's Room at the library? That's Sadie as well. She was one of the chief benefactors of the library, you know. Yes, wise, charitable, strikingly beautiful."

"But she never married?" Sean interrupted, forgetting himself.

"What a *sexist* remark!" Miss Sawyer blared. "And that's *two* interruptions! Three strikes and you're out! No, she did *not* wed—not everyone does, you know, particularly people who are more concerned with social welfare and the March of Civilization—though one can hardly describe these last several decades as anything other than a crawl, backwards—but I digress. Now be quiet and listen. Will you be quiet?"

Sean nodded. It was especially nice, being the orphan he was, to realize how deeply his family's roots went into Nawshant's history.

"Good. Now, Sadie Sutherland was born sometime in the early 1820s, I believe—I can't say for sure—and she was already somewhat mature and settled when the Great War between the States was fought, by which I mean of course the Civil War. We can't imagine now how all-consuming that event was back then, nor how highly and hotly passions were running. Nawshant was much smaller then, consisting of several dozen great houses—like mine, I might add, and yours too, for that matter—and a number of more modest but still utterly charming dwellings for the sailors, tradesmen, servants, and fishermen who lived here then. A lovely, democratic mix of classes—as it remains today, I am glad to say.

"Aunt Sadie was deeply involved in the Abolitionist Movement, which sought to ban slavery. She frequently attended meetings in Boston, and even went on speaking engagements to other communities throughout New England. Oh yes, she was a tireless campaigner for the abolition of slavery, oh, and a founding member of the Boston Female Anti-Slavery Society—which you've no doubt heard of."

When Miss Sawyer paused weightily and raised one eyebrow, Sean realized this was a question. He raised both hands helplessly.

"Ouf! *Doubly appalling!* What are they teaching you in that school? Well, the Boston Female Anti-Slavery Society was formed in the 1840s by a group of prominent women from the Boston area, including several from Nawshant—including Aunt Sadie. They were quite ahead of their time. Sad to note, this was a time when citizens took an active part in their democracy, rather than sitting idly on their overstuffed, tasteless couches watching rubbish on television, as too many do today. Or *texting*, which, as you know, I WILL NOT TOLERATE in my presence. But at any rate—-uhm, where was I?"

Sean smiled weakly, for Miss Sawyer could text like a 20-fingered pinball wizard.

"Permission granted to speak for three seconds."

"The Boston Female Anti-Slavery—"

"Oh yes yes yes. Now, the assumption is that New England, as a hotbed of Abolitionism, was solidly 100% against slavery for years before the War. Hogwash! There were many here in New England who loathed the Abolitionists, and were themselves actively profiting from the slave trade, directly or indirectly: ship owners, merchants, people involved in the cotton trade, clothing manufacturers, and the like—as well as many newly arrived immigrants, whose leaders told them freed slaves would take all their menial jobs away. In fact, Sean, a howling mob of 5000 once descended on a meeting of the Boston Female Anti-Slavery Society at which 45 members were present. Including, in all likelihood, your Aunt Sadie. Justin has told you none of this?"

Sean shook his head weakly.

"Ouf, that man! Always has his head in his work—always did—always will! Well, anyway, the Boston Police tried to remove the women—for their own safety—from the interior of the church, which was where the meeting was being held—but our Ladies refused, saying they were happy to die for freedom right then and there. The police finally took them out against their wishes, and escorted the Ladies through the violent, cat-calling mob.

"Now at the same time, the Underground Railroad was in effect. As you may know—I'm assuming nothing at this point—this was a series of houses or hiding places stretching up from the South, where escaped slaves could hide in safety as they made their way north. Once the poor souls reached Free States they were ordinarily safe; but after the passage of the Fugitive Slave Law in 1850—of heinous memory—it was unlawful not to return escaped slaves to Federal authorities, and so most of the escaped slaves after this date headed for Canada. As I say, this whole system was known as the Underground Railroad, and it was so secretive that people involved with it often knew only the location of the next safe house ahead—nothing more. Part of the Underground Railroad passed right through Nawshant, and while it's never been proven to historians, all the locals here who know anything about anything assume that Sadie Sutherland was deeply involved—as were the Hutchinsons. Sadie fed the escaped slaves, and housed them, and cared for those too weak or sick to make it further, hiding them somewhere and putting her own safety on the line.

"Well, in the course of all this work, Sadie met a bachelor minister about her own age—late thirties or early forties, I suppose—still very young of course by today's standards, but not by the standards of that time—and he was as passionate an Abolitionist as she. When it looked like the coming war was inevitable, it leant a further urgency to their work. The Minister—I'm trying to recollect his name now—Samuel, Samuel—Dimmesdale? No, that was the minister in *The Scarlet Letter*—Dimsworthy? Samuel Dim-something. Sadly all I can think of right now is Dim-Sum, because I haven't dined yet— it'll come to me. Anyway, he and his church's congregation purchased an old schooner, re-named her the *Southern Cross*, and made arrangements to travel secretly to Wilmington, Delaware, to pick up a number of escaped slaves, some three or four dozen in all, who had just one last chance to get out before the war started. Turn on the hose for me, will you Sean?"

Sean snapped out of the reverie Miss Sawyer had cast him in, and did as he was bid. Miss Sawyer quaffed deeply, exclaimed *ahhhhh!* in great satisfaction, and resumed her tale.

"Water water everywhere, and plenty for us to drink—speaking of things nautical. Did you know, Sean, that Thoreau says water is *the* only drink for the wise? For the most part I agree with him, though if I were a betting woman I might venture that he never had the opportunity to sip a small glass—or two—of fine sherry just before dinner.

"But anyway—I'm not sure how seaworthy the *Southern Cross* was. And I believe most of the men manning the ship, including Minister Samuel Dim-whatever, were well-intentioned-but-land-lubbing members of his flock who wouldn't have known the difference between an ebb tide and a jib if you shoved their face in the water. At any rate, the voyage seemed destined for doom right from the start. Somehow they missed Delaware entirely—now granted it's small, but how does one miss *an entire state?* Instead they came ashore somewhere along the South Carolina coast. As you can imagine, the locals were not exactly enamored of their presence, and the crew avoided wholesale lynching only by the last minute intercession of the local minister, who apparently had been a classmate of our Samuel at Harvard Divinity School some years earlier. Talk about Divine Intervention!"

Miss Sawyer laughed loudly at her little joke, and Sean thought it prudent to do likewise.

"That's enough, Sean— stop guffawing, it wasn't *that* funny. Well, they set out again, and this time they made Wilmington— though it took them several tries, if you can imagine. They took on about three dozen escaped slaves and another sympathizer or two, then headed northeast, deciding to stick close to the coast. Perhaps by then they realized they didn't know what in the world they were doing."

Miss Sawyer paused, and plucked at a spent purple and white petunia blossom in an old terracotta pot beside her. Then she turned to Sean and arched her right eyebrow ominously as she held up the flower.

"This particular variety of Petunia, Sean, bears the rather unfortunate name of *Fluffy Ruffles*—though there is something about the name's insouciance that I salute. But one would never think, in a world that includes *Fluffy Ruffles* petunias, that this same world would contain in its broad compass the kind of...*horrific sea tragedy* I am about to relate." Miss Sawyer gazed at Sean and smacked her lips in anticipation.

"A week later," she continued, slowly, lowering her voice to a dour mumble, "as the ship and crew sailed past Long Island, they couldn't know—how could they know?—that they were heading into the savage maw of—" here Miss Sawyer paused dramatically, "the...*worst*...Northeaster...in...years: specifically, the Big Blow of '60! As the poet wrote, *Christ save us all from a death like this, on the reef of Norman's Woe!*"

Sean gulped again. Miss Sawyer was warming up to her task. She had half-turned to face Sean, and her wide, vacant eyes shone with the kind of light that only comes with the recitation of delicious gossip—or the retelling of a disaster in which nobody one knew was involved.

"MARITIME DISASTER!" she suddenly brayed, waving both meaty arms, and Sean jumped in his squeaky red metal chair. "Well! It was the same sad story Sean—all too often in those days, I'm afraid—the deepening swells, the plunging barometer, the towering waves, the mizzenmast going by the boards, the screams and confusion and panic as the rigging collapses onto the deck in a shuddering heap. You're clinging on to something—anything!—as the waves break over the creaking, listing hull, and you watch frozen with fear as your ship disintegrates under your very eyes, all the while viewing the *seething* watery grave that awaits you, or the merciless rocky cliffs dead ahead!"

Sean gulped again and swallowed his gum in consternation.

Miss Sawyer had now closed her eyes, and her head was shaking solemnly while her right hand made futile, wave-like motions. When she spoke again her voice sounded very distant.

"The *Southern Cross* was spotted by a frigate as she dangerously drifted round Race Point at the tip of Cape Cod; and then three hours later, the attendant at Boston Light made note of her—and by this time her Main Mast had gone by the boards. Now—would you believe it? The sea and wind took her in their terrible grip, and pushed the *Southern Cross* round the Brewster Islands, and into Broad Sound. Yes! Our very own Broad Sound! The *Southern Cross* met her doleful end when she slammed into the rocks of—can you guess? Permission granted to speak—but not for very long."

"East Point?"

"Guess again."

"First Cliff?"

"Again."

"Second Cliff?"

"One more time."

"Not—not Third Cliff?"

"Yesssssssss!" Miss Sawyer hissed, almost pouncing on Sean she came in so close. "Third Cliff!"

"But that's…that's 200 yards from my house—Aunt Sadie's house," Sean said in a faltering voice. "You can see Third Cliff, from all the east-facing windows at Greystones. I mean, we're on Third Cliff."

"Exactly." Miss Sawyer agreed dramatically. "You're on Third Cliff. And you can see Third Cliff from all your east-facing windows. You can see it now—and you could see it then. And your Great Great Great Aunt Sadie saw it as well, as she was awaiting the return of the ship—and her secret lover!"

"What?"

"Yes! It's *terribly* romantic, and tragic, and all too true! Why, their love letters are probably somewhere up in your attic! And no more interruptions! You see, the minister Samuel was Sadie's beloved, and he and Aunt Sadie had secretly planned to marry as soon as he returned from his ill-fated mission of mercy! But can you imagine? How ironic! How tragic, that the ship should crash at Third Cliff, with Sadie a front row witness to the whole calamitous thing! The storm struck them in Long Island Sound, and they could have—and *should* have—wrecked somewhere down that way—or if not, then certainly along the treacherous sandbars of Cape Cod's lee shore. But no! They smashed *right on Third Cliff! Under Aunt Sadie's nose!*"

Miss Sawyer's eyes were riveted now on Sean—and he couldn't interrupt anymore, even if he wanted to. How weird was this?

"It was the bells that drew Aunt Sadie to the window, you see," Miss Sawyer continued after what seemed a very long time. "There used to be an old clanging bell out there long ago, floating right off Third Cliff. When the waves were slamming particularly rough against Third Cliff, the buoy's bells used to peel out deep and ominously. *No Come Near Me! No Come Near Me!* the locals used to think those bells said—every different buoy around here had a different signal, you see, a different voice, and the locals had various little sayings to mime the call of each one. But above and beyond the bells, Aunt Sadie had a bit of the psychic about her as well—and I suppose it was this that drew her to the window on that fateful day, as much as the bells.

"Well! It's horrible enough to witness a tragedy like this, Sean, when the victims are strangers—simply horrible! But imagine what it's like to witness such a thing when you realize your beloved is aboard!"

Sean, congenitally disposed of an active imagination, pictured just such a thing—and saw himself looking out Greystones' second floor window while a ship carrying Matt—of all people—shattered against the granite of Third Cliff as if the ship were made of glass.

His heart gave a sudden wince, ending at the back of his throat.

"What's the matter, Sean? You look like you've seen a ghost!"

Sean came back to the here and now. Miss Sawyer was staring at him with concern.

"Permission granted to speak for a moment. Are you feeling ill?"

"Oh no, it's…nothing. What happened to poor Aunt Sadie?"

"Well you might inquire," Miss Sawyer answered, sitting back in her chair and folding her hands. "She dashed down to the Cliffs and had to be restrained from leaping into the boiling black sea to save her lover. Not all hands died, you know—two or three crew members were tossed ashore more dead than alive, and half a dozen or so of the poor miserable escaped slaves survived as well, two of whom stayed with Aunt Sadie until the day she died.

"But Minister Samuel, alas, was not among the survivors. His body washed ashore on Tudor Beach two days later."

Tudor Beach. One of five beaches on Nawshant, on all of which Sean had spent delightful, carefree afternoons, alone or with his friends. Sean shook his head as he pondered the inscrutable mystery of bad things happening to good people.

"She…went *strange* after that," Miss Sawyer said carefully. "Sadie, I mean. Not right away—she was too strong-willed for that. She threw herself doubly into her Underground Railroad work after Samuel's death—and then the war came and all. But the love of a strong-willed person can be an all-consuming thing. People began to see her at the top of Third Cliff, throwing wild roses into the sea. Or sometimes staring out the thrown-open windows of her third-floor bedroom, even in the most frigid weather. Yes, yes, she had moved her bedroom up to the third floor of Greystones, as that had and has the best view of Third Cliff. That whole floor was the servants' quarters up there, that's how they did it in those stays, but that didn't bother her in the least. And then she began…well, I suppose *wandering* is the only word for it—inside the Thicket, gathering flowers. Or along Third Cliff. She had become quite quiet and thoughtful—far-away and vacant, if you know what I mean—but when storms came up the coast, as they often did and still do, she would become kind of—franticly morose.

"Then some time later another change occurred— now she became at times joyous, almost giddy—as if she were carrying a lovely secret. When these fits struck her, she would put on the ancient dress she was to have been wed in—an antique white lace affair, with blue and yellow flowers appliquéd round the waist. She'd put flowers in her hair and the old tulle veil over her face, as if she were off to the marriage that had never taken place. People would see her standing, or sitting, but in both cases waiting—not at the church, never at the church—but at the top of Third Cliff, or in the part of the Thicket right behind Third Cliff. She was out in all weathers—wearing her little satin slippers and her wedding gown, and what a pathetic sight when these thin, exquisite furnishings became filthy and muddy and torn. *But Samuel's coming!* she would happily announce to anyone who found her and tried to escort her home. *Samuel's coming and I must be ready...*

"Ahhh me. The only ones who could talk any sense to her at these times were the two former slave women I just mentioned, two sisters who were now in her employ. They would go out searching for her with lanterns and hurricane lamps when she vanished like this, and bring her home when they found her. *Yes'm, Reverend Samuel IS coming, but not tonight he ain't, he's not coming tonight,* they would tell her, gently leading her home. They were so devoted to her! Strange to say, Aunt Sadie had little recollection of these occurrences the next day, and then she'd be back to her old self for a month or two, until the fit took her again. The two sisters—I'm not remembering their names now— had that wedding outfit made over and over again on the sly, for the next time the fit took Sadie, using a seamstress in Boston who was paid well to keep her mouth shut and her fingers nimble. But of course the word got out anyway, for Sadie would be seen out and about, acting in this strange and queer manner. I suppose it was the late 1880s by this time."

Miss Sawyer sighed deeply, and shook her head. Her eyes became faraway again, and she rubbed her chin thoughtfully.

Finally Sean cleared his throat.

"Oh! Oh. Pardon me, Sean I was thinking...I was thinking of something from my own past. Well, at any rate, these fits of Sadie's became more and more frequent. And then one night—it was sometime in May, 18...89?—and a beautiful night it was, you know May! Sadie called the two sisters into her room, and asked them to help her get dressed 'for my wedding.' She was older and quite arthritic by then, and could walk only with the help of a cane in each hand—I suppose all the exposure out of doors over the years hadn't helped matters. She seemed very much excited this night, more so than usual I mean when these fits took her, and yet full of a quiet, smiling urgency. The sisters dressed her with care, and finished off by weaving wisteria flowers—from the vine right outside her window—into her streaming white hair. And then Sadie rose, gazed at herself in the mirror for a bit—and then, kissing both sisters on the cheek, bid them adieu. They begged her not to leave the house that night, despite the clemency of the weather—but she told them they no longer had to concern themselves with her—at which of course like sensible women they panicked. She ushered them out of the room, and closed and locked her bedroom door, remaining inside.

"Well Sean, would you believe it? That was the last time anyone saw your Great Great Great Aunt Sadie, dead or alive."

"How...what do you mean?" Sean couldn't help asking.

"I don't recall having given you permission to speak—but there it is— she was never seen again. The two sisters were frantic, and tried to force the door—but to no avail. They ran outside and out back to where the stables were—that's the Quinn's house now, you know, your little friends' the Twins' house— and roused Patrick, I think that was his name—he was the groom, the man who took care of the horses, and he lived above the stables—and brought him back up to the third floor, where they eventually found another key and opened the door. What do you think they found?"

Sean, mesmerized, shrugged his shoulders.

"Well, the windows were thrown open, and the drapes were dancing in the delicious, wisteria-scented sea breeze—but no Sadie. Now as you know, her bedroom wasn't and isn't that large a room—but such as it was, they searched it. They opened the closet. They looked in the wardrobe. They peeked under the bed. But she was gone.

"Full of almost hysterical dread, they rushed outside, and scoured all the grounds, beginning, naturally, with the area right beneath Sadie's window, three floors below." Sean knew this area well, for it was the same place he landed every time he snuck out via the wisteria vine.

"But they found nothing. Nothing, that is, except—guess."

Sean shook his head.

"Two canes, lying on the ground. Sadie's canes. Nothing else."

"But…when did they find the body?" Sean asked.

"They never did Sean, aren't you listening? They never did. Half the town was roused from sleep that night to aid in the search, for she was loved by all— and the other half joined them the next day. They combed the whole town, even the Thicket, impossible as that sounds. When that turned up nothing, they brought in hounds. But they would go no further than the spot where the canes were found, directly beneath her window and three stories down. No further. The scent apparently vanished there.

"And most remarkable of all—the very night she…vanished, if that's the word for it—well, would you believe it? That evening was the thirtieth anniversary of the wreck of the *Southern Cross*."

They both sat in subdued silence for a while, until the last trill of a robin brought them back.

"So now," Miss Sawyer continued, heaving a great sigh, "they say she walks—or at least they *used* to say that, when I was a young girl. Why, my great Aunt Regina claimed to have seen her, one night when she was strolling home from the Hutchinsons. Aunt Sadie—or the ghost of Aunt Sadie, I should say—was sitting on a large boulder near the Thicket, moonlight streaming through her, gazing into a hand mirror and arranging her veil. Others claimed to have seen her walking along the top of Third Cliff—not wringing her hands, but smiling and looking around, as if she expected someone.

"Well, that's my tale, Sean, and this is why I say if there is a ghost in the Thicket, she's quite benign by all accounts, and besides, a blood-relative of yours, so nothing to worry about. And now I must say I'm famished. I'd invite you in for a bite, dear, but I've a million things to do."

"Oh, no, that's okay, Miss Sawyer," Sean mumbled, rising from his seat as stiff, sore, and wonder-whacked as if he had just sat through a gripping three-hour movie. "Margaret will be wondering where I am, it's almost dinner time. Uhm…thanks. That was quite the story."

"You're welcome, Sean. And I'll see you tomorrow afternoon?"

"Oh, right, yes."

"Good! And uhm…bring some grass seed, won't you? It seems some lawless hooligans have driven over a section of my south lawn."

Miss Sawyer winked at Sean, laughed, then vanished inside her kitchen door, whistling Vivaldi.

CHAPTER NINE

A CAPRICIOUS TRIP TO THE LIBRARY YIELDS RESULTS

Sean was more than halfway home when he heard a bellowing, *DIM-SWORTH!* coming from the direction of *Lily Vale*—more birds around him decamped—so he knew Miss Sawyer had remembered Reverend Samuel's last name—or perhaps she had looked it up in one of the thousand brittle-paged books in her own personal library.

Whoa, what a story, Sean was numb with it. To think all this had happened in and around his home—to a member of his own family. But it wasn't just fascinating—it was tragic too, and he felt such empathy for Aunt Sadie. The grief she had been subjected to—how horrible.

But something was nagging at Sean—he couldn't put his finger on it. It wasn't the Matt business, but something Miss Sawyer had mentioned in her story. Not a main part of the story, but something she had said in passing. A flashing part of his subconscious mind was telling him he should have made note of this detail, it was somehow important—but he hadn't, and now he couldn't remember what it was.

He took the long way home—he shuffled, as only Sean could, as he wanted to digest Miss Sawyer's story—and this brought him only one street away from Nawshant Road; and it was on a little rise on that street that the old gabled, ochre-colored stone library sat, as it had sat for over

140 years. Breaking into a trot, he decided, despite the time, to make a quick pilgrimage and check out Aunt Sadie's portrait in the Children's Room. He had to see her, right now.

Dashing up the granite steps, each one adorned with a giant stone urn overflowing with pink geraniums and variegated ivy, he passed through the open, ornately-carved oak doors, and breathed deeply of the library's enticing aroma.

It was hard to say when the library was more evocative—here in the nice weather, with the sunset streaming through the lead-glass windows and the massive old trees just outside casting their lacy shadows on the creaky wooden floors; or in the winter, when the vast stone fireplace, which was lit every day from mid-October to April, poured forth its delicious smell to mingle with the quiet odor of books. Sean chided himself for not coming here more often.

"Well well well, hello Sean!" he heard lowly. Turning, Sean saw Kevin Nelson, the assistant head librarian, a dark-haired, gray-eyed man in his late-thirties, Sean guessed. Sean had always liked Kevin, for his laid-back, funny ways, and cheery disposition—and he felt a sudden spurt of sympathy, for Kevin was gay and lived on the other side of Nawshant with his partner Steve, who worked at a large bank in Boston and ran in that city's annual Marathon.

"Hello, Mister Nelson," Sean smiled, approaching the front desk, where Kevin was sorting books.

"Never mind the Mister stuff, it's Kevin," he answered, extending his hand across the ponderous front desk, which must have weighed as much as a minor planet and several of its satellites. "Where've you been hiding, Sean? We don't see you in here anymore."

"Oh, one thing and another," Sean said evasively. "Why? It hasn't been that long, has it?"

"Well, let's see," Kevin said, sliding a pile of books off to the side. He got on the computer and a moment later said, "Huh! The last book you took out was *Make Your Own Kites*. What does that tell you?"

"Ahhh…that I'm young at heart for almost eighteen?"

"Well," Kevin laughed, "there's one explanation—though Computer says no. You took that book out four and a half long years ago."

"Wow!" Sean laughed, rubbing again at his chin, and surprised to find his now three-day old goatee there. "I should read more. You got any good detective books, like?"

Kevin rolled his eyes. "Only about 4000 of them. If you want, I'll pick out a few good ones for you, and you can come by tomorrow or Monday and pick them up."

"That would be awesome Kevin! Thanks!" Sean secretly yearned to ask if they also had a book entitled *How to Tell If You're Gay, or Not*—but he was far too self-conscious to ask. That was the problem with the self-help books one really needed—how ever to get one's paws on them with no one knowing. *Hey Honey, did you take out this "How to Divorce Your Husband Without Him Knowing?" book?*

Not that Sean didn't trust Kevin. It wasn't about that at all.

"So what's up today?" Kevin asked. Kevin always talked a scooch loud because he was deaf in one ear, Sean remembered.

"Eh, not much really, I just stopped by to take a look at that picture of my Great Great Great Aunt Sadie in the Children's Room."

"What?" Kevin asked, leaning forward closer.

Sean repeated himself.

"Ah yes, good old Aunt Sadie Sutherland," Kevin sighed, putting one hand across his chest. "She of the broken heart."

"You know about that too?" Sean was shocked. He was looking forward to telling the tale for the rest of his life; but now—who else knew?

"Duh," Kevin answered. "Librarians are usually treasure troves of local history, since this is the first place people who are doing research on things like that come to. So, yeah, sure, I know all about Aunt Sadie."

"Does everybody?"

"Well, everyone who knows their Nawshant history. But that's only about one-tenth of the local-yokels. Why?"

"Oh, because Miss Sawyer just told me the story like half an hour ago. The story of Sadie, I mean. I know it sounds weird that I didn't even know my own family's history, but—"

"So she told you about the *Southern Cross*? And the Minister? And how she went a little nuts after the wreck?"

"Yeah, that's the one."

"And the bell and everything?" Kevin persisted.

Sean froze.

"What bell?" he asked.

"The buoy bell out on Third Cliff."

"Well…yeah. You mean like…how they rang the day of the disaster and everything?"

"Yeah, but more like how she got rid of it. It's not a *they* by the way, but an *it*. There was just one big-honkin' bell out there on that buoy."

"Oh. And Aunt Sadie got rid of it?"

"She did indeed. Hold on a sec." Kevin's cell phone rang. He turned around and took the call, murmuring as he spoke—but Kevin's murmur was loud enough for Sean to hear—and if Sean strained and moved just a speck closer—which he did—he could hear the caller too.

I shouldn't be so nosy, Sean chided himself—but then again, he rationalized, he was a paid detective now—wasn't this part of the job description? Keep your eyes and ears open?

Sean put one elbow on the shiny wooden counter and half-turned away, trying to look nonchalant as his eyes ran down the stacks of books off to the side. Apparently it was Kevin's partner Steve calling and, though Kevin said he was busy and couldn't talk, the call was strictly a personal one: Steve had returned home from work and was waiting in the couple's backyard hot-tub, and he described in brief but explicit detail what would happen when Kevin got home.

This wasn't quite what Sean had expected— not that he'd been expecting anything in particular. But—just like when Miss Sawyer talked about witnessing one's beloved drowning right in front of one's eyes, and Sean had thought of Matt, Sean now, more or less involuntarily, threw himself a few years into the future: he had an office in the village downtown for *Sutherland Detective Agency*, and Matt was calling from their fabulous oceanfront home up by First Cliff to say that he was waiting in their hot-tub, and he would do thus and so as soon as Sean got home, and hopefully that would be soon. Sean shifted and blushed.

"I have to *go!*" Kevin laughed, hanging up and spinning around.

"Sorry about that," Kevin grimaced. "So—what were we saying?"

The flush that Sean felt riding up his face was almost hot enough to make him run for water, and it spread further and darker, naturally, the more he tried to will it away.

"Ahhh…" Sean blurted.

"My God! You didn't hear him, did you?" Kevin blurted.

"Ahhh…hear who?" Sean stalled. "You were ahhh…we were ahhh… saying…" For the life of him, Sean couldn't remember what they had been talking about.

"Oh, I know! Aunt Sadie and the buoy bell," Kevin said, mock-slapping his forehead—but he avoided Sean's eyes and looked like he was coloring a little himself.

"Oh yeah yeah yeah!" Sean said, a bit too zealously.

"Well, yeah, like I was saying, Aunt Sadie got rid of the buoy-bell right along Third Cliff, which was a hundred yards or so from her house—your house."

"She did?"

"Well, wouldn't you? Every time the seas got a little rough it would clang out there, and she could hear it—I'm sure it made her crazy. So, she had it discreetly removed, and paid to have a bigger and more modern buoy anchored a little further off-shore. Which is still there, of course.

Third Cliff Buoy."

"Oh sure, I know that. We sail around it all the time. I didn't know Aunt Sadie had it put out there."

"Yeah, there's a little plaque on it to that effect. People understood what Sadie had done. Plus it was actually safer to have the buoy further out, to give ships a bit more of a warning. Oh, and her father was the one who put the first buoy bell out there anyway, or actually her grandfather, so I guess it was their own property, more or less."

"He did?"

"Sure. There'd been another nasty wreck out there when he was young, and he never forgot it. Frederick Sutherland was that guy's name. Your... let me see…Great Great Great Grandfather."

"Really?"

"Really," Kevin answered, his eyes lighting up with the zeal of a dedicated librarian dispensing information.

"Miss Sawyer never told me that," Sean mumbled dubiously.

"Who you going to believe," Kevin asked, feigning outrage, "me or a jailbird?"

"A jailbird? Miss Sawyer *was in jail?*"

"Shh!" Kevin hissed. "Ah, she didn't tell you that story I bet! Well, she wasn't really in jail—just the cell in the basement of the Nawshant Police—though I do think they kept her overnight. You never heard?"

"No!" Sean was dumbfounded.

"Well," Kevin said, leaning both his elbows on the edge of the shiny wooden desk and coming closer, "you don't have to tell her I was the one who told you, because I like my job. Though to tell the truth, she's not ashamed of what happened at all, and tells everyone who'll listen that she'd do it again in a heartbeat."

Kevin looked around again, to make sure no one could hear them. "This was before you were born. She was still teaching at the High School then, and only worked here nights and weekends. I had her for English back in the day—and of course she was mad into gardening then, like now—always was. Anyway, there was this family who moved in next door to her, *nouveau riche* and kind of jerky. They let the place go a bit, and then they started selling off their land and building tiny tacky new houses there—first one, then a second. Miss Sawyer couldn't stand them. They were always cutting down old trees on their property, because the Man of the House couldn't stand bird-poop on his big-butt car. Well, Miss Sawyer came home from school one night, and she saw that this ancient Mulberry tree that was right on the border of the two properties had been hacked down right to the stump. Well, she went *off!* I guess her grandfather had planted that tree way back when, and birds nested in it and all that. Miss Sawyer didn't even get out of her car, but drove right up the neighbor's driveway and *rammed hell* out of the neighbor lady's Lincoln. Then I guess that felt so good, she backed up and did it again! And then again!"

"Oh my God!" Sean laughed. "Call me crazy, but I can see her doing that!"

"But wait, that's not even the best part," Kevin continued, coming even closer and lowering his voice, after looking around again. "It seems that the neighbor lady and the tree-cutter guy were actually…uhm, how old are you now anyway?"

"I'll be eighteen in January," Sean answered, wondering what this had to do with anything.

"Oh. Well, it seems the Lady of the House and the tree-cutter guy were in the back seat of the woman's car at the time and they were… uhm…getting to know each other a little better."

"No!" Sean laughed.

Kevin nodded.

"They arrested Miss Sawyer—I mean, really, they had to—who kept begging the police to let her do it one more time before they hauled her off. But all charges were dropped later that night when Miss Sawyer threatened to spill the beans about what was going on in the car—plus

I guess the tree really was on her property. And of course Miss Sawyer's cousin was governor then—that never hurts. The boys in blue were glad to be rid of her, for she had them stepping and fetching something fierce. But word about what happened got out anyway—you know Nawshant. And two days later the *For Sale* sign was up at the neighbor's house."

"Oh my God," Sean commented. "I can't believe it, but I can too. But wait—there's no new houses next door to Miss Sawyer's."

"Not any more there's not. Miss Sawyer bought the whole property next door through a blind trust, then had the two smaller new houses plowed into the ground. They weren't quite finished yet with the second one. She had a big party and invited all her friends to come and watch the demolition. Even drove the bulldozer herself for a while, said Someone Who Was There. She rented out the big house to a company that wanted to hold retreats there, then she sold it ten years later and doubled her investment. That's the Bigelow's house now, as you know."

"Wow. Quite the wheeler-dealer, huh? I wonder if—"

Sean stopped as his eyes ran through the main hall of the library, out into the quaint and charming Reading Room, where the fireplace was sited—though of course it wasn't lit this evening. He had spotted someone poring over books and papers on one of the tables—and it looked an awful lot like that weirdo real estate lady Dottie LaFrance.

"Hey, Kevin—do you know who that woman is?"

Kevin turned. When he looked back at Sean there was a Cheshire-cat smile nailed on his face and his eyes were closed. "*What's your budget?*" he hissed, in a very credible imitation.

Sean covered his mouth to keep from laughing. "I thought so."

"Yeah, that's good ol' Dottie LaFrance, of Manchuso-LaFrance-and-O'Shaughnessy—I've heard her say that so often, I'll be saying it on my death bed. She's some real estate agent. The woman's in here at least twice a week—has been since the middle of summer. I had to give her some Tough Librarian Love her first month here though, as she kept hitting on the patrons, which people can't stand. She's been okay since then, though she sure keeps me hopping. If it wasn't so slow here most times, I'd say she was a royal pain in the butt."

"What…what's she doing here? What's she after?" Sean asked.

Kevin raised one eyebrow. "This isn't a private club you know. Anyone can come here. And what people research and check out is private—though a previous political administration in our nation's capital begged to differ." Kevin looked around him again. Then he leaned in closer and whispered, "I'll tell you as a friend, not as an assistant librarian. Old stuff. Boring stuff. Deeds, title searches, land sale records, town zoning ordinances and easements, mostly stuff like that."

Then Kevin leaned back and eyed Sean quizzically. "What's it to you anyway? And what's all this detective stuff you're all of a sudden interested in? What's going on?"

"Oh, just curious," Sean said vaguely, looking up at the ceiling's medallion and chandelier.

"Liar!" Kevin hissed. "C'mon, tell! I just told you stuff!"

Now it was Sean's turn to look around, and he kept an especially keen eye on Dottie in the other room as he leaned closer to Kevin. It occurred to Sean that Kevin might be a good ally and confidante to have, since he knew so much about Nawshant's history and people.

"Alright, but you have to promise not to tell anyone."

"I can't even tell Steve?" Kevin asked.

"Okay, just Steve. But you have to swear him to secrecy."

"Scout's honor. Okay, give."

"Well," Sean said, leaning in closer against the desk, "Mrs. Hutchinson—you know her, right?"

"Duh. She's one of the Trustees here."

"Alright, well, she's been hearing—bells. She says someone's been ringing a bell late at night—she's heard it like twenty different times. She says it's coming from the middle of the Thicket and it isn't bike bells or ships' bells or anything tinkly and dinky like that, but a big-ol' honkin' bell—like a church bell. She told Professor Singleton about it last week, and he thinks she's getting senile—but somehow I believe her. Anyway—she's hired me to get the bottom of it. Don't laugh, okay?"

"Why would I laugh?"

"I don't know—cuz I'm young and everything. But I really want to solve the mystery—I…I think maybe I'd like to go into this line of work."

"That's great!" Kevin answered, but he seemed vaguely absent-minded as he said it. "She ahhh… says it's coming from the Thicket?"

"Yeah."

"Humph."

"How come?" Sean asked. "What are you *humphing* about?"

"Well, I was just thinking," Kevin said slowly. "The buoy bell I was telling you about? Well—"

Just then Bert Stevens, a local author in his late sixties who wrote books about beekeeping, came up to the desk with a small pile of books to check out, and the gossip session came to an abrupt halt.

"Hello, Sean! How are you and yours down at your hive?" Bert laughed at his own joke, while Kevin rolled his eyes behind Bert's back.

"Hi, Mister Stevens, very well thank you, and you?"

Mr. Stevens eyed Sean fiercely, then pronounced, "The Missus has the chilblains!"

"Oh no," Sean answered—whatever that was. "I'm so sorry."

Mr. Stevens laughed in his opened-mouth, silent way.

"No Sean, that's not true. The Missus in fact ran off ten years ago before I got sober, and who can blame her? She should've done it twenty years ago. No Sean, that was a line I read thirty minutes ago—*The Missus has the chilblains!* Don't you love it? And don't you love the English habit of understated euphemism? Here in my hand I have a, well, 'spine-tingling thriller,' in the words of the back cover, and no doubt it must be, as it concerns itself with a series of murders at a posh English tennis club. The murderer's M.O. is an ice pick—and he gets them in the ear with it! Here in America we'd entitle such a book *The Bloody Ice Pick Digs Ear Deep* or *Bloodbath at the 19th Hole* or some such grisly, over-the-top thing. But look at this!"

He held up the book in question. Sean saw that the title was *The Unpleasantness at the Fairfield Club*. Kevin laughed out loud as he checked out Mr. Stevens' books.

"That is funny," Kevin said. But Sean wasn't sure he got it.

"Goodbye, gentleman. Kevin, Sean."

"We live in a town full of eccentrics," Kevin commented as Mr. Stevens passed through the open oak doors.

"Duh," Sean said. "You have a flair for the obvious, Kev." This was actually one of Margaret's lines, but Sean used it when he could.

"The mouth on you!" Kevin cried, but he laughed as he said it.

"I owed you that for the other *duh* you gave me earlier," Sean smiled. "Alright, where were we? You were about to say something about Aunt Sadie's bell buoy."

"Right, right. Well—is that a goatee you're growing?"

"Oh, yeah," Sean smiled, blushing a little and rubbing it self-consciously. He waited for Kevin to compliment it—but he didn't.

"Anyway, I was just thinking," Kevin went on. "You don't think there's any connection between Aunt Sadie's bell and this one that's ringing in the Thicket, do you?"

Sean made a face of confusion. "How could there be? What happened to the buoy-bell Aunt Sadie got rid of?"

"No one knows. But you know once or twice since I've worked here, some scholar or historian has come up from Pennsylvania looking for information about it. They seem to think it was of historical value or something. Which I suppose any two-hundred year old bell would be."

"Why Pennsylvania?" Sean asked.

"Because that's where the bell originally came from. Your family was originally from Pennsylvania—*duh!*" Kevin snapped.

"Ha ha. They were? I didn't know that."

"Yeah. They were all Quakers from Pennsylvania. Probably came over with William Penn. One of the Sutherlands came up here after the Revolutionary War to marry a Nahant woman. He would've been Aunt Sadie's father—or, no, grandfather."

"The dude who first put the buoy bell out against Third Cliff," Sean said. "My Great Great Great Grandfather Frederick you mentioned earlier."

Kevin smiled. "Yeah…how nice that you're paying attention. But they weren't dudes then, they were *gentlemen*. And God knows, gentlemen are scarce as hen's teeth nowadays, more's the pity—present company excepted, of course."

"Of course," Sean said. "Ahhh…who was William Penn again?"

Kevin made a face of feigned outraged disbelief.

"What are they teaching you at that school nowadays!" he cried, doing his Miss Sawyer imitation now. Kevin was a great mimic, and Sean had to laugh. "I bet you heard that once or twice this afternoon."

"Right?" Sean agreed.

"Well, Penn was the gentleman who founded Pennsylvania. Penn's Woods, that's what the name means. They were from England and Germany mostly, and came here for religious freedom."

"Oh—is he the really happy dude on the oatmeal box?"

Kevin glared at him.

"Oh, sorry. Is he the happy *gentleman* on the oatmeal box?"

"I'm not even going to dignify that question with an answer."

"Some help you are!" Sean scoffed.

"Shut up and listen! Anyway…I was just thinking…what if Aunt Sadie's out in the Thicket, ringing that ol' buoy bell?"

Sean eyed Kevin. He was serious. Sean tried to ignore the chill running up his own spine.

"Why not?" Kevin whispered. "They say she's a ghost anyway."

"Yeah, but not for forever. That's what Miss Sawyer said, that no one had seen her for a wicked long time—since Miss Sawyer was a girl."

"An eon, I'm sure," Kevin said. "Ah, the cruelty of youth!"

"But I can't believe you!" Sean remonstrated. "You're serious!"

"Well…maybe just a little. A lot of people in the old days said they saw her. They weren't all kooks either."

"That's just hearsay," Sean said, "and way before our time."

"It's in the book," Kevin said defensively.

"What book?"

"*Ghost Tales of the North Shore of Massachusetts*. There's like three or four chapters on Nawshant's very own ghosts, and Aunt Sadie is one of them. What? Don't tell me you're one of the seven billion people in the world who's never read that book?"

They stared at each other for a minute.

"What shelf is it on?" Sean asked. "And are you just trying to get me to read?"

"Now would an assistant head librarian ever do something like that?" Kevin asked, putting a hand to his chest. He turned back to the computer and typed something into the machine. "God forbid you should read." Kevin fell silent as his eyes scanned the records. "Humph, that's funny. Someone took it out last month—and hasn't returned it yet. Thirty lashes with a wet noodle and a nickel-a-day fine."

"Bummer," Sean sighed. He was hoping to feed his ghost-story addiction this weekend—after all, it wasn't every day one could manipulate Miss Sawyer into a foul mood. Plus of course it would behoove him to read up on all the local ghosts—especially Aunt Sadie. He couldn't believe his great great great aunt—or the ghost of her—was mentioned in a real book. He really couldn't wait! He wondered if he could get the book online somewhere else.

"Well, that's not the funny part, that it's been checked out," Kevin added. "You'll find this astonishing, no doubt, Mister Make-Your-Own-Kites, but people do take books out from time to time. But what the funny part is…well never mind, I can't tell you what the funny part is."

"C'mon!" Sean hissed. "I told you stuff!"

"I know, but if I tell you this, that'll be two 'stuffs' I told you, and you only told me one stuff. Tell me something else, and I'll happily violate every principle of ethics a librarian should observe, and sing like a canary."

Sean thought hard. What could he tell Kevin that he didn't already know? A sudden smile came to his face—

"A-ha!" Kevin hissed. "You thought of something! Tell!"

"Okay, but don't say I told you!" Sean laughed. He paused dramatically. Kevin leaned in closer. "Miss Sawyer had a *major* meltdown this afternoon," he whispered.

"Ah!" Kevin replied knowingly. "So that's why she told you the story of Aunt Sadie and the *Southern Cross*! I was wondering!"

Sean's face fell. "You mean you know that too? That she only tells stories when she's in a sh—ahhh…bogus mood? And don't say *duh*!" Kevin's mouth was just forming to make a "d" sound.

"You must have ESP," Kevin said dryly. "By which I mean of course, Extra Smelly Pits. Yes, Sean, I would say everyone in town—or at least we older folks who had Miss Sawyer for English at Nawshant High—knows that you have to get her well and righteously angry before the good stories spring forth. Fresh water from a foul spring, eh? My God, if I had a dollar for every time we accidentally-on-purpose pushed the poor dear over the edge, just so we could hear a ghost story instead of listening to her recite Shakespeare, I'd be able to—"

"God forbid you should hear Shakespeare!" Sean interjected.

Kevin narrowed his eyes at him.

"You're way too flip for someone your age. You sure you're not….oh, never mind."

"What?"

"I'll ask you when you're 18. We live in the age of self-righteous witch hunts, and I like my job too much to get in trouble. Alright, give me all the chapters! About Miss Sawyer's meltdown, I mean."

Sean lowered his voice and told Kevin the details of Miss Sawyer's less than stiff-upper-lip reception of the unhappy news of her hemlock's infestation, and her resultant acting out.

"That one will never die of an ulcer," Kevin commented when the tale was told. "Hilarious! Wreaking havoc on her own Holy Ground of a lawn—and smacking bugs with her pocketbook! God, I love that woman."

"That's nice. Okay, your turn. Spill your guts."

Kevin looked around again. Then he leaned in closer and mumbled, "Well, the person who took out *Ghost Tales of the North Shore of Massachusetts* was…and don't worry Sean, we have another copy in the Young Adult section…that person was…"

Here Kevin smiled so broadly and, one would have thought, painfully, that his eyes vanished into slits.

Sean could feel his own eyes growing wide in shock.

"Not—not her?" Sean asked, pointing a discreet baby finger into the reading room.

"Yup," Kevin nodded, his grin only slightly diminishing. "Miss *What's-Your-Budget* herself. Dottie LaFrance!"

"Humph, that is funny," Sean said, though he wasn't smiling. He fell quiet for a moment—more evidence that Dottie wasn't all she said she was. Or…well, was Regina right about his own overly-active imagination? What if Dottie was just interested in this town, that's all, in wringing whatever money she could out of it through real estate deals—in which case she would obviously, and rightfully, do her homework and find out as much about Nawshant as she could. Or maybe she was a ghost story aficionado, like Sean. Or maybe she moonlighted as a ghost-buster. Sean pictured her intoning, *Step into the light, come into the light!* in her raspy, nasally twang, and laughed suddenly when he pictured her asking even those who had "crossed over" what their budget might be.

"Alright, that's it, it's ten of seven and I have to start closing and get home, or Steve will die of loneliness."

"Oh, is that what it's called now?" Sean asked innocently. "*Loneliness?*"

"Oh you little twerp! You did hear!"

Sean laughed and this time Kevin was the one who blushed.

"Not another word, Sean Sutherland, or I'll ban you for life. Follow me if you want that book, it's this way."

Several moments later, Kevin handed Sean a small hardback book with a clear plastic covering. The cover illustration depicted the infamous Lady in Black chasing a terrified soldier over at Fort Warren on George's Island, her arms outstretched as if to snatch and her cape billowing in a moon-tossed wind.

"Subtle cover art, eh?" Kevin asked. "Well, enjoy! Oh, and here's Aunt Sadie's portrait, right through here." They stepped into the Children's Room, empty now except for the sunset streaming through the windows. "Beautiful, wasn't she?" Kevin mumbled.

Sean must have seen the large picture hundreds of times before, as there was a time when he and Margaret visited the Children's Room at least once a week, when Sean was younger. Certainly it dominated the whole east wall, and there was something commanding in the way the fair features and dress of Aunt Sadie leapt out in contrast to the almost-black background of the work. But he had never known until this moment this was his great great great aunt. The flesh of his flesh and the bone of his bone. Why hadn't Margaret told him? Maybe she herself didn't know—after all, she had worked for Justin for almost twenty years over in England before the two of them moved to Nawshant and Greystones, and there was no large nameplate or anything identifying the subject of the painting. Just a little metal tag near the bottom of the frame. Sean leaned in closer to read the words inscribed thereon: *Go On.*

"Go on?" Sean asked. "What's that mean?"

"No one really knows," Kevin answered.

Oddly, Sean could see something of his cousin Kyle around Sadie's eyes—though not of himself. Sadie was dressed in a billowing gown that wasn't the color of cream, or the color of snow, but something of both, depending on how the artist had depicted the sun falling onto his subject. Sadie's light blue watery eyes showed intelligence, but something else beyond that—something almost dreamy and fairy-like. She was sitting up in a small skiff, and an open green leather-bound volume was resting in her lap, with Sadie's hands folded on top of it.

"Was this painted before the wreck of the *Southern Cross*, or after?" Sean whispered, almost reverentially, as if a part of Sadie were present there with them, listening.

"Oh, before," Kevin answered. "She'd never sit for a portrait afterwards—especially in a boat. They said she never set foot in a boat again, after the wreck. Gosh, it's too bad we have such a tight budget here, it really should be cleaned."

"How do you mean?" Sean asked. "It's dirty?"

"Well, Mrs. Hutchinson told me once that it sat for about a hundred years right over the fireplace mantle in the Reading Room. All the smoke darkened it considerably I guess, because she insisted the background was light blue, not black, with the sky and water and all, and had lots of details in it."

"What kind of details?" Sean asked.

Kevin shrugged. "I guess we'll never know. Alright, listen, stay another minute or two if you want, but I need to get those other deadbeats out of here."

"Oh yes, we wouldn't want Steve getting too, uhm…*lonely now*, would we?"

"I'm not playing with you anymore, you're too sharp for me," Kevin said, leaving the room, but laughing as he did.

Sean studied the portrait for another minute, sitting down in one of the tiny kid's chairs at a table opposite the east wall. It was probably just his overly-active imagination (again) and romantic nature instigating this, but he became aware of something in Sadie's eyes, almost calling to him, as if she had something to say to him. Strange.

Then he left, dashing down the front steps before Dottie LaFrance could see him, and listening with chagrin to the library's bell-tower tolling the hour of seven. He was now OLFD (Officially Late For Dinner) and Margaret as a result would be on the warpath.

But such, amazingly, was not the case. Uncle Justin and Professor Singleton (the latter was over for dinner three or four nights a week) were comfortably ensconced in their chairs in the Snuggery, alternately reading their newspapers and chatting; and Margaret was busy making her usual pre-dinner racket in the kitchen, alternately singing and cussing, as she pulled things together.

"Hi, Uncle Justin, hi, Professor!" Sean said, taking a seat across from the two gentlemen. He lowered his voice. "Ahhh...I'm not late?"

"Oh, yes dear boy! Errr, that is, no! We're dining late tonight."

"We *are*?" Sean asked. "What world crisis brought this on?" He lowered his voice further so Margaret of the Very Large Array wouldn't hear him. "Did the earth fall out of its orbit?"

Professor Singleton thought this funny.

"Actually, no, Sean," Uncle Justin answered. "Your cousin called about an hour ago. He apologized most profusely and begged most earnestly if he might come home at 7:30, as something vital and necessary—which escapes my memory now, I'm sorry to admit—was keeping him late at school. That is, he must have been most profuse and earnest, as he spoke with Margaret, and she came out shortly thereafter to inform us that we would be dining at 7:30, rather than 7:00."

For the taking of a breath, Sean couldn't answer at first.

"Wow, the Mountain comes to Mohammed," Sean muttered. "She'd never do that for me!"

"Nonsense, dear boy!" Uncle Justin remonstrated. "It's just that you'd never call, but instead come in thirty minutes late."

Sean said nothing, for this was true enough.

"Oh, by the way, Uncle Justin," Sean said, "what can you tell me about Aunt Sadie Sutherland? Miss Sawyer told me a wicked cool story about her today. And an old bell buoy that used to be out on Third Cliff—well, no one knows what's become of it."

"Aunt Sadie, Aunt Sadie," Uncle Justin ruminated, lowering his magazine, tugging on his moustache, and staring at the ceiling. "Oh, yes! Used to live on the third floor here, where your cousin is now. Wasn't she lost at sea?"

"Jumped out the window, didn't she?" Professor Singleton ventured from behind his magazine. "Look here, Justin! It says that the Germans have cloned a disease resistant *Ulmus americana…*"

Knowing further questions were futile in the present, botanically-rarefied company, Sean, in his quest for knowledge, made so bold as to venture into Enemy Territory, which the kitchen always was shortly before meal time.

Alas, Margaret wasn't any more helpful—in fact, distinctly less so. She was red-faced in her Holy-of-Holies, with her nose in a cookbook and a bowl of light-colored, fragrant batter in her hands, making, "!#@$%!! Madeleines" in her own words—"and it's the last time I'll ever try them! The Divil himself wouldn't have any luck with them! Excuse my French, Sean, but it's your own fault, and it is, too! You shouldn't come in here during—*Zero Hour*! What do you want anyway? It isn't to help, I daresay!"

"Uhm…yeah, sorry Margaret. I was just wondering—would you happen to know anything about my Great Great Great Aunt Sadie?"

This being a certain type of book, Margaret's answer is not recorded herein.

CHAPTER TEN
THE PLOT THICKETS

Generally speaking, Friday nights during the school year were tame sometimes lame ones for Sean, Matt, Regina, and Timmy (or "The Gang of Four," as they sometimes called themselves) since most Saturday mornings found them engaged in various activities of a highly energetic nature: namely, lacrosse, football, and field hockey. They might hit a movie, or the mall (though lately Regina had vetoed this latter activity as being "too bourgeois and depressingly soulless") or watch a movie over someone's house, or hang-out down at the beach with some of the other kids from town. But they had made no plans yet for tonight.

During dinner that evening at Greystones the social tables were somewhat turned, in that Kyle seemed almost *happy*, to Sean's astonishment, and Sean found himself encased in a thoughtful silence, as he digested all he had learned from Miss Sawyer and Kevin Nelson. Afterwards Kyle actually helped Margaret scrub the pots and pans and empty the dishwasher, two seemingly-ritualistic activities Margaret ordinarily allowed no one else to do: mere mortals could not possibly hope to meet her imperial standards, and vestal virgins were a rare commodity in town. But Margaret—more remarkable still!—actually praised Kyle for the job he did: *I believe we could set you to herding cats at a crossroads, and you'd give a good accounting of yourself!* Sean heard her beaming. My God, the whole world was turning upside down…

Uncle Justin, Sean, and, especially, Professor Singleton, were still in the dining room, finishing up the remnants of dessert—Margaret's "#@$^%!!" Madeleines, which had turned out, of course, *parfait*. Even Sean had been yanked out of his pensive ennui after a bite or two.

"My dear lady," Professor Singleton had said at one point, actually rising to say the words. He cleared his throat, half-closed his eyes, and folded his hands behind his back, almost knocking his chair over. "I have been fortunate enough to have munched these delicacies at patisseries ringing the Bois de Boulogne, the Champs Elysees, the Left Bank as well as the Right—and I have *never* consumed anything so light, so ethereal, so exquisite! *I will not believe* this is your first attempt at making them. Bravo, madame!" My God, was he tearing up? Over a cookie?

"Thank you, Professor," Margaret answered, quite seriously. She chewed on her cheek for a moment; then added, "Truth be told, this is actually my third attempt at them; my first two weren't fit to serve. I might add that this is the type of culinary endeavor that can only be successful when undertaken with much scheming and perseverance."

Then she decamped back to the kitchen, leaving Professor Singleton still standing with a rather confused look on his face.

In typical Margaret fashion, she had made lemon-water Madeleines, orange-water Madeleines, rose-water Madeleines, vanilla Madeleines, chocolate Madeleines, almond Madeleines, mint Madeleines, lavender Madeleines, and lemon-balm Madeleines, the latter three iterations infused with fresh chopped herbs from her gardens out back. It had all started when she was cleaning out a section of the attic two months earlier and had found half a dozen or so Madeleine baking trays from, perhaps, a century ago. This had raised her culinary curiosity, the end result of which was visible—and edible—this evening. She had also announced a desire to read Proust, "the man who made them famous." In her opinion this latter contribution to Humanity far outweighed anything the man might have written. Professor Singleton still hadn't been able to decide which Madeleine rendition was the most superb— not from a lack of trying, as he had sampled three or four of each version, claiming as he munched that the problem was still insoluble without "further evidence."

Sean got up to join Margaret and Kyle in the kitchen, thinking he might take advantage of Kyle's loquaciousness and make some social in-roads with him; but Kyle went back to the dining room as Sean entered the kitchen, and Sean heard his cousin ask Uncle Justin if he might go out for a while—to which Uncle Justin warmly assented—and once again Sean felt hurt, just when he thought Kyle might be warming up.

Why didn't he ask me go with? he kept wondering. *And where's he going anyway?*

Lonely and a little down, Sean slunk up to his bedroom to make a few calls and see what might be up for the night. He would sneak out to the Thicket later, but that wouldn't be until 11-ish or so.

He had tons of homework for the weekend, but the idea of doing it on Friday night was depressing. He could read about the ghosts of Naw-shant in the new library book Kevin had given him—but Sean wanted to undertake that exciting task when he was in a better mood than the one he found himself in now. He needed to be with people now, people who cared about him and who longed for his company.

He called the Twins first—but nothing doing there. He shared with Regina the news that the Quinn's house had, back in the day, been the sta-bles at Greystones (which Sean had never known until Miss Sawyer told him) and that the groom—the guy who took care of Greystones' horses, some guy named Patrick—had lived above the stables, maybe right where Regina's room was now.

"Wow, cool," Regina said, but she yawned as she said it. She add-ed that Timmy and she had company, the Devaney cousins from New Hampshire, and therefore they were "stuck" with them for the night. But

Sean was more than welcome to come over and hang if he wanted to, she said, "although they're playing the piano now with Moms, and they're annoyingly lousy at it."

This wasn't exactly what Sean was in the mood for, so he made his excuses and hung up.

He laid back down on his back and wondered what he was in the mood for.

He didn't have to wonder long—he really wanted to see Matt. But of course he was hoping that Matt would call him first.

Over the next fifteen minutes, Sean dialed Matt's number eleven times, always clicking off before the call went through—before finally letting it connect on the twelfth go-round. It wasn't that he didn't want to talk to Matt—quite the contrary—it was that he knew he needed to say something to Matt about what had happened the other day between them, and Sean didn't know if he was ready for that, or could find the right words. What he really wanted to do—and he winced as he realized this, even as part of him rejoiced—what he really wanted to do...

He really wanted to kiss Matt.

That was it in a nutshell. To see Matt and just kiss him. That would say everything Sean wanted to say and let Matt know how he felt. Besides, it might throw some light on Sean's confused state. If it felt weird or gross then at least Sean would know. If it felt awesome, then he would know that too.

Matt's line rang. Once. Then twice—

"Oh...oh, hey Sean," Matt answered. "What's up?"

"Hey," Sean replied, with a bit of a confused chuckle. "It sounds like... it sounds like you're a little surprised I called."

"Oh, ahhh...no, not...not really. What's up?"

Sean felt his brows scrunch down. This was the second time Matt had asked this—almost like he was wondering why Sean had called—and for ten years they had called each other several times a day, and it was always effortless.

"Ahhh…am I bothering you or something?" Sean wondered. He wouldn't have been so forward if he wasn't in such a down mood.

"No, no, I just…I'm trying to get ready here and—"

"Oh, what's up?" Sean asked sarcastically. Here was someone else who hadn't invited Sean to do whatever it was they were doing.

Just then Sean heard Matt's mother's two Papillon dogs going nuts as the doorbell rang at Matt's house.

Matt, your friend's here! Sean heard next over the line.

"I gotta go, Sean—talk to you tomorrow?" Matt said.

"Ahhh….yeah, sure. Sounds…good."

"Okay later."

"Right."

Sean remained motionless for some time, lying on his back on his bed, staring at the ceiling. To bring the pain and confusion to a more exquisite point, he leaned over, donned ear buds, and played *If I Were Your Woman* approximately as many times as the Misses Sawyer and Worthington had "boulevardiered" around Nawshant that afternoon. He wondered how his mood—so high, blithe, and, well, *gay*, this afternoon—could plummet to such dismal depths this evening.

Where the frig was Matt going? How come he hadn't included Sean in his plans? Like he always did—since they had been eight! Even if they were just doing nothing! Why had Matt been so evasive? Was it because Sean was bow-legged? Or that his ears stuck out too much?

Uncle Justin always said that taking things personally was always the first option where matters of the heart were concerned, when one was seventeen going on eighteen; and so Sean, being no exception to this rule, slid off the bed, walked across his room—not without looking at the silvering sea as he did, he could never cross his room without stealing a glance at the ocean—then he placed himself in front of his dresser's mirror, surrounded by the growing violet dusk and a not-entirely intolerable sea of despond.

He narrowed his eyes critically and took stock. Front on; from the left side; from the right side.

His face looked pretty good—he hadn't had a zit in about a month now. His eyes were still blue, his hair still blond, his thin eyebrows still dark. He pressed his hands against his ears and pushed them against his head.

He wouldn't be half-bad looking, he thought, if his ears didn't stick out so much—even though one time when he had mentioned this belief to Regina in confidence when they were talking about what they perceived to be their own physical flaws—she had snorted, "Oh, c'mon Sean, get over it, everyone thinks they're adorable."

Well, maybe everyone but Matt.

He unbuttoned and threw off his flannel shirt, then peeled off his T-shirt. He flexed both arms, took a deep breath, and inflated his thin chest: yes, there could no doubt, he had a bit more muscle than the last time he had checked this (Monday), because of his working out. The school had installed a mini-gym in the basement over the summer, and he and Timmy and Matt had started working out after school when they didn't have practice. Was it, then, his bow-leggedness?

He hopped up on his bed and kicked off his trousers. Dressed only in his boxers, he walked to the edge of the bed, then back again backwards, watching himself in the mirror.

Yes, undoubtedly he was bow-legged. He sighed.

Well, even if it was this, there was nothing Sean could do about it. Besides, he reminded himself, *it was just yesterday* that Matt had half-sung the words of that song to him! *If I were your woman/And you were my man/You'd have no other woman/You'd be weak as a lamb…If you had the strength to walk out that door/My love would over-rule my sense, and I'd call you back for more—*

He slunk down onto his bed and stared at the ceiling again, utterly confused and hurt. It didn't make sense. How could Matt be so fickle, singing him a love song yesterday—and then giving him attitude, rushing him off the phone, and going out without him tonight?

Well, fine. If Matt wanted to give him attitude, let him. Sean didn't need him. He was fine without him. He'd give Matt attitude right back, see if he wouldn't.

Sean waited to feel better after reaching this decision. And waited… and waited…

He woke when he heard a light rapping. Sean struggled back to consciousness and limped to his bedroom door. It was Uncle Justin.

"Oh—hi, Uncle Justin—what time is it?"

"It's just gone ten-thirty. Ah, I'm sorry dear boy, I've woken you. I was just saying goodnight and checking in on you. You were very quiet at dinner. Everything tickety-boo then?"

"Oh, oh, yeah—thanks, Uncle Justin, I was just…tired I guess."

"Well…go back to sleep then, Sean— and always remember, if there's ever anything you'd like to talk about, you know you can tell me in complete confidence. You may especially rely upon my confidence, as I would be just as apt to forget an hour later!"

Sean warmed at his Uncle's sincerity and self-deprecating humor—what a great guy. Maybe Sean would talk about his confusion over Matt with Uncle Justin—but not right now.

Sean opened his arms and hugged his uncle hard.

"Goodnight, dear boy then, and sleep well! Margaret says goodnight as well, she went up some time ago."

"Did…uhm…Kyle come home yet?" Sean whispered.

"Oh my, yes—thirty minutes ago. Said goodnight and went up."

"Where was he?" Sean asked further.

Uncle Justin hunched his eyebrows.

"Oh dear!" he murmured. "I don't know! I never asked!" The happy, somewhat-bemused smile deserted his face. "I only inquired as to how his evening had been, and he said it had been fine. Should I have asked where he'd been? I hate to pry, but I would so like to do my duty by him!" Uncle Justin was so self-conscious about being a good guardian.

"I'm sure he wasn't getting into too much trouble in good-ol' Nawshant," Sean smiled. "No, I'm sure you did the right thing."

"Well, you young people see so much more among your peers than we old fossils do. As time goes on, if you notice anything I should be aware of in your cousin's behavior, please let me know."

"I will, Uncle Justin—goodnight."

"Goodnight, dear boy."

Sean sat down on the edge of his bed, a little whacked-out from his unplanned nap. "She does have corporate breath," he heard himself mumble, as if he had dreamed of Dottie LaFrance during his nap. "She does, and I don't believe for one minute she's into realty."

He took emotional stock—somehow, he didn't feel quite as bummed as before he'd fallen asleep. Perhaps because—he had a job to do! Now! Up at the Thicket!

He dressed in black again even though his one black T-shirt smelled a little off—well, one had to make sacrifices and occasionally "live rough" when one was a professional detective. He donned the dark raincoat he had worn last night, even though the evening smelled dry and fine, as the wind played with the curtains in his room. He found his flashlight, and jimmied his notebook and a short pen into his back pocket in case he should need to jot down any facts—or take any depositions!—while he was out and about skulking.

He sat down again on the edge of the bed and waited for the night-sounds of the house, and its occupants, to sift down into stillness. He heard Uncle Justin padding down the hall from the bathroom, then closing his bedroom door. Uncle Justin was an uncanny sleeper: since he traveled so much, he had gotten used to sleeping in strange places and therefore slept like a dead thing when back at his *dulce domum*, Greystones. Sean would give him five minutes.

He was impatiently counting off the time on his watch when he heard something upstairs, directly above. It startled at first—in all his years here, no one had ever slept in the room above Sean—Aunt Sadie's room—but then he realized it was his cousin. The walls, floors, ceilings, and beams of Greystones were built of solid Maine oak, and his cousin seemed to move as discreetly as a cat—no surprise there—yet still Sean could just make out stealthy movement above him. Kyle was probably getting ready for bed. He wondered vaguely if Kyle would play in the varsity football team's game tomorrow, since he had practiced with the team this afternoon. He wondered again what Kyle had done this evening, and with whom, if anyone, he had done it. Did it have anything to do with Kyle's distress signals, flashing from his bedroom window at midnight last night? Was that the person Kyle had gone out to meet? But how could he know anyone else in Nawshant yet? He had been stand-offish in school all day, and, regardless, he couldn't have known anyone last night when he was flashing the signals, as he'd just arrived here. Another mystery!

But perhaps, Sean thought—remembering Professor Singleton's invocation of Occam's Razor—the simplest explanation being in most cases the correct one—Sean was making things more dramatic than they were. Maybe Kyle had just gone out this evening for "a wander" (as Margaret called an aimless walk), bopping around Nawshant, getting to know his new home better. Plus Kyle had already demonstrated some kind of fascination with the ocean. Maybe Kyle had just walked along the cliffs, listening to the music of the sea—though it still bothered Sean a little that he hadn't been invited. Sean, loving Nawshant as he did, would have been more than happy to show his cousin the sights. Plus now he could tell Kyle a little bit of their family's history, especially that part concerning Aunt Sadie, and take him over to Third Cliff and—

Sean bolted upright. His eyes narrowed and his right knee started bouncing furiously.

He suddenly recalled the thing his subconscious mind had been try-ing to push up from the mud. A little bell went off, as it were, when he recalled certain of Miss Sawyer's words: *Aunt Sadie had a bit of the psychic about her, you must know—and I suppose it was a premonition that drew her to the window on that fateful day the* Southern Cross *went down on Third Cliff, as much as the bells…*

Sean gulped. He got up and carefully opened his bedroom door and stepped into the hall. Then he took two steps and placed himself in front of the large Palladian window just outside his room.

The waters right off Third Cliff, perhaps two hundred yards away, were silvered with the rising moon. Sean realized with a shiver this was the exact spot from which Aunt Sadie had watched the wreck—*and it was the same place where Kyle had stopped last night, seemingly mesmerized, wondering aloud if some tragedy had occurred at the spot he was looking at—the waters of Third Cliff!*

This was the thing that had been nagging at Sean all evening.

Sean didn't know if he had believed in psychicness before this, or the Sixth Sense, or ESP, or whatever one would call it—but how could he not, now? Had Kyle "seen" the wreck of the *Southern Cross* when he first got here last night? He thought of Sherlock Holmes—his favorite detective—and how he was always telling Watson that, when every other explanation had been eliminated, the remaining one, however improbable, must be the correct one. How else to explain Kyle's weird behavior, other than to say that there was such a thing as psychicness, that it did apparently run in the family, and that Kyle had it in spades?

It was incredible—but there was no other explanation that Sean could come up with to fit the data.

Sean slipped back into his bedroom. His mind worked quickly. While he doubted he had inherited any of this aforementioned psychicness, he forgot nothing, and did get these odd "hunches" once in a while—which almost always proved to come to pass. He was having one now, and that was that this whole business—the bells ringing in the Thicket, Aunt Sadie's buoy-bell, the wreck of the *Southern Cross*, his cousin's psychic abilities, the figure he had seen last night—were all connected, all smaller pieces of the same story—

He couldn't say why he felt this, but he did.

He looked at the clock. It was 10:55 now and one thing he did know for certain was that he had to get up to the Thicket before it got any later. While Sean sensed now that there were many different roads leading into this mystery, it had only one heart—and that was somewhere in the dark tangle of the Thicket. But he had to enlist his cousin's aid eventually, he knew now, if Kyle had the supersensory gifts that he apparently did— my God, what mysteries *couldn't* the two of them solve together, between Sean's nosiness and memory, and his cousin's ESP? Plus his cousin was big, and strong-looking, and could probably by all appearances kick some butt if he had to—a skill not entirely useless when one was a professional detective.

Okay, let's go, Sean whispered aloud, pulling his raincoat hood up over his head, for purposes of concealment. But was his cousin asleep yet for heaven's sakes? Sean doubted Kyle would ever squeal on him if he saw, or heard, Sean shinnying down the wisteria—but on the other hand one never knew with these Southern, red-state, straight-laced types, with their odd love of law and order, rules and obedience: best to take no chances. If Sean had had a drinking glass in his room, he would have stood on his bed and, putting the glass to his ear, placed the closed end of the glass on the ceiling to listen in on whether Kyle was still up, knowing this trick magnified sounds wonderfully.

But, somewhat sloppy as Sean might have been in his living arrangements, Margaret was not: she stormed through his room every morning at precisely 11:15 like Sherman going through Georgia, sucking up everything in her path.

Thus, there was no glass in his bedroom.

Well, why not climb UP the wisteria and take a peek in Kyle's room to see if he's gone to bed? he thought.

Why not indeed?

Quiet as thought, Sean raised both windows and moments later had a firm grip on the wisteria. While he was always excited when he did this, tonight for the first time poignancy was added to the usual emotional agitation: this was the very plant Aunt Sadie had known, the very plant the two ex-slave sisters had plucked flowers from to dress Aunt Sadie's hair on the last night anyone had seen her alive—the very plant that had lavished its benign, sympathetic scent on the woman in love, as well as the aging woman of grief.

How many times had Aunt Sadie breathed in its fragrance? How often had she absently stroked the frilly softness of its leaves and tendrils as she gazed out her window, mourning the lover who wouldn't return?

Sean felt her with him as he started climbing up. Again he got the odd feeling that she had something to communicate to Sean, that she wanted Sean to solve the mystery, was *with* Sean in some strange way.

His heart started racing and he couldn't say why.

It was a little slower going up rather than down, and he saw almost immediately that a light of some kind was coming from the bedroom above. For most people this would have been enough to indicate that someone was still up-and-at-em—but Sean wasn't most people: he wanted to know things, he liked to see things—

—and, as long as he was halfway up, he decided there was no harm in a little peek. He began inching his way up toward his cousin's quarters. Quietly, carefully, gingerly, he came to the bottom of the window sill, then raised his head, as slowly yet irrevocably as a moonrise.

He almost lost his vice-grip on the ankle-thick vines, so startled did he become at what he saw when his eye inched beyond the sill: it was only, as it turned out, his cousin, wearing a full football uniform—in fact, the

Nawshant Mariners' blue and white colors; but with the pads and helmet on, Sean for a moment mistook Kyle for some unidentifiable behemoth of a thing, stomping around his cousin's bedroom.

So apparently Kyle had made the varsity team after all.

Sean tightened his grip and relaxed, from panic down to keen curiosity. Of course anyone might do the same—try on their uniform before their first game—Sean had done it himself sophomore year before his first lacrosse match. But there was something all too human and weirdly touching in his stand-offish and friendless cousin doing it; and Sean watched with a sharp and inherent interest, observing a fellow human thinking themselves unobserved, and doing something in private they never would by the gaudy light of day.

Sean, an intrepid student of humanity, could have watched for half the night as his cousin tried on, as it were, along with the uniform, various poses in front of the ancient mirror in the bedroom; and he was moved, too, because he knew this was the same looking-glass that had mirrored Aunt Sadie in her antique finery the last night of her life; but it was high time, in fact well beyond high time, to get up to the Thicket.

He was just lowering himself away, as slowly as he had raised himself, when something hanging from one spike of the ancestral four-poster iron twin bed caught his eye. It was a navy-blue hooded sweatshirt. On its backside was the number 17.

Sean felt his eyes enlarge and his mouth pop open. As if to further confirm what he now suspected, beneath the dangling hood rested a pair of large boots, sitting on the floor atop folded newspaper—and Sean could see the crusty remnants of mud around the boots' edges.

Only one explanation: as bizarre as it seemed, it was his cousin that Sean had seen last night in the Thicket. It was Kyle's boots that had made the tracks he and Mrs. Hutchinson had discovered this morning. Sean tightened his grip lest he fall with the force of this revelation. Kyle had been the phantom menace, hiding out in the Thicket last night! But why?

Why? What could have brought Kyle up to the Thicket at midnight last night? He couldn't possibly have followed Sean, for the figure—his cousin—was already in the woods when Sean first got there.

Utterly confused— each fresh revelation only seemed to make things more inexplicable—Sean lowered his body in immeasurably tiny increments until he reached his own room. What did it mean? Would Kyle visit the Thicket again tonight, after he got done wearing out the mirror in his football uniform? There was only one way to find out.

Sean crept over to his desk and pulled from the top drawer a roll of scotch tape. Taking as much time as he had five minutes earlier, he re-climbed the wisteria vine and attached two pieces of tape between the glass window and the wooden sill of Kyle's bedroom window—if Kyle tried to go out again tonight this way, the tape would break and Sean would know next time he checked it. To be on the safe side, Sean climbed back down, slipped out his bedroom door, stole down the hall, and attached another piece of tape between the door leading up to the third floor and the door frame. Now both exits from Kyle's room were taped. If Kyle were to sneak out again tonight—and so much, Sean thought, for the law-abiding, rule-loving generalization he had applied to him earlier—he would have to either climb out his window, or open that door. There was no other way. Sean would know.

He spent a precious three minutes writing out the details of what had just occurred, then shoved his small notebook back into the pocket of his black jeans. It was time to go.

For the third time in ten minutes, Sean slipped out the west-facing window of his bedroom, but finally this time he headed downward, blessing the fresh westerly breeze that made the wisteria vine shimmy and rattle against the house: there was no way his cousin would hear him. Just to be on the safe side, Sean waited five minutes once he touched *terra firma*, staring up at his cousin's window. Nothing—he saw no movement of any kind across the window, and the tiny light was still on. Kyle was no doubt still playing his imaginary game of football in front of the old mirror.

Sean weaved through the shrubbery, trying to avoid the light of the blossoming moon as he did. The night was cooling, but it was still fine and mild. As he stole through the gardens behind the house, he snuck into the tool shed. From this musty, earth-smelling place he took a small but rather efficient-looking branch-pruner, and a pair of old leather gardening gloves so thick Sean didn't think the thorns growing round Sleeping Beauty's castle would make a dent in them. Although everything in the shed had been here years before Justin and Margaret arrived from England, this place too (and, by association, everything in it) belonged irrevocably and indelibly to Margaret, she of the green thumb and sharp tongue. Sean felt a tad guilty at this pilfering, but he would return everything on his way back.

IF you come back! a voice sounded in his head.

Shuddup! Sean murmured back, but it was no use: the Three M's (murkiness, mysteriousness, and midnight) were gathered all round him now, and, being alone again and about to go back to the Thicket, his imagination was having a field day. Why oh why had he ever watched all those horror movies growing up? Every wind-rattled bush seemed to whisper *Ha-Ha-Ha!* a la Jason; every stripped-bare branch seemed to have Freddy's filleting fingernails attached to it; and that huddled form on the Fogerty's front lawn could just be a Halloween figure stuffed with leaves—but from this angle it sure looked like a not-quite-dead zombie, its mouth drooling for a fresh snatch of human flesh!

"Oh God, get a hold of yourself!" he whispered as he slipped by the Quinn's house. He told himself he was looking for a diversion from his current mode of paranoid thinking; but he knew deep-down it was more than likely just his nosiness that made him creep up to the Quinn's living-room window for a quick peek, for he saw lights on. He pressed his face against the bush-shadowed glass.

My God, poor Timmy and Regina! The Devaney cousins were still at it! Three very stout girls and an even stouter boy were all crammed onto the piano bench, attempting four-part harmony or something while Mrs. Quinn was keeping time with her long willowy body and serving cookies. Regina and Timmy were rolling their eyes at each other and yawning their heads off.

Sean laughed and next slipped past the Spillane's house. Here lived Will and Michelle, two of Sean's favorite urchins in all of Nawshant. As Uncle Justin had brought Sean up to help out whenever he could—that was the Quaker way—Sean had tutored the two children in math and science for a few months a year or two ago—until it became obvious that they knew more about these subjects than Sean did.

He came onto Crow's Nest Lane. The quick but revelatory vision of Timmy and Regina suffering agonies of boredom had done the trick—at least temporarily—and gave Sean something else to think about as he made his furtive but steady way up to the Thicket—not that he didn't have enough to think about already.

The night was sweet and lovely—there was a certain *je ne sais quoi* in the air, a whiff of poignancy as it were, as if summer were sorrowful at having to go south, the way of the robin and the redwing, already: it hated to be called "last summer" so soon. The rising moon edged things with its breeze-blown silvery light; from right offshore a foghorn sounded its eternal lament; and he could just hear, less than one hundred yards away, the sea and shore continuing their ancient conversation.

He turned a corner and there before him was the Thicket, as brooding as ever, as untouched by the sweetness of the night as if it were an iceberg just towed in from a Soviet gulag. All thoughts of the night's deliciousness drained away from Sean as if a plug had been pulled.

He gulped. Well, rather than go into the Thicket here—where it was especially thick and impenetrable—why not hike a little further up the road, and come in through its (hopefully) soft underbelly, from Mrs. Hutchinson's back grounds? She had said he could, right?

Sean immediately seconded this motion—though truth to tell, the idea's favorability in his mind had more to do with delaying the inevitable than anything else. He broke into a light trot, staying in the middle of the road where it was quietest—the sides of the road were ankle deep with potato-chip-sounding crunchy fallen leaves.

He passed Third Cliff—and all its astonishing evocations—then five minutes later left Second Cliff behind him as well, as he ascended to the highest part of Nawshant. Three minutes later he came upon *Linger Longer*, the ancestral estate of the Hutchinsons, sitting on its own high promontory, and bordered by the sea on two sides. It was shining in the moonlight like a gemstone—a veritable Yankee Taj Mahal, built on the proceeds of the spice trade almost three centuries earlier.

The crushed-seashell driveway up to the three-story, Federal-style mansion was perhaps two hundred yards long, and Sean ducked into the shade of the ancient sycamores that lined either side, for the moon was brightening as it rose. He skirted far to the left of the imposing home as he approached it, eventually passing the side greenhouses and coming into the old, south-sloping apple orchard: for the first 150 years of its existence, *Linger Longer* had also been a self-sufficient farm, specializing in the apple and dairy trades: no living off the trust fund for the old Yankees, when there was good money to be made in apples and dairy goods. Sean tried his best to avoid squashing the many windfalls lying on the ground, pouring forth their sweet pomace odor. A small family of raccoons slunk off at his approach, initially startling Sean now that he was on Full Alert. Then he smiled warmly and squatted down to observe their camp-breaking, one of them still clutching a juicy apple in its flashing white teeth. Another one half-turned and hissed at Sean as it slunk away, its small banditti face humorous despite its obvious annoyance at having this bacchanalia interrupted. Sean chuckled, then stood and looked beyond the sloping field to what was undoubtedly the most expansive ocean view in Nawshant, if not on the entire North Shore of Massachusetts. It was said in the old days that from here anyone could see ships coming in from Europe two days before they reached Boston and one day before they reached Salem. Right now, Orion, *the glory of the autumn skies*, as Uncle Justin called this constellation, was raising his bow above the moon-drenched waters of the North Atlantic; at the horizon's end, a large cruise-ship was heading south, seeking, like the birds, warmer climes.

But the view meant nothing to the raccoons, presumably; and Sean himself, dreamer that he was, had to be just as prosaically impervious to its star-spangled charms—at least for tonight: his task lay elsewhere. He turned away and continued his downward march through the orchard.

There was still a boutique-batch of apple cider pressed every fall at *Linger Longer*. It was distributed to local markets in a very limited edition —*Linger Longer Cider*—and the equipment for same sat near the bottom of the orchard, shining in the moonlight and looking for all the world like a hillbilly's still gone high-tech.

Sean stopped—like a sudden wall, there twenty feet beyond was the other side of the Thicket: dark, dense, and as solid-looking as if it were cast in stone. Even the moonlight failed to make a dent in its iron-black surface, seemingly withholding its illuminating charms to scatter them on less gloomy recipients. The squeaky wheel gets the grease, Sean thought, and perhaps moonlight, like fortune, favored the merry, as Margaret often said, lavishing her lights on those who smiled back.

Okay, cut with the philosophy and get your butt in there, Sean told himself. He withdrew the (hopefully) trusty pruner from his back pocket, feeling like David taking on Goliath. Since the Thicket here was as impenetrable as it was down at its other end, any random spot along its edge seemed as good a place of entrée as another. There were no trails going in—though hadn't Mrs. Hutchinson said there were? Or were they further in, or off to the sides?

At any rate Sean didn't see any. The crickets plumbed the night's depth as if they were mariners and the Thicket their ocean. His nose itched;

otherwise all was still. Sean felt he was on an uninhabited island a thousand miles out to sea. The far-off foghorn sounded again, and this time it sounded like a warning: *Nooo-Gooo! Nooo-Gooo!*

Sean gulped again, wiped his sweaty palms on the sides of his jeans, and found one last thing over which he could stall: he took out his notebook from his other back pocket, stepped into an almost neon-blob of moonlight, and jotted, *Friday night at three minutes before midnight. I'm just about to enter the Thicket from the southwest end of Linger-Longer, Mrs. Hutchinson's estate. My cousin Kyle was the figure I saw in the Thicket last night—I can't say why. Saw a raccoon family of four a few minutes ago eating apples.* He closed the notebook, self-criticizing, imagining a reading public raising a disdainful eyebrow at the lack of drama: *A raccoon family eating apples, is it? Well, I never! Hardly seems blood-curdling to me! And you call this a mystery?*

A sudden image of Matt being up here with him came—this would've alchemized the evening into a romantic, screwball-comedy, rather than a gloomy and terrifying solitary vigil. He shoved the image away. Then with a sigh, and no thought—he didn't want to find other things to delay him, and he knew he would if he gave the matter another moment's contemplation—Sean put on the leather gloves and plunged in, pushing aside the rubbery trunks of two staghorn sumacs, skirting around a wild cherry, and ducking under and eventually through the sharp limbs of a chaotically-branched jack pine draped in thorny brambles.

He began hacking and pruning. He told himself he wouldn't think of anything until he had cut 100 branches, and these he counted off as he advanced.

The first thing that struck him when he reached 100 was the darkness. Spots of moonlight drizzled down here and there, but these intermittent will-o-the-wisps became less and less frequent the further he went in. Next was the smell of the place—earthy, funky, heavy with life and redolent of decaying vegetation at the same time—very unlike the sea-rinsed odor that permeated most of Nawshant. The third impression was that his progress was a tad easier than he had imagined it would be. The only time he needed his pruner was when he came upon curtains of thorny-briars. There were many of these, bright green even in the darkness, and amazingly fecund, some of them running all the way to the tops of tall trees—but certainly not as many as at the southern end of the Thicket, where they seemed to form a continuous blockading maze.

Remarkably, he proceeded. Possessed of a decent sense of direction, Sean made generally southwest as he went, his plan being that he would head right for the heart of the Thicket. With any luck, he thought he might—if he reached this central place—continue along southwest until he came out somewhere near Third Cliff and Ocean Road, close to home. He doubted he'd make it that far—it was almost a mile away—but that was his plan. If he accomplished this, then the next time he came up here he could travel along a line perpendicular to this first southwest/northeast one, and then set up a kind of plot of the place, and go from there. But what if this was all for nothing? What if there were no bells? What if Mrs. Hutchinson was just hearing things, after all?

He became amazed at his progress, once he got the hang of the thing: prune, swoop down, advance, prune, swoop down, advance—it was now 12:27 and, though it was impossible to tell for sure, Sean guessed that he might have come, more or less in a straight line, one quarter of a mile, un-believably halfway to the very center of the Thicket. At this rate he might reach the heart of the Thicket in twenty minutes, the other end by 1:30 in the morning—if he kept at it.

Except for the crickets, it was so quiet and still here.

Five minutes later he slowed, as he thought he saw a light in the distance before him. He stopped, stood on tip-toes, peered, and advanced slowly.

Huh. Yes, undoubtedly it was a light, but its form and source were hard to fathom from here. He stole forward. The light grew. Whatever it was, it was steady, and didn't seem to be electric. He bent down a bit and advanced further still. The light continued to brighten, almost throbbing now. What the?

Five minutes later, Sean crawled to the very edge of a moon-drenched clearing, so bright after the darkness that he almost squinted. This was the source of the light, a wide hole cut right into the Thicket and seemingly gathering all the moonlight in the world into it. He peered across, then right, then left: the open space seemed to be roughly circular, and about forty yards in diameter. His pulse began thudding again, so he waited in the shadows. But all was still, all was quiet.

He carefully stepped out into its openness, feeling vulnerable. There wasn't a vine, bush, or tree within the opening, though there were dozens of stumps large and small, as if this place had been recently cleared. It was almost perfectly circular—it had to be man-made, for how could this have happened otherwise? He looked upward—the sky appeared above him as if he were viewing it through a tunnel; like the ones Uncle Justin's had seen down in Chile, the stars were so many, they seemed to overlap.

As Sean's eyes adjusted, he saw a rectangular pile of something near the opposite edge. Skittish and alert as a deer, he approached. It was a pile of rough-cut logs of various sizes, cut into firewood—maybe half a cord in size, more or less neatly stacked. Sean examined the ends of the logs: not too fresh, but not too old either. Someone, or a number of someones, had done this probably about a month or two ago. But who? Why? This was all conservation land and supposedly off-limits—but more than that, this showed that someone had been in here quite recently, and done a considerable amount of work.

Again it seemed that every fresh revelation only increased the depth of the mystery—and once more Sean had the odd feeling that this, too, was somehow tied in with the greater mystery of the bells.

He grew incrementally bolder and examined the clearing more close-ly. After five minutes he was through to the other side of it, and had found for his pains two discoveries: a circle of blackened rocks at the other end—where someone had obviously made fires—and an empty can of *Tru-Sweet* brand cling peaches "in their own juice." A number of black ants were still inside the can, making a beggars' banquet of the sweet stickiness—so this must have been a very recent meal.

How bizarre! He took out his notebook and drew a quick rough map of this place, and where it lay along his path.

The clearing, he wrote beneath his sketch. *Found a stack of wood and an empty can of peaches.* Again he envisioned his bored audience: *peaches and woodpiles! Bah! That was hardly worth calling our attention to! What about a corpse?* But there was no corpse, to Sean's delight—both for selfish and altruistic reasons.

When he was done with this, Sean retraced his steps and found the place where he had entered the clearing. He broke a sumac branch at this spot so that he could keep his path straight, and also, on the way back—if he were forced by unseen circumstances to return this way—find his way back to *Linger Longer* along the path he had just blazed.

He was halfway across the clearing when the bells began.

At first it felt like the sudden noise of them would kill him, drop him dead on the spot. Their sound rained down an icy chill from Sean's brain to his feet, and his sides began quivering.

Not knowing what else to do, but feeling incredibly vulnerable here in the open, he dropped down to the ground—he was capable of nothing else at this point—and forced himself to pay attention as they pealed on: deep and sonorous, yet oddly ominous, there was no way in the world that anyone could ever mistake them for the dinky bells of bicycles, or the distant chimes of ships or buoys. So much for Professor Singleton and Occam's razor! Sean's head nearly snapped as he looked this way, then quickly that way, expecting any moment to see a ghostly Aunt Sadie floating by in her moth-ridden bridal dress. The pealing seemed somewhat distant, but at the same time way too close for comfort. Undoubtedly they were ringing before him, the direction he was making for. So there *were* bells! So there *was* a mystery!

And then they stopped—as suddenly as they had begun.

For a second Sean contemplated a career as an accountant; then he peeled his spleen off the ground, as it were, stood up, and, with shaking hands, pulled out his notebook and wrote with a trembling hand, *Just heard the bells—it's 12:57 on Saturday morning and they are deep and clanging. They're coming from somewhere in front of me, somewhat distant but not too far off at all. Definitely in the Thicket.*

He put his notebook and pen away. He gulped. The quiet now was eerie, beyond creepy. Now what?

He tried to think of a good reason to turn around and run home: it was getting late; he had a game in the morning and needed his rest; he… he might be over his head, and should've brought someone with him.

But he knew these were all lame; he knew it as well as he knew what he had to do next. *If I think about it I won't go*, he told himself.

With another rearward glance at the clearing to mark his spot by the broken sumac, he re-entered the Thicket directly across from where he had left it. Prune, swoop down, advance, don't think, prune, swoop down, advance, don't think, he repeated like a calming mantra, but his progress was snail-like and frustrating—and it wasn't just from his growing fear and the trembling of his hands: after the icy brightness of the clearing, this part of the Thicket was a sea of ink, darker than ever.

Ten shaky minutes later it grew instantly darker still, and Sean looked heavenwards just in time to see a towering Man-o-War cumulus cloud swallow up the moon. *Uh-oh.*

He knew now that he had been mistaken in thinking it dark before; for here now all round him was the real thing, and even his hand in front of his face could not be seen. In panic he jerked his head upwards again— and was somewhat calmed to see two or three reassuring stars shining through the dense filigree of the trees and bushes around him.

A sudden idea took hold of him and he dissed himself for a dummy for not having thought of this before. He turned on his flashlight, then sliced a long length of vine—he didn't have to search far, they were dangling everywhere. He quickly stripped the vine of its leaves, then wrapped it around his head, tying the ends eventually around the flashlight, which he now placed on top of his head. In this way he fashioned a kind of head-lamp—like the ones coalminers wore in movies.

It worked too well. Within minutes, hundreds of white-winged moths, and twice the mosquitoes, were fluttering around his face; and then he saw the eyes, and panicked outright: bright, laser like-eyes that picked up the light from his head-torch and threw it back at him ghostly-green and mega-creepy. There were three pairs of them, perhaps twenty yards away and stationary, the middle pair higher than the others. The creatures the eyes belonged to weren't raccoons, for they stood too high off the ground. They must be coyotes, for people around town had seen them here and there by night.

Sean's instincts took over, snatching as it were the steering wheel of his will and driving directly to out-and-out over-the-cliff panic. Yelling out in terror, he backed up so quickly that he stumbled over something behind him and fell backward to the ground, the force of his fall knocking his odd head-gear astray and plunging him into blind wild darkness. He covered his face instinctively in case the wild canines should leap upon him first and ask questions later—then he realized he should get up as quickly as possible. But he had become enmeshed in a wall of thorny brambles, and it seemed the more wildly he struggled, the more entangled he became. He heard crashing movement through the woods in front of him—were the coyotes coming to get him, or had his cries and thrashing noise scared them off?

All of the above took about ten seconds to occur. Sean tried to push down his tsunami of panic, reminding himself that while coyotes did often attack small pets left unguarded, there had been only two incidents of coyotes attacking people in the Commonwealth of Massachusetts in the past fifty years. He knew this because his sophomore biology class had made a special study of them. In both cases the usually human-shy canines had been rabid.

Yeah, I know that, and you know that, his panic spoke to his reason, *but do they know that?* But as nothing happened over the next several minutes, Sean lay motionless and tried to regroup. Gradually the thick poultice of cricket-sound enveloped him again, and the thudding in his ears slowed. One by one he began prying thorny vines off his clothing. This took some time, as more often than not the supple, whipcord-like brambles would spring back and barb onto his pants and jacket again; but eventually, with the help of his pruner, he was able to free himself to the point where he could stand again.

"Oh my God," he mumbled, trying to stretch his anxiety away. He took a few steps forward just to make sure the coyotes were gone—they were—then he went back to where he had fallen and began feeling around in the tar-like darkness for his flashlight. He assumed this would take mere seconds—but such was not the case: five minutes went by, then ten. Then fifteen. How could his flashlight have rolled so far away?

Then he heard approaching footsteps. He thanked heaven he hadn't found the flashlight after all. They were coming not from behind him, not from in front of him, but from off to the left. A chill of spangled horror squirted through him. He squatted, then froze, hardly daring to breathe. The sound grew nearer. Now he could plainly hear, in addition to the light footfalls, the passage of someone through the wild tangles. Whoever they were they were proceeding cautiously, slowly—as if they were hunting for something—hunting for *him*, Sean suddenly realized, for no doubt they had heard his screams of panic.

Off to his left he now saw a darker form passing through the bushes and brambles—it was a man, a tall one, hooded in a sweatshirt, heading right for him. His pulse began thudding wildly again, and he crouched down closer to the ground. *I just don't have enough courage to be a real detective!* he self-scolded. *I'm just too much of a—*

But then he remembered—his cousin! It *must* be his cousin! While it was far too dark to see if the number 17 adorned the back of the dark sweatshirt, there could be no doubt, right? Hadn't Kyle been up here last night, with his hoodie and attitude? And now that Sean was getting used to the dark, it kind of looked like Kyle too, for splotches of moonlight would occasionally splash across this person's face—

Sean, wisely or not, decided to have a little fun at his cousin's expense. After all, he had been scared out of his wits twice tonight—and why not pay Kyle back for the terror he had caused Sean last night at the other end of the Thicket? He could be full of surprises too.

Creeping as slowly as he could, he inched toward the direction of the figure—but this was hardly necessary, as the person was coming right for him, moving slowly, looking around, almost sniffing the air. He was carrying a thick long stick in one hand, a cudgel sort of thing that looked like it meant business. But what was Kyle doing up here? Had he managed to bird-dog Sean? Well, Sean would know soon enough—after he scared Kyle's liver out.

The figure drew closer. Sean reached out his arm, and waited. The figure came nearer, then stopped two feet from Sean, looking around, his imposingly large body stiffened and tensed.

Sean plunged his arm through the tangles and grabbed the figure just above the ankle.

A sudden inrush of breath punctured the night-silence. The figure lurched back, breaking Sean's grip. He raised his stick to swing away. The mother-ship of a cloud broke then. A splash of white moonlight smeared upon the form's face.

It was not his cousin.

CHAPTER ELEVEN
FOLLOWING A STRANGER HOME

What happened next occurred within a blur, a frenzy of time that was more an explosion than the normal linear progression of things: the figure swung back his stick, and howled out—if Sean was hearing him correctly—"*Satyr City! Satyr City!*"

At the very moment Sean realized the man was about to bring his weapon down on him, the thick club whistled through the briars, barely missing Sean's head—in fact he felt the threatening breeze of the stick as it swooshed by him. When Sean saw the face of the stranger in the moonlight, he didn't know how he could have ever mistaken this person for his cousin. The stranger's face was scruffy, older, fuller, small-eyed, pockmarked, and twisted with fear. And now that he heard the voice, it was different as well—entirely; but still, if Sean was hearing correctly, twanged with a bit of a Southern accent.

Then the moon vanished. Sean and the stranger were plunged into darkness.

Sean bolted off at a frantic run, one part of his brain amazed at how fast he could vamoose, brambles or no, when panic was hogging the driver's seat. Thorns scratched his face, vines snatched at his ankles, and once he ran smack into a (thankfully small) birch trunk; but these were nothing—he didn't pause long enough to see if he was being followed.

He found that he was making little gasp-cry-whimpers of effort and alarm. *God, I sound like a frightened TeleTubby*, he thought. He tripped once over a rock and was up again before he was even aware that he was falling. He came to the circular clearing and covered its width in a dozen breathless bounds. The moon took pity on him and came blaring out again, and now his pace doubled—not for nothing was he the fastest kid on the lacrosse team—for he could more or less now see the path he had cut on his way here. He came upon the end of the Thicket ten frantic minutes later, amazed at how quickly it had appeared.

He burst through the darkness into the streaming moonlight. It wasn't until he was halfway up the apple orchard at *Linger Longer* that he stopped, doubled over and gasping for air. He found what he was looking for—an especially gimungous, moon-shadowed apple trunk that could have hid three of him. Throwing himself against its backside, he inched his head around its lichen-encrusted, scaly trunk—and waited while he snatched breath, his eyes riveted to the place in the Thicket from whence he had just emerged.

He stole a glance at his watch: it was 1:21 in the morning.

He took stock, and became aware that his face and hands were trickling blood in about twenty different places. The gloves! They had fallen off or he had dropped them somewhere. Oh no, and the pruners too! Uh-oh! There would be no end to Margaret's indignation. He envied Uncle Justin's antique fastidiousness—never was the man without a handkerchief. Sean had never carried one in his life, and tonight was no exception—his raincoat sleeves would have to do as he smeared the trickling blood away as best he could, all the while keeping an eye on the Thicket, should his attacker still be pursuing.

Of course the watched pot never boils, Sean told himself, and the spied-on path seldom produces any travelers: but in this case it did. Sean was just about to abandon his post and head for home when a blobby, deeper darkness mingled with the shadows of the Thicket, and then separated and emerged from that darkness.

It was the stranger again. He was still carrying his stick.

Sean felt the hair on the back of his neck stand up, a heretofore unknown phenomenon that he had always dismissed as an old chestnut. He withdrew further into the tree's welcome umbrella of darkness.

But it seemed the figure was no longer looking for Sean—for the man made a furtive beeline over to the large stainless steel cider press, of all places, at the end of the orchard. Looking around as he did, the man squatted down, opened a cabinet at the bottom of the still, and withdrew a box that was heavy enough to require both his arms. He set the box down on the ground, then pulled something from his pocket—Sean couldn't see what it was—and placed it inside the cabinet. He shut the door, lifted the heavy box off the ground, then, looking around, snuck back into the Thicket.

Well! Whatever next!

Sean waited five heart-thudding minutes before he took out his notebook again, and wrote, *Suspect-With-Stick just observed at 1:37, sneaking from the Thicket and taking something from a cabinet in the cider-making thing. Don't think it was random pilfering, as it seemed like he was expecting something to be there. Will now go to see what he left.*

Well, after all, there wasn't any rush to do *that*. It was some ten minutes later—though it seemed an hour—and Sean was sure the figure had really withdrawn—when, going tree-to-tree, he stole his way back down to the cider press. He waited five more minutes at the last tree, just to be sure.

With a pounding heart, he approached the cider press, took one more glance behind him toward the Thicket, then squatted down and opened the cabinet.

There were two shelves inside: a large one, and a smaller on top. The larger one—presumably where the box had just been—was now empty.

On the top shelf there was a small white envelope. Taking one more look behind him, Sean snatched the envelope, closed the cabinet door, then ran back up the slope to the same concealing tree. He shoved the envelope into a blob of moonlight to see what it might be.

It was somewhat grimy with dirty thumbprints, and torn in one corner. Scrawled across the front of it was written, in pencil, *Thank you.* The flap of the envelope was tucked into the back, not sealed. Sean was startled to open it and find a newish one hundred dollar bill inside. Stuck to the back of the bill was a yellow Post-it note, with little flowers and Easter bunnies printed along its top edge. On this was written, in blue pen, *Yes, we came up here to scatter his ashes. Milk, tea, sugar, canned beans and fruit and corn, chicken, hamburger, potatoes, rice and beans.* Below that was written, in a red pen, *cigarettes, same kind as before. Beer, any kind but nothing fancy. Newspapers. Thank you, God will bless you, no questions and no cops.* The list was signed at the bottom, *Three Spirits.*

Three Spirits? Who the heck was that? *Three Spirits?*

Sean read the note again, then again. Then he decided he better copy it down verbatim, in his notebook: so frazzled was he by the night's experiences, he didn't trust his memory.

Of course most of it was just a simple grocery list—anyone could see that; but the opening *we came here to scatter his ashes* and closing *no questions and no cops* lent an ominous air to the message—not that things weren't ominous enough. Had "they" (whoever "they" were) killed someone, burned him, then scattered his ashes? My God—

When Sean was done with his note-scribbling—always stopping to look over his shoulder, and his pulse thudding madly in his ears—he tucked the envelope back into itself. He waited a few more minutes just to be sure he wasn't being observed, then crept shadow-to-shadow back down to the cider-press, and returned the strange missive and its $100 bill from whence they had come. He retraced his steps to the hiding-tree, then tried to decompress, gather his wits, and remember everything that had happened.

It certainly had been a busy night: the discovery of the clearing; the clanging of the bells; his encounter with the coyotes; the stranger with the club, and his attack; the stranger's retrieval of a package in the cider-press; the weird grocery list and C-note he had left behind.

Well, it all must mean that a number of someones were hiding out in the Thicket, code name *Three Spirits*—escaped convicts perhaps; and someone was providing them with the goods they needed to survive. But whom? And why? And why were they ringing the bells, if it was them?

Though he had learned much tonight, Sean felt he was no closer to solving the mystery of the bells. Where were the bells? Why were they in the middle of the densest woods in town? Why was someone ringing them? And what the heck did *Satyr City*—the weird words the stranger had cried out—mean?

It was unfortunate that he had panicked and turned tail, for Sean sensed that he had been very close at that moment to where the bells were sounding. On the other hand, who in their right mind would've stuck around to take a few whacks from Three Spirit's club? Sean wasn't at all ashamed or abashed at his flight— what was it Mrs. Hutchinson had said? *He who retreats today lives to fight another day?* Was that it? Regardless, Sean heartily concurred. *We concurred and then we had vegan con carne,* Sean thought, remembering a joke Matt had made once in English class when they were doing oxymorons.

For a reason he couldn't put his finger on, Sean was reluctant to head home, and leave the shadowy and relatively safe concealment of his apple tree. His head wanted to go home—in fact he ached for his bed: he was emotionally and physically drained after the night's adventures, and he was anxious to wash his many cuts and scrapes. He had a lacrosse game in the morning, and it was already so late.

But something else was telling him to, well, linger longer. His instincts had served him well enough in the past for him to listen to their whisper-ings now. He crouched back down to a kneeling position, and withdrew further into shade. He glued his eyes back on the Thicket.

The moon rose higher. The shadows shifted, and Sean with them. He was just about to give up when the figure of Three Spirits re-emerged from the Thicket, though at a slightly different place this time around. He was no longer carrying his club—but as he emerged, Sean saw the moonlight glint off a not large but not too small hunting knife that Three Spirits sheathed back in its case; then he shoved the whole affair in his back pocket.

Sean cringed lower behind the tree. Uh-oh. Three Spirits had gone back to wherever—an island, perhaps, like Gollum going back for his ring—to fetch his knife! To finish the business, and silence forever the one who had seen him—Sean!

Sean blessed the cloud that covered the moon as Three Spirits advanced up the slope of the orchard. He was about twenty feet away when he passed Sean—but he was looking neither right nor left.

As he had last night, Sean refereed a quick battle between his fear and his curiosity. If he had more time to think about it, his fear might have carried the day; but he didn't, and before Sean knew what he was doing he found himself stealing from tree to tree, making his way up the sloping orchard, keeping an eye on Three Spirits. The latter was making right for *Linger Longer*—did he plan on breaking in?

Apparently not—as Sean pursued, Three Spirits quickly passed the greenhouses, lurched around the west wing of the estate, then headed down the edge of the long driveway, still looking neither right nor left nor behind. He might be out taking a Sunday afternoon stroll, albeit a rapid one, for he had lost all his skulking furtiveness.

Sean had to do a quick dash down the last part of the driveway to keep up. He was just in time to see Three Spirits take the bend onto Ocean Road as it descended from First Cliff—on which *Linger Longer* sat—down in the direction of Second Cliff. Where the heck was he going?

Sean had to quicken his pace, for this part of Ocean Road was especially twisty. He was perhaps thirty yards behind his suspect, and he blessed his own keen eyesight and swift feet. So what if his ears stuck out and he was bowlegged? He had what he needed to be a good detective, although, in time, he hoped to develop a bit more courage, for he found he was trembling as he pursued the stranger.

Second Cliff was passed and then the road plunged down to Third Cliff—and still, Three Spirits was keeping on a determined course, as if he were heading for—Greystones!

My God, Sean thought, what if Three Spirits had somehow recognized Sean—although Sean could swear he had never seen the stranger's face before—and now he was coming to "get" Sean at home?

I'll know if he takes the left onto Crow's Nest Lane, Sean thought. Three Spirits did so, to Sean's alarm; even more disturbing, he cut through the Quinn's side yard with no hesitation whatsoever; this was the little-known short-cut that led directly to the back gardens of his home! No one but Sean and the Twins ever used this!

I've brought danger to Uncle Justin and Margaret! And Kyle too! was Sean's next thought, but just then the moon reappeared in all her revelatory glory. As Three Spirits walked around the back corner of the now-darkened windows of the Quinn's house, a bright number 17 was clearly emblazoned on the back of the stranger's sweatshirt.

Sean stopped dead. This was impossible! But—well, either this was his cousin Kyle, and not Three Spirits at all; or Three Spirits had somehow made off with his cousin Kyle's sweatshirt. Not likely.

Sean raced around the corner of the Quinn's house, then a minute later stopped in the shadow of Margaret's toolshed, leaning his body against its old chestnut hewn planks, now smoothed by scores of years of rains and suns into a smooth patina.

He leaned his head around the corner, snatching at his breath, and waited. He tried to ignore the blood still oozing from his myriad facial cuts. Five minutes became ten, then fifteen—finally, as Sean watched, a light came on in his cousin's bedroom.

So it was Kyle, and not Three Spirits at all! But what had taken him so long to get inside? Kyle—for whatever inexplicable reason—had come out to the Thicket again tonight. Clearly Kyle and Three Spirits were two different people—after all, Sean had seen Three Spirits' face close-up— but Kyle must have been in the Thicket at the same time Three Spirits attacked Sean. Kyle no doubt had heard the bells too. This was Kyle's second night in a row in the Thicket. Sean had to assume that, somehow, Kyle knew about the mystery, and, like Sean, was trying to solve it. But how Kyle had found out remained inexplicable.

Sean waited in the chilly, moon-drenched gardens to see if his cousin might fling open his window again, as he had last night, and send distress signals up to the heavens. But he didn't. After ten more minutes the light went out. Presumably, Kyle had gone to bed.

Sean snuck over to the shrubbery, then made his way through the bushes to the bottom of the wisteria plant. He was halfway up to his own room when he decided he would check on the tape he had placed on Kyle's window. Was that how Kyle had snuck out? It showed nerve if it was, for Kyle could have had no way of knowing if the wisteria would support his weight all the way down from the third floor.

But no, the tape was still intact, both pieces of it. Hmmm. He must have snuck out through the more conventional means then, of going down the third-floor stairs, and then down Greystones' main staircase. But that had taken nerve too—to say nothing of crafty wariness, for that way led directly past Margaret's bedroom, a dragon's lair of unceasing watchfulness and its door always open to "get the air, don't cha know."

Sean took seven minutes in total to lift up his bedroom windows, so careful was he. He didn't snap the light on, instead lighting the candle on his bed stand, by the flicker of which he wrote out a full account of all that had happened.

As he was finishing, his eyes began to blur together, so exhausted was he. But on a hunch, and to satisfy his own curiosity—which would have kept him awake in any case—he inched off his bed, almost crawled to the bedroom door, opened it, then snuck down the hall, flashlight in hand, to check the tape on the third-floor doorway.

This tape had not been broken either.

Sean scrutinized it three times just to be sure. For about the tenth time tonight, he was utterly at a loss. "What the—?" he heard himself mumble. *Kyle hadn't come this way either.*

An hour later an exhausted Sean was still awake, trying to puzzle this latest conundrum out. But he was no closer to finding an answer. Kyle had left the house—but why? More mysteriously, *how*? *There was no other way out, other than the window, or the door.*

And yet he hadn't come either of those ways.

Once again Sean thought of the Holmesian Maxim, which stated that when the false was eliminated, whatever remained was true, however improbable: if Kyle had not exited Greystones by either the window or the door—and Sean had proof that he hadn't—then he had left by some other means. But there was no other means that Sean knew of.

So— it *must* be a way that Sean wasn't aware of.

Greystones had somewhere, then, a secret passage, and Kyle had discovered it.

CHAPTER TWELVE

A RASH OF NEW DEVELOPMENTS

"Sean! Sean!"

From some rarefied height 20,000 leagues above him, and him down a deep well, Sean heard the sound of knocking, and his voice being called as if through deep waters.

He stirred, flopped over, and mushed deeper into his pillows. After the adventures of last night, he was still wearied to stupidity. Under no circumstances was he ready, willing, or able to greet the new day.

But it was probably only a dream—

"YOU, Sean!" Oops, apparently not—*"Sean! Sean Sutherland!"*

Uh-oh—an iron dismay settled onto him. It was Margaret, and when she invoked his last name, it undoubtedly meant she thought him guilty of one or more of the feasances: mis, mal, or non.

He opened one swollen eye and squinted at the clock on his bed table. He let out a snort of outrage—for heaven sakes it was only seven o'clock— a *whole hour* before he had to get up: an eon when one is exhausted and seventeen. What the—

"Sean Sutherland! Get out of that bed, you bold thing! Was it you who broked into my toolshed last night and stole my gardening gloves and my favorite pruner? If so, what is the meaning of this? What have you done?

Why, you've *ruined the entire year for me!*"

Double uh-oh—she was being overly-dramatic too this morning.

Margaret, of course—like a dragon atop its pile of treasure—knew all within her province down to the last lusterless doo-dad, and each item's exact location at any given time. Whether she ever used any of these things was totally beside the point. Talk about a rude awakening—

He was tempted to sing out, *Blame it on the Bossa-Nova,* a silly line Matt was always using. That was the name of a song Matt's mother often played during her painfully hip parties, when "interesting" guests sipped exotic Martinis and danced campy dances from the '60's—

But Sean guessed this was not the time and Margaret not the person for such abstruse levity, so instead, "Yes, I did take them Margaret," he answered, in a stiff and groggy moan. "So sorry—I'll replace them this morning and explain everything later."

Of course *I'll-explain-everything-later* maneuvers like this one might work in the movies; but seldom did they satisfy in real life—and never with an opponent as formidable as Margaret.

Sean had forgotten to turn the lock on his bedroom door—really, there was hardly any need, other than the teenage fatwa for inviolate privacy—and so Margaret stormed in, but not without her obligatory triple-knock and loudly-brayed, "I'm coming in!"—as if she were the Ninja Turtles or something.

"Where are my things?" she hissed, doubling over and bristling like a hedgehog; but when she saw Sean, groggy eyed, messy-haired, and resignedly complacent with his head propped up on the pillows, she flung her hands to either side of her face and ejaculated, "Mother of All Sorrows! Is it the Bloody Flux you've got, my little lamb?"

Yes; for while Margaret talked a good game of brusqueness, any sickness, accident, or other perceived threat to her charges brought the love and devotion she felt for Uncle Justin and Sean flooding to the fore. She bounded across the room like a grizzly mom, depositing herself on the edge of Sean's bed, all thought of her hand-pruner and gloves gone by the boards: for it was a changed Sean that greeted—however reluctantly—this new day's dawning.

Sean wasn't sure at first what Margaret was alluding to, and he looked at her queerly, with a tilt of his sleep-addled head. Then he recalled the Death by a Thousand Cuts he had almost endured last night in the Thicket as he fled from his assailant.

"I must look gross," he told Margaret's owl-gray eyes, over-swollen now with deep alarm. "But really Margaret, I—"

"Gross, is it!" she exclaimed, as she made futile gestures at his face, not knowing exactly what to do with the dozens of oozing cuts and scrapes—to say nothing of the erupting rashes—spangled across Sean's visage. "The martyred Saint Sebastian looked a sight better when they cut him loose from the tree! What in the world has happened? What do you look like? A thing to be shuddered at, that's what! Oh no!"

Sean couldn't recall ever seeing Margaret so beside herself!

But there was good reason. Unbeknownst to Sean, the harmless-looking vine he had appropriated last night to serve as a makeshift flashlight-holder was none other than an especially robust and ill-minded poison ivy strand, which had been sitting wickedly in the midst of the Thicket lo these many years, waiting for human flesh as pink, sweet, and blemish-free as Sean's to work its magic on; nor did Sean immediately realize—although he had been scratching in his sleep all the short night long—that many of the plants he had, rather intimately, become more acquainted with in his panicked flight were the dreaded *Rhus vernix*, or, as Uncle Justin could have instantly translated, poison sumac: evil cousin of poison ivy and the bane of short-sleeved birders. It was infinitely more virulent than its milder cousin.

Greased by the skids of Sean's innocently-itching fingers, these two had made all kinds of inroads throughout the short night on Sean's previously unbesmirched flesh, skipping around, it hardly needs to be added, those areas of skin already open and raw from the cuts and scrapes of the thorns and brambles. In fact, it was difficult to find—other than his eyes, nostrils, and mouth—a place on Sean's face that was not cut, scraped, or rash-ridden—hence Margaret's hysteria.

"Did you burn yourself in the night, my lamb?" Margaret continued shakily, on the verge of a crying jag by all appearances; then without waiting for answer she leapt up from the bed and began hunting for Sean's cell phone, wailing out, "Call 911! Call 911!"

"I'm fine Margaret, really—" Sean began.

"Holy Saint Finbar! He's gone delirious too! *Call 911! Call 911!*"

A rapid pattering of footsteps was heard skipping down the hall; Uncle Justin, already dressed and with his morning paper still in one hand, scurried into the room, followed quickly by Kyle, clad only in boxers and sporting a surprisingly well-developed physique that Sean found himself gawking at. Kyle was holding his phone in one hand, already raised and poised for action. *Oh leave it to you*, Sean thought.

"My my my! What have we here?" Uncle Justin cried, flinging a hand to the side of his face; but his concern was tempered by the cooling curiosity of his scientific nature, never capable of being entirely quelled in minds like his, even in the midst of emergencies. *He'd be measuring the teeth of the lion that ate him*, as Margaret had said.

"Calm down everybody!" Sean yelled, raising his voice in an attempt to extinguish the growing conflagration among the members of his household. "I...couldn't sleep last night, so I took a walk, and I... I tripped and fell into a bramble bush—that's all."

His cousin's eyes narrowed suspiciously as Sean said the words, and it was then that Sean spied similar scratches and cuts, not on Kyle's face, but on his hands. Kyle saw where Sean's eyes were looking, and he quickly withdrew his hands behind his back. They locked eyes, and Sean knew instantly—and he knew that Kyle recognized this too—that they both totally understood the other: they each knew the other had been out in the

Thicket the night before.

My God, Sean thought. *It's like we can read each other's minds.*

But at the same time Sean reached out one hand from beneath the covers to absent-mindedly scratch his strangely itchy scalp; and when he did, Margaret sang out, pointing, "Misery me! Look at that, will yez? The pox is on his hands too! Call 911!" and she fell to outright blubbering.

"Now now, my dear!" the always-calming voice of Uncle Justin broke in. He put on the reading glasses that were forever dangling from his neck, and came in for a closer look. "It appears that these are, in fact, nothing more than superficial cuts and abrasions, nasty looking as they are. Complicated by what is most definitely Poison Ivy, and, perhaps…yes! Poison Sumac!" He turned with a smile to the almost hysterical Margaret and put a reassuring hand on her quivering shoulder. "Nothing more than that, my dear! But let's give Doctor Hallissey a call, just to be on the safe side."

Doctor Hallissey was actually retired, and had been since before Sean was born; but he still made occasional house calls for especially favored patients. The doctor's wife approved, for it got the old gentleman out of the house. He was known for his long-winded and frequent declamations on a) politics; and b) conspiracy theories; and when he was house-bound, Mrs. Hallissey bore the difficult weight of these never-ending Jeremiads.

The mention of his name, as usual, acted like an elephant sedative upon Margaret, for Doctor Hallissey was the kind of old-fashioned, no-nonsense medico she put her faith in—plus his grandmother on his father's side had hailed from the same village Margaret had grown up in on the west coast of Ireland.

"Oh yes! Call Doctor Hallissey! Yes, do!" Margaret cried. "In fact I'll call him myself, right now!" and she took off as if for a bet down to the kitchen, where she had a little office in a corner of the huge pantry.

Sean really liked Doctor Hallissey—even though he was old-fashioned; so old-fashioned that Sean wasn't sure his prognostications were to be entirely trusted. The good doctor frequently gave voice to the old shibboleth that what couldn't be cured by butter, whiskey, or a good laugh could not be cured, and sometimes Sean thought the old gentleman actually believed this verbatim. He loved to force-feed fish liver oil into his patients, and was also a grand hand at bandaging, of which his little black bag seemed to contain vast longitudes and latitudes. Sean wouldn't have been surprised, so archaic was the doctor, if he showed up at their door one of these days carrying bellows, a pitchfork, and a blood-letting kit. His favorite word was *flibbertigibbets*, the name he gave to maladies that he thought might be hypochondriacal in nature—or, possibly, that were unknown to the good doctor. *Nothing more than the flibbertigibbets*, he'd pronounce with a smile.

In fact, that term had come into proverbial use in Nawshant, thanks to 50 years of the doctor's ministrations, and was used to describe a general but indefinable and vague malaise that was usually destined to pass quickly. One could still hear native-born third or fourth graders explaining to their mothers or fathers that they couldn't possibly attend school that day, as they had the *flibbertigibbets*, though they sensed they'd be well enough to go out and play by lunchtime.

But what Sean enjoyed most was that Doctor Hallissey—like everyone else in Nawshant, with the exception of Margaret and Mrs. Hutchinson—and those too young to get the stories right—was a profligate gossip.

It would be unkind, and, possibly, untrue, to suggest that this had been the cornerstone of the doctor's very successful practice over the years in Nawshant. But such were the savory gems Doctor Hallissey dispensed— along with medical advice, which was ignored more often than not—that everyone in town gladly toiled under the illusion that they alone were the recipients of these tasty tidbits: what was *actually* wrong with Ken Shaw; where Jen Lee had really gone off to, and why, when her parents told everyone she was studying art in France—and hoped and prayed that whatever dish the doctor uncovered in their own homes would not be carried as quickly as the doctor's bandy legs could take him to the next house down the lane, and the thirsty ears therein. (Mrs. Hutchinson and, especially, Margaret, on the other hand, were silent as the tomb when it came to dishing the dirt—which is why they were sought after more than anyone else when locals felt the need to disburden their restive souls. In the case of Mrs. Hutchinson, it was felt by all—rightly or wrongly—that this had to do with her high breeding; her education in a Swiss boarding school; her station in life as a last pillar of an ancient and highly distinguished family that had first come over on the Mayflower and given the Commonwealth more than its share of governors, congressmen, and senators; and of course the estimated size of her very weighty purse. In the case of Margaret, a different explanation was assigned, one that concerned itself with Margaret's frugal nature— like a tidal surge, everything came in, people said, while nothing went out. Miss Sawyer had expressed it most succinctly to Sean one day when the former was in an especially unlovely mood: "Everyone adores Margaret, of course," she had snarled. "But when it comes to the pennies and the gossip, she's as tight as a crab's ass—and that's watertight. Now that's not a vulgar expression, Sean, but, rather, a nautical one." For her part, Margaret thought Miss Sawyer talked too much, and had said more than once, "That one spends the whole length of the day without her two lips touching each other." The two women had always struggled to be cordial.)

Margaret brayed up the stairs a moment later, shouting the news that Doctor Hallissey was "very very highly imminent,"—crises made Margaret's word choice lean toward the dramatic and somewhat bizarre—and next they heard—even though the house was, as always, immaculate—a sound that resembled a herd of panicked animals trying to find the door, and they knew by this that Margaret was "picking up." Sean knew too that she would be up to his room momentarily, scouring and scrubbing to beat the band—an Oompah band at that—so he slipped from bed and took this opportunity to high-tail it into the bathroom to address his heretofore neglected morning chores. He noticed that his cousin had slipped back upstairs by then, and Uncle Justin said that he would be down the hall in his office awaiting the arrival of the doctor, and Sean should just sing out if he needed anything.

Sean shut the bathroom door, snapped on the light, and nearly swooned when he saw "the cut of himself" (as Margaret would call it) in the unflinching mirror. He cried out at the sight, which brought Uncle Justin back to the bathroom door in a heartbeat; but Sean dismissed him, saying it was just that he had caught a good look at himself in the mirror.

My God! Matt would never want to go near him now! And how could he go out in public? He looked like something out of *Star Wars*, when they did that exotic alien cantina thing!

He showered—*ouch!*—then dressed, yanking on part of his lacrosse uniform and barely able to keep his hands—which were just as bad as his face—off his maddeningly-itchy scalp. When nothing of a dramatic nature happened for a minute or two—Margaret had finished with his room while he was showering—Sean did what all animals and some smart people do in such situations: he slipped back into bed for an additional forty winks, for he was still exhausted.

Five minutes later there came a pleasant knock upon the bedroom door, and here was Uncle Justin, tray-laden with heavenly-smelling breakfast. Sean found that he was ravenous, and he ate in bed quickly and, apparently, in a very ungenteel fashion, for Uncle Justin watched him (sitting on the edge of the bed and never saying a word, bless him) with increasingly expanding eyes and a finger on his lip.

"Dear boy, I see that you've dressed for your lacrosse game," he said when Sean finished, "but I just got off the phone with Sam McKinley at the University—our local expert in diseases of a dermatological nature?—and he says that it would be best for you not to compete in anything involving bodily contact for a bit, as you might be somewhat contagious should you rub up against someone. Plus, as your condition seems to be in a most eruptive state, quiet rest might be best for a few days, don't you know."

Sean's face fell, but he nodded acquiescence—at least he wouldn't have to be seen like this.

"I'll call your lacrosse professor—I mean, coach!—if you like, and explain—and at least this will not cause divided loyalty on my part. Kyle will be playing in the football game this morning, which is happening at the same time as your lacrosse game, so at least I shan't have to disappoint either of you by bounding back and forth from one event to the other. Like a tennis ball, what?" Uncle Justin tittered at his own joke. "But the good news is, Sam said if Doctor Hallissey does bandage you…as he will of course—well, they can come directly off as soon as he leaves. Sam said it's best to let the air get at it, though certain ointments that he prescribed I will pick up later at the pharmacy."

"Then why did we bother calling Doctor Hallissey?" Sean asked.

"Oh well, he's not totally incompetent, you know!" Uncle Justin exclaimed, tugging at his moustache and stealing a glance behind his back to make sure Margaret wasn't within earshot. "Set my arm beautifully he did, when I broke it many years ago. I was a little younger than you are now."

"Oh. How'd you break it?"

"I was…errr…sleeping over a friend's house and…well, we were sneaking out his bedroom window via a large wisteria vine, and I slipped and fell."

Sean opened his mouth, then shut it abruptly.

"Plus don't you know," Uncle Justin continued, lowering his voice, "a visit by Doctor Hallissey will soothe our Margaret like the hand of God. She puts a good deal of stock in his opinion. My, what a *wreck* the poor thing was when she first saw the state you're in! You *do* know she just *dotes* on you, Sean?"

"I forget that sometimes," Sean agreed, though he was warmed to his core. "By the way, Uncle Justin—can I ask you what a word means without you making me look it up in the dictionary down in the library? I mean, considering the state I'm in and everything. And I'm so comfortable now in bed and all."

"Oh, of course, dear boy, of course! What's your word?"

"Uhm...*satyr.*"

"Satyr! Well," Uncle Justin answered, half-closing his eyes and putting on his best pedagogical air. He cleared his throat, leaned backward, and folded his hands delicately on his lap. "In fact, there are several meanings for *satyr*, S-A-T-Y-R, noun. The first one that comes to my mind is probably the one that is least frequently heard among the lay public—and that would be when it is used to describe any of the various butterflies of the family *Satyridae,* which are characterized by brown wings adorned with these extraordinary, eye-like spots, and, among the males...oh. Oh, I see this is probably not want you want, Sean. Very well then, let's try its most popular meaning, shall we? Which will take us back to the days of Roman Mythology— ahem. Now, this type of satyr would be a woodland humanoid creature with pointed ears, two legs, and the short pointy horns of a goat, and a...uhm...unbridled fondness for...errr...well...*unrestrained revelry.* Which, don't you know, brings us to the third meaning of the word, and this would be when it is applied to a person, ordinarily a man, exhibiting these kinds of...uhm...behaviors."

An old horn-dog, Sean thought, mentally translating Uncle Justin's words into an understandable, though undoubtedly less lovely, vernacular. "Oh," he said. "So Satyr City would be...a place full of satyrs?"

My God, Sean wondered, *was it some kind of sex and party club they were running up there in the Thicket?* That seemed highly unlikely...but that's what the stranger had cried when Sean surprised him, Satyr City. But maybe it was just what they called themselves—like a secret password or something—or a call for help—

"Satyr City? Humph. Yes, I would imagine, though I don't believe I've heard the term before. One might think it a euphemistic sobriquet for a place in ancient Rome where the satyrs, for example...held an annual convention, like the Lion Clubs or something," (Uncle Justin tittered again) "but when we took Latin back in high school, Old Miss Barnes— she was way before your time—made us know Roman Mythology cold— so I don't think there is such a reference to be found in the literature."

Uncle Justin's eyes said that he wanted to ask why Sean wanted to know all this; but his delicacy, and respect for Sean's privacy, made him hold back. It had always been like this, and such regard for one's own space, mental as well as physical, was one of the virtues Sean loved best about his uncle.

"But what *did* you want with Margaret's gardening tools?" Uncle Justin asked, tactfully changing the subject, Sean knew, now that he had imparted all that he knew of the topic. "The dear woman raised *mountains* of ruckus this morning, I can tell you— you know how she is with her things. She was, well, *itching* to wake you at 5:30, if you'll pardon my pun. But I asked her to give you until seven. I didn't know you were developing horticultural interests, Sean."

Sean couldn't be sure, but there seemed to be more than the ordinary twinkle in Uncle Justin's eye. Sean opened his mouth to answer—though he was clueless as to what the nature of his equivocation would be—when the doorbell chimed with theatrical timing and the lower chambers of the house filled up with the hale and well-met-good-fellow voice of Doctor Hallissey. Uncle Justin winked at Sean, then went downstairs to greet the doctor—not that Margaret wasn't doing an ample job already, for even from this distance they could hear her fussing and clucking over the doctor as if he were a rajah on an elephant.

Just then Sean's cell phone went off. It was Timmy.

"Hey."

"Hey. You ready to kick some? We'll be over in five."

"Dude, sorry, I won't be playing. I'm like…you should see me."

"What's up?" Timmy sounded incredulous. "How can we win without my co-captain?"

"I have wicked bad Poison Ivy. And Poison Sumac, and…a whole bunch of scratches on my face. I'm contagious. Doctor's orders."

There was silence for a moment.

"Are you pulling my leg?"

"No, no way. Call me after the game and come over."

"What the heck happened?"

"I'll tell you when you come over." Sean knew this was one way to get Timmy over here quickly after the game, and he decided now that he needed Timmy. "Good luck! And don't forget to keep your head up!"

"Alright. Oh, Regina wants to know if you came over last night at 11:30ish and peeked in our living room window."

"Yeah, that was me—you guys looked like you were having the time of your lives!"

"Dude! I never want to hear a piano again. Who knew *Feelings* could be done in four-part harmony—for two hours? What was up?"

"I'll tell you later. I gotta go, Doctor Hallissey's coming up the stairs as we speak."

"That's a relief anyway. It can't be serious if he's there."

"Be nice. Later."

"Later."

As Sean clicked off, the large frame of Doctor Hallissey eclipsed Sean's bedroom doorway—and he already had a cup of tea in his right hand, along with what looked like Madeleine crumbs on his starched white shirt and navy-blue tie—the doctor still dressed when he came a-calling. Even the doctor started when he saw Sean, and a bit of tea sloshed out of his cup—but Margaret was just behind Uncle Justin, who was just behind the doctor—my God, it was a procession—and she quickly wiped up matters with the hunk of fresh paper towel that was always tucked deep within the hidden treasury of her ample bosom.

"Well well! What have we here, then?" the doctor boomed. He smelled, as always, of rubbing alcohol and, naturally, chalky bandages. His leonine white hair was dressed as usual in a pompadour and was wet with the fragrant witch hazel that was one of his many hallmarks. Margaret scurried in before him and placed a chair at Sean's bedside, which the doctor soon overflowed. He examined Sean's face closely, hmmming every few seconds as he did.

"Very good, Margaret and Justin, we don't want you anymore," he eventually declared, not bothering to turn. "Nothing to be alarmed at, just Poison Sumac, Poison Ivy, and a good many scrapes and bruises. Looks worse than it is, eh? We'll have him right as rain in no time."

"Thanks be to God!" Margaret hissed under her breath, crossing herself. "Shall I boil water, doctor?" Most of Margaret's medical knowledge came from the Victorian novels she read at night, many of them involving young women who had gotten themselves "into a fix."

"Not unless you want to make me another cup of that delicious tea!" the doctor laughed. "You can shut the door on your way out." He waved them out of the room with his massive right hand.

The doctor reached into his black bag, took out a few cotton balls and some kind of ointment in a jar, and began applying same to Sean's face, his sausage fingers working more gently than Sean could have imagined. Sean hoped the doctor wouldn't start on politics, for then he'd be here forever—

"Now, I won't talk politics, for like most young people I presume you're ignorant as the swallows when it comes to the demise of our democracy," the doctor began, and Sean inwardly groaned. "That's right! Give 'em a smart phone and a music box with earphones and they're happy, what? Rome can burn for all they care! Now in my day—"

Sean made a whimper of feigned pain, knowing the doctor was, despite his bluster, compassionate, and, more importantly, that the simplest interruptions often derailed the good doctor's train of thought.

"Oh, sorry young man, I'll go easier. So…where was I? You can't remember either, eh? Oh, Justin tells me you were out hiking last night?"

"Oh, yeah Doctor, that's right, see I ahhh…couldn't sleep and I got a little restless and—"

"What's her name?" the doctor hissed, coming in closer as if for an invasion of Sean's personal space and winking at him. "A little romantic rendezvous, eh? Don't tell me! I was a boy once and therefore have much experience in the matter of boys, and from that experience I can tell you I don't have a great deal of respect for them! They're a bad lot, as a rule!" But the doctor was chortling.

Oi. Sean knew this topic—however awkward it might be when it came up with an old person—was infinitely preferable to a political harangue. So he thought quickly. He also knew the doctor might be more apt to let fall an indiscreet bit of news if he himself was fed first. Sean may not have been feeling his best, but he wasn't sick enough where a little gossip wouldn't interest him—in fact, Sean never had been that sick...

"I...I wouldn't want this to get around, Doctor, but I was supposed to meet—uhm...Regina Quinn," Sean lied.

"Ahhhhh!" the doctor smiled. "That red-haired vision! The Queen Genevieve of Nawshant! Lovely as a summer's day!"

"Uhm....yeah, right. We were going to ahhh...take a little walk." Sean would have a little fun on the doctor's part, and Regina's as well—for he knew the news would be all over town by the third quarter of this morning's football game. "You know what I mean!"

"Indeed I do! Why, when I was courting Millie..." Here the doctor launched upon a labyrinthine tale peopled with, seemingly, vast nations of young ladies. Sean became lost within seconds; but that was fine, he was enjoying the feel of the fragrant ointment on his abrasions. It actually felt wonderfully soothing. But his mind came back to the doctor all in a rushing instant when he heard him say the secret words, as it were: *Linger Longer*.

"Uhm...pardon me, Doctor?" Sean asked, being careful as he sat up in excitement not to push the doctor from his chair.

"I was just saying, I bet you can't tell me what's been going on less than a mile from your own nose, right up at *Linger Longer!*"

Sean thought quickly and feigned a yawn. Bug-eyed enjoinders, salivation at the mouth, and cries for *more!* made the doctor parse out what he knew in miserly strands; pretend to be only vaguely interested, on the other hand, and the whole tale flooded out like rushing water from a burst dam.

"Oh, I have no idea," Sean said drowsily. He yawned again.

"I thought not! Well now, two weeks ago I got a call from—well, let's just say, the regal elderly stateswoman who presides at *Linger Longer*. You know me—I name no names."

"Right," Sean said, wondering how in the world he and the doctor's noses didn't grow exponentially at this.

"Well, it seems she had a…ahem…*workman* doing a few chores for her up at the estate. Poor devil'd had a little accident for himself. Could I come up right away and tend to him? Well I did, and when I got there I was ushered out back, and there in the last greenhouse was this fellow with a nasty slice in his foreleg. Mrs. Hutchin—the regal lady, I mean—seemed quite distraught. When I suggested we get him to the hospital so they could take an x-ray—I thought he might have nicked the bone—they both wouldn't hear of it—seemed very alarmed, in fact. So I stitched him up, right there in the greenhouse with all the camellias, and Mrs. Hutchinson assisting. Twenty-seven stitches in all, and as neat a job as you'd see in a long day's walk, if I do say so myself."

My God, Sean thought—this must be the stranger he had seen last night—the one who had almost clubbed him! *Three Spirits* himself!

"Now here's the thing," the doctor continued, lowering his voice and coming in closer. "She told me over the phone he'd been chopping some wood for her; but when I sent her into the house for more iodine, he told me he'd been digging up old tree roots in the rhubarb patch."

"Humph," Sean said, idly picking at a scab at the end of his elbow. But his heart and mind were racing. "Imagine that."

"Well, *you* can't tell me he's just a workman! Above and beyond them not getting their cock-and-bull story straight, he was a deep devil—one glance and you could see that—smooth, I mean— nothing to say. Not that he had the appearance of a scoundrel, I don't mean that at all. In fact he seemed full of quiet integrity. And Indian too, by all appearances—Native American, I mean. You know what *that* means!"

Sean hoped the doctor wasn't going to imply that Mrs. Hutchinson was having an affair. It was tres embarrassing when old people talked about stuff like that—but what did he mean, the guy was Native American? Sean had seen him last night and he looked no more Native American than Margaret did.

"Uhm, no, I don't," Sean answered.

"Well! If you knew your World War II history and the Navaho Code and all that, you'd know! He's a *government* agent, and there's probably a team of them up there building some satellite so they can spy on us some more!"

"Uhm…he was an Indian? How do you know?" Sean tried to ask the question as nonchalantly as possible, but his pulse was quickening.

"Well! Reddish-brown skin, long and smooth jet-black hair parted down the middle, dark eyes! They recruit them you know, they make our best government agents. Why, during World War II, like I was saying, when it came to making and breaking codes, Navahos were routinely…"

Here the doctor went off again, and Sean barely listened—the important thing was that the person who had been wounded that day wasn't the same man Sean had seen last night. That meant there was more than one person hiding out in the Thicket—at least two of them—Three Spirits and then the Indian guy—but then again, the note had said "we came up here to scatter his ashes," whoever the deceased person was. But that wasn't the point—the point was, Mrs. Hutchinson knew about them—or at least about one of them—and she was aiding and abetting them—*and she hadn't told Sean.*

CHAPTER THIRTEEN

BEDSIDE MANNERS

Sean could hardly believe it—Mrs. Hutchinson was holding out on him—but *why*?

Maybe she was part of it—whatever "it" was: some vast, international conspiracy involving high-tech gadgets, an East German *femme fatale*, a cryptic note found clutched in the hands of a body floating in the Volga River, and Interpol—but then, why had she hired him to solve the mystery? It made no sense—or maybe they were blackmailing her! Perhaps she had had—in her youth—a torrid, Boston marriage affair with another woman, and—

"Oh don't be so dramatic," he told himself. "Occam's Razor, dude, Occam's Razor."

At any rate, Sean worried for the first time that he might have to involve the local police—which he hated to do—since there was more than one of the bad guys up there hiding out in the Thicket. He so wanted to solve this mystery himself. But, though he wasn't vain, he liked his face very much, thank you, just the way it was now—well, not *right* now—and didn't take a cotton to the idea of it being rearranged by, not one, but two ex-cons wielding sticks. Or whatever.

Or was this just a workman Mrs. Hutchinson had hired for the day, as she had told Dr. Hallissey?

As the doctor prattled on, he took from his bag a roll of medical tape big as Sean's head, and the chalky smell of it quickly stained the room. Sean inwardly groaned as the doctor—who must surely be a frustrated make-up artist, Sean thought—wrapped him as if for ancient Egyptian burial. After what seemed hours, the doctor finished. Sean was careful to keep his hands under the covers, lest the doctor wrap them too.

"There! You'll be good as new in a few days!"

"Pmthanks, Docphtor," Sean mumbled through the tiny opening his mouth had become. It was difficult to talk.

"I'm leaving you some of this ointment, which you can put on twice a day—once in the morning, and once before you go to bed. Then have Margaret put those bandages back on again."

"Whaft is that stufmf anymway?" Sean asked. "Itf feelps really good-mph."

"Haven't the foggiest!" the doctor laughed, rising up and checking his luxurious white mane in Sean's bedroom mirror. "I got it at the new Health Food Store down in the village—one of the young Seaver girls opened it last spring. She called it *Heal-All*, and said it was especially effective for Poison Ivy, Poison Sumac, and minor cuts and abrasions. I picked it up, as I thought it might come in handy sometime. *Herbal Therapy*, they call it. I'm not such an old dog that I can't learn new tricks!"

And with that, the doctor laughed himself out of Sean's room, and down the hall to the main staircase.

Sean was up before he could say Uncle Justin's Friend from Dermatological Diseases. The first thing he did was apply some of the ointment—which, really, was wonderfully soothing, and redolent with the smell of mint and bayberries—to his hands. Then, standing before the mirror—my God, he looked like the Invisible Man—he carefully unwrapped the yards and miles and leagues of bandage, feeling thirty pounds lighter after he did. He put on his favorite lucky ball cap—a green Red Sox one, with a red *B* in front and a red shamrock on the back—so that he wouldn't absent-mindedly scratch his scalp any more, then made his bed—he could never write in his notebook while lying on an unmade bed—and plopped down, pen in hand.

He had to sort everything out, put everything in order, set priorities, and he knew he could do this best by writing it all out. Again, there were many cords which led into the mystery of the Thicket Bells, and he needed to decide which one of these tangled threads to follow next. Once the bed was made he had to find his lucky pen—this was green too, and thick, and it made a wonderfully-pleasant scratching noise as he wrote—and then he was off.

As Sean scribbled, he kept one ear cocked to the commotion downstairs, for apparently Margaret had invited Doctor Hallissey to have some breakfast (which, judging by the tiny remnant of dried egg on the left side of the doctor's face, would be his second breakfast this morning). He prayed the doctor wouldn't come back upstairs, and find Sean *sans* bandage. But the doctor was generally a creature of habit, and once the sufferer had been dispensed with, the real business could be addressed—gossip, and the gastronomical and potable delights of whichever house he happened to be visiting.

Sean kept his other ear cocked in the direction of the ceiling, for Kyle was moving about briskly in his room above, probably getting ready for his game. How had he snuck out last night?

Sean kept writing.

"Hope you feel better," Sean heard behind him a minute later, in a soft drawl, and he actually cried out weakly so startled did the sound render him. He turned and saw Kyle filling up his doorway, all decked out in a navy blazer, dark dress slacks, white shirt, and striped tie—apparently he, like the doctor, dressed for the occasion—or maybe it was catchy. In his left hand Kyle carried a big blue nylon duffle bag, stuffed with, presumably, his football uniform and pads.

Sean didn't know if he should tell his cousin that no one, not nobody, not no-how, ever dressed for games in Nawshant—it was all way too casual for that. This wasn't Kansas for heaven's sakes, or any one of those other states unfortunate enough not to have a coastline; and, sure, people liked football and all but, *Mon Dieu*, it wasn't a *religion* the way it was in some places. People had *lives* up here.

But Sean realized this revelation probably wouldn't make any difference to Kyle, who apparently did his own thing regardless—plus it might not be welcome.

"Oh, thanks," Sean said, closing his notebook and sitting up on the edge of his bed, stiffening. The vibe was always so *intense* when he and his cousin talked for some reason. "Ahhh…congrats on making the team and ahhh…good luck with your game there."

"Thanks."

"Who you playing again?" Sean tried to remember but couldn't.

One of Kyle's eyebrows lifted, as if he couldn't believe Sean didn't know.

"Glowchester."

"Uhm…I'm sorry, who?"

"G-L-O- U…" Kyle began spelling the word.

"Oh, pronounced GLAW-ster," Sean said, looking down and trying not to smirk. Gloucester was the perennial bad-ass powerhouse that won the title every year, and more often than not won the Division Three Super Bowl for the entire state. There must have been something in the Gloucester water, because even the wimpy water boys for their team resembled double-sided refrigerators in ill humor. Kyle would have a baptism by fire—*if* he even got in the game. "Uhm…good luck, Kyle."

Sean tried to inject more optimism into his voice than he felt.

Kyle nodded curtly. They were staring at each other and Kyle seemed reluctant to move away—as if he wanted to say more, but couldn't find the words. His eyes shifted back and forth, his mouth opened, and then shut.

Sean decided to take the initiative once again, for he had just thought of something.

"Can you come here for a second, Kyle?" Sean asked.

This time both of Kyle's eyebrows—they were thin and dark and exactly the same as Sean's—went up, as if he were puzzled.

"Why?" he asked.

"Just come here—please?" Sean repeated, as kindly as he could. Kyle strode forward to the side of Sean's bed. Sean reached over and grabbed the jar of Heal-All ointment from his night table, then swung around to face Kyle again. Sean opened the jar, swiped a dollop of the stuff with his fingers, then said, "Give me your hand. The doctor gave me this stuff and it's really good for...uhm...cuts and stuff."

Above and beyond being a kind act, Sean thought this might make his cousin open up to the point where they could talk to each other about the Thicket, and compare notes, and Sean could find out how Kyle had learned of the mystery—and how he had left the house last night.

But Kyle of course hesitated. They were still staring intently at each other, Sean sitting on the edge of his bed, and Kyle towering over him. Sean's pulse quickened a little. Finally Kyle, still looking at Sean, grudgingly held out his left hand with a just-audible *tssk* of annoyance.

Sean ignored this and applied the salve, working it in circles onto the top of Kyle's large, smooth, but rash-ridden hand. Gradually Sean became conscious of a very strange sensation, electricity almost, that seemed to build and ooze all through him, starting with his fingers.

"Okay, now the other," Sean said, but his voice was shaky.

Kyle complied, and the sensation grew. Kyle must have felt it too, because he suddenly yanked his hand away as if he had been shocked; he gasped lightly. Sean looked up at his cousin and their eyes locked once more. There was a bead of perspiration on his cousin's face that hadn't been there a second ago, right between his eyes, and he was panting a little. So was Sean. Now they both looked puzzled.

"Th-thanks," Kyle mumbled. "I've…I have to go now."

Sean tried to say something, but he couldn't. He was almost dizzy. What the heck had happened? But as Kyle left Sean's room, once again he froze at the turn outside Sean's door, and his head yanked towards the Palladian window, as it had done Thursday night when he'd first arrived here. Almost against his will it seemed, Kyle appeared to be nailed to the spot, his eyes glazing over as he looked out the window onto Third Cliff.

"You were right, Kyle," Sean heard himself quietly say. "Something *did* happen out there. Something tragic."

"*The Southern Cross*," Kyle mumbled after a moment. Sean's mouth fell open. Then Kyle seemed to yank himself away.

"I've got to *go!*" he hissed, almost as if he were speaking the words to someone else. He turned his back and bounded down the hall, then down the stairs.

"Well well, who have we here, eh?" Sean heard next, the patrician voice of the doctor booming up from downstairs as Kyle was introduced. There was mumbled conversation, much of which Sean couldn't pick up, (despite his best efforts) mostly pleasantly banal.

Sean sat back down on the edge of his bed, dumbfounded. His hand still tingled from when he had touched Kyle—talk about electricity. My God, it was like…poking a wet finger into an electrical socket, almost. What the heck did that mean? And Kyle had had another "vision" or "fit" or whatever you might call it, as he passed by the window again. And, he knew about the *Southern Cross!* How had he found out about *that*?

It was a few more minutes before Sean could snap out of it and return to his journal—he had to make note of these two new developments as well. He tried to put the whole thing together and make some sense as to what his next step should be. He had the day to himself, for he knew Uncle Justin and Margaret would go to Kyle's game, and then they were having luncheon at Professor Singleton's—the five course meals served by the professor's housekeeper could never be called simply lunch—and

Sean meant to take full advantage of the ensuing peace and quiet and get some serious sleuthing done.

A few minutes later—he was almost finished with his journaling, and was coming up with a plan—Sean heard the sound of a beeping horn just outside the front of Greystones. His heart gave a little jump—okay, a *big* jump—was he hearing things? It sounded like Matt's car—

Sean flew to the window—it was Matt, in his mother's maroon Subaru wagon, complete with twenty-seven (at last count) dangling "energy crystals" here and there throughout the interior of the vehicle. Being the kind of halcyon day that only late September in New England can bring, Matt's mother had no doubt taken her motorcycle to work ,and given Matt her car for the day—and he had come instantly here! *Yes!* Matt had come to see him before his football game, and to make it all up from his weirdness of last night!

A sudden joy pumped through Sean, and he felt again the love he had sensed when he was watching Matt walk home the other night. *God, I really must be gay*, he thought—but what of that—he'd tell Matt everything that had happened, get him as into the case as Sean was, and then…and then…

Of course Sean couldn't kiss Matt right now, not in the contagious condition he was in; but somehow he'd let Matt know that everything was cool between them, and that Sean was as anxious as Matt to take their friendship to the next level— just to see—

Sean tingled as he pulled back the curtains and lifted the window. Matt was already out of the car, and leaning against it in his sexy, insouciant manner. But his face shone with the same look he had worn the other evening, when they had been alone together on the lacrosse field—he looked beautiful and, my *God*, Sean now noticed that he was all dressed up too, in off-white chinos and a navy blazer, white shirt and a baby-blue paisley tie. He looked so slick! But what the…? Matt *never* dressed up, even on those special occasions when everyone else did, and Sean actually gulped at how stunning he looked—his hair kind of off to the side and the September sunshine doing things to it, and—

Just then something cold and discomforting began squirting through Sean's stomach. Matt's face was shining, but...he wasn't looking up at Sean's window. What the—

Oh no. He was looking straight ahead, and a moment later...Kyle walked into view, as he headed toward Matt's car.

Matt had been looking at his cousin Kyle.

He was here to pick Kyle up—not to visit Sean.

Sean yanked himself back from the window, lest he be seen. A cloud of sorrow passed over his heart. He watched as the two young men shook hands; and then—Matt reached out and squeezed the top of Kyle's shoulder affectionately. Even from here, Sean could see his cousin turning crimson as he walked around to the passenger side of Matt's car and, after stowing his gear almost reverently in the back seat, he got in and immediately fastened his seatbelt. Matt did too—something else he *never* did—and then the car scooted off with a scudding squeal of rubber. Matt was showing off, as he always did when he was in his brighter moods. And he hadn't even once glanced up at Sean's bedroom. *Jerk!*

And then it occurred to Sean—of course, how had he been so blind as not to have seen this last night? Matt had gotten together with Kyle last night! *That's* where Kyle had gone! It was Kyle who had called for Matt—

Of course. It was obvious. *Double-jerk!*

Sean's pain took on a green-eyed tinge, and he felt his eyes narrowing as a thorn pierced his heart.

Of course of course of course. They had been practicing together yesterday evening, Matt and Kyle, and at some point had made plans to get together last night.

Sean half-fell onto the edge of his bed with the power of this realization. It was like someone had just booted him in the gut.

Matt and Kyle had been together last night.

Well, so what if they had? the voice of reason asked.

But Matt didn't invite me. Why? What was he trying to hide?

Nothing, probably—they were most likely just going over some plays together, that's all.

But the way Matt was looking at Kyle just now—and he didn't even look up at my window!

A vast melancholy overcame Sean, different from the one that had troubled him last night. That had, in a weird way, almost felt good, to self-indulge in a he-loves-me-he-loves-me-not pity party, and play "that" song over and over again on the boom-box, and wax lugubrious and teenagey-in-love; but this was more serious. It went straight to Sean's heart, and made him feel so bad it frightened him.

He stared at his bed, and longed to drape himself back onto it, never getting up again; and play that tune over and over until he wept.

But he didn't want to go there. He was a sensitive soul, and had been lucky thus far in that he had only known one heart-breaking sorrow in all his life (other than the loss of his parents, which he was too young to consciously feel when it happened). That had been the death of Biscuits, the little black-and-white long-haired Jack Russell Terrier that had been Sean's shadow for more than a decade. Uncle Justin had got it for Sean's fourth birthday, telling him that Biscuits, too, had lost his parents, for someone had abandoned the whole family of dogs on a bitter winter's night, and Biscuits was the only one to have survived, buried at the bottom of the sack. He had lived for twelve years, and Biscuits and Sean had been the sight and light of each other every day of that time. He had died of old age a year and half ago, and Sean still missed him like a limb. He still often woke up of a morning by searching his hand out across the covers to find the reassuring lump of devoted warmth; and then when he realized the bed's emptiness, and what it meant, he jumped up instantly so he wouldn't go there. It was still too painful.

And this was the same kind of pain. Only worse.

He was afraid to go there.

Besides, he told himself, he had too much to do.

He forced himself up and walked over to the corner of his room. Above his desk on the wall was a shrine, to wit, mounted black and white, or sepia, 8 x 10s of his favorite detectives. He'd been collecting them since he was a kid. Here were the perennially adolescent and hopeful Hardy Boys of Bayview, maybe not the brightest bulbs in the circuit but certainly decisive and bold; and the ever-resourceful and intelligent Nancy Drew; Sherlock Holmes with his pipe and deerstalker hat, rousing Watson because the game was afoot; Inspector Poirot with his perfectly manicured moustache and supercilious—yet bumbling—eyes; and Miss Jane Marple in all her tweedy perseverance, just sitting down with a cup of tea to give a rigorous third degree to the Countess of Shrewsbury. Or whomever.

He sighed deeply.

None of them had ever married, to the best of his knowledge—my God, he didn't think he could ever recall any of them even going on a date for heaven's sakes! And who could blame them—when hearts were fragile as frozen lace? Instead they had buried their unconfessed sorrows and secret pinings, steeled themselves against the distracting temptations of jasmine-scented vixens with come-hither gams—or well-dressed, smooth-tongued devils with la-dee-da ways, as the case might have been—and served humanity by getting to the root of crimes that had left the regular authorities pickled in perplexity.

Perhaps his would be the same fate. He sighed deeply, and ran his fingers along the portraits, hoping that some of his idols' moral fortitude—emotional saltpeter, as it were—might invest him by osmosis.

He closed his eyes. It was bad enough to be rejected by Matt—it was worse to see Matt with his cousin. Not that, of course, anything romantic would develop there. After all, his cousin had uttered that rather unlovely homophobic remark about Massachusetts and gay marriage.

Help! he whispered.

As if in answer, the front door slammed—that was the doctor leaving—and immediately the pitter-patter of Uncle Justin and the heavier hoof-beats of Margaret's footfalls could be heard ascending the stairs.

Sean leapt back under the covers just as they sailed round the corner of his bedroom door. They burst into the room and planted themselves on either end of his bed.

"My little lamb!" Margaret cried, resembling a speed-reading mime with the intensity and rapidity of her futile gestures. "Did he make it all better? But why in the name of all that's sacred didn't he bandage you? Is it *modern* he's getting?"

"Ahhh, well, he...uhm...he said that—"

Sean threw a desperate glance at Uncle Justin.

"Oh, yes, he said that...he said that the air *must* get at it," Uncle Justin pronounced decisively, standing up, and fiddling with his pince-nez as he always did when he...stretched the truth for Margaret's sake. "I believe, Margaret, you were off fetching the maple syrup when he told me all that. Otherwise infection might set in. If that happens, then..."

Here Uncle Justin laid it on thick, emitting a mile-long string of Latin names for various fungi and bacteria—and what they might do. Margaret's right hand clapped itself onto her sternum, then her throat, then the side of her cheek, then finally her mouth as he progressed. Sean thought of the strong-man sledgehammer test-of-strength at the Carnival—Uncle Justin had, undoubtedly, just made Margaret's bell ring.

"I'm really feeling much better," Sean smiled.

"Excellent!" Uncle Justin chirped. "We'll be off then to Kyle's football match, and then after that to Professor Singl—"

"Ho-no!" Margaret chortled. "Maybe *you* will, Professor. But someone needs to stay with my poor boy, and if you think that I'll be after abandoning my post when—"

Oh no! Sean had to snoop this afternoon, and Margaret would be an insurmountable roadblock to all such activity! Once again he looked desperation at Uncle Justin, and shook his head as slightly as he dared while Margaret, her eyes closed, went on about her devotion.

"Errrr, well, we best be going, Margaret," Uncle Justin continued, fidgeting violently with his pince-nez. He took out his pocket-watch and consulted it. "Sean will become contagious in…exactly twenty-seven minutes from now, according to Doctor Hallissey. Uhm…air-borne, you know. But only until five this evening."

"Contagious, is it?" Margaret cried. "Did you think *that* would stop me? I already told you—"

"Did I tell you Margaret that Professor Singleton is trying out a new cook this afternoon?" Uncle Justin asked.

Margaret was out of Sean's bedroom so fast that the door slammed behind her in her gale-force wake. "Call us Sean if you need anything!" she bawled as she raced down the stairs. If there was one thing Margaret couldn't resist, it was the chance to meet another "culinary engineer" (as she called herself) in town—and see if the newbie "had the goods;" —and of course on the odd chance that she could purloin a new recipe or two.

This news was no surprise for Sean, though he thanked God for it— Professor Singleton seemed to wear out cooks faster than he could hire them, and it was in sympathy of them (as well as, of course, the pleasure of his company) that Uncle Justin and Margaret invited him so often to dine at Greystones.

"Thanks Uncle Justin!" Sean sighed. "I'd like to get some…studying done."

"Of course, dear boy! We all need a little peace and quiet! But, like Margaret says, do call if you need anything, or if something comes up. I say, you are feeling alright? You seem a little—"

"I'm really fine, Uncle Justin, thanks," Sean said, lifting his chin and stiffening his lip a little. Work was the antidote for a broken heart—he had read that somewhere, and that was just what Sean intended to do with the rest of this morning, and the afternoon as well.

"Well, alright then. Good luck…studying!"

Five minutes later Sean heard the front door slam, and then a minute after the crunchy-gravel sound of Uncle Justin driving off with Margaret down the long driveway. He reached under the covers and took out his notebook, consulting the list he had made half an hour earlier, before—well, before *that thing* happened, which had upset him so much.

He looked at his list again:

1. *Go back to the Thicket and snoop some more*; Well, duh, that was obvious;

2. *Find out how Kyle left the house last night;*

3. *Find out how much Kyle knows, and how he knows it;*

4. *Ask Mrs. Hutchinson what she knows about Three Spirits and the Indian guy, and why she's leaving them food, if in fact it's she that's leaving the food;*

5. *Try to find out more about Aunt Sadie, especially the bell that she had relocated; where is it? Is that the one that's ringing?*

6. *Call Kevin at the library and see if they have any private papers or documents that Aunt Sadie might have left;*

7. *Infiltrate the Thicket some night very soon dressed as a Satyr;*

8. *Find out what the average satyr wears;*

9. *Ask Matt why he wants to break my heart.*

Sean crossed out the last item, over and over until the letters were no longer legible.

"Alrighty then," he said aloud. "Time to get busy." He couldn't really leave the house today, looking like this, and feeling like this—the rash, though its crazy fire had been somewhat diminished by the Heal-All, still stung, itched, and burned like mad. So he circled Numbers Six and Two from his list. He could make calls from here, he could snoop around here, and certainly the mystery of how Kyle was getting in and out of the house without exiting through doors or windows was an acutely local one. He could call, too, Mrs. Hutchinson, and confront her with what he had seen, and what the doctor had told him—but wait, no—that conversation might go better in person:—then he could judge—if Mrs. Hutchinson got crafty or hesitant—if she were hiding anything.

He called the library immediately, and Kevin answered.

"So, what's this I hear about you and Regina Quinn?" was the first thing he said when Sean identified himself.

My God! That had to be a new record, even for Nawshant!

"Lies, all lies!" Sean joked. "No seriously, we're good friends, that's all."

"I see," Kevin said, but by the way he dragged out the phrase Sean could tell he didn't see at all. "How good?"

"Never mind all that—how was your uhm...night last night?" Sean asked, as innocently as he could.

"Oh stop, you little twit! Next time I see Margaret I'm going to ask her to box your ears! What do you want, anyway?"

"Well, since you asked so nicely...would you have any private papers of Aunt Sadie up there? Notes, letters, journals, anything like that? I know she wasn't Eleanor Roosevelt or anything, but—"

"Actually Sean, you should check the Historical Society. We used to collect things like that, but a few years ago when the Historical Society moved to a bigger space in the old school, we gave them all that stuff, so we could expand the Music Room."

"Oh. Okay."

Sean didn't even know Nawshant had an historical society.

"Want the number?"

"Sure, that would be great. Thanks Kevin."

"Just doing my job."

Sean noted down the number.

"They're only open from four to seven on Friday nights and nine to eleven on Saturday mornings, Sean—someone should be there now, but you better hurry up."

"So why I am wasting time talking to you? Thanks, Kev! See ya!"

Sean clicked off before there could be a retort. It wasn't often he—or anyone—got the best of Kevin Nelson.

He dialed the number for the historical society.

"Nawshant Historical Society, this is Miss Sarah Sawyer speaking, how may I help you?"

Added to Sean's surprise that Miss Sawyer was there was the sudden recollection that he was supposed to cut her Central Park-like lawn this afternoon, for her dinner party tonight. He'd forgotten that!

"Miss Sawyer? Miss Sawyer, it's Sean! Sean Sutherland!"

"Well hello Sean, how are you? What a pleasant surprise! I don't ordinarily volunteer here, but Dolly called me this morning with a terrible… well, we shan't go into all that now, but anyway, here I am! When duty calls, Miss Sarah Sawyer responds! Now, number one Sean, why aren't you at your lacrosse game? And number two, what are you doing calling here?"

"Oh, ahhh, I have wicked bad poison ivy and poison sumac, Miss Sawyer— and I'm stuck in bed for a few days—"

"What?!"

"—but don't worry, Miss Sawyer, I'm sure Timmy will be able to cut your lawn instead." Timmy often worked for Sean when the season was busy.

"Ahhh, the brother of your girlfriend! How sweet!"

"Miss Sawyer, she's not—"

"Well, I certainly *hope* he cuts it! And this afternoon, Sean! Not a month from now! But I *am* sorry, despite my preoccupation with my lawn—that's just dreadful! Did I ever tell you of the time when I took a terrible tumble into the most vicious patch of poison ivy, and it was the day before school started when I was still teaching? And Mary Elizabeth Cronin had just done my hair, and I was walking home, minding my own business as you understand, when suddenly…"

Sean looked at the time on his cell phone nervously—though he could still hear Miss Sawyer loud and clear as she launched herself upon a veritable Lake Superior of a story. It was three minutes before eleven, and if precedent was any precedent, Miss Sawyer would slam down the phone at exactly 11:00:00, and not a second later. She was nothing if not the soul of punctuality itself—especially when she was on the clock.

Sean listened as patiently as he could while Miss Sawyer went on about modern hairstyles, the vulgar habit of using orange juice cans for hair rollers, and four hundred other things. Finally at 10:59, Sean closed his eyes, squeezed the phone, and did the unthinkable: he interrupted Miss Sawyer.

"MissSawyerI'msorrybutdoyouhaveanypapersofmyGreatGreatGreat AuntSadieupthere?" he blurted. "It's kind of important."

"Well!" Miss Sawyer expostulated, and Sean could almost feel his hair blowing over the phone from the strength of the air she let out then. But what she said next made Sean lurch up in the bed. "What's all this about Sadie Sutherland? Is your school doing a project on her or something? You're the *third* person since yesterday to ask about her, and if we have any of her papers!"

"Uhm…wow! That's funny, isn't it?" Sean half-laughed, but his heart was going wild. "Uhm…anyone I know?" he ventured, raising his voice a little too much.

"Now Sean Sutherland, you *know* I can't give out that information! Haven't you ever heard of the…errr…Privacy Act? Or something?"

"Well, I have heard of the Freedom of Information Act," he answered. He took a deep breath and played his trump. "You know, Miss Sawyer, now that I think of it, I bet Timmy will be *exhausted* after his lacrosse game. I'm so sorry, but I don't know if your lawn will—"

"You blackguard!" Miss Sawyer exclaimed. "This is blackmail! Alright, listen—I was reading over the private log of inquiries this morning—not much else to do here, you know!—and it seems your new cousin stopped by last night, just as they were closing up shop at 7, asking the same thing. Isn't that wonderful, Sean, that he's so interested in the family history!"

"Ah…yeah, that is wonderful," Sean answered slowly. My *God!* It seemed everywhere he went in this mystery, Kyle had got there before him—how could that be?

"Oh, well, and then this morning," Miss Sawyer went on, her voice lowering into mincing disgust, "there was that—ghastly woman who came in here. I told her three times there was absolutely no way I was going up to the attic to find the thing she was looking for, especially for a *real estate agent*. My GOD, Sean! Have I never told you about—"

"What was her name, Miss Sawyer?" Sean interrupted again.

"Oops! Sorry, Sean! It's *just* gone eleven and I *can't wait* to get out of here! Thank you for calling the Nawshant Historical Society, where yesterday meets today! And have a nice day!"

With that, the phone clicked off.

Great.

Sean sat up straighter, his mind spinning. He took up his pen again, and began writing out these latest revelations. But just as he was getting going, the phone rang.

"Hello?"

"Yes Sean, hello, I'm calling you back on my cell as I'm driving home. Now, you *will* see that Timmy cuts my lawn this afternoon, won't you, dearest Sean?"

"Okay, I promise. What was the real estate agent's name, Miss Sawyer?"

"Oh, *her!* Uhm, Totty Au Canada or something."

"Dottie LaFrance?" *Why* were people screwing up this name???

"*Yesss!*" Miss Sawyer hissed. "That's the one!"

"What did you tell her?"

"Well, I told her what I'm telling you, and what your cousin was told, no doubt. We have nothing here of Aunt Sadie's, nothing. I checked myself this morning. Although…"

Here Miss Sawyer paused archly.

"Although what?"

"Why don't you call Timmy now and get his word that he will cut my grass this afternoon. Can you do that? And then I'll tell you...*everything!*"

Everything? My God!

"But Miss Sawyer, he's still in the middle of the lacrosse game now. I can't call him right now!"

"Nonsense! I'm driving by the field this instant and I can see that it's *intermezzo*. The cheerleaders are making fools of themselves in the middle of the field with their low-cut, vulgar outfits. Haven't any of these young women read Freidan or Steinham? But...I say, there is quite a commotion down on the football field, though. I wonder what's the fuss?"

"How do you mean, like?"

"Oh, never mind Sean. Where were we? Ah yes, call Timmy, now. Call me back, I'll wait."

Sean rolled his eyes.

"Okay."

Thirty seconds later—

"Yeah?"

"Hey it's me. Are we winning?"

"It's tied. We could sure use you, they're good, but we're awesomely okay so far."

Whatever that meant. "Can you cut Miss Sawyer's grass later this afternoon?"

"Maybe. How much?"

"She gives me $200 cuz it's huge, but still that's half of what the last guy charged her. I'll give you $180."

"Capitalist swine! Okay, I'll do it."

"Thanks. Come over later."

"Okay. Oh, what's all this about you and Regina? I thought it was Matt you had the hots for."

!!!!!!!!!!

"I'm losing you, bad connection! I'll see you this afternoon!" Sean cried, rubbing his sleeve back and forth over the mouthpiece.

My *God*, whatever next! How the heck did Timmy know *that*?

"Hi, Miss Sawyer, you still there?"

"Of course I am—where else should I be? Well? What did your chum say?"

"Done deal."

"EX-cellent! Oh, I am glad!"

"Okay, so what did you tell Dottie LaFrance?"

"Oh, well, according to the computer—everything's been cross-referenced on the computer you know, old Fred Barnes did it last winter—but why wouldn't he, what else has the poor soul to do? Did I ever tell you—"

"About what you told Dottie LaFrance?" Sean interrupted. "No, but you were about to."

"Ouf, you're incorrigible this morning, Sean Sutherland! *Why* is that it's so hard to have a *conversazione* with young people nowadays? Anyway—I looked on the computer and we have only one paper related to Aunt Sadie—I bet the rest are somewhere in your attic. Anyway, this reference is from John Singer Sargent, the painter who did the portrait of her that's up the library—one of Nawshant's treasures, I must say! It's in a letter he wrote to someone or other, and in it he happens to mention that Aunt Sadie *insisted* on having the bell included in her portrait after the Reverend died—the buoy bell that sat right off Third Cliff, her family's buoy bell. She apparently insisted that it be added to the portrait, some years after the original portrait had been completed. That's all."

"And you told this to Dottie LaFrance?"

"Certainly not! I did nothing of the sort! I wouldn't give her the time of day if she asked me on bended knee! I told her we had nothing, and then in fact, *I showed her the door*. But that was only after she called me… after she called me…well, I *shan't* tell you what she called me."

"You said you'd tell me everything."

"Ouf! Alright. She called me…that vile woman called me…you'll *hardly* believe it…an old buffalo."

Sean could feel seven different throat and mouth muscles straining as he did all in his power not to laugh out loud, for somehow the slur was apt, and all he could envision was Miss Sawyer pawing the ground with one foreleg, steam blowing from her shaggy nostrils. He was thinking, too, that he would have paid to see this, the battle of the alpha females. But the important thing—*Aunt Sadie's bell was in the painting! The painting that Kevin said needed to be cleaned! But what did that mean, exactly?*

"Well, I must run, dear Sean—good luck, and many thanks! A million things to do, you know. Oh, best of luck too with your itches! Try Heal-All, you can get it down the village at the new health food store! *Ciao* for now, and say hello to your sweet little redhead for me!"

Sean rolled his eyes again as he hung up the phone. He got busy again with his journal so he wouldn't think about what Timmy had just said regarding Matt. *Dottie LaFrance. Dottie LaFrance. Dottie LaFrance* he wrote. She was up to something—her and her corporate breath!

He looked down at his journal. On the side of this sheet he had doodled a quick sketch of Aunt Sadie's portrait, the one that hung in the library. So she had made the artist come back, long after the portrait was finished, and paint in the bell—but why? He picked up the phone and called Kevin back.

"Hey, it's me again."

"Oh hello, me again. Funny, you sound like that wise-guy Sean."

"That's my evil twin. Hey listen, Kev—about that painting of Aunt Sadie. How much would that cost to have cleaned professionally?"

"Funny you should ask, Sean, because I price it out every year when we put the budget together—but the Selectmen always 'X' it out, along with 10,000 other things I'd like to do up here. Those stingy queens! I list it for $3000, but we could probably get it done for about $2000."

"Wow, that much, eh?"

"Well, we're talking about a Sargent painting here. You know, *the* John

Singer Sargent? It would have to be done by a professional conservator—not Margaret with a jug of Spray-and-Go."

"Okay, well, consider it done. How fast can they do it?"

"Excuse me?"

"How fast can they do it? I'll pay for it. Consider it a gift from the Sutherland Family. I've got some money in the trust fund, so no worries."

"But you already give the library $2000 a year from your trust."

"I know. So this year I'll give $4000. How fast?"

"My God, Sean! That's…wonderful! But—well, there's a lot of red tape—we'll have to get the trustees together and have them vote to accept your kind gift—that'll take me three minutes of phone calls. And then, well, we just have to find a conservator. They'll come out and pick it up—"

"They can't do it there?"

"No, Sean, *they can't do it here.* If we're lucky it'll take a month."

"A month!"

"I know that seems like a year to the young, but, yes, a month. Maybe I can find someone who'll do it more quickly. Unless, of course, you want to handle it."

"Oh, no Kev, you can find someone more qualified than I could."

"Okay, I'll give the trustees a call and get the ball rolling, then call a few conservators. Maybe they'll even come out today and pick it up. I should move it anyway, the painting I mean."

"Why?"

"Oh, because we have a leak in the ceiling from the storm the other night and the town is sending someone over on Monday to fix it. Nowhere near the painting, but still better safe than sorry."

"Right. Okay, thanks Kevin."

"Oh no, *thank you,* Sean! I'll send the papers down for Uncle Justin to sign. Should I call *The Tides* and tell them the good news?"

"Oh no! Keep it unanimous."

"By which I believe you mean—anonymous."

"Yeah, that's it. I always have trouble with those two."

"Wonderful. We'll keep it anonymous. In which case the news will be all over town by tomorrow. Bye!"

Sean hung up the phone and repositioned himself cross-legged on the bed, his chin resting in his hands. A month! He couldn't believe he had to wait that long to get a look at a depiction of Aunt Sadie's bell! But what else could he do? Again, he wondered what had become of the bell, and if it was the same one that was ringing in the Thicket. But what did Dottie LaFrance want with all this info?

Sean folded his arms, closed his eyes, and thought. But after five minutes—all he could think about, really, was how itchy he was—he was no closer to an answer. He only knew she was on to something. Kyle was too, and they were—the two of them, and Sean—at about the same place. But Sean felt that he himself was missing one key ingredient to the puzzle— which Kyle and Dottie had.

He *had* to talk to Kyle and find out what he knew!

Sean's eyes shifted, looking at the ceiling. Kyle wasn't home—

Of course, it wasn't very nice to go snooping in other people's bedrooms, especially other people that one happened to be related to. You could get away with it when you were a pesky kid—but Sean wasn't a kid anymore, though no doubt a few people still thought him pesky—

But still, the case, like the show, must go on, and if one had to give up a love-life to pursue crime, then perhaps one also had to make the additional sacrifice of burdening one's conscience with deeds that one otherwise would never dream of doing.

Or something. And while he was up there snooping, now was as good a time as any to find out how Kyle was sneaking out of the house.

He had to go upstairs.

He was about to get the surprise of his life.

CHAPTER FOURTEEN

THE TWINS JOIN THE CASE

Sean leapt off the bed. Even though the house was empty—present company excluded—he tiptoed down the hall, opened the hall door crack-by-crack, and crept silently up the stairs—or as silently as creaking stairs allowed. *Sa-dee! Sa-dee!* they seemed to rasp.

"That's just your imagination, dude," he murmured. No doubt this was true; and yet Sean almost could feel her presence, if only because Aunt Sadie had swept and crept up and down these same steps thousands of times a century and a half ago.

It was so strange—a few days ago, all Sean knew of Aunt Sadie was that one of the rooms on the third floor was named after her—nothing more. Uncle Justin's forte had never been family history, and while Sean had had some vague knowledge that the Sutherlands had been in Nawshant for hundreds of years, and that some of the old codgers were memorialized in portraits here and there in Nawshant's public buildings, that was the limit of his understanding.

But quickly Aunt Sadie had become almost a living, breathing person to Sean. He knew now a good deal of her history—her fiery determination to help end the scourge of slavery; her passionate love for another, waiting until her middle age to flower; her grief and tragedy.

But that wasn't even the half of it: she was taking shape within his heart, it seemed; a glowing, nebulous tremble inside him, becoming clearer by the day. But after all, why not? Her long dresses had swept these very stairs; her fingers had lightly grazed these walls; she had peeped into these same mirrors, and them gazing back; she had looked out the windows here—in joy, and in almost incomprehensible horror and sorrow. The very walls were moist with her heartbreak, you could say.

And Sean had a face and body now to assign to this almost palpable presence, since he had for the first time really *looked* at her portrait in the Children's Room of the Library: the light-filled, knowledgeable, compassionate eyes; the same jug ears as Sean, partially concealed by her upswept hair, and a glistening pearl dangling from each lobe, small enough to be elegant but utterly devoid of the ostentation that besmirched, Sean thought, his own modern times of vulgar excess. If fortune had favored Aunt Sadie as being of Old Money, then much was expected of her in return, and she had tossed herself into the trenches as she wrestled the evils of her time—slavery, poverty, ignorance, and disease, the enemies of most ages. Not for her, the idle lifestyle of the rich and infamous.

He recollected when he was a child, exploring these same numinous stairs that linked the second and third floors—how Magellan-like had been his sense of wonder and discovery then! Each riser seemed a mini-Matterhorn in those days, and the dust-covered piles of volumes stacked on each side of the steps must contain, Sean thought then, ancient secrets, whispered incantations, and stories to both enthrall and terrify. Untold generations of spiders and their cobby nets festooned every nook and cranny; there was even a resident bat, haunting her Gothic cathedral of a stairway as well as any grimacing gargoyle. And rounded globs of dust—Matt called them *ghost turds*—rolled around everywhere.

Of course, all that hadn't lasted long—not with Margaret—and now the stairway was as immaculate and dust-free as every other surface in the house. Sean wondered where Margaret had exiled the old books to—

probably the attic, as the basement tended toward mustiness. And the bat had been let out via an upstairs window—exterminators could starve under Uncle Justin's benign watch.

Sean opened the door at the top of the stairway, then took a right. The house narrowed somewhat as it rose, so this floor was a bit smaller than the second floor. Still, there were six rooms up here, three on each side of the hall. This had all been the servants' quarters in the old days. The walls were light butter yellow, the wooden door frames and wainscoting darkly shiny with mahogany varnish, and a long Oriental carpet in shades of green and maroon ran the long length of the hallway.

Sean passed Margaret's domain first—she actually had two rooms up here: her bedroom, and then her magnificent sitting room, complete with fireplace. The next room down on this same side was used as a guest bedroom—it had a fireplace too—and the three rooms on the opposite side—the same side as the staircase—were: another old bedroom that was never used; an old storeroom filled with spooky, sheet-draped furniture and portraits; and then Aunt Sadie's room, now Kyle's.

He stopped as he stood before Kyle's closed bedroom door. He paused, his hand on the doorknob—

In the same way that he had witnessed a number of battles over the past few days between his fear and his inquisitiveness, he now felt an interior taffy-pull between his curiosity and his conscience. His own privacy had never been invaded by Uncle Justin; nor could he deny that he wouldn't care for someone doing this to him—and when in doubt over a course of moral action, he tried to let the Golden Rule—Do Unto Others As You Would Have Them Do Unto You—be his guiding light. This had been Uncle Justin's continual advice, and it had always served Sean well.

But on the other hand, he reasoned, if he were Mrs. Hutchinson, he would want someone to solve the mystery; so if he snooped now, wouldn't that be doing unto Mrs. Hutchinson as he would want Mrs. Hutchinson to do unto him? But still he hesitated, his hand on the doorknob, as he felt the moral buoyancy of this rationalization float away.

He finally decided that he wouldn't go snooping in Kyle's room, as far as yanking drawers open and rifling through notebooks—much as he, well, itched too. He would limit his investigation to strictly trying to find out how Kyle was getting out of the house—that was all. He might observe things lying about—but he wouldn't go trolling under beds and tearing through notebooks. Before his conscience could rebel, he turned the door handle and walked in, shutting the door quietly behind him.

The first thing that struck Sean was the Spartan quality of the room. The old iron-framed four-poster twin bed, the ancient, free-standing looking-glass, a chest of drawers, and the antique desk and its ladder-back chair were the only furnishings. Unlike Sean's, Kyle's bedroom was immaculate. The bed of course was made; there were no Pisa-piles of things tippy-stacked on the desk; no rumpled clothes draped over the chair; and no shoes lying sideways-up, tossed helter-skelter on the floor wherever fate—or Sean's kicking feet—had happened to let them fall.

There was a faint smell of pine in the close air, and Sean now recognized this as the same odor that drifted around his cousin. The three windows were closed, despite the fresh benign breezes of the day—perhaps his cousin, being used to a warmer clime, liked it that way. Good grief, Sean thought—if Kyle thought it was cold now, let him wait until the frozen winter came like an old sailor's curse. That would be one rude awakening.

It looked like Kyle had only made two changes to the space in his brief time here: a navy-blue blanket emblazoned with *Piedmont Military Academy* in aggressive yellow letters adorned the bed; and two framed 8 x 10s—one of a man in military uniform, the other of a woman—rested atop the desk: Kyle's parents, Sean assumed. He tiptoed closer, and did a double-take: the man looked like a twin of Sean's own father, except the hair was darker than Sean's dad's had been.

Sean sighed deeply, then peeked out each of the three windows here in turn—my God, the view of the ocean from two of them was magnificent, as well as thought-provoking—for here were Third Cliff and its deep waters in all their shining delight—and tragic recollections. No, there was no question— the wisteria vine only came into contact with one of the windows here, and if Kyle hadn't snuck out that way—which he hadn't, because the tape on the windowsill had never been broken—there was no way he was getting out the other two windows. It was thirty feet off the ground, and sheer all the way down. Nor did the wisteria—or any tree, for that matter—grow close enough to the house anywhere else near the third floor, so the windows in the other rooms could be discounted as well. There was a metal fire escape just outside one of Margaret's bedroom windows, which Uncle Justin had insisted on having built when they first moved here—but the idea of Kyle sneaking into Margaret's bedroom undetected was unthinkable.

Okay, so if Kyle wasn't getting out through the windows, or via the third-floor stairway, "how the Dickens" (as Margaret would say) was he getting out? It must be from this room—

A sudden thought occurred to Sean: hadn't Aunt Sadie disappeared from this room in the same inexplicable manner? Hadn't the two ex-slave sisters been ushered out of the room, and then some time later, with the help of the groom Patrick, opened the locked door—only to find Sadie gone?

A sizzle shimmied down Sean's spine—*yes, this must be the answer to the unsolved riddle of Sadie's disappearance, as well as Kyle's! There was a secret way out of this room! There had to be!*

Old houses like these were riddled with secret passageways—

But where was it? And how had Kyle found it so quickly?

Sean numbly pulled out the ladder-back chair from Kyle's desk, and plopped down with the weight of this realization. It had to be! His head swirled as he turned around, eyeballing this space: this was a corner room, so two of the walls bordered the outside—he could dismiss them, there was no way a hidden passage would fit there; a third wall bordered the hall—Sean leapt up and opened the bedroom door, and, keeping one eye on the inside wall and the other on the hall, measured the width of it: again, no way. It was no more than six or seven inches thick. No hidden passage there.

Sean's eyes fell on the last wall, the one between this room and the next one down, the old storeroom. This had to be it. He walked over to the closet door, and turned the doorknob. It was locked.

First check. Sean didn't realize he had been holding his breath until a big gush of it swooned out in his disappointment. His cousin must have done this—his cousin must be keeping his things somewhere, and there was no place for this other than the closet—

"Now if I were a closet key," Sean mumbled, looking around, "where would I be?"

While he had vowed he wouldn't go prying, this was, of course, an extenuating circumstance—and once the top drawer of his cousin's dresser had been breached, there seemed no point in not opening others. He found the old brass key in the third drawer down.

"Bingo," Sean mumbled. "This must be it!" It was.

An old cedar smell seeped out to him as he opened the closet door, swirled with Kyle's pine smell again, and something else: lemon verbena? Lavender? For a moment Sean had a view of a hot summer afternoon: still, quiet, though spritzed in cicada sound, and even the wood beams pouring their odor out in the benign heat. There was a swish of a long dress, a wisp of lemon-verbena/lavender scent; then the vision left. He was back to the now.

Here was a large closet indeed. Facing Sean were four pairs of Kyle's pants, a half dozen shirts, several T-shirts (even these were hung up and looked as though they had been ironed), some belts and ties, and a few jackets, all seemingly arranged by category and, my God, color. An ancient, half-faded mirror no more than a foot square shone behind a gap in the clothing; Sean jumped when his own poxy face leapt out at him. Taped to the mirror were two sayings, clearly new additions, which had been printed out by all appearances on a home computer: *"My strength is as the strength of ten, because my heart is pure."*—*Sir Galahad* was at the top of the mirror, while at its bottom Sean read, *"God speaks to man chiefly through visions and dreams"*—*Carl Jung.*

Humph. Imagine his cousin quoting Jung.

Whoever Jung was. *Read more and stop being so ignorant!* he chided himself.

While the mirror had clearly been here a long time, probably since Sadie's day, these words were obviously a new addition, put up during the last day or two by Kyle. They evoked in Sean an odd compassion for his cousin: what a funny customer he was. And obviously, from the second saying, Kyle realized he had some kind of extrasensory gift for seeing "visions"—although perhaps he didn't see this as a gift?

On the floor in front of Sean rested Kyle's big black trunky-suitcase; to the right the closet ended, but to the left it went on, and on again: Sean looked above him and found what he was looking for, a light bulb with a chain dangling from it. He snapped it on, then made his way to the end of the closet, rapping on walls as he did. He felt a tad foolish but, well, this was how it was done, no? But from nowhere did the hollow sound he was looking for echo back to him, except for the ceiling—but that was to be expected, the attic was right above. Besides, the ceiling boards, the floor board, the wall boards—all were nailed into place.

He stepped back outside the closet. Second check. He made a face, then winced, as even this caused pain. There *must* be a secret passage—and it *had to be* in the closet. Somewhere.

He stepped back inside, and shoved the hanging clothes aside. "I'd go insane if I tried to manage everything in my life as tightly as this," he mumbled. But nothing doing behind the clothes either. He was trying to get the goods back in their precise geometrical order—something that seemed beyond him at this point—when his cell phone rang to the tune of *If I Were Your Woman*, which he had downloaded last night. But its suddenness shocked him so that he banged his head on the wall behind him as he jumped.

It was Timmy, singing a ditty which he was apparently making up as he went along:

"We won, we won, we really really won,
we didn't think we would but then we did,
we won, it was a lot of fun,
I thought we possibly could and then we did,
we won, we beat them by just one,
we didn't think we should but then we did,
we won, it was a lot of fun—"

"I catch your general drift, dude," Sean laughed, rubbing the back of his head. "That is awesome! Way to go!"

"It was wicked close, but quite the awesome game you missed! How you feelin'?"

"So-so. How'd the ahhh…football team do?"

"Oh, no idea, dude. They could lose every game from now until the year 3000 and I wouldn't bat an eyelash—oh, except for Matt's sake, of course."

"Of course. Where are you now?"

"Coming up your front stairs."

"Cool, I'll be right down."

A minute later:

"Holy s—, Batman!" Timmy cried when he saw Sean's face. "You weren't kiddin', huh?"

"Cut with the potty mouth dude, we can't use cuss words."

"Why not?"

"Because! I'm writing down everything that happens. Maybe some-day—okay, maybe someday this will be like a Hardy Boys or Sherlock

Holmes book for people to read—"

"What will?"

"I'm involved in a…mystery! And so see we can't be going around saying—"

"S---, p---, f---"

"Yes exactly," Sean interrupted. "The seven deadly words. Alright, you better come in."

"Duh, I was planning on it anyway. Why the drama?"

"I have a lot to tell you."

"About you and Matt? I already know, though of course I'd love the details."

Sean froze, then wheeled around.

"No, it's not about that, but—how do you know anyway? Has he been talking?"

"Who, Matt? Like he would!" Timmy laughed. "By the way, you got anything to eat? I'm starving here."

"Yeah, probably. Walk this way." They stumbled out into the kitchen, both of them limping, the old joke between them.

"So how do you know about…about me and Matt?" Sean repeated a minute later, handing Timmy a sandwich. "I'm admitting nothing, by the way, by asking this question."

Timmy shrugged. "This looks awesome dude, thanks. It was Regina told me, as you might expect."

"Regina!" Sean cried. "Je—"

Timmy held up a finger. "Don't say it, dude. Hardy Boys and all."

"Right. But how does she—"

"She can just tell. The way you guys look at each other. Where your eyes go and all that. She asked me about a year ago what I thought and I said I never noticed. But then after that I started paying attention and I told her I thought she was right. So big deal! Ask him out."

"But…my God!—how could you guys see it before I did?" Sean asked.

Then he cried, "I'M SO CONFUSED!"

"Maybe you didn't want to see it."

"Maybe. Well, anyway, something—we kinda had this…moment the other night. After practice, and—"

"What'd yez do?" Timmy asked eagerly, in between boa-bites.

"Nothing! We didn't—nothing! We just—I don't know, he was like staring at me, and I was staring at him, and time—time kind of slowed down, and then, like, well, he—said my name and then reached out and ran his finger down my face, and then I told him…I told him he was beautiful, and then like…he came in like…like he was going to kiss me, and I kind of panicked and jumped up and said I would race him back to the school and everything, and then he left after that and since then he's been distant and weird and giving me attitude."

Timmy nodded his head and took another gargantuan bite.

"Heph probablyg thinkphs youf—"

"Mmphg smrgg mmphh mmphh," Sean imitated. "Not helpful."

"Sorry, it's your fault, this sandwich is so freakin' good. He probably thinks you freaked when he tried to kiss you, and that you think he's a weirdo now or creepy cuz he tried to pull something gay on you and you weren't into it but didn't want to totally *ewww* on him, cuz he's your friend like."

Sean felt his head lurch back and his mouth open. He hadn't thought of that—Matt didn't know! It made perfect sense—Matt had taken a chance by trying to kiss Sean, and Sean had jumped up and run away!

"Aha, I'm right again!" Timmy cried. "Why am I always right, I wonder? So just tell him. Take him out on a date."

"Well, yea, I didn't really think of that and I think you're right, I swear. But now there's another problem—"

"There always is," said Timmy. "Tell."

"—which is…he's been hanging out with my cousin now. In fact, Matt picked Kyle up this morning and was all ga-ga eyed when I looked out the window, and me thinking he was coming to see *me*. And I'm pretty sure they got together last night and—and—"

"Did the nasty?" Timmy suggested.

"No!" Sean cried, when he could catch his breath. "No! Are you kidding me? My cousin's like from Georgia, and his first night here he was like ragging on Massachusetts for being first with gay marriage and everything—"

"Maybe he's a closet case. Remember what Mrs. Eddes told us last year in Psych class? The people with the biggest problem with it are probably freaked out cuz it's too close to home, like."

Sean eyed Timmy thoughtfully, then shook his head.

"I don't think my cousin's gay. I'm not even sure I am, I just…just know how I feel about Matt…"

"Maybe you're a Mattsexual and not a homosexual," Timmy opined, seriously. They looked at each other, then burst out laughing.

"I just don't know," Sean sighed a moment later.

"Well, I think you are but what do I know. Maybe you're bi. What do you think about when you—"

"Hardy Boys!" Sean warned, raising his finger.

"Alright, ahhh, dream. By which I mean fantasize of course."

"Yeah, dude, I got that."

"Well? Answer the question."

"Ahhh…kinda personal dude, huh?"

"Not really," Timmy shrugged. "When I, ahhh, dream, I think about Nancy McDigby and her two hottie sisters, putting on a show for me at their bedroom window and me just walking by minding my own business like usual. And they're like tearing off their clothes they're so worked up, but they keep their high heels on, right? And then they like toss their heads back, and open and close their mouths, and lick their lips and shake their hair, like this—" Here Timmy jumped up and demonstrated—"and start running their hands up and down their—"

"Oh, where is my phone when I really need to video something? But like I told you ten minutes ago," Sean added dryly, "I catch your general drift. Well, I guess I have thought once in a while about…about Matt, and…and maybe a few other guys, but usually they're with girls and…and stuff like that."

"Ever think about me?" Timmy asked matter-of-factly, guzzling down his glass of milk in one long gulp.

"Dude!" Sean laughed. He was glad his face was a mess, as he felt himself reddening like a thermometer in a cartoon. "Ahhh….I…I dunno. Maybe once or twice when we were younger."

"Oh, that's cool. If you didn't, I was gonna ask *what am I, chopped liver?* Too bad I'm not gay though, huh? I think we'd make a nice couple and stuff. Probably wouldn't fight much."

Sean was so surprised by Timmy's cavalier attitude that he didn't know what to say. But then again, both Timmy and Regina always spoke what was on their minds—that was just one of the things Sean loved about the Twins.

"Can we change the subject though? I'm trying not to think about Matt right now."

"Oh, sure, dude, sorry. How's about we talk about what kind of dessert you might have kicking around."

Sean got up and opened the refrigerator door behind him. "All we have is these French cookies from last night," he reported, after a rummage. Timmy instinctually stretched a quick hand to the bowl on the second shelf; he stopped cold when Sean added, "Margaret made these."

"Never mind. She'd kill me. She's probably got them counted."

"No doubt, bro," Sean answered, "but I'm her *little lamby* today cuz I'm sick, so I have like Amnesty International going on until I get better. So take a few and I'll say it was me."

"Thanks, dude, you truly rock. So what did you want to tell me?"

"Okay. Ahhh…I've been hired to solve a mystery."

Timmy's head snapped back. "For real? Who?"

"Mrs. Hutchinson. She's been hearing bells in the Thicket, at night. Church bells, like big tower bells, from the middle of the Thicket."

"Huh! And she's not cray-cray, you think?"

"No."

"Weird! What'd she hire *you* for?"

"To solve the mystery, duh! Remember how I solved the mystery when Mister—"

"Oh yeah yeah yeah, the old-timer who was hearing voices. So you finally get to play Sherlock Holmes like you always wanted."

"Exactly," Sean agreed.

"How much?" Timmy demanded.

"How much what?" Sean asked, confused.

"How much dough are we talking here?"

"My God! For an artist you seem awfully money-fixated."

"Just lookin' out for my buddy!" Timmy laughed, squeezing Sean on the shoulder. "Jeez, these are good! French, you say?"

"*Oui oui.*"

"So how much?"

"Dude, we haven't even discussed money! Give it a rest!"

"You need a business manager," Timmy said flatly. "Want me to have a few words with the old gal? She's loaded, you know. *Rivers* of money. But then again, so are you guys, everyone says."

"Not like her we're not. But I don't want you to be my business man-ager—I want you to be my assistant." Sean paused dramatically and raised one eyebrow. "We have to go on a mission tonight."

"AWE-SOME DUDE! I'm in! The Devaney cousins are staying over again if you can believe it, and anything would be better than four-part harmony of *Jeremiah Was a Bullfrog*. God! Me and Regina love Moms, but she's got execrable taste in tunes. She thinks it's *campy*. We think it's *gar-barge*. So what's on for tonight?"

"Before we get into that, let me bring you up to speed. Come up to my room and I'll fill you in. Just don't interrupt though until I'm finished, cuz it's a little complicated. God! I sound like Miss Sawyer now! C'mon."

Once upstairs, Timmy sprawled out on Sean's bed, packing the pillows behind his head. Sean, pacing across his room, and gesturing as necessary, filled Timmy in regarding the dramatic events of the past forty-eight hours. By the time Sean was finished, Timmy was off the bed and pacing too.

"So you think those guys hiding out in the Thicket are like ex-cons or something?" he asked. "And you think maybe the bell that's ringing is the same one that Aunt Sadie had moved away from Third Cliff a hundred and fifty years ago or so?"

"I don't know—maybe," Sean said, relieved to have someone at last that he could tell the whole tale too. "Maybe yes in both cases—that's what we have to find out."

"And what about that weirdo lady with the ahhh…corporate breath? What's her name, Doughty Au Canada? What's she up to?"

"What is up with her name being hard to remember?" Sean asked with a laugh. "That's what Miss Sawyer called her too—but it's Dottie La-France, dude! Where are you getting Doughty Au Canada?"

Timmy shrugged. "Dunno. France, Canada. Montreal, the Canadian National Anthem at hockey games? *Voulez-vous*? You know?"

"Not really. What are they teaching you in that school? But anyway, I don't know what she's doing. But you'll remember I suspected her from the first."

"Right, her and her corporate breath, we've covered that ground already, though I still have no idea what you're talking about. And wait, how does your cousin know about all this?" Timmy asked. "I thought the dude just got here like two days ago?"

"He *did*, that's what I can't figure out at all—but right now—dude, listen: I think there's a secret passage in Greystones."

Timmy's green eyes blazed. He plopped down on the bed's edge.

"Oh, go there, Sean dude."

"Well! How else is he sneaking out? I told you about the tape on the door and the windows—plus, remember how Aunt Sadie just like *vanished*? And no one ever found her? Anyways, I just know there is—and that's what I was doing when you called, checking out Kyle's room upstairs—which used to be Aunt Sadie's room. Like I told you. I just *know* there's a secret passage up there somewhere."

"So what are we doing down here then?" Timmy asked, leaping up from the bed. "Let's go! Plus it all makes sense! If your Aunt Sadie was helping runaway slaves from the Underground Railroad, naturally they'd be mad secret entrances and tunnels all over the place!"

Sean felt his mouth open again. "Dude, wow! Oh my God I never thought of that!" he blurted. "You're right! But ahhh…you don't, like…ahhh…think it's like…just wrong? To go snooping in Kyle's room?"

"Oh God, no. No way. The dude's holding out. We got a case to crack. Lives might be at stake!"

"Alright, let's go then," Sean announced. "But take off your shoes, they're muddy as hell."

"Can we say *hell*?" Timmy asked.

"Oh, I dunno. Alright, they're muddy as heck."

"Potty-mouth, potty-mouth," Timmy taunted, waving a finger.

A minute later they were upstairs in Kyle's room. Sean, talking in a whisper for some reason, explained to Timmy what he had done so far, and where he had looked.

The phone rang again, they both jumped, and Sean snatched at it before Timmy could figure out the love-song it was playing.

"Your sister," Sean whispered as he picked it up. "Hey, what's up Regina?"

"Don't you *hey* me! What's all this about me and you being an item? It's all over town! And for once I traced it all the way back to the source—

Doctor Hallissey just told me you said we had a date last night!"

"I was just joking because I didn't want to tell him where I really was—sorry! But never mind all that, get over here, now! I have a mad mystery I'm involved in, and me and Timmy are on the verge of discovering a secret passageway up on my third floor."

"Oh, oh, oh my God! Don't do a thing until I get there!"

"Okay, but hurry! The front door's open."

"You should have asked her if the line was secure before you told her that," Timmy commented, pointing.

Sean made a face. "Don't make a meal out if it, dude," he said.

Three minutes later they heard Regina hello-ing from the front hall. Sean scampered down to get her—forgetting again to forewarn about the state of his face. Once that was duly explained, and Regina calmed with cherry juice, Madeleines, and explanations, Sean repeated the strange events of the past two days, bringing Regina up to speed.

"Sean, you were so right, Dottie LaFrance is *definitely* not a real estate agent!" Regina pronounced when Sean had finished. They were up in Kyle's room by this time. "There's something about her gives me the heebie-jeebies. She's hot on the trail, Sean—we just have to make sure we discover…whatever it is we need to discover, before she does. Ohmigod, this is where your cousin *sleeps*?"

Reverently, Regina approached the monkish twin bed. She bent at the waist and smelled both pillows deliriously, her red hair spilling down and mingling with things.

"Ohhh!" she sighed, closing her eyes. "Pine smell, cutgrass, something, something else…heaven." Then she opened them and turned to the boys. "What?" she demanded.

"Oh, my God—oh my God, Sis, I wish you could see yourself now," Timmy commented, his hands on his hips. "Get a hold of yourself! Whatever happened to *I am Woman, Watch Me Not Date Anyone in Nawshant?* What happened to your roar?"

"Darling Bro—you want to hear me roar? Fix me up with that stud-muffin and you'll hear me all the way out to Lynn Shore Drive."

"Too late," Timmy answered, stifling a yawn. "Matt's already got his hooks in him."

"*What?*"

"Guys, please!" Sean interrupted. "That's not really true, plus business first! We don't have much time before Kyle gets home! C'mon! Let's find the passage!"

As Regina rearranged the pillows the way they had been, mumbling under her breath, a chunk sounded from behind the bed as something fell to the floor. They all looked at each other, then simultaneously made a dive for it. Regina got to it first and pulled out a spiral-pad notebook, open, from under the bed.

"Gimme!" Timmy cried, making a snatch. Regina pulled it into her breast.

"Never!" she blurted. "Mine! I got here first!"

"Guys, please! Let's not pry," Sean said. "I promised myself I wouldn't snoop too much up here."

"You're right," Regina said. "I'll put it back under the pillow where it was. Lemme just take a whiff first."

She inhaled, her eyes closed, then slowly lowered the book, and all three of them gathered round to look at the open page.

"I mean, it's not really snooping if we just happen to see the page that's open, right?" Timmy asked.

There was only one long sentence written on the open page, in precise, blocky pencil, but it was circled several times in a cherry-red.

"*Dottie LaFrance has been to the Historical Society,*" Sean read aloud. "*Proclaim liberty throughout the land unto all the inhabitants thereof.*"

They all exchanged ponderous looks.

"See, I told you that Dottie chick was in on it," Regina said. "She's got a bad vibe. She's no way a real estate agent. She's after something Sean, and your cousin knows it!"

"But what?" Sean asked. "And geez, how does he know it? He's only been here two days! And what's this other stuff mean, about liberty?"

"That is the question, dude," Timmy answered, rubbing his chin.

"That's three questions," Regina told her brother, as she carefully put the notebook back where it belonged, under the pillows.

"Duh," Timmy responded. "You have a flair for the obvious, Sis."

Regina opened her mouth to retort, but before she could Sean interjected, "C'mon, time's wasting. Let's find that hidden passage! We can try to figure out what the other stuff means later."

"Can we invite Sis to our secret mission tonight?" Timmy asked.

"Oh, as if you wouldn't, now that you mentioned it," Regina answered warningly.

"Of course, of course," Sean said. "Come on."

They huddled into the closet. They took turns knocking on the walls and floors.

"Did you move this big-honkin' suitcase thingy?" Regina asked.

Sean lurched his head back.

"Duh!" Timmy laughed, seeing from Sean's expression that he hadn't. Timmy slid it back, out into the bedroom. Under the trunk was a section of old carpet, about three feet square, frayed at the edges and of a deep maroon color. It was fastened to the floor with black tacks.

"Pull it up!" Timmy squealed. Sean and Regina raced to undo the tacks, from opposite sides.

"Don't lose the tacks," Regina said excitedly. "Give 'em here."

The last tack was out. Regina wrapped them all in a wad of tissue paper, then carefully shoved the folded wad into the back pocket of her sweatpants. Sean lifted up the rug and tossed it behind him.

The floor underneath was cut into a square panel on three sides. The fourth side was hinged. Two wooden knobs were clearly meant to be pulled up.

"Oh my God!" Regina gulped.

"A trap door," Sean hissed.

"The secret passage!" Timmy blurted. "We found it!"

Sean pulled at it. The wooden flap was heavier than it looked, and Regina took the other knob as together they lifted it back, though either one could have done it on their own, albeit with a bit of a struggle.

There was a gaping black hole before them.

"My God," Regina whispered.

Three faces clustered together at the opening. An ancient smell—something like decrepit dirt—wafted upward.

A stab of light shot down between them, piercing the darkness.

They could just make out the beginning of an old wooden staircase, vanishing down into a musty black darker than ink.

CHAPTER FIFTEEN

THE CLUE IN THE TUNNEL

"Whoa!" Sean moaned, when he was finally able to speak. "Let me go get flashlights! DO NOT GO DOWN WITHOUT ME!"

"Hurry UP!" the Twins hissed—simultaneously. This kind of synchronized outburst happened so often with the Twins no one thought it odd any more. As Sean fled the room, the Twins fluctuated between their excitement—and the possibilities of bugs in this passage, and their respective moods, numbers, and appetite. Sean, hearing them, had to chuckle—neither Regina nor Timmy would ever be entomologists.

Now while it was true that—if cleanliness were a crime and Sean hanged for it, as Margaret was always saying, he would have died innocent—he did know where everything in his room was at any given moment. He was also much of the opinion that one couldn't have too many flashlights. He thundered back up the stairs a minute later, carrying seven flashlights: three black, two blue, and two yellow.

"God, you're prepared," Timmy commented, snatching the yellow one. "You stick up the hardware store?"

"Take two each, you never know," Sean said, clicking them on to test them. "Okay, listen—it's almost 12:30 now, so we have to move fast. The home football games are always over by one, so Kyle could be home any time after that."

"Yeah, but they tailgate after, with the parents and food and everything," Timmy commented. "It's the reward for anyone who suffers through one of our football games."

"You never know with Kyle," Sean answered. "He's not exactly the social butterfly type."

"Where's Uncle Justin and Margaret?" Regina asked.

"They're at the game too, then they're having mad high lunch with Professor Singleton—so they won't be home until late. Okay, we have to make this quick. I'll go first. My God, I can't believe this! It's been here all along and we never knew! Hold my light, Regina."

Sean lowered his legs down the square hole, swinging them freely through the air until they hit solid, loud-echoing wood. He discerned that he was on a somewhat wide platform, the top of the flight of stairs they had just spied a moment ago.

"Glad your tap-dancing lessons paid off, dude," Timmy said, "but do you think this is the best time?"

"I'm just trying to find out how big this platform is," Sean answered. "Okay, oh, it's easy," he added, vanishing down the hole. "There's a railing here and everything. Oh! And there's some kind of built-in ladder on the side here, against the wall!" He tapped his hand, signaling where the top of it was. "No need to jump down to the platform."

Regina came next, almost squealing with excitement, then Timmy. The Twins were still in their grass-stained athletic uniforms from this morning. Soon all three of them stood crammed together on the top landing, wide-eyed in amazement. Their searching lights showed a narrow and very steep stairway plunging down to darkness, with a wooden railing on its right side. The three sleuths' electric torches lit up a silver skyline of cobwebs, and the dank odor was overwhelming. They looked around, their mouths plopped open in shocked silence. Just seconds ago they had been in a room at Greystones, the sunlight flooding in on a typical Saturday; now—

"You should close your mouth, Bro, it makes you look dumb," Regina advised Timmy.

"And you should take your own advice, Sis," Timmy rejoined.

"Should we close the trap door behind us, do you think?" Sean wondered. "Speaking of open maws."

"No, I'd freak," Regina said. "I can't stand closed-up places."

"Me neither, dude," Timmy said. "Both of us can't, ever since we were trapped in the womb together for nine long months. Don't do it."

They both folded their arms and stared at Sean.

"That answers that, then," Sean commented. "But if Kyle comes home—"

"Oh, that's not going to happen," Regina said, with a dismissive gesture. "We won't be in here long—how far can it go?"

"Besides, the dude doesn't own it," Timmy quipped.

"Yeah, but we had to go through his bedroom to get here," Sean commented. "Major invasion of privacy, no? And I think Kyle is just starting to open up a little and trust me. Alright then, we'll just have to make sure we're in and out quick. We better go single file. I'll test each step as we move down." He grasped the railing beside them firmly, trying to rattle it. "It looks solid, but take it slow, just in case. Be careful, okay?"

"Okay, Mom."

"And we should put our phones on vibrate, just in case."

They descended. Sean checked each step before he put his weight on it. He fought the OCD urge to touch both sides of the wall.

"Step one's okay…step two's okay…" he whispered.

"Look at the footprints!" Regina cried, and it echoed wonderfully. "Sean, those aren't yours!"

Sean jumped, whacking his head on the low ceiling in the process. He turned, his hand on his heart.

"Can you not shout out like that when you have to say something please?" he asked, blanching as he did.

"Oh—sorry Sean. But look!"

Sean turned, and shone his light where Regina's was. It was true—they could all see large boot-prints trailing down the dusty stairway, which looked nothing like their own sneaker footprints.

"They're Kyle's," Sean observed, shining his light ahead of him.

"Don't smell them now, Sis," Timmy advised.

"Dry up."

"C'mon, the footsteps keep going, let's go," Sean urged, whispering still—for sounds were amplified wonderfully in the dark chamber. Every footfall—every breath—seemed to rebound off the walls.

Sean's mind was spinning—so this was the answer! Not only to how Kyle was getting out, but also to where Aunt Sadie had gone. She had to have come this way when she vanished——

A sudden thought occurred to him, and he gulped: what if they found Aunt Sadie's body down here? That would be deeply creepy—and kind of sad, too—

"Wait!" Timmy exclaimed. Regina and Sean, almost at the bottom of the stairs, both snapped around, glaring.

"My God, Timmy Quinn, don't scare us like that!" she scolded.

"Oh sorry guys—but look at this!"

Timmy was halfway down the flight, and bent over, retrieving with pincer-fingers something between the stairway and wall.

"What's that?" Regina asked.

"A wicked old newspaper," Timmy hissed. Sean and Regina climbed up to Timmy's stair, all three cramming together on the same step. Timmy, holding the paper in both hands, blew off a blanket of dust, and they all read *WAR IS DECLARED!* on the thin yellowed paper, which was somewhat mealy in texture. Underneath this bold headline were others:

LINCOLN CALLS FOR VOLUNTEERS;

A PROCLAMATION;

THE ATTACK ON FT. SUMTER.

"Oh. My. God," Regina said. "This is the start of the Civil War!"

"*Harpers Weekly*, April 27, 1861," Sean read aloud from the top of the page, in a reverential hush.

"Wow," Timmy murmured. "I bet'cha this is worth a couple of bucks. How much, do you think?"

"Really? Is that all you can think of a time like this?" Regina accused. "My God! This is like—this is like holding history in our hands! Think of the people who touched this paper, and read it, and freaked out as they did! This has a proclamation in it from the man who was president then—*Abraham Lincoln.*"

A hush fell among them.

"Where exactly did you get this, Timmy?" Sean asked.

"Right under the stairs here," Timmy answered, shining his light behind and below them. "I already checked, there's nothing else there."

"Maybe it fell out of an old scrapbook that's somewhere else," Regina commented. "My God, I have goose bumps."

"Me too," Sean said. He felt he had entered not only a secret passage to another space, but to another time. "Okay, we can look at it later. Set it down for now Timmy and we'll get it on the way back. The Historical Society should get that."

"The who?" Timmy asked.

"Don't tell me you never heard of the Nawshant Historical Society!" Sean chided, winking at Regina.

"What ARE they teaching you at that school?" Regina mumbled.

They resumed their single-file descent along the narrow steep stairway. Sean noticed occasional rusty hooks on the wall, big ones—he wondered if they were made to hold lanterns or something. They reached the landing at the bottom—a flat platform of plain, unvarnished planks, about four feet square, identical to the first platform. The stairs turned and continued down.

"There's another flight," Regina announced.

"I bet this is my bedroom right here, or actually, my bathroom," Sean whispered, rapping lightly on the walls. "If we had more time, I'd have one of you knock while I raced around and listened."

"It must be," Regina said.

"You been in his bathroom that many times?" Timmy teased.

"No more than you."

"There's no connector anyway going from there to here," Sean said, examining the walls closely with his light. "It's all sealed up." He turned and flashed his light down the next set of stairs, then Regina joined him on the platform, then Timmy. They could see another landing way below them, also thick with dust—and Kyle's boot-prints. The festoons of cobwebs were even thicker and more numerous here.

"God, Margaret would have twenty field days in here, cleaning all this," Regina observed.

"Okay, let's keep going," Sean said. "Watch out for the cobwebs. One's okay…two's okay...three's okay….hold up!" he suddenly hissed. "Step four here is broken!"

"Careful!" Regina shouted.

Sean, putting his weight against the wall, put his right foot at the very edge of the broken plank, then descended to the next step. He turned, and shone his light on the clean break. With his other hand he reached out for Regina's hand, then Timmy's, and helped them over.

"I think your cousin broke this one," Timmy said, once he was over. "Look! The break is fresh, and you can see half a boot-print on either side of the break."

"Thank God he didn't hurt himself!" Regina sighed.

"You're right Timmy, look," Sean said, flashing the light to the wall beside them. There amidst the dust and scattering spiders they could clearly see a few smeary hand-marks, where Kyle—no doubt frantically— had tried to regain his balance.

"Wow, he was brave to come down here all by himself," Regina commented. Sean and Timmy rolled their eyes at each other, even though they each secretly agreed with Regina. "By the way, any of these spiders poisonous, do you think?"

"Uhm....ahhh," Sean vacillated.

"What he's saying Sis is, do you want the truth, or a nice lie."

"Well, uhm…there are only two poisonous spiders in our area," Sean explained. "The Black Widow, and the Brown Recluse. But they're pretty rare, and they only bite people if you invade their space."

"Oh. Like we're doing now, you mean?" Regina asked, cringing down to avoid yet another dangling cobweb, while Timmy rapidly wiped off the sleeves of his lacrosse shirt, making little mumbly frantic noises.

They reached the next landing without further incident. Again there was a turn, and before them, another flight of stairs, the third one thus far. This time no landing could be seen at the bottom, just a rumpled earthen floor. Halfway down the stairway the wooden walls became replaced by round gray-and-sand colored boulders.

"My God, where's this go to, China?" Timmy said.

"This must be the Snuggery now," Sean said, lightly rapping on the wall at the landing. "No connection here either. And now," he continued, carefully descending the next seven steps—each flight thus far had had twelve steps—"we must be past the basement. We're underground now."

"I always wanted to be an underground artist," Timmy said.

"You won't be a stand-up comic, anyway," Regina observed.

They slowed down and touched the smooth boulders. It grew decidedly colder, danker.

"Oh my God," Sean said. He had reached the bottom of the stairs, and was shining his light before him. The Twins quickly caught up.

They found themselves at the head of a long, somewhat low tunnel, with stone-wall sides, and a planked ceiling supported by occasional beams of thick wood that resembled unfinished trunks more than lumber. Here and there they could see large outcroppings of ledge, and the tunnel twisted and turned to accommodate these, and then vanished around a particularly wide bend about thirty yards ahead.

"It must have taken an army of people to do this," Regina commented, when she could speak again. "Wow, I am really impressed! This feels like a dream, doesn't it?"

"To think this has been here all along, and we never knew it!" Timmy whispered. "I read somewhere that when pirates dug tunnels to hide their treasure in, they killed the people who dug it for them, once the work was through. Dead men tell no tales!"

"This is no pirate tunnel," Regina scoffed, looking around as she said it.

"This is where Aunt Sadie went when she disappeared—I know it," Sean hissed. "You don't think—do you think her body is down here, speaking of bodies?"

They exchanged glances.

"Only one way to find out, I guess," Regina answered.

"I'm kind of twisted around," Timmy said as they slowly progressed. "What direction are we headed in, do you think?"

"It's really disorienting down here," Sean agreed. "You can understand now how people get all messed up and lost in caves and old mines. But if I had to guess, I'd say we were headed out back, behind the house."

"Towards our house, yeah, I agree," Regina murmured.

Their amazement grew with every step.

Turning a bend in the tunnel where a gargantuan boulder sat, they saw that the tunnel went on, and on again.

They began to find things—setting on the rocky ground, or leaning up against the cave-like walls: several very thick bottles, their glass a light green in color and their bottoms rounded; a smooth wooden stick or club of some kind, which they eventually decided was the handle of an ancient pick-ax; several stout branches, about 18 inches long, with their ends charred and burned; and the body of a bird, so old and dried out it looked mummified.

"I think it's a swallow," Sean said, leaning down to examine it more closely. "He must have flown in and couldn't get out."

"The poor thing!" Regina gushed.

"There's got to be a way out, then," Timmy commented.

"Hey, these were torches," Sean said, picking up one of the thick branches and examining it. "This is some kind of pine—*Pinus resinosa*, by the looks of it, which they used in the old days for torches since it has so much resin in it."

"You sound like Uncle Justin now," Regina smiled.

"I guess some of it had to rub off," Sean admitted with a chuckle. "That's the red pine, and really easy to identify."

"Yeah, if you're a Brainiac," Timmy commented.

"Do you still think we're heading out back?" Sean asked, turning to Regina. "We've been going a ways. We're off our property now."

"I don't know," Regina answered, shaking her head and looking around. "There's been so many twists and turns. I can't believe this! But wasn't Greystones bigger in the old days? Didn't you say our house used to be the stables, and where the groom lived and everything?"

"That's right," Sean agreed. "Greystones went all the way to the ocean in two directions in the old days. I wonder if—God, that would be wild if it ended up going all the way to the shore."

"Guys, not to change the subject, but we could have like intense parties down here!" Timmy exclaimed. "This could be like party central!"

This time Regina and Sean rolled their eyes at each other.

"Well don't break out the togas yet," Regina cautioned.

"What?" Timmy asked. "Tell me we couldn't! We could hang the walls with torches, and people could come dressed all Goth like, and then—holy—!"

This time Timmy, as well as Sean, forgot about the Seven Deadly Words; for they had just turned a corner—they were walking three abreast now—and there, in front of them at another twist in the tunnel, and painted on a massive piece of smooth ledge, were words—some kind of message in big bold foot-high letters. They scurried forward to read the two lines sprawled across the massive boulder:

PROCLAIM LIBERTY THROUGHOUT THE LAND
TO ALL THE INHABITANTS THEREOF

"My God," Regina said. "That message again. What Kyle wrote."

This was no piece of idle graffiti: the words had been painted in blue, with maroon shadowing, and each letter was fancy with filigrees and serifs. The faded state of the letters told that this was no recent work.

"That's Bookman Old Style," Regina pronounced in a whisper, running her hand along one of the letters.

"Popular during the Civil War," Timmy added.

"How do you know that?" Sean asked.

"Summer school last year," Regina answered. "The Museum School, a graphic arts class. We had to learn font types by heart. *They're the tools of our trade!*"

Timmy laughed in remembrance, as obviously Regina's last words were in imitation of their instructor. "It's really easy to identify."

"Yeah, if you're a Brainiac. But what do the words mean?" Sean wondered aloud. "I know them from somewhere."

"Kyle's notebook," Regina said.

"Duh," Timmy said.

"Well, yeah," Sean agreed, "but somewhere else too. They're kind of ringing a bell but I can't put my finger on it."

Regina stared at Sean, her eyebrows scrunching.

"I know what you mean," she agreed finally, saying the words slowly. She tucked some of her hair behind her ear. "Ringing a bell—"

"Look!" Timmy hissed. Sean and Regina both jumped, then rushed over to where Timmy was standing. His flashlight was pointed at the last letter of the last word. Beneath this they could clearly see three small initials, painted in simpler blue lettering: *PJQ*.

But it was what was painted on the smooth rock beside the initials that made Sean's heart leap up: a bell, about four inches square.

"Oh my God," Regina whispered.

"Wait a minute!" Sean said, "wait a minute!" He turned and fled back down the tunnel in the direction they had come.

"Where you going, dude?" Timmy called out.

"We should all stick together!" Regina cried, but Sean wasn't listening.

The Twins gave chase, their beams of light flashing helter-skelter. They found Sean around the next bend, furiously shining his light back and forth on another piece of exposed ledge.

"What are you doing, dude?" Timmy asked.

"I know I saw it, I swear I did," Sean was mumbling. "Yes! Here!"

The Twins rushed over and saw what Sean was looking at: another bell painted onto the rock, again in blue, and the same size as the first one they had just recently discovered back at the big letters.

"I knew I saw a flash of blue back here, but it didn't register," Sean explained. "I just thought it was a shadow or something. Plus I was so anxious to see where the tunnel went I didn't think more about it."

"Well we still haven't figured that out," Timmy commented. "Where the tunnel goes. And we don't have much time—"

"There's another one over here!" Regina cried, and Sean and Timmy turned to see Regina back at the next turn, toward Greystones. They hurried over and saw the same type of bell, again painted in blue.

"Look, and there's another!" Sean said, and, sure enough, there was another bell, this time on the opposite wall, and behind them twenty feet in the direction they had come. "I bet we passed about a dozen of them on the way—they're all over the place!"

"But what do they mean?" Timmy asked. "Taco Bell next exit?"

"They must be some kind of sign," Regina said.

"Of course!" Sean added. "Duh! This was probably originally made for the Underground Railroad, to show people where to go, like blaze marks along a trail. They probably used this passage to usher people on to the next stop, in case Greystones was being watched."

"Why would anyone watch Greystones?" Regina wondered.

"It was against the law to hide a runaway slave after 1850," Sean explained. "And since Aunt Sadie was a well-known Abolitionist, it would make sense to watch her. She was one of the founding members of the Boston Female Anti-Slave Society."

"Sounds like an awesome name for a band," Timmy said. "I'd check them out for sure! But none of these other bells have the initials. What were they again, *PFQ*?"

"*PJQ*," Regina answered. "I remember only because I was thinking they were Great Uncle Paul's initials. Paul Quinn, dad's uncle."

"PJQ must've been the guy who painted the words back there on the wall," Sean mused. "Whoever he was. He wasn't a Sutherland."

"Or the woman who painted them," Regina added.

"Right, or the woman. But it does make sense to have bells showing the way to freedom. You know, like Liberty Bells and all that."

Regina's head snapped up and she stared oddly at Sean.

"What are you saying, Great Uncle Paul painted those words and these bells?" Timmy joked.

"Oh my God, I've got it!" Regina cried out loud, putting both hands on her head. "I can't believe how dense we've been! Oh my God! Could it be true? Timmy, do you remember when we went to Phila—"

But at the same instant Sean wheeled around behind them. He raised a cautionary finger, then hissed, "Quiet! What was that?"

They froze at the noises, clearly coming from above them.

CHAPTER SIXTEEN
THE FACE IN THE TUNNEL

Their eyes darted back to the Greystones' end of the tunnel. They all heard the next sound: a door closing, and what sounded like feet walking around: the noise was muffled. Instinctively Sean and the Twins cowered together in a half-crouching knot.

"Oh my God," Sean moaned. "The tunnel must act like some kind of echo-chamber—someone just came into my house!"

"Kyle!" Regina whispered. She clapped a hand on her mouth.

"What do we do?" Sean asked. Everyone had deer-in-the-headlights eyes.

"C'mon c'mon, we have to think of something fast!" Timmy said. "We can't stay crouched here like Charlie's Angels."

"I'll distract him!" Regina blurted. "Tell me what to do!"

"Alright, alright," Sean panted, trying to think of something. "Get... go up to his room fast as ever—you've got to beat him up there. Shut the trap door, then put his suitcase back and shut the closet door and lock it—I left the key on top of his desk. Then put the key in the third drawer of his desk, that's crucial. The *third* drawer. Then if you have time, sneak down to my room. Wait there until he starts coming up the stairs to the second floor. Then go to him—tell him you were looking for me, and waiting for me cuz you heard I'm sick. Ask him if he knows where I am."

"Then tell him I must've come by and taken Sean out, to…to get medicine or something," Timmy blurted.

"Okay, okay," Regina said, tucking hanks of nervous hair behind her ears. They all started moving as quickly and noiselessly as possible down the tunnel. "Third drawer down, third drawer down. Oh God, I've got to tack the rug back on the floor too!"

"I forgot about that!" Sean rasped. "Hurry! But be quiet!"

"Don't worry," Timmy counseled, patting Sean's shoulder as Regina tore off. "She's an awesome sneak when she needs to be."

"Don't explore the end of the tunnel without me!" Regina hissed back, as she vanished around the last bend.

Sean and Timmy trotted after her, their ears pricked. They reached the bottom of the stairs just as Regina reached the top. They strained to hear any sounds coming from above—they needed to know where Kyle was now.

"C'mon, Regina, c'mon Regina," Sean whispered, his pulse thudding in his ears. He clasped his hands together.

They heard some kind of *whoosh* above them and off to the side—again, the sound was muffled, but unmistakable.

"Water," Sean said.

"A toilet flushing?"

"Right," Sean agreed. "Thank God he had to go."

"You never read about the Hardy Boys having to go," Timmy said. He was silent for a moment then whispered, "Or, really, any detectives for that matter. *While Holmes took fingerprints, I myself rushed behind a large Hydrangea, as I had to take a furious—*"

"Hardy Boys!" Sean cautioned lowly. "And don't make me laugh! Plus I don't think literature would be improved by a recital of bodily—"

A glob of dull light from the stairway way above them was rubbed out, like a cloud passing over the moon.

"Regina's shutting the trap door," Sean whispered. "Now she must be putting the tacks back in the rug."

Timmy whispered, "C'mon, Reggie, go, go!"

"She hates it when anyone calls her Reggie," Sean murmured.

"Duh," Timmy whispered, "she can't hear me now, dude."

Sean thought it better to make no response.

Next they heard footsteps, walking around—directly overhead.

"He's in the hall now," Sean mumbled into Timmy's ear, so quietly he could barely hear the words himself. They were still pressed together in consternation. Despite the dampness and chill, Sean could feel sweat collecting under his arms. "Okay, go out in the kitchen, Kyle—you gotta be hungry after the butt-whopping you must've just got."

As if in answer to Sean's plea, they heard Kyle's light but firm tread travel off to the left—toward the kitchen. Timmy and Sean exchanged noiseless high-fives—there *might* be a chance they wouldn't be caught. The footsteps traipsed back and forth, back and forth. Each second delivered more hope. From far above on the other side, they barely heard a soft but certain click echoing down the stairs—Regina had just locked the closet door! Another silent high five was exchanged.

"We're good, I think," Sean whispered into Timmy's ear. "Just another minute—"

But then Kyle's footsteps grew louder. They passed directly over them: not four feet, Sean guessed, above their heads. A light sprinkling of dust filtered down onto them—Sean and Timmy looked desperately at each other—Kyle had left the kitchen and was making his way out to the main hall, to the stairway!

"Stall him!" Timmy hissed, clawing Sean's sleeve in his frantic state. "Call him on his cell!"

"I don't know the number!" Sean whispered back.

They clutched each other in alarm as they heard the steady thumping of feet as Kyle ascended the stairs up to the second floor.

"Too late!" Sean cried. "Not enough time! He'll definitely catch Regina in his bedroom—and how's she ever going to explain *that*?"

There followed a long delay; they strained, and heard footsteps sounding very far away.

"He's going down to my room, probably to see how I'm feeling," Sean cringed. "Great! Just when we were starting to get along a little. He'll never forgive me."

A moment later the sound of someone climbing stairs was repeated, but this time duller, less distinct—Kyle was now on the stairway leading from the second to the third floor.

"We might as well go up and face the music," Timmy sighed.

"No, wait," Sean answered. "Just in case, wait a minute. We can get up there fast enough if we have to come to her rescue—let's just wait."

But even as Sean said the words, they both moved up the first few steps of the staircase—it could only be a matter of minutes now.

The seconds plopped by, torturously slow. Sean and Timmy were frozen, waiting for the other shoe to drop. But nothing happened.

Still they waited. Sean took his phone out and marked the time. A minute went by, then another. They looked at each other in confusion, mixed with a bit of cautious relief.

More minutes crawled by; then more still. They relaxed their hold on one another.

"Why's nothing happened yet?" Sean whispered.

"Dunno," Timmy said. "But no news is good news, right? She must have hidden herself somewhere. She's wicked crafty like that. Remember how she'd always win hide-and-seek?"

"Right, right." Sean consulted his cell phone again. "Okay, it's been… ten and a half minutes since Kyle went up to the third floor. You'd think if he was going to catch her, he would've by now."

"I hope. So…what do we do now?"

"I dunno. I guess we wait."

"For what?"

"Well…" Sean's whisper trailed off. *For what* was right.

"We can't get out this way," Timmy said, nodding up the stairs, "until your cousin leaves his room—and even if he does—"

"The closet door's locked," Sean remembered.

"Bingo. So we have to wait until he leaves, and Regina gets the key again."

"What if he doesn't leave?" Sean asked.

"Don't ask me!" Timmy hissed. "He's your cousin!"

"What's that supposed to mean?"

"It means *I'm confused*, dude, and starting to get a little claustropho-bic, that's what it means! You know I freak in closed spaces!"

"Alright, chill dude, we can always go out the other way. Bah!"

Just then Sean jumped and let out a cry—but it was only his cell phone, vibrating away in his hand.

"Sorry, just my phone," he said to a panicked-looking Timmy.

"It's Regina!" Timmy hissed.

"No, it's…I don't…I don't think I know this number…and yet-"

"Answer it! Have them send help! Money, guns and lawyers!"

They trotted back down the tunnel to get further out of earshot. They passed the first bend, then the second, and third. On the fourth vibration Sean answered and whispered, "Hello?"

"Sean?"

"Yeah?"

"It's me."

Sean couldn't place the voice, though it was somewhat familiar—but whoever it was, they sounded upset.

"Ahhh…who's me?" Sean asked in mumble.

"Kevin, up the library. Why are you whispering?"

"Oh, uhm, I'll explain later Kev. But why are you—you sound a little messed up."

Kevin let out a deep sigh.

"I am. In fact I'm very messed up. I can't talk long—the police are on the way. As soon as they get here I'll have to go."

"The *police*?"

"We won't be getting the painting cleaned, Sean," Kevin said, and his voice shook as he said it.

"Why not?"

"The painting was stolen. Last night or early this morning."

"Wha—who..."

"It's gone, Sean."

"Holy—God, Kevin! I can't believe this!"

"I can't either. Listen Sean, I'm just going to ask you this once." Kevin sounded more serious than Sean could recall. "I'm not going to tell the police you wanted to have it cleaned, because then that involves you, and I'm sure the FBI will be involved before too long, as the painting is worth about ten million."

"*Ten million*?" Timmy's eyebrows leapt up at Sean's words.

"At least. So everyone who works here will be suspected. But anyway, let me get this over with—I *know* you didn't, and I'm sorry—but I just need to ask—you didn't have anything to do with this, right? Or know anything about it?"

Sean was taken aback—still, he could see Kevin's position.

"No, Kev." Sean swallowed. "I swear on my parents' graves."

"That's good enough for me, Sean. Okay, cops here, gotta run."

Sean felt like he'd been whacked on the back of the head with a 2 x 4 as he hung up. This whole time Timmy had been plucking at his sleeve, asking interruptive questions to the point where Sean had to finally push him off, as the go-away waves weren't doing it.

"What?" Timmy asked. "What was all that about ten million?"

"The painting's been stolen—the one of my Aunt Sadie up at the library? I just called Kevin an hour ago because I was going to have it cleaned, because there's a rendering of the bell in the painting, though you can't see it anymore because the painting's all dark with age."

Timmy's eyes grew bug-wide.

"Holy...! That's the same bell she had moved from right off Third Cliff, right?"

"Yeah—but whether it's the same one that's ringing now, I don't know. Timmy, Kevin told me the painting is worth...*ten million.*"

Timmy put a hand behind his back as he slowly lowered down into a sitting position on the dirt-and-rock tunnel floor.

"My God," he gasped. "Dude...you mean...you don't mean that's an *original* Sargent? I always thought it was a copy!"

"Maybe a lot of people did, which is why it was safe up there—until now. No, it's the original, the real deal. My family gave it to the library about a hundred years ago."

"Dude, a Sargent just sold for $24 million like a year ago—even Ms. Daniels doesn't know that's an original, I bet." This was the head of the Art Department at Nawshant High School. "I mean...my God, dude, I can't tell you how many times I've looked at that painting over the years. It's kind of like an unprovocative *Madame X.*"

"Whatever that is," Sean commented vaguely, his mind reeling. He plopped down beside Timmy on the cold and bumpy dirt floor.

"What are they teaching you in that school?" Timmy joked. "*Madame X,* by Sargent, is one of the 'BIPs' of the world—that's Big Important Paintings. It's a full length portrait of a woman—this New Orleans-born high society babe named Madame Pierre Gautreau, born Judith... Judith...Avegno. It shocked the French so much, Sargent had to screw out of Paris after it was exhibited at the Salon in 1884."

"What was it, a nude?"

"No—though the almost strapless dress was part of the problem. It's the way she's depicted—probably the way she was in real life—larger than life, sexy, rich—and just dripping with attitude—disdainful of the *hoi polloi.* Character, clothes, and soul, that's Sargent. There's even a rumor Madame X's profile is really that of a hottie guy Sargent knew. You knew he was gay, right?"

"Ahhh…no," Sean said carefully.

"Oh sure. Sure he was! So was Leonardo, and Michelangelo, Caravaggio, oh and Warhol, and Hockney of course…should I go on?"

"Oh no, no need to wear yourself out," Sean said carelessly.

"Oh, okay. I just don't want you to feel bad about being gay."

"Who says…who says I feel bad?" Sean blurted. "And who even says I am?"

"Ssssh! Well that's just it, you shouldn't feel bad! But Regina's really the one you should talk to about Sargent. She knows a lot more about him than I do. Hey, didn't you say Dottie LaFrance was snooping around this morning, looking for that letter Sargent wrote?"

"I did. That's *exactly* what I said."

"Do you think she's behind this?"

"I dunno," Sean said slowly. "At first I was thinking yes—but now it's like—I don't know. Would she still be around town snooping this morning if she stole it last night?"

"Maybe she wouldn't," Timmy said. He thought for a minute. "But if she was the one who stole the painting, she's probably on her way to Asia or Saudi Arabia or something by now. To a private buyer, I mean. They're the only ones that would touch something like that."

Sean turned and looked Timmy in the eye.

"How do you know all this?"

"Because I'm an *artiste*! It's my *thing*, man."

"Shhh!" Sean hissed, "not so loud!"

"Sorry, dude. It's just my passion. It's like you and—you and…ahhh…"

"Solving mysteries," Sean pronounced. "And skateboarding."

"Right, that's what I was trying to think of."

Just then Sean jumped once more—though not as much this time. It was his phone again. This time it was Miss Sawyer.

"Hello?" Sean murmured.

"Oh Sean, it sounds like you've just woken up, and I am sorry to bother you—but have you heard the *dreadful* news?"

"Yeah, I just did, Miss Sawyer."

"Well I've just got off the phone with the state police—they're running the investigation until the FBI arrives—demanding that they seal the Commonwealth's borders!" she wailed, so loudly that even Timmy next to Sean recoiled a bit. "Oh Sean! How *ghastly!* I always said we needed a modern security system at our library! And now…now our treasure is gone!" Miss Sawyer broke down crying—and Sean felt genuinely warmed. She really cared about Nawshant: its people, flora and fauna, art, and quality of life.

"There there, Miss Sawyer, don't worry, I'm sure we'll get it back," Sean soothed. "Did you…happen to tell the state police that…uhm … people…were inquiring about Aunt Sadie's papers and everything?" Sean sure hoped Kyle didn't get dragged into the investigation—or himself for that matter.

"I most certainly *did not!*" Miss Sawyer briskly sniffed. "Sean, rule number one when dealing with Official Authorities: *never* volunteer information. Wait, I say, until one is asked. That is my motto!"

"Oh, that's wise," Sean sighed, in relief for his and Kyle's sake.

"However," she quickly added, "I'm afraid I *did* happen to let spill from my lips the fact that that…*termagant*, Doughty Au Canada was, *just* this morning, searching for a letter Sargent wrote *about that very same painting*. I suppose it was the state of shock I was in that made me so indiscreet."

Here Miss Sawyer cleared her throat pompously.

"No doubt," Sean said, trying not to laugh.

"Yes. Anyway Sean, as a member of the Sutherland Family—the same family that was generous enough to donate this priceless work to the Nawshant Public Library—let me express my condolences. Now, not to change the subject, but when *is* your chum coming up to cut my grass?"

Now it was Sean's turn to recoil from the phone.

"Oh, here he is right now, Miss Sawyer," Sean explained, shoving the phone at Timmy, who wasn't quick enough in getting away.

"Oh, *hi, Miss Sawyer!*" Timmy beamed, while at the same time he was shaking his fist at Sean. "Yes, I most definitely will be up soon—I'm just... just a little stuck right now in a...uhm...chore, like. I won't be too long! Okay, bye! You're welcome!"

Timmy wheeled on Sean.

"Great! How the frig am I supposed to get up there now?" he hissed. "I could use the money too!"

"You'll have to get up there," Sean replied. "She'll turn us both into mulch if you don't."

"Well then..." Timmy said, and they both looked down the other end of the tunnel. "I think we should head off and go out the other way."

"Maybe," Sean said. "I just hope Regina's okay. But Timmy, what if there's no other end?"

Timmy's eyes popped. "There must—you trying to freak me out?"

"As if! No, what I mean is what if the other end has been...well, like long-sealed up or something. Would you freak?"

"Freak? Oh God no. I'd just run back screaming to your cousin's closet and kick the friggin' door down. But no, I wouldn't freak."

"Well, that's good to know," Sean answered dryly.

"But you're spewing nonsense, dude. Remember, this is how your cousin's been getting out—so of course it has to lead *somewhere*."

"Duh," Sean laughed, smacking his forehead. "Why didn't I think of that?"

"I dunno—maybe there's not enough oxygen down here or something. You know what? I think we should call Regina and see what the heck's going on. Dude, thank God you told us to put our phones on vibrate. How'd you know?"

"ESP, I guess," Sean said, as humbly as he could. "Maybe it runs in the family."

"Extra Smelly Pits, right. C'mon, let's call her."

"Are you sure?" Sean asked. "Did you really think her phone's on vibrate?"

"I saw her do it."

"Okay, call."

"Why do you sound so bummed now?" Timmy asked.

"Oh, I really wanted us to solve this ourselves," Sean groaned. "Now like the state police and FBI are coming in, and I *know* the art heist has something to do with the mystery of the bells—I know it!"

"Your ESP again?" Timmy teased. "Maybe that's what you should call your detective business someday—*ESP Consultants: Guessing the Solution to Your Mysteries for the Past Ten Years.*"

Sean shoved Timmy away as they both laughed.

"Don't worry, Sean-dude. Even if it is all connected, and even if the big dogs solve it—it's not like this'll be the last mystery on earth."

"True," Sean admitted, feeling marginally better.

"And either way," Timmy continued, pausing dramatically until Sean looked at him, "I'll still be your best friend."

"Oh, get out of town!" Sean laughed. "Okay, call her."

Sean held his breath as Timmy called Regina. Almost immediately she picked it up.

"Yea," Timmy said. "Yea. Okay. I dunno. I dunno. Yea. No. Okay. I gotta cut Miss Sawyer's lawn and I'm almost freakin' cuz we're trapped down here. Yea. Yea. Okay. Good luck. Call me as soon as you can, if something changes. Love you, later."

"Well?" Sean hissed, grabbing Timmy by the forearm as they both stood up.

"She thinks Kyle went out, but she's not sure."

"Out? We didn't hear anything."

"Yeah, but maybe he snuck out, she's sure he did. He hasn't been in his room for half an hour."

"Where is she?"

"Under the dude's bed."

"Under his bed?"

"That's all she could do. He was coming up the stairs when she was ready to go down them to your room."

"Good grief, what a nightmare," Sean groaned. "What else?"

"She said if we tried to find a way out in the other direction, she'll only hate us for a year instead of forever."

"That's good of her. What's she going to do?"

"She's gonna sit tight for a bit yet. She thinks we ought to try to get out the other end, and then come back into the house through the front door and make sure Kyle's really gone. Then she can come out. After, of course, a few more sniffs of his pillow."

"Okay. Well then—let's go."

In walking away from the stairs to take Sean's calls, the boys had come almost to the Writing on the Wall, so they rounded the next bend and there were the words again.

"It seemed longer the first time," Timmy observed.

"Really," Sean agreed. But they slowed down again once they came to *terra nova*. After two more bends—one immediately after the other, and both trending right—they came to the longest straight stretch thus far—some thirty yards in length, they guessed.

"Amazing," Sean muttered. His respect for, and attachment to, Aunt Sadie swelled exponentially—what a woman she had been, of conviction, dreams, and determination, to plan and oversee this prodigious work— all so the marginalized might be free.

"Listen!" Sean said as they rounded the bend at the end of the long stretch. They both stopped, and strained to listen

"My God!" Timmy hissed, a smile of amazement lighting up his face and his green eyes blazing. "The ocean!"

"Where's it coming from, exactly?" Sean asked.

But it was hard to say—nowhere and everywhere.

They moved along, and the sound slowly ebbed away. By this time the color of the bedrock walls had changed—no longer were they gray and white; they were reddish grey and brown now—like the stones and cliffs along the eastern shore of Nawshant.

"Oh yeah, we're getting close to the ocean," Sean mumbled. "As the sound of it indicated a minute ago." He said the words as lowly as he could, for a strange feeling—of apprehension and lurking danger—was beginning to creep over him. He tried to shake it off.

He slowed as they approached the next bend.

"What's up?" Timmy whispered, turning to him. They were back to whispering again.

"I don't know," Sean said, dropping his voice further. "I...I just have this funny feeling." He stopped moving altogether. He beckoned Timmy closer with a wave, and leaned into his ear.

"Call me crazy but I'd just feel safer if we went round the next bend real slow. I got this weird feeling something's there. And shut off your light. I think we'll be able to see a little without them. I just have intense heebie-jeebies all of a sudden."

Timmy made a face, but complied.

The flashlights went off. At first it was indeed pitch—but shortly their eyes adjusted, and they could see just enough to proceed at a snail's pace. The odor of dank dampness grew, and now the reek was tinged with the unmistakable aroma of the sea. They reached the edge of the bend, and Sean stopped again, shaking his head.

"What do you think it is?" Timmy whispered.

"I don't know," Sean shrugged. "Let's wait another minute before we go round the corner here."

They did, their hearts beating in rapid tandem. As time went on Sean's ominous dread swelled. When he felt he couldn't take it anymore, he tugged Timmy by the elbow, leading him on.

They came to the corner. They leaned against the damp cold stone and inched their faces round the bend of bedrock. They waited for their eyes to adjust.

After a minute of dread, they could just barely discern that—amazingly—the tunnel split at the next bend, some twenty feet away. The extension of the tunnel to the left was utterly dark, and its gaping black maw seemed deeply scary and nasty, as if a river of unseen black creepiness were oozing from it. The part of the tunnel that went to the right had just the slightest dull glow to it, as if infinitesimal chinks of light were coming through, further along. It was by this vague light that they could see—again, just barely—a large object leaning against the opposite wall of the tunnel, some ten feet away. Although there were still some rocks on the floor of the tunnel, there was now sand mixed in as well.

They jumped into each other when they saw the object and, unfortunately, Timmy dropped his flashlight in his panic. It wasn't a cheap plastic model but a heavy metal and rubber affair, and it clanged something fierce as it bounced and rolled along the rocky floor before finally coming to a rest. The noise of it seemed like a thunderclap as it clanged and echoed all around them.

The sudden silence that followed seemed beyond eerie.

"Sorry," Timmy whispered.

Sean shrugged. His heart was still thudding up by his throat somewhere. They did nothing for another minute, and found that they had clutched on to each other again.

"What do you think it is?" Timmy finally asked, tossing his head toward the object against the wall ahead.

"I'm not sure," Sean whispered back. "Whatever it is, it's big. It's not alive, anyway."

Sean was convinced—he didn't want to share this with Timmy yet—

that it was some kind of sepulcher, a grave or monument, for his Aunt Sadie. He pictured a great stone slab, and Aunt Sadie's now dried and desiccated body lying atop it, skeletal hands clutching dead flowers. And perhaps her ghost floating around it! Goosebumps rose on his neck and arms, and he felt as he had when he was a child, and lost in the woods—he wanted to run home and hide under the covers. But, of course, his curiosity would never hear of that.

"I'm going to shine the light on it now," Sean said, so lowly into Timmy's ear that he had to repeat the words twice. He gulped. "If anything happens, we'll just book it back to the stairs as fast as we can. Ready?"

Timmy nodded, taking a deep breath as he did.

"On the count of three then…one…two…*three*."

The light came on and sliced across the dark, dank air.

A face jumped back at them.

Sean's worst fears had come true—it was the ghost of Aunt Sadie! There was a loud ringing in his ear, and his vision began swimming. But even as it did, something else told him that this was not the case—there was something too reflective, too artificial, about the face. At the same time Timmy grabbed onto Sean again and gasped out loud. He turned to run, but before he could Sean grabbed back and held tight. "No, look!" he cried.

It was, indeed, the face of Aunt Sadie…as John Singer Sargent had depicted it. It was the stolen portrait, still in its tarnished gilt frame, leaning against the stone wall, a few thick blankets at its feet.

"Oh my God," Sean gasped loudly. "It's here!" He wasn't sure he felt relief, or greater shock.

"Uh-oh," Timmy murmured in a nervous pant, looking around in panic. "Dude—nobody leaves a ten-million-dollar painting just hanging around. I think we're in deep do-do."

"You can say that again," a strange male voice said, coming from the darkness beyond the painting.

CHAPTER SEVENTEEN

LIGHT AT THE END OF THE TUNNEL

Now it was Sean's turn to drop his flashlight in panic—just when it would have been handy, to see who the stranger in the tunnel might be. Perversely, now that they had been discovered, his flashlight plunked to the sandy ground with a quick, almost noiseless thud, and the darkness swallowed up the sound. They were plunged into a sudden, terrifying darkness—not that they weren't terrified already.

Immediately a blinding light knifed into their eyes, as whoever was standing behind the painting blasted his own flashlight in their faces. Timmy cried out, but Sean didn't notice Timmy's violation of the Seven Deadly Words rule—because he was breaking it himself.

Now, Sean had never considered himself brave—if anything, quite the contrary. Later, when he thought about what he did next, he always attributed his behavior to his fear, rather than some kind of heroism. After all, what if this stranger had a gun? As difficult as life was at this current instant, Sean had no desire to leave it just yet.

So—hardly knowing where the idea came from, but going with his instincts—he shoved Timmy away with a suddenness and strength that surprised them both. Sean scooted down in the other direction and scrambled into the darkness, figuring the stranger's flashlight could only cover one of them at a time. He prayed he wouldn't bash his face against the stone wall.

"Hey!" a voice cried, but at the same time Sean scooped up a clump of sand and flung it, aiming just above where the flashlight was shining. He was targeting the eyes of their assailant—

But instead he apparently got the stranger in the mouth. The tunnel was instantly filled with a choking, coughing sound that bounced off the walls horribly. At the same time Sean cried, "Get 'im now, Timmy!" The two of them leapt on the coughing stranger, knocking their assailant to the ground. Oddly, the stranger offered no resistance whatsoever, even when his coughing subsided. Sean quickly pinned down the person by sitting on their stomach, while Timmy held one of the assailant's arms back. Weirdly, for the second time today, Sean felt a bolt of…well, it was almost like electricity—jigging through him. It must have been his nerves, Sean half-thought—but he was almost beyond thoughts, and his jagged pulse was coming in crazy thuds.

Sean grabbed the stranger's flashlight lying on the ground, then blared it on the person's face.

"H'it's me!" Kyle sang cheerily, in his little Southern accent.

"You!" Sean panted. His surprise knew no end. "You!"

"Mind if I get up now?" he asked politely. "I'm a mite sore from the game s'morning."

Sean rolled off his cousin. Kyle got up, then wiped sand from his mouth with a crisp handkerchief he took from his back pocket.

"Huh. James Mason used that trick in *Journey to the Center of the Earth*," Kyle commented. "I had disremembered that."

"Hey! That's my word!" Timmy protested.

"*That's* what made me do it, probably," Sean said, ignoring Timmy. "A bourgeois trick, I think his enemy called it. That's one of my favorite old movies."

"Well how 'bout that," Kyle said easily. "Me too."

"You guys have so much in common," Timmy called over his shoulder. He was over at the painting already, oohing and ahhing.

Kyle turned to Timmy. "You can call your sis now and tell her she can come out from under my bed. The coast is clear."

"You *knew*?" This time it was Sean and Timmy who made the synchronized outburst.

"Not at first," Kyle said, carefully wiping off the back of his pants. He had changed out of his football gear and was wearing chinos and a green plaid shirt, tucked in, with a belt. "But y'awl don't allow for the rigidity of personality types—like mine. See, there was this strange smell in the room—that got me thinkin'. And then, three long red hairs on my pillow. Finally—I keep the closet key in my third drawer, but face *up*, not face down." He turned to Sean. "So! You running tours of my bedroom now?"

Sean shifted uncomfortably.

"Ahhh…" he stalled, feeling himself reddening. "I…see, I was convinced there was a secret passage, right? Because I saw you last night, coming back from the Thicket. I'm…I'm really sorry, Kyle, if this seems like a violation of privacy. I am, really. Ordinarily I'd never do something like that, I mean it. If there was any other way to get to the secret passage, I would have ta—"

"Not to interrupt," Timmy interrupted, "but I think you guys might be missing the bigger point. We happen to have a ten-million-dollar painting here that someone stashed until they could come back for it. The whole town will be crawling with state police and FBI by sunset. We better figure out a plan of action."

Kyle grimaced at Timmy's words.

"Uhm…no one's coming back for it," he said. "Not here anyway."

"How do you know that?" Sean asked after an awkward silence.

"Because I put it here," Kyle answered simply.

"You? *You?* But…where'd you find it?" Sean stammered.

"I was the one who took it from the library last night," Kyle answered casually. He looked down at his fingers and started cleaning a little sand from one of his nails.

"*You!*" Sean exclaimed. Involuntarily he took a step backwards from his cousin.

Kyle, his hands on his hips, nodded. Timmy drew closer to Sean's side, thinking any moment Kyle would start opening fire on them or something. Who knew what someone would do for ten million?

But Kyle just kept standing there with his hands on his hips.

"Uhm...okay," Sean said carefully, after a long silence and a few false starts. He could barely get words out of his mouth, such was the power of his amazement. "Anytime you'd like to tell us why, Kyle..."

But how dare he! Here Uncle Justin had brought Kyle into his town, into his home—and this is how Kyle repaid him! By stealing art and, when the truth came out—as it inevitably would—bringing disgrace to the Sutherland name!

As usual, Kyle stared at Sean for a bit before replying.

"I think you guys are in over your head," he finally muttered. "Not to worry though—I b'lieve I can handle this on my own."

"Oh right!" Timmy chortled. "Like Sean's gonna be an accomplice to the fact, and let you get away with grand larceny!"

Kyle turned to Timmy. He was smirking. "I'll just tell you this much—though I have to say it's nice to find y'awl have faith in my integrity. I didn't steal it. I never stole a thing in my life. I took it for safekeeping—so someone else wouldn't steal it, like they were planning to. Tonight, or last night."

"Oh please," Timmy sighed.

Kyle threw him a quick glance that wasn't friendly. Timmy looked away first, suddenly noticing a scab on his elbow.

"Oh, I get it," Sean said, his voice rising involuntarily. "So we're in over our heads—not because you just committed the art heist of the decade, but because you're trying to solve the mystery yourself. And, of course, you know so much more about it than us mere inept kids do."

"Never said that," Kyle said calmly, after a minute of very uncomfortable silence.

"Well, fine," Sean chortled, "if that's the way you want it, fine. Too bad though, cuz you might find out some stuff from *me*. And there's about a thousand questions I want to ask you—like how you know about this, and how you discovered the secret stairway, and who you think was planning on stealing the painting tonight, and why, and who's living up in the Thicket, and how you came to know about the Bells, and if you heard them last night like I did—"

"Pick one," Kyle said flatly.

"Excuse me?" Sean said.

"I said, pick one. Question. I'll answer it."

Attitude! Of course, Sean also *really* wanted to ask about Matt and Kyle, and what, if anything, was going on between them—but all that would have to wait. Business before heartbreak and all that.

"Alright, I will ask one question then," Sean blurted. "How do you know about the mystery?"

"Naw, don't ask him that," Timmy moaned.

But it was too late.

"There's a heating grate in my bedroom. I reckon it must go right down to the dining room, for I heard voices coming from there the first night I got here. And when I leaned my ear against it, I heard Uncle Justin's friend telling the story of the Bells. I was...a little down, and the mystery kind of took my mind off things. So I thought I just might go out that night and take a look around, and see if it was all true."

"That's when you discovered the secret stairway," Sean said.

"That's right," Kyle agreed.

Well, that made perfect sense. Since he was a kid, Sean had been taking advantage of the wonderfully-echoing effect of the various heat shafts at Greystones, and overhearing all kinds of conversations—

Sean realized with a sinking heart that he should have asked a more pertinent question—like who was planning on stealing the portrait tonight, and whether that had anything to do with the mystery of the bells. Sean wasn't so sure anymore that everything was connected—and just minutes ago he had felt positive everything was.

He was visibly squirming to ask more, but with his pride he wanted to keep to the agreement. He knew Kyle would think less of him if he asked another. But still, his cheeks were aflame at Kyle's words about Sean and Timmy being over their heads! And him the same age as Sean and Timmy—talk about attitude!

"Well, I've really got to go now," Kyle smiled. "I've got a mess of homework, and then there's a victory party tonight I'd like to attend."

"A victory party?" Timmy asked dubiously. "The Gloucester football team invited *you* to a victory party?"

For the first time Kyle laughed, and his whole demeanor changed. "I was just hoping you'd ask that!" he chuckled. "No, they didn't—because they won't be having one."

"Ahhh…okay, I'll bite," Sean said, somewhat facetiously, after a silence. "Why exactly won't Gloucester be having a victory party?"

"For the simple reason," Kyle answered, smiling like the Cheshire Cat, "they didn't win. We beat them today. 38-24, to be specific. The party I aim to attend is at Matt's house."

Sean and Timmy exchanged mouth-breather glances. This triumphal report seemed the most shocking news of all—even after the discovery of the painting, and who had "borrowed" it. The Nawshant football team had hardly won a game in memory, and there was even talk of dropping them down to lowly Division Four—where desperate football teams from towns with scant population often had to resort to shanghaiing reluctant freshmen for fodder. For the Nawshant Football Team to win a game at all was news to shock and bewilder; for the locals to beat Gloucester, the Butt-Ugly-Bad-Boys of the Division, stretched credulity.

"We beat 'em?" Timmy mumbled, in bewilderment.

"Oh, I'm glad you got your team spirit back!" Kyle chuckled. "It's we now, huh?"

Timmy made a face, but found no suitable retort within his depleted arsenal of wits. Sean knew his friend was still feeling sketchy down here in the claustrophobia of the tunnel.

"Well, like I say, I need to run along," Kyle continued, "and I believe I overheard you say a little while ago, Timmy, that you had a lawn to cut. You wouldn't want to keep the lady waiting, I'm sure. I suggest we all go back t'other way, through my closet. It wouldn't do at all to have this hidey-place discovered right now, as, like you say, Timmy—it *is* Timmy, right?—the town will be crawling with Law soon. If it isn't already. And they'll probably be looking for me soon." Kyle turned to Timmy again. "Best call your Sis now and tell her to unlock the door."

"Why would they be looking for you?" Sean asked. "That's not another question by the way, it's just…conversation. Did someone see you… uhm…borrowing the painting last night?"

"I don't believe they did," Kyle answered matter-of-factly. "I was some careful. But I was making inquiries about the painting at the historical society last night, and I expect that will be remembered and reported by the woman who assisted me."

"Oh, that," Sean said, with a dismissive gesture of his hand. "No, it won't. Miss Sawyer already said she wouldn't say anything about you asking that. I already spoke to her about it."

Kyle's eyebrows lifted. Sean thought he saw—for the first time—admiration and gratitude in his cousin's eyes.

"Thank you," he said, with a slight bow of his head. "Much appreciated." He paused for a moment. Just then Timmy's phone rang.

"Regina," Timmy said.

While Timmy took the call, telling his twin what had just happened, and asking her to open the closet door as they would be there soon, Kyle lowered his voice and mumbled to Sean, "Just for that, I'll answer one more of your questions."

How patronizing he was! But Sean couldn't let himself be bothered by that now. This time he thought before he asked. His eyes locked with his cousin's.

"Does the art heist have something to do with the bell mystery?"

Kyle's eyes narrowed, and once again Sean saw respect there. This was, apparently, the right question.

"It has *everything* to do with it," Kyle said, lowly but fiercely. "This painting here might be worth ten million—which, to tell the truth and shame the devil, was a big-ole surprise to me. But they're after bigger fish than that. *Much* bigger."

"It's not the painting," Sean answered, more or less talking aloud. He was getting some kind of strange, intuitive feeling. "It's…what the painting reveals. That's why they wanted it."

One of Kyle's eyebrows lifted, as if in surprise that Sean knew this much. "That's what I reckon. Or maybe a diversion, one or t'other."

Their eyes were still locked. *Who's they?* Sean longed to ask. *And what's the bigger fish? What could be bigger than ten million? And how the frig do YOU know so much?*

But he knew he couldn't. He bit his lip to keep hot words from bubbling off his tongue, and clutched his hands behind his back so he wouldn't shake Kyle by the shoulders in frustration—and desire to know.

"He knows because you got your hair all over his pillow!" they heard next, accusingly, from Timmy as he spoke with his sister.

They started idly walking back down the tunnel. Timmy hung up his phone a bend or two later.

"What'd she say?" Sean asked.

"She says she's entering a convent tonight, she's so embarrassed," Timmy laughed. "Dude, listen," Timmy added, turning to Kyle, "we have to join forces. Didn't you ever hear the one about strength in numbers?"

As usual, Kyle stared at Timmy for a while before answering.

"Yes sir. But I also heard the one about *loose lips sinking ships*," he said in his soft drawl. "And then there's the other one, about *three may keep a secret, if two of them are dead*."

"Benjamin Franklin," Sean said. But his mind was spinning, while his heart seethed. So, Kyle thought they were over their heads, eh? And couldn't keep secrets? He'd show him!

They came back to the bottom of the stairway without further conversation. Vague daylight was spilling down the stairs—evidently Regina had already unlocked and opened things—probably, Sean thought, in her acute embarrassment she had already fled home. A second later this was confirmed: the front door slammed above them on the first floor, after a flurry of footsteps.

"I believe Elvis has left the building," Kyle remarked, turning to the boys and smiling.

When they reached the top stairway, Timmy stopped to pick up the newspaper again, where he had left it on a dusty step.

"What's that?" Kyle wondered.

"That's the only question you're allowed," Timmy threw over his shoulder in reply.

"Turnabout is fair play," Kyle smiled.

"It's an old newspaper section we found on the way down here, between the stairs and the wall. It came out the day the Civil War started."

"By which of course you mean *The War of Northern Aggression*," Kyle said. They assumed he was joking. "I'd love to take a look at that sometime."

"Well then, I'll let you borrow it—sometime," Timmy answered. But Timmy was joking—he opened the page and held it up for Kyle.

"Well ain't that something," Kyle murmured, as his eyes eagerly devoured the story. A minute later they resumed their journey upward, Timmy giving the paper to Sean.

They passed through the closet and came into Kyle's room. The sudden light blinded them. Kyle—he was being facetious—carefully lifted up the overhanging end of his bedspread.

"Anybody to home down there?" he chimed.

But of course Regina was nowhere in sight.

"We'll let you get to your studying," Sean said.

"Much obliged," Kyle answered. "And I'd also appreciate it if you two didn't say a thing about the painting. Not just yet. Everything's comin' to a head, so it won't be long."

"Oh, as if, dude," Timmy snapped, speaking for them both.

They slunk out of the room while Kyle locked the closet door.

"We didn't even find out where the tunnel goes!" Timmy mumbled as they slunk downstairs. "You should've asked him that!"

"I know," Sean said. "But I think what I asked him the second time was important. We know now everything is connected! That's crucial! But—my God, what attitude he has!"

Sean forgot his own rule about not speaking badly about his cousin in front of others.

"Tell me about it," Timmy agreed. "Well, I gotta say it's nice to be out of there, regardless. And I guess I better get doing." He wearily pantomimed the act of grass-cutting.

"Not yet," Sean whispered. "Quick council of war, in my room. We have to make plans for tonight's mission."

They came into Sean's room, opening the closed door. They found Regina lying on the bed, her hands covering her face.

"I have to *moooooovvvve!*" she bawled, in a hissed whisper, as soon as the door was shut. "I can never face him again!"

"Oh don't be so dramatic," Timmy said. "We just faced him and it wasn't all that. He's got wicked attitude anyway."

"How'd you get back here so quickly?" Sean asked. "I just heard the door slam not ten minutes ago."

"I just snuck back in now," Regina panted. "I had to go get something at home."

"You look like the cat who swallowed the canary," Timmy accused. "What's up?"

"In a minute. First tell me everything." Regina sat up on the bed's edge. They quickly updated her on what had happened. She was as shocked as they had been to hear that:

a) the Sargent portrait of Aunt Sadie had been stolen;

b) it was an original, and worth over ten million;

c) it was now resting against the wall of the secret tunnel;

d) *Kyle* was the one who had stolen it;

e) but he had only "borrowed" it so that someone else—the bad guys presumably—wouldn't steal it, and that "they" were really after much bigger fish, according to Kyle.

When Regina had absorbed these startling developments, they broke it to her slowly that the football team had beaten Gloucester. After a glass of water and a quick trip to the bathroom to splash water on her florid face, she returned to the bedroom, where Timmy added the finishing touches to the update, stressing Kyle's admonition that they were *over their heads*.

"Oh really," Regina commented, her eyes shifting. "Well—isn't that… well. *We'll* see who's over their heads. How dare he! He's like a… he's like a big luggy…Gronkowski. Nice to look at maybe on a football field, but would you really want him in your living room?"

"The Big Gronkowski!" Timmy laughed. "That was funny for you. Not to be confused with one of the premier films of all time, *The Big Lebowski*—"

"Oh, you mean the most overrated film of—" Regina interrupted.

"The last cult film of all time, a film that perfectly captured the zeitgeist of—" brayed Timmy, closing his eyes and raising his voice.

"Faux zeitgeist, conjured zeitgeist of stereotypes, shallow as celluloid—" Regina cried.

"Only a few could penetrate its many layers and implications—"

"Yes, masters of single entendre, like Timmy Quinn—"

"Guys, please!" Sean interrupted. This was one of the few topics upon which the Twins utterly disagreed, and said movie title had not only forever prevented them all from going bowling again, but the very title had become a four-letter word among their set—although Matt sometimes invoked it just for provocative laughs. "If you guys start beating that dead horse again," Sean added, "we'll never get anywhere." The Twins both crossed their arms and glared at each other.

"Okay, thank you. Now, Regina, didn't you have something to share with us?"

"I do, but…" she gave Timmy, who was smiling by now, one last narrowed-eyes stare. "Alright, alright…the thing is—are you ready?" She leapt off the bed and folded her hands in front of her.

"Ready for what?" Timmy asked doubtfully. "For you to return to your senses?"

She stuck out her tongue at her brother. "Oh go bowling with yourself, why don't you! Okay, look. I mean listen! I solved the mystery," she said lowly, but her green eyes were on fire.

"Hold up!" Sean hissed. He respected Regina's intelligence enough to know she wasn't just—well, whistling Dixie. But it had grown awfully quiet over their heads, and Sean pointed to the heating grate in the corner of the ceiling.

"Talk about invading privacy!" Timmy hissed. "He's been listening in! That's how he knows all about this stuff!"

"I don't think so," Sean whispered back. "I haven't talked about it much here. But let's not take any chances. Keep our voices down." He turned to Regina. "Well? You solved it? When?"

"Just now, I think," Regina hissed. She started bouncing up and down in her excitement.

"But…but how?" Sean asked, disappointedly.

"Oh, don't feel bad, Sean!" she cooed. "You see, you didn't have *this!*" She reached under her baggy sweatshirt and pulled out a tattered old volume, its corners dog-eared and its brown leather covers cracked and stained.

"What is it?" Timmy hissed.

"Ditto," Sean said.

"This," Regina said dramatically, holding up the volume, "is the diary of Patrick Joseph Quinn."

"Who he?" Timmy wondered.

"PJQ! The initials!" Sean cried. "Wait a minute! Patrick? Was he—this wasn't Aunt Sadie's groom, was it?"

"Oh, he was more than her groom," Regina gushed. "But yes, that's him! He was the guy who took care of the horses and everything, which is what a groom does, but he also oversaw the construction of the secret stairs—and he was me and Timmy's *great great great grandfather!* Aunt Sadie left him the stables and all the land around it in her will, and the Quinns have lived there ever since!"

"Oh my God!" Sean said. They all three looked at one another, feeling a further deepening of the affection they'd always shared. The roots of Quinn-Sutherland devotion ran deep indeed.

"My God, we're…like family almost," Timmy murmured.

"Right?" Sean answered. "But what…how did you find it, Regina? What does he say?"

"Right before Kyle came home, when we were walking through the tunnel, remember I said something about figuring it out?" Regina explained. "It didn't hit me at first, but then when I was under Kyle's bed I knew I'd seen those bells painted on the wall before—somewhere else. I finally realized it was in this old book that me and Timmy found one snowy day when were like six or seven, exploring our attic. I didn't really understand much of it then, so I put it away in the back of my closet, and just remembered it when we were in the tunnel. After Timmy told me Kyle knew I was under his bed, I ran home and got it, then came back here to your room. But look at this!"

Regina opened a section near the end of the volume. They all stared as they saw two full-page drawings of a bell—one drawn from the front, the other from the back—with the same words written on the bell as were written on the wall of the secret tunnel—and Kyle's notebook: *Proclaim liberty throughout all the land and all the inhabitants thereof...*

"It's the Liberty Bell!" Sean gasped. "Of course! That and the North Star were the symbols of the Abolitionists, Miss Sawyer said! But—"

"I still don't get it," Timmy interrupted.

"I think I'm starting to," Regina said. "Timmy, don't you remember when we visited Philadelphia, with Moms and Dad and Grandma, and went to see the Liberty Bell?"

"Yeah, so what?"

"We need the Web," Sean said.

"Exactly!" Regina agreed. "But notice that *this* Liberty Bell isn't cracked."

"I'm so *confused!*" Timmy hissed.

"You won't be in a minute," Sean said.

"Not sure about that!" Regina laughed.

They dashed over to the computer and Sean quickly entered *Liberty Bell* on a search. "Okay, listen to this little history lesson," Sean said. He read aloud: "The bell now called the Liberty Bell was originally cast in the Whitechapel Foundry in the East End of London. It was hung in the tower of the building currently known as Independence Hall, which was called the Pennsylvania State House, in 1752. It was an impressive object—12 feet in circumference around the lip, with a 44-pound clapper.

"What's a clapper?" Timmy asked. "An old-fashioned rapper?"

"Uhm, *no, brother dear,*" Regina explained. "That would be the big thing inside the bell that whacks against the side."

"The Pennsylvania Assembly," Sean continued, "ordered the Bell in 1751, to honor the 50th anniversary of William Penn's 1701 Charter of Privileges, which was Pennsylvania's original Constitution. It speaks of the rights and freedoms valued by people the world over. Especially modern were Penn's ideas on religious liberty, his liberal stance on Native American rights, and his inclusion of ordinary citizens in enacting laws. As the bell was made to commemorate the Charter's fiftieth anniversary, the quotation on the bell, *Proclaim Liberty throughout all the land unto all the inhabitants thereof*, from Leviticus 25:10, was especially apt, since the line in the Bible immediately preceding *proclaim liberty* is, *And ye shall hallow the fiftieth year.* What better way to honor Penn and hallow that 50th anniversary than with a bell proclaiming liberty?

"Unfortunately, the clapper cracked the bell on its first use. It was recast twice, once adding more copper to make it less brittle, and then adding silver to sweeten its tone when people complained of the bell's sound. From 1753 until 1777, the bell, despite its crack, rang mostly to call the Pennsylvania Assembly to meetings. But by the 1770s, the bell tower had started to rot and many felt ringing the bell might cause the tower to topple. So the bell was probably not rung at all to announce the signing of the Declaration of Independence, or even to call people to hear its first public reading, on July 8, 1776. Still, officials moved the bell, with 22 other large Philadelphia bells, to Allentown Pennsylvania in September 1777, so that invading British forces would not confiscate it. It was returned to the State House in June 1778.

"In February 1846, repairmen attempted to repair the bell, but in a subsequent ringing for Washington's Birthday later that month, the upper end of the crack grew and officials resolved to never ring the bell again."

"And what does this have to do with the secret tunnel?" Timmy asked.

"Hush," Regina said. "Soon! Be patient!"

"But by then," Sean continued, "it had been around long enough to gain a reputation. Because of its inscription, abolitionists started using it as a symbol, first calling it the *Liberty Bell* in the *Anti-Slavery Record* in the mid-1830s. By 1838, enough abolitionist literature had been distributed that people stopped calling it the State House bell and forever made it the Liberty Bell."

"There's the connection," Regina said. "It became a symbol of the Abolitionist Movement. But there's something missing."

"I know it," Sean agreed, "but we're not going to find it here." He thought for a moment, playing idly with a pencil. "Try the diary."

The binding of the old journal had cracked, and all the pages were loose already, so they split it up into three sections, each taking one, and got busy reading. "We're looking for anything at all that mentions the bell, or the tunnel," Regina told her brother.

"Here's the last page," Timmy said a minute later. "He was losing his eyesight, poor guy. *My eyes fail me now, so I'll write no more in this book, having said what I have said. And forever grateful I am to the best woman I ever knew, a queen of light in this dark vale of life.*"

"What a poet he was," Regina mused. "That must've been our great great grandmother he was talking about. How romantic."

"Uhm...I don't think so, Sis," Timmy said. "Not to burst your pink bubble, but there's a sketch here that looks like Sean's Aunt Sadie."

Sean on the left and Regina on the right leaned in to get a closer look at the drawing. Done in pencil, it was undoubtedly the same woman depicted in the stolen portrait, though considerably older. Underneath the sketch were the penciled words *Go On*. The sketch was quite well done.

"*Go On!*" Sean said. "Those same words! They're underneath the portrait of Sadie at the library!"

"You mean down in the tunnel," Timmy corrected.

"But what do they mean?" Regina asked.

"No one seems to know," Sean answered. "At least Kevin up at the library didn't know. What's the date there at the bottom of the sketch?"

"June 17, 1912," Timmy answered. "It's the last entry."

"And the first is April 3, 1849," Regina said, referring to her pages, which constituted the opening section of the volume. "I think he was in love with her! Sadie, I mean. Listen to this—it's on the first page all by itself—like a dedication or something:

The people were saying
No two e'er wed,
Without one had a secret,
That never was said.

"Then the next line—that would be the very first line in the diary itself—is *Thanks be to God, we have found a home and work, Maire and Liam and myself, with a kind lady in this town of Nawshant, an ocean away from beloved but blighted home. Maire will do the washing, Liam will assist the gardener, and I am to work with my beloved horses.*"

"What's he mean by *blighted*?" Timmy mused.

"They came over from Ireland during the Great Famine," Regina answered. "Don't you ever listen to Dad and his old stories?"

"Not always," Timmy said. "Nostalgia is the enemy of art! Old art is the problem! New art the solution!"

"Okay, c'mon, we've got a job to do here," Sean said. "Let's get back to reading our sections."

"Listen to this!" Regina hissed a minute or two later. *November 7, 1850. The Mistress is sorely vexed by the passage of the Fugitive Slave Law—there is talk of nothing else in the house, from the rising of the sun until its setting. She is very concerned for the Visitors.*"

"Visitors—that's got to be the escaped slaves!" Sean interrupted. "And 'the Mistress' is obviously Aunt Sadie. What else?"

"Nothing else there," Regina said, skimming the pages. "Wait! I've got something! *February 14, 1851. The Mistress has bestowed the highest honor upon me, and that is her trust. Since the fire in the stables two springs ago, and my saving of the horses and rebuilding of the place, I have come up leaps and bounds in her eyes. She asked me this evening—the snow was just ending, and you never saw such snow—if she could trust me with a secret;* *'To the grave, Patrick, mind, to the grave,' she said, and I had never seen her* *so earnest. I told her she could; aye, she little knows what I would under-* *take, for her smallest whim."*

"Oh yeah, he loved her," Timmy commented.

"I bet you he's talking about the secret stairway and tunnel!" Sean added. "He says she was worried, and that's when she came up with the idea of the secret escape route!"

"Well, he got married on April 7. *This evening I married Maggie, a* *very nice girl who has been taking care of the Tuttle children. God bless our* *union.* Humph. That's short and to the point."

"What was he doing writing in his diary on his honeymoon night?" Timmy wondered.

"Here's more," Regina continued. "*May 17, 1851. Started work this* *day on the Mistress's Project. I have Liam and Ned and Maggie, and the* *two boys, to assist me, no one else. It is a prodigious task; but I would move* *mountains for the Mistress, and these others will move mountains for me.* *We are starting from the cellar and working up.*"

"That's gotta be the stairway!" Sean cried.

"Shhh!" Timmy remonstrated, pointing at the ceiling vent again. "Sorry. I wonder who those others are he mentions?"

"Maybe his brothers, and their kids. Maggie's his wife," Regina answered, flipping a page. "Our great great great grandmother. This is so fascinating! I have to read this again when we have more time. There's so much in here about the horses! He loved them—I bet he was like a horse-whisperer. Oh wait, here we go: *August 17, 1851: Finished the Mistress's* *Project this afternoon, and blocked off the cellar; there is talk of a connec-* *tion—we shall see. September 28, 1851: We made the most remarkable dis-* *covery last month: we have connected to a long stretch, running from here* *to there—the Mistress believes it was made in the old days of smuggling.*"

"They found part of the tunnel when they were digging," Sean said.

"It was already there, or part of it anyway."

"From here to there," Timmy repeated. "What's that mean?"

"It must mean it ran from here, to one of the other old houses, or maybe to the sea," Regina opined.

"Alright, that's all interesting," Sean added. "But...isn't there anything at all about the bell? That's what we really need to find. I think I've got the section that covers the Civil War."

Sean's room fell into hushed silence as the three investigators sifted through the pages, skimming as fast as they could.

"Got something!" Sean cried, and the others jumped. "*May 26, 1859: A date none of us will ever forget. A terrible blow has fallen. The Mistress is out of her wits with the brain fever. We have lost the* Southern Cross, *and most of the passengers, including her dear friend the Reverend. I would sit like a dog at the door of the Mistress, but there is too much to be done. I fear she will never be the same. She has lost her one true love, though not the one who would have loved her to the end, had our stations in life been different.*"

They fell silent for a minute.

"Right outside this door is where Aunt Sadie saw the wreck from," Sean commented lowly, a lump in his throat.

"That is so sad," Regina said. "I don't know which is sadder, that Aunt Sadie's boyfriend died, or that Patrick went his whole life worshiping a woman he couldn't have. Our own flesh and blood. I always think of people from the old days as being...I don't know, in black and white and somehow—somehow less human or...that's not exactly what I mean."

"This would make an excellent rap song," Timmy commented.

"Thank God you're such a doofus!" Regina laughed, rubbing her brother's shoulder.

"It's funny he'd write that openly though," Sean said. "Wasn't he afraid someone would read this and find out?"

"Probably his wife and family couldn't read English," Regina explained. "Most of the Famine Irish spoke and wrote only Irish, not English, if they could read and write at all. Maybe that's why he wrote his diary in English." The Twins themselves could speak, write, and read Irish, taking part in a yearly Irish Immersion Camp the last two weeks of July, in Upstate New York. In fact they spoke it to each other when they desired to speak confidentially, much to the chagrin of certain teachers at Nawshant High—and, of course, to Sean.

"Here's more," Sean said. "Oh my God, listen. *December 22, 1860. I asked the Mistress today shouldn't we be beginning the Christmas decorations and such. When she looked at me it near killed me, and t'was all I could do not to comfort her the way I wish to. She told me to do what I would, and so we pulled down a tree from The Neck, and filled the house with garland and trimmings. Maggie tied ribbons everywhere and all of our spirits were lightened. I think it did the Mistress a good turn. But later when I was gathering the hay I saw her through the window on the second floor, staring out. You could hear the bell tolling as plain as day. She asked me later this evening—there's a gale coming from the eastward—to haul it in as soon as I could. 'But mind, Patrick, not in this storm!' she said. 'Never in a storm!' She looked like a ghost then, and my heart near broke for the black pain in her eye. So in it will come.*"

By this time Timmy and Regina were wide-eyed with interest. They had rolled onto their sides, their chins perched on their hands, and were hanging on Sean's—or, rather, their Great Great Great Grandfather's—every word.

"*December 23, 1860. This morning the Mistress said at breakfast not to touch the bell until she had made arrangements to have a replacement set further out in the Sound. It was a dark day, stormy and wild, and the bell tolling something fierce. Odd how we never seemed to pay it much mind before the disaster, and now it seems it's all we hear, a very death knell to our spirits. The Mistress gave orders to have her own things moved upstairs— that's where it all begins, or ends, and that room has been vacant since we finished, though that's all the servants quarters up there. The view of Third*

Cliff is unobstructed from up there—that's not good, to my way of thinking. It's a dark day, and there's a cloud of sorrow over my heart. I fear the mistress is not well.

"February 11, 1861. There is nothing but talk of war in the village. Three Visitors left this morning, and they told tales of men and militias gathering in the Southern States."

"Escaped slaves, he means!" Regina cried. "I'm sure of it! Oh my God—right here, in this house! In the tunnel!"

"If war comes, it will be ugly, and I fear it. I will not go, for my duty lies here—but Liam says he will go if it comes to a fight. Yesterday in the forenoon a new buoy was dropped out in the Sound, about a quarter of a mile offshore. Please God we shan't hear its toll when the wind's out of the east or northeast! This morning Liam, Ted, and myself, and John and Ned Drake from the village, pulled the old bell ashore. The Mistress said t'would be heavy—a ton or more, she said, and it was all of that, and the very devil to get ashore. It's a grand ornate thing, with a Bible quote and all. We had to saw it away from the wooden harness it tolled from, which was waterlogged, and a harder day's work I've never done—but the Mistress wanted it done in one day, she said it wouldn't do to leave it. How we ever got it up on the wagon I'll never know. It's there yet, in the barn, and the Mistress says a Tinsmith will come in the spring to get the green off of it, and restore its varnish. She's out there still, staring at it—I can see the glow of her lantern from where I write."

"It's the Liberty Bell!" Timmy gushed.

"Yeah, but…it can't be," Regina said. "We saw the real one in Philadelphia, remember?"

"The Sutherlands were Quakers," Sean mused after a minute's silence, putting the papers down. "Kevin said one of them came up here after the Revolutionary War from Pennsylvania, to get married. Which was when Greystones was built. So there is that Philadelphia connection."

"It might be a replica," Timmy said.

"Maybe," Sean said. "At any rate we know it came in from offshore—now we have to see what happened to it. Alright, come on, let's get through the rest of the pages."

They got busy again, and the only sounds were their breathing, and the shifting of ancient, crisp paper.

"Here's sad news," Sean said at one point. "*July 2, 1863. There is a great...something,* oh, *battle, being fought in Southern Pennsylvania as I write this, and it still rages, from what we hear over the telegraph wire. From Liam's last letter we know he must be in it, for he said they were leaving Maryland, and heading into the Northwest. God between those we love and all harm!*

"*July 5, 1863: a black day. We have word from the telegraph that Liam has been killed in action, may God rest his sweet soul—my dear baby brother. One of the Mistress's brothers, George, fell as well. The Mistress had warned him against going, for they are all Quakers, and do not take up arms. There is a black cloud of sorrow over the house. But we all must go on, as the Mistress is always saying. I can write no more.*"

"Sad," Regina muttered. "But there's the answer to one question anyway. *We must all go on, as the Mistress is always saying.* That must've been Sadie's mantra. That's why it's written under her portrait."

"You're right!" Sean blurted. "I never would have caught that, but you're right! *Go on...*" They all fell silent.

"That's the last entry for like a year," Sean finished.

The Twins fell silent. They slowly went back to their pages.

"*My third son was born last night,*" Regina read aloud a few minutes later. "*We will call him Liam.* Timmy, that was our great great grandfather, I'm pretty sure." They all looked at each other.

"Wow," Sean said. "We're...we're all like family. Not that you guys weren't before this." The Twins smiled. They went back to the book.

Sean put his papers down first.

"I'm done. There's nothing else on the bell," he said. "I'd really like to read these again sometime, taking my time. Some of them are like poetry. There's one point he writes about *a lusty fellow, a robin I suppose, singing his heart out just beyond the window.* Funny to think there's robins outside my window now—hear them?—probably descendants of Patrick's. There's so much history in here—and life."

Regina finished next, tucking her papers back into the leather binding and shaking her head slowly.

"Nothing," she said. "But beautiful nothing. Life, like you said, Sean. And sorrow and joy along with it."

They both turned to Timmy, who was still reading. It looked like he had about five pages to go. Regina made a reach for the top sheet but Timmy whacked her hand away.

"Mine," he blurted.

Sean and Regina rolled their eyes and settled down to wait.

Sean focused on Timmy's face, which was a regular barometer of whatever he was feeling. Sean grew excited when he saw Timmy's eyes narrow. When they expanded, Sean asked, "What, *what*?"

Timmy held up a finger. Sean groaned, rolling onto his back.

"Can you read at any more of a glacial pace?" Regina blurted.

"Where's Aunt Sadie buried?" Timmy suddenly asked.

"Uhm…can't say for sure. Oh, wait, no, she's up in Mount Linden Cemetery, right here in town. There's a big monument there to the Sutherlands. I remember seeing her name there once."

"I don't think she is, dude," Timmy said. "Check this out—I think it's the missing link: *June 11, 1867: It's a hard thing we did, but it's done now. He lies beneath the bell, and let no one disturb him again. She'll go there too when her time comes. Please God, that will be a long way off. Jamie is five years old today. 'Do you know how much this is worth?' she asked me, tapping the bell before we moved it. 'I don't,' I answered. 'More than this whole house, and all that's in it,' she smiled. 'But for all of that, I wish I'd never seen it.'*"

Timmy looked up at them, his mouth set. "That's all," he said.

"Read it again, slow," Sean said.

Timmy did so.

"They're buried together," Regina said. "He—Patrick—must've moved the reverend's body from wherever it was, and buried it again somewhere...somewhere. And that's where Sadie's buried too. With the bell over it."

"In the Thicket," Sean said, with a shiver.

"Undoubtedly," Regina said. "And that's the bell that's ringing."

"And when Sadie vanished, she must have gone into the tunnel to die, and then later Patrick took her body out and buried her with Samuel."

"That's it," Timmy and Regina said together.

They all sat quietly, glancing at each other and blinking.

"It doesn't explain why the bell was so valuable," Timmy said.

"Right," Sean said. "Right. But definitely it is—and was. Even then. Aunt Sadie knew that."

"But *is* it the same one that's been ringing?" Regina asked. "We don't know that yet for sure."

"It's too much of a coincidence not to be," Sean said. "It *has* to be! But why *now*? And who's doing it?"

"The bad guy you saw," Timmy said.

"Well, we're no closer to finding out why it's so valuable," Regina said, stuffing Timmy's share of the papers carefully back into the leather binder. "But—"

"But I think I know who might be able to tell us," Sean said. "Oh, besides my cousin, that is."

"What a loser for not sharing!" Regina blurted. "I don't like him anymore for that, that big Gron—oh, never mind. Not that much, anyway."

Sean just shrugged.

"Okay, who?"

"Kevin Nelson up the library told me that ever since he's worked there, one or two people—that's what he said, one or two people—have come up from Philadelphia, or at least Pennsylvania, asking questions about Aunt Sadie's bell. Like historians or something."

"Or at least they said they were historians," Regina sniffed.

"How do they know about it?" Timmy blurted.

"From some other source, obviously," Sean said after a minute. "Some other source that we don't know about. Maybe Kevin knows who those people were, and we could call them."

"Don't you think Kevvie Boy has his hands full?" Timmy asked.

"I wasn't thinking of Kev," Sean said. "I was thinking of his boss. While those Philadelphia people might not have spoken to her personally, you can rest assured nothing happens in the library that Miss Sawyer doesn't know about. Plus she'd never let a little thing—like, say, a $10 million dollar art heist—stop the business of her *library*. In fact she told me on the phone a little while ago she was 'bopping' down to the library for fifteen or twenty minutes to make sure they didn't close it. Kevin had called her saying that's what Captain Curry, the chief of police, wanted."

"I'm sorry, I can never take him seriously," Regina chuckled. "He sounds like a cartoon character, running around making the world safe for Indian food."

"That was funny for you!" Timmy laughed, pointing at his sister.

"I'm going to call her now," Sean said.

"Nawshant Library, who's this?" a voice growled over the phone.

"Ahhh…" Sean began, totally surprised that Kevin or Miss Sawyer hadn't answered. But he was required to say no more; next he heard an outraged. "How *dare* you!"—Miss Sawyer—and then what sounded like a struggle for the phone.

"Nawshant Public Library, please hold for one moment!" came next— Miss Sawyer's voice—and then she continued, addressing whomever it was that had had the temerity to answer the library's phone without her explicit permission—probably poor Captain Curry.

"I've a good mind to go down to the police station and answer *your* calls, demanding who it is!" Miss Sawyer went on. "And we *never* ask our patrons whom they might be! State Police? I don't give a…a hooey WHO you are, NO ONE answers the phone here at the Town of Nawshant Public Library *except for employees* of the Town of Nawshant Public Library! Close the library? I should say not! I've just had that out with your captain and told him that, pursuant to Town of Nawshant By-Laws, Chapter 37, Section 4, Paragraph 3, lines 1-17, such power as the setting of operating hours and emergency closing times resides with the Head Librarian—that would be me—and only in the Head Librarian, until such time as she—or he—might be removed by the Board of Trustees of the Town of Nawshant Public Library, and unless you have a note from the Board of…no no, we're open, come *in*, Mrs. Johnson, do come in, that detective novel you ordered came in yesterday! Now, where was I? Oh yes! *Don't* make me call my cousin the governor again, sir!"

Sean put his call on speaker-phone so the Twins could also enjoy this dressing-down. It was five minutes—and a shouty five minutes at that—before she finally took Sean's call.

"Nawshant Public Library, this is Miss Sarah Sawyer *Head Librarian* speaking, thank you for holding, how may I help you?"

"Hi, Miss Sawyer, hi, it's Sean with a quick question. I'm so glad you're still open!"

"And why shouldn't we be?" Miss Sawyer brayed.

"Right! Well anyway, some time ago, I think there were a few—or maybe just one—visitors to the library from Philadelphia, asking questions about Aunt Sadie's bell, and—"

"Aunt Sadie, Aunt Sadie, *Aunt Sadie!* That's all I've heard today! My heavens, you'd think she was Madonna! Though I worship her of course, and emulate her—whenever possible and practical. Aunt Sadie, I mean. Go on?"

"Anyway—I was just wondering if you might remember who those people were—I…I'd like to speak to one of them about a little…oh, just a little unimportant detail of family history. But, like I was saying, apparently one or two people have come up over the years, from Pennsylvania I think, asking questions about her bell."

"Oh, yes, Sean, that would be…oh, what was his name? Left a card I think in case we should ever have some information for him about Sadie's old missing buoy bell. Lovely old gentleman. I wasn't here that day but Kevin told me all about him and I've spoken with him once or twice over the years on the phone, and if I—DON'T TOUCH THAT GET AWAY FROM THERE! Pardon me, Sean. Anyway, Sally, Sally dear, be a love and go knock on the Men's Room door and tell Kevin to stop hiding in there and come out at once! I need the card of that old gentlemen from Philadelphia who's come by once or twice. Yes, Sally, now, not two weeks from now! Has your chum finished my lawn yet, Sean?"

"Oh, ahhh, he's just leaving now, Miss Sawyer."

"Oh? Only now? Well, I do hope he finishes in time. As egalitarian as I may be, it is awkward to have workmen pottering about when guests arrive. To say nothing of the ear-assaulting roar of two-stroke engines. Because you see, I'm still planning on having my little soiree this evening—despite recent developments of a most alarming nature. Ah, there you are Kevin! Where did we put that card that old gentleman left, inquiring about Sadie Sutherland's bell? Yes, this *is* Sean on the phone, how did *you* know?"

"Get me a pencil and paper," Sean hissed, covering the mouthpiece.

Two moments later he clicked off the phone, just as another battle royal was starting between Miss Sawyer and someone else.

"Charles Biddle Hallsley, Pennsylvania Society for the Preservation of Antiquities and Artifacts," Sean announced, lifting the paper like it was a holy relic.

"There's a mouthful," Timmy observed. "With a name like that he never said a Hail Mary."

"Keep it on speaker-phone?" Regina asked, rocking back and forth on the bed nervously, her hands wrapped around her knees.

"Okay." Sean dialed the number with a pounding heart.

"Who's calling please?" the woman who answered asked, after Sean had inquired for Mr. Hallsley.

"Uhm…Sean Sutherland."

"Hold please."

"What's that?" Timmy asked.

"It's the Muzak version of *Comfortably Numb*," Sean reported wearily.

"I'm sorry, Mister Hallsley is in a meeting now. Is there something I can help you with?"

Regina was shaking her head frantically, gesticulating wildly.

"Don't take no for an answer!" she hissed.

"Please, Ma'am, this is important—tell him it's Sean Sutherland, calling from Nawshant, Massachusetts. I think he'll take my call."

"As I said, sir, Mister Hallsley is in—"

"Please? Just give him that message, please? While I hold?"

She didn't say yes, but Sean heard a sigh, then next Muzak, Sweet Muzak again as he was put back on hold.

It seemed like a very long time, but finally a man's voice came on, breathy, brittle, and excited.

"Mister Sutherland," he half-panted, in an old-fashioned, scholarly voice, somewhat similar to Uncle Justin's, but less bemused and without Uncle Justin's English accent.

"Yes," Sean affirmed, gulping.

"From Nawshant, Massachusetts?"

"That's right, sir."

"Descendent of Samantha Sutherland, known as Sadie?"

"Yes."

There was a long pause.

In a trembling voice, Mister Hallsley then asked, "Is this…by any chance is this about the bell, Mister Sutherland?"

"It is," Sean answered, his own voice trembling.

"Have you…you haven't found the bell?"

My God, Sean hoped the poor old dude wasn't having a stroke!

"Well…we think we know where it is," Sean answered.

The next pause was longer. Mister Hallsley's breath was coming in fast halts as he said, "Mister Sutherland, I have been waiting all my life for this call. We can't of course offer you what the bell is actually worth, but a number of foundations have already guaranteed our organization certain sums, should the bell ever be located. Mister Sutherland—excuse me, Mister Sutherland, this is a very emotional moment for me—Mister Sutherland, we would like nothing better than for the bell to come back to what many of us feel is its proper home, here in Pennsylvania. We are prepared to offer your family $250 million dollars for its return."

CHAPTER EIGHTEEN

YOU CAN RING MY BELL

"Mister Sutherland? *Mister Sutherland?* Are you there?"

"Uhm…y-yeah. I mean yes, I'm here, sir."

Sean felt as if he were speaking from a different sphere—my *God!* *$250 million!* Kyle wasn't kidding when he said "they" were after bigger fish than the Sargent painting!

Regina's mouth resembled the opening of Boston's Callahan Tunnel, while Timmy got up and broke into a frenzied little dance on the bed that was part jig, part…well, Watusi or something. Apparently he was assuming that as a supporting member of the investigative team, his share of the $250 million would not be an insignificant one.

"When did you actually *find* the bell, Mister Sutherland?" Mister Hallsley asked. "What kind of condition is it in? Would it be convenient if I came up later this evening for a look at it? I'm most anxious to see it."

"Well, we uhm…actually haven't *found* it yet, Mister Hallsley," Sean confessed. "But we think we know the general area where it's at. See, someone's been ringing a bell in this conservation land just up the road, and we think it's the same bell that Aunt Sadie—hid away."

"How very bizarre!" Mr. Hallsley answered. "Good heavens, I hope they're not abusing it! But you refer to a conservation area—would that be the Thicket? Is that what you call it?"

"Yes, that's right," Sean answered, surprised that Mr. Hallsley knew the name.

"So it's *not* currently on Greystone's property?"

"No. Not that I know of."

"Well, it's probably in that part of the Thicket that was donated by your family—a hundred years ago or more."

"I didn't know we had done that," Sean said. "I thought the conservation land was all once Hutchinson land."

"Oh no," Mister Hallsley answered. "Mrs. Hutchinson only added to what your family established a long time ago."

Suddenly Sean remembered what Kevin up the library had said— when he told Sean what Dottie LaFrance had been researching. *Oh, nothing important—old land deeds, titles, records of real estate sales, things like that...*

"What...what difference does that make anyway?" Sean asked. "Whose property the bell is on?"

"Well, it makes all the difference in the world, and yet no difference at all, Mister Sutherland, depending upon which side you look at it. Some might say one could regard the bell as buried treasure, as it were, in which case it's Finders, Keepers, I'm afraid. Others would say it's the property of the Sutherlands, and therefore anyone else who took it would be in violation of the law. I think a lot of it depends on what kind of circumstances we find the bell under. I was thinking the odds are a lot better of you folks finding it if it was on your own old property. Certainly if you found it that would make things easier than if...other parties came across it first."

Timmy's dance came to an abrupt halt.

"Mister Hallsley, what exactly *is* the bell? Why is it so valuable?" Sean asked.

"Ah! You don't know," Mr. Hallsley answered. "I presumed you did. Well, before I tell you that, Mister Sutherland...excuse me, but do you

mind if I only reassure myself? We thought all the Sutherlands had vanished from the Nawshant area. There were none living there on the two
occasions I visited. Would you mind telling me a bit about yourself?"

"Oh, okay. Ahhh, my name is Sean Sutherland, and my parents…
died when I was a year old. We were living in California then. My Uncle
Justin—Justin Sutherland, who's actually my father's uncle—adopted me
after that. He was teaching in England, and when he became my legal
guardian he came back here to Nawshant. It just so happened Greystones
was for sale then, the old family home, so he bought it. We've lived here
since."

"Ahhh, another missing link!" Mr. Hallsley exclaimed. "We didn't
know that! I wrote to your Uncle Justin many years ago, when he was
teaching in England; but I'm afraid he couldn't tell us very much at all."

"No no, family history's not his thing," Sean admitted.

"Well, it *is* good to know that the Sutherlands are back."

Mr. Hallsley paused again to catch his breath.

"So how much do you know about the bell?" he asked.

"Well, we know that it came up from the Philadelphia area a long
time ago. The Sutherlands put it out on Third Cliff to serve as a buoy, and
then they brought it in again when—well, there was a wreck out there and
everything. And then it kind of vanished. It was moved, but then it seems
to have vanished. Oh, and we know it looks like the Liberty Bell."

"Indeed it does," Mr. Hallsley answered. "In fact, you could say it *is*
the Liberty Bell."

"I told you!" Timmy hissed, breaking into his dance again.

"But…but that's in Philadelphia," Sean stammered.

"Yes, of course, the original," Mr. Hallsley explained. "But the Sutherland Bell is an exact replica, *without* the crack—and it's less than thirty
years younger than the original. It's really quite priceless. You see, during
the Revolution, the British occupied Philadelphia for a time, starting in
October of 1777. Several weeks before they arrived, the largest bells of the

city were removed from Philadelphia and hidden away, as people knew the British would in all probability melt down every bell they found to make cannon balls. The Liberty Bell was taken at that time to a small village known as Northampton, today's Allentown, specifically to the Zion Church, where the pastor hid it beneath the church's floorboards. It stayed there for over a year, until later in 1778 when the British abandoned Philadelphia.

"But while it was in Northampton, one of your ancestors, a wealthy man by the name of Frederick Sutherland, whose father had been a very dear friend of William Penn, apparently commissioned the making of an exact duplicate, in case the British should discover the hidden bell and destroy it. You see, the bell was originally built to commemorate the freedoms celebrated in Penn's charter; it wasn't known at all as the 'Liberty Bell' until much later. And so it was in commemoration of Penn, and his founding of Pennsylvania, rather than any other associations, that a second bell was cast, in secret. *Without* the crack, as I say. And this was kept with the Sutherlands when it was finished.

"Just after the Revolutionary War, the son of that Frederick, who was also called Frederick, married a woman from Salem, Massachusetts, and he relocated to Nawshant, where he and his wife eventually built Greystones. We don't know if he took the bell with him at that time. Perhaps, perhaps not. Their eldest son—you guessed it, also named Frederick—witnessed a horrible shipwreck on the shores of that same Third Cliff when he was a child, and apparently never got over it. One of the first things he did when he took over Greystones was to have the bell set as a buoy just off Third Cliff. So either Frederick III had the bell hauled up from the Allentown area then, or the bell was already there."

At this, Regina raised her hand—like she was in class.

"Excuse me, Mister Hallsley," Sean said. "My friend Regina is here, and she'd like to ask a question."

"By all means, Mister Sutherland."

"Oh, please call me Sean."

"Yes, hi, thank you," Regina began. She cleared her throat. "Why would they use the bell as a buoy, if the bell was so valuable?"

"Well, for several reasons," Mr. Hallsley answered. "First, it was valuable, but not all *that* valuable, when they first put it out there, which would have been around 1820—because the Liberty Bell was not yet the famous Liberty Bell that it was about to become a decade or two later. The second reason I would say is just good old fashioned practicality—they needed a bell, they had this bell, so they put it out there on top of a wooden float. Bells were quite rare and valuable.

"And now, Sean, you can help me. Why was the bell removed from the Third Cliff area? You said something about another wreck."

'I did," Sean answered. "Sadie was involved with the Underground Railroad, as you might know. She met this du—a guy by the name of Reverend Samuel Dimsworth, another abolitionist. He sailed a ship down to Wilmington, Delaware, to pick up some more escaped slaves just before the Civil War started. He was bringing them back to Nawshant, but they hit a storm. The ship—the *Southern Cross*—actually wrecked right on Third Cliff, while Sadie watched from the windows of Greystones."

"How ghastly!"

"I know, right? But the worst part was, they were going to get married when he returned. She already had her wedding dress and everything. They were lovers."

"Fascinating. But how tragic! What happened then?"

"Well, Aunt Sadie could hear the bell whenever the wind was from the east, and naturally it filled her with grief whenever she heard it. So she asked her groom, the guy who took care of the horses, Patrick Quinn by name, to pull the bell in, and they replaced it with a regular ocean buoy, further offshore. Then they had a tinsmith come up and clean the bell a bit. Later—well, we think…we think the Reverend Dimworth's body was moved somewhere into the Thicket, and Sadie's buried there too, and the bell is above them. That's what we guess anyway. But you can't imagine how wild the Thicket is. It's not a case of going up there and finding it."

"How on earth did you discover all this?" Mr. Hallsley asked. He sounded astounded. "It's the missing connection we could never make, try as we might! We assumed the bell vanished in a storm. And yet there were whispers that it hadn't, that it had been moved to some secret location. It's that hope that has made this the quest of my lifetime. But again, how can you be sure of all this?"

"We found Patrick's journal, Patrick Quinn, the guy who worked for Aunt Sadie as the groom. By the way, Mister Hallsley, Patrick was the great great great grandfather of Regina, who you were just talking to, and her brother Timmy, who's also here—they're my best friends."

"Ahhh, so that explains it! Fascinating, *fascinating!* You know, all my life I've been searching for the bell, and writing a book about it—but of course I couldn't finish the book without knowing what had become of the bell, so I abandoned the project years ago. But what a story this will make! You say you've been looking in the Thicket?"

"Yes, we have— though it's slow going in there. But we're going back tonight. Mister Hallsley—uhm—there's other people looking for it too. I'm...I'm not sure how they found out about it, but they did, and...well, we don't think they're the nicest people in the world."

"Oh no!"

"I'm afraid so."

"Ah, it was ever thus," Mr. Hallsley sighed. "The dark underbelly of the priceless artifacts search. Hard to avoid entirely, I'm afraid, when one is dealing with invaluable things. *Do* be careful! Oh dear! But, as I say, would you mind if I came up and joined in the search? If I can be of some assistance in any way, I assure you that all credit will still be given to the Sutherland Family, and to them and them alone will remuneration be made, should we both find it together, and should your family elect to part with it."

"Oh, ahhh…." Sean dithered. He looked at the Twins.

Timmy shrugged and Regina whispered, "Sure, why not."

"Of course, Mister Hallsley. Let me give you my cell phone number, and please call me when you get into town."

"Thank you, Sean!" Mr. Hallsley panted when he had jotted Sean's number down. "I can't…I can't even *begin* to tell you what this conversation has meant to me! If I can get arrangements to get there late this evening, I'll call you when I get settled. If it's too late, I'll contact you first thing tomorrow."

"Great. And thanks, Mister Hallsley."

"Thank *you*, Sean!"

They hung up their respective phones. Sean and the Twins sat in an open-mouthed silence for a bit…

…while Mr. Hallsley, equally stunned, continued sitting at his desk, a light in his eyes, and his hands trembling. Elsewhere in the same building, the person who had been listening in on the conversation hung up, then dialed a number.

This person's hands were trembling as well.

"Hello, Dottie?" the person said lowly, when the party had been reached. "I have some very good news. It *is the bell*. We know that now. I also have some further instructions: we've got to act *now*. We've got to get the bell out of there tonight. Yes, that's right, tonight. No matter what, Dottie. No matter *who* gets in the way. Other people know about it, these teenagers, and now Hallsley. *Tonight*."

Back at Greystones, in Sean's bedroom, Regina was the first to break the stunned silence.

"*Holy—*"

"Don't say it, Sis!" Timmy warned. "Hardy Boys and all. But can you *believe* this? $250 million dollars!"

"That's not *that much*," Regina stammered. Then she gulped. "It's only—a quarter of a—billion."

"Right, *only*. You're forgetting about movie rights, book rights, product tie-ins—the Liberty Bell duplicate play-action figures, complete with Timmy, Regina, and Sean, the kick-butt investigative team…"

"C'mon guys, this is way serious," Sean interrupted, even as he laughed. "We've got to get up there tonight. It'll be a good chance too, because Kyle won't be up there—"

"Why not?" Regina asked.

"Oh. Ahhh, Matt's having a victory party," Sean mumbled.

"You're not going?" Regina gasped.

"Oh, ahhh…I haven't…exactly been invited. Yet," Sean said. "But even if I was, this is more important, obviously. I just…I just have the feeling tonight's the night, that if we don't find it tonight, they will."

"So what's the deal on tonight then?" Regina asked. "Let's make some plans."

"It'll be dark by 6:30. Let's meet here at 5:30. We have to dress up as satyrs."

"As what?" Timmy gawked.

"Satyrs—I already told you. I looked up what they look like on the web late last night. Remember when I told you that guy screamed out *Satyr City*? It must be like a secret club they have up there, to tell who's on their side or something. We have to dress the part."

"Really?" Timmy asked. "Dude, I think you're being a little—"

"Oh my God! It's like Matthew Bourne's all male *Swan Lake*!" Regina gushed, overriding her brother. "Remember Timmy when Moms and Dad took us to see that? I'll do the make-up for us, and I'm sure my old ballet leggings will fit us all."

"*Make-up?*" Sean blurted. "Who said anything about—"

"We have to look the part," Regina repeated.

"And what do we tell Margaret and Uncle Justin when we try to sneak out of the house dressed like cedars?" Timmy wondered.

"It's satyrs, dude. S-A-T-Y-R-S," Sean corrected.

"We'll tell them…we'll tell them we're going to a Halloween party!" was Regina's idea.

"At the end of September?" Sean wondered.

"They'll buy it," Regina countered. "It's not like it's March or something. But wait—they'll never let you out of the house, Sean, dressed like a Satyr or otherwise. Not like that. Not Margaret anyway."

"I'll figure something out," Sean said. He'd probably have to use the Wisteria vine again. "Timmy, you better get up to Miss Sawyer's and cut the grass."

"Oh, dude, hello? Why should I cut the grass for a lousy $180 when I'm going to be a millionaire soon?" Timmy protested. "I mean…I mean, you are planning on giving us a little reward, right ol' buddy?" He wrapped his arm around Sean's shoulder and winked at his sister.

"Oh, sure," Sean answered. "But you *have* to cut the grass—she'll kill us if you don't."

"I know," Timmy answered, getting up from the bed. "I was just getting in touch with my inner fat lazy country-clubber, for practice. Okay, we'll all meet here at 5:30 then. I'm out of here."

After the Twins left, Sean realized he was starving. He went down to the kitchen and found—not to his surprise—a ready-made sandwich wrapped in wax paper in the refrigerator, with a post-it note attached that said, *For when my little lamb gets hungry.* Oddly enough it was a lamb sandwich, leftovers from a meal this week. Sean thought it odd that, while Margaret never missed a trick, the gift of irony had never been hers.

He ate at the kitchen table and was just taking a last swig of iced tea when a frantic knock came at the window over the sink. He jumped, the glass fell and shattered, and he wheeled around to find Regina's mug pressed against the window and displaying twenty degrees of urgency.

Once his heart stopped racing he waved her in. He was almost finished cleaning up the damage when Regina burst into the kitchen, her eyes like fried-eggs and one raised finger pressed against her lips.

"Oh my God, *what*?" Sean asked.

"Where's your cousin?" she whispered, pointing to the heating vent in the ceiling of the kitchen.

"Right, right, right," Sean agreed. He jerked his head upward and a moment later they found themselves back in Sean's room, the door shut. But that wasn't good enough for Regina—she took Sean by the hand and pulled him into his bathroom, then shut that door too and ran the water in the sink at full blast.

She drew close to Sean's ear.

"Google Earth," she whispered.

"Ahhh…what about it?" Sean wondered.

She shut off the water and dragged him by the hand back into his room. She plunked down at Sean's computer, then called up Google Earth, the program that showed images of earth taken from satellite cameras. Sean remembered how they had all looked at their houses when they had first discovered this site years earlier.

"I didn't even think of that," Sean murmured. "What a great way to get a view of the Thicket, and map it out!"

"It's a great way to do a lot more than that," Regina whispered, turning around and looking up at him. Her eyes were still buggy-large and drenched with…something. Sean's curiosity expanded.

She called up Nawshant, then zoomed in a bit on the Thicket.

"What part of the Thicket is this?" Sean asked.

"Smack in the middle," Regina whispered. "See anything?"

"Not really," Sean answered. The screen showed a tangled mass of gray-brownish, somewhat blurred detail, punctuated with the crisscrossing shadows of what must have been humongous trees. "What exactly am I looking for?"

Regina bit her lower lip, then eyed Sean dramatically.

"You're looking for this," she said. She clicked on the *show only build-*

ings button. The tangled mass vanished, leaving a small dark object near the center.

"What did you just do?" Sean asked.

"I think it must be infra-red or something, and shows buildings and objects by their higher temperature, and not any trees or anything," Regina explained. "Don't ask me. But don't look at the object itself—look beside it, here at its shadow."

Sean leaned down closer to the screen.

"Oh my God." The shadow was—undoubtedly—in the shape of a large bell. "That's it!" Sean hissed. "That's definitely it!"

"I thought so too!" Regina answered. "But I wanted to get a second opinion. Can you believe it, Sean? There it is!"

"It *would* have to be right in the middle like that," Sean said. "It's just as far in, whether we go from the south, by Ocean Road, or from the north or east, from Mrs. Hutchinson's. Or west, from the old cemetery."

Regina snapped her head up. "*Promise me*, Sean Sutherland, we won't be going in through the old cemetery! That would totally creep me out. I won't do it. Timmy won't either."

"But it's so peaceful there!" Sean protested. "I go jogging in there sometimes. Uncle Justin's always in there bird-watching, and—"

"Good, fine, you guys keep doing that," Regina answered. "But there's no way you're getting me in there. Especially at night. Don't you remember Miss Sawyer's story about the haunted graveyard she told us during Story Time when we were like ten? And half the mothers in town complained because the terrorized kids couldn't sleep for weeks?"

"Oh please, don't tell me you're still bothered by *that!*" Sean accused. "The one where the kid is taking the shortcut through the graveyard at night, on a bet, and he walks by an open grave, and just as he's almost past it a cold, bony hand reaches out and grabs him by the ankle, and the next day when they found him all his hair had turned white, even though he was only ten? And all along it was friends playing a trick?"

"Uhm, yes Sean, that would be the one," Regina answered, shivering. "Plus tonight's the full moon, which makes it *tres* creepier. You're not getting me in there. Not even for $250 million."

"Geez, weren't you going to leave any of the money for me?"

"Oh stop, you know what I mean."

"Alright, well, I guess we don't have to," Sean said. "As long as it's just as far from all directions, it really doesn't matter from what side we go in from." Secretly Sean loathed the idea of going in from Mrs. Hutchinson's property, because he felt that was where Three Spirits and Cut Leg were hanging out. But Sean had already blazed a bit of trail there last night, and this route would, he had to admit, be infinitely easier than starting from scratch somewhere else.

But they'd be sitting ducks, especially with the full moon.

"Okay, we'll go in from Mrs. Hutchinson's," Sean sighed. "We'll take the trail I made last night. That'll be the easiest way to do it. It's just going to be so hard to find the bell though if it's covered under 150 years of brush and vines and growth."

"But it can't be, can it, if someone's ringing it?"

"Oh—oh, duh, you're right!" Sean answered, mock-slapping his forehead again.

"But my God Sean, what are we even *talking* about? You can't go in there like that! I just thought of this! You'll get even more poison ivy!"

"Don't worry, I feel better," Sean lied. "It looks worse now because… because I just put some more stuff on it."

"You should never lie, Sean, you're the worst liar in the world."

"Well…no really, I'll be careful. Besides, we'll wear gloves and stuff and just take it slow. I only got this when I panicked and fell and ran into bushes. Oh, and tied one of them round my head."

"Yeah, that would do it," Regina agreed, staring again at Sean's scarified face. "Okay, I gotta get going. I'm going to pull our costumes together—Moms already said she'd help. I'll see you back here in a few."

After Regina left, Sean busied himself assembling on his bed the gear they would need that night—flashlights, gloves, and rope (he didn't know why they might need rope, but he had the feeling they would.) He then text-messaged Timmy and asked him to pick up pruning shears and loppers at Kendrick's Hardware down in the village on his way. *AND DON'T SPILL THE BEANS!* was Sean's final message.

He was just contemplating a nap—wow, Kyle was being *intensely* quiet upstairs—when Uncle Justin and Margaret came home, Margaret bellowing the Nawshant Fight Song to wake the echoes, and Sean not even knowing there was such a ditty. Again came the sound of panicked animals roistering up the stairs as they both stampeded into Sean's bedroom—to check on his progress, Sean assumed.

But no—

He cleared off the bed, threw the gloves and other items under the covers, then climbed in as quickly as he could.

"What did they do? They thoroughly thrashed them! Can I be more specific? Yes, I'd be happy to be, they *destroyed* them! They put them to full rout!" Margaret brayed as she charged into the room, putting her hands on the ends of Sean's bed and shaking his mattress in her shocking zeal.

"Who?" Sean couldn't help exclaiming.

"Who did these things? Why, our Kyle, and the rest of the team!" Margaret answered, looking at Sean as if he had just sprouted a second head. "And who did it more than anyone? Our Kyle, and your Matt, that's who! What am I saying? Why, I'm saying they put them to headlong flight!"

Your Matt, Sean thought. If only!

Sean looked at Uncle Justin, for confirmation of all this.

"It's all true!" he announced, rubbing his palms together. "While I can't say I appreciate or follow football's many intricacies and procedures, Kyle was certainly the hero, as was your friend Matt, both of whom were carried off the field on the shoulders of their teammates."

"What was it?" Margaret continued. "It was grand, just grand! Why, it's the biggest thing that's happened in this town for years! And how is our lamb feeling?"

"Oh, ahhh, better, thanks, Margaret. Uhm, actually… something else happened today—or rather, last night, but it just came to light today, that I think might be remembered longer. The painting up the library of Aunt Sadie was stolen."

"Really?" Uncle Justin asked, but he was already checking his text messages. "Ah. So that's why there were so many police cars around this afternoon. Shocking, I say. We were wondering, weren't we Margaret? *Good heavens!* An arctic tern was seen in Andover this morning! I must be off! No, no dinner for me, Margaret, please, as I shan't be back in time! Do you need anything from the outside world, dear boy?"

"Ahhh, no, I'm fine, really," Sean answered. "But," he continued, turning to Margaret, "they claim that painting of Aunt Sadie is worth ten million dollars!"

"Is that so," Margaret wondered vaguely, polishing Sean's television screen—it was already immaculate—with the loose end of her jacket belt. "Who would ever credit such a thing? No one, that's who."

"But…" Sean looked helplessly from one to the other. It was obvious the abduction of Sargent's painting meant less than nothing.

"What does my lamb have a taste for, for dinner?" Margaret asked next. "What are your choices this evening? Why, anything at all!"

"Oh, ahhh, I don't think I'll be all that hungry," Sean stalled. "I had that nice sandwich you left me—just a few minutes ago I had it."

Margaret opened her mouth to protest. Sean threw a frantic look at Uncle Justin and shook his head—it just wouldn't do to have Margaret obsessing over him tonight when it was D-Day—and he needed to be long gone by the time the dinner hour of 7:00 rolled around.

"Oh, uhm, yes, yes, didn't Doctor Hallissey say something about not eating much this evening, so as to give the medication a chance to work better?"

"Oh?" Margaret wondered.

"In light of all this," Uncle Justin added, "and, you know, Kyle already told us he won't be home for dinner this evening, as he has a celebratory party to attend—you should take the night off, Margaret."

"Oh. Hmm. Well! What would I do with such a night off? Why, I would call Nancy Dennison, and suggest we attend a movie."

"An excellent idea!" Uncle Justin said, smiling too broadly. Sean hoped he wouldn't overdo it—Margaret could smell a ruse a mile away.

"But I'll fix a little something for yez all, in case you get hungry later," Margaret said, nodding decisively, her mind made up.

Sean could hardly believe his luck! Timmy and Regina and he could put on their Satyr outfits and leave Greystones without incurring either the suspicions of Uncle Justin or the remonstrations of Margaret!

Margaret scurried off to make her arrangements, while Uncle Justin took off in hopes of finding the arctic tern. They both left the house within ten minutes, checking in once more on Sean, and calling out goodbyes and congratulations to Kyle upstairs as well.

But there was no answer from Kyle.

"He had studying, but maybe he's asleep," Sean suggested.

"And why wouldn't he, the day's he had?" Margaret answered. But Sean suspected Kyle had left some time ago.

He had. In fact right at this moment, Kyle's limp hands were being tied behind his back, and a thick swath of concrete-colored duct tape was sealing his mouth shut.

CHAPTER NINETEEN

SATYR SUPPER

Sean figured he'd better sleep while the house was quiet, as he was sting-eyed sleepy. He had two hours before the Twins were due.

But his restless mind and achy heart would have none of it. He told himself that he should be happy, so very happy, for Kyle and Matt in their triumph this morning; and, really, how…*wonderful* that they'd been carried off the field together! The two victorious heroes!

"I *am* glad for them," he insisted; but even as he mumbled the words, he found his fists and toes clenched with the intense effort this forced magnanimity was requiring. He realized an old truth: wanting something and having something were two entirely different things: *If wishes were horses, beggars would ride*, as Margaret said.

He let out a breath and faced the unlovely truth: no, he wasn't happy for Matt and Kyle *at all*. In fact, dredging up the look on Matt's face when he had picked Kyle up this morning, and the way Matt had squeezed Kyle's shoulder in obvious and open affection—a part of Sean wished the Nawshant Football Team had been utterly…what was Miss Sawyer's unlovely phrase?—oh yes, *bitch-slapped* this morning, and that Kyle himself had been sacked a new state record number of times.

And as far as Matt was concerned—Sean didn't want to dwell much on negativity, but the first image that came to Sean's mind involved Matt going out for a long one, and the dermatological benefits of a deep and cleansing full-body mud-bath.

He shoved these images out of his head, shocked at his own pettiness. He knew he'd never sleep if he didn't stop thinking of it all.

But next, anticipatory visions of what might happen tonight in the Thicket rushed in to fill the void, accompanied by a realization of the shocking news that people were willing to pay $250 million dollars for the bell. And this wasn't all it was worth, the man had said! My *God!* But was it the same bell? Well, really, how could it not be? It had to be! Hmm, what would Sean do with all that money? There really wasn't anything he needed—but he could sure help a lot of people…

And when Sean succeeded in lashing *those* images out from his wired mind—he became so itchy he thought he might scream.

But in time the mad burning passed, and Sean felt himself finally going under from sheer exhaustion. To further calm himself, he replayed in his head the lullabies Margaret used to sing to him when she would put him to bed at night, especially right after Sean arrived here, when he was a bewildered, newly-orphaned one and two year old. He repeated the songs to himself, and felt his whole body relaxing. Thoughts and images of Aunt Sadie drifted into him, as if of their own volition: her smiling face; her poise, passion, and conviction; her shining eyes, just as Sargent had depicted them. A gentle, relaxing warmth stole over Sean, like an interior sun, and then it was spreading all over, and then—

His phone vibrated in his back pants pocket, making him leap up in cattle-prodded alarm and cry out. *Urg!* It was Timmy.

This better be important, Sean thought.

"Hello?"

"I just thought of something," Timmy began immediately.

"Congratulations. What."

"Do you think Eddie Hartigan's older brother Ralphy is gay?"

"*What?*"

"I said, do you think Timmy Hartigan's older brother Ralphy is gay. He just walked by here a little while ago, and he was walking in kind of a…oh I don't know—a *languid* way."

Sean made a face of sour exasperation.

"You woke me for *this*? And what do you mean, *languid*?"

"No, I just thought you might know, dude. What's that thing you people have where you can instinctively spot another gay person? Gaydar? Is that what you people call it?"

"*You People?*"

"You know what I mean."

"I'm not sure I do. Maybe you can tell me the word *you* people use when you think someone might be straight. I can't believe we're even having this conversation at a time like this! Finish the lawn yet?"

"I'm about…three-fifths of the way done. Maybe four-sevenths."

"Oh. Can you be a little more specific?"

"Alright, well, we can have this conversation when you're in a better mood, dude. I was just trying to give you dating alternatives in case it didn't work out with Matt. Later!"

"*I'm in good mood now!*" Sean roared.

But Timmy was already gone.

Sean rolled his eyes and leaned back into the pillows, realizing sleep was impossible now. He got up and went into the bathroom, then carefully splashed water on his face in an attempt to alleviate the itches.

He came back into his sun-flooded room and plopped down on the edge of the bed. Now what?

His eyes drifted ceiling-ward again. My God, Kyle was being quiet up there!

Well…as long as Sean was hanging around, doing nothing but fidgeting and waiting for the approaching night, he thought he might as well go upstairs and see if…if Kyle was okay. If his cousin had fallen asleep, maybe he wanted to be woken? Or, possibly, Kyle needed help with his homework? Maybe that's why he was being so quiet—he was stuck on a calculus problem.

Or something.

Sean got out of his bed, left his room, and walked down the hall. Or maybe Kyle…

"Oh, be honest," Sean told himself when he reached the third floor. "You just want to get back in the tunnel, kiddo."

Of course he did. He couldn't believe that Kyle had talked them into coming back to Greystones before Sean and Timmy had discovered where the rest of the tunnel led—or, more accurately, where the two ends of the tunnel led.

The secret stairway/tunnel was the biggest discovery in Sean's life, the biggest mystery, ever—and it was in his own house!! And yet, he didn't know where the tunnels ended! How had that happened?

Well, he and Timmy had been surprised, confused, and alarmed, especially after their "struggle" with Kyle; and the next thing Sean knew, they were back in Kyle's room, Kyle having shepherded them along like compliant farm animals. Plus Sean had felt (as he rightly should have, he admitted) a tad guilty for sneaking into Kyle's room, and thus had offered no resistance. And now on top of it all—Kyle was the hero of Nawshant! A media darling! The flavor of the month! His third day here! And Sean was—just a forgettable, broken-hearted, bow-legged also-ran on the lacrosse team, with a face that currently looked like ten miles of bad road.

He crept up the third floor stairs noiselessly, then entered the hall. But a sudden tsunami of a sneeze from nowhere blasted out of him— perhaps the result of some residual dust from the tunnel. Whatever its cause, the echoing explosion ended any idea of stealth.

So he boldly approached Kyle's door and rapped freely.

"Kyle?" he called, when the knock went unanswered.

Nothing.

He waited a few minutes, then carefully turned the knob.

The door was locked.

Great—well, that ended that. But what a…jerk! Keeping Sean from further exploring the tunnel that led from Sean's own house to—to wherever it went. Just for spite.

Or was Kyle just demanding that his privacy—so recently and egregiously violated—be respected?

Sean lay down to await the Twins when he returned to his own bedroom, not feeling so well and his emotional mood matching. Of course sleep was out of the question now, but he'd just *rest his eyes* for a bit. As often happens in cases like these, Sean promptly fell into profound sleep.

He dreamt—and in his dream he was cold, a piercing, maddening cold he had never felt in waking life. He was pitching back and forth, and all around him was dark and obscured. There was a roaring wind, a moaning, and other ghastly sounds he couldn't name: but their sum total was chaos. Chaos, horror, and a growing sense of doom.

By degrees the light grew, though it still remained dark around the edges of Sean's dreamy frame of view. He realized the pitching was not of his own volition. He was on a ship, a large wooden one, and it creaked and shuddered wildly as a storm broke upon it. Lightning flashed. Waves reared back, gathered up concrete strength, then crashed over the gunwales; the wind was a rising shriek. The ship leapt and pitched, and it was hard to tell, so difficult was it to keep his eyes open from the sting of the salt water, whether the biting, gale-driven precipitation was sleet, snow, or ice.

A low moaning—human voices smeared together in despair—was the bass to the winds piercing soprano. The pounding crash of waves on rocks was too loud, too close.

In his dream Sean looked up, and saw a large stone house upon the back hill, barely visible through the pelting roar. It was Greystones. A dim light shone from a window in the house, and a figure was perched behind the glass, frantic in its gestures. Sean became aware that the figure was a woman; she was dressed in a flowing black gown; her hands were shielding her eyes, in an attempt to see better; then the hands would be clapped against the woman's mouth, in horror. She repeated these two gestures over and over, a frantic marionette.

There was a ripping, a roaring, and then a stupendous crash. A frozen-wet sail fell like a crushing shroud upon Sean; he struggled, and then an icy flood enveloped him. His mouth opened involuntarily, filling up instantly with storm-driven sea water. He was pulled underwater, kicking and flailing, his feet inextricably tangled in rope. He was launched out of the sea at one point; a wave picked him up like he was a match-stick; it pulled him back, then reared and hurled him forward. He was underwater again and the cold was killing him. He opened his eyes and saw death before him, the jagged, black-green stone of Third Cliff, on which he would now be dashed. He put his hands in front of his face—

Then everything flipped. Sean was now the figure in the window, his face pressed against the old, wavy glass on the second floor of Greystones. He was watching the death-throes of a large wooden ship as she was being hurled onto the rocks of Third Cliff. Someone was clinging to what was left of the mast; Sean screwed up his eyes and saw that it was his cousin Kyle. Sean's heart lurched up into his throat, and he found himself making the same frantic gestures the woman had, minutes earlier. A wave crashed over the ship, and when it was gone, so was his cousin. *No!* he screamed—

Someone grabbed him from behind—

"Dude! *Dude!*"

Sean bolted upright, panting and rigidly awake. Timmy and Regina were on either side of him, their eyes wide with concern. They both leapt back at the sight of him.

"What?" Sean asked, his heart still racing.

"No, your face is still kind of a shock, dude," Timmy said.

"You were freaking in your sleep," Regina said. "You okay?"

"Oh, boy," Sean exhaled. He looked around. It was so nice to see his friends there with him. "What time is it? It was…wow. That was like the most intense—Kyle was…wow." Sean stopped to wonder—was this similar to what Kyle experienced when he had one of his "fits"?

"What was the dream?" Regina asked, sitting on the bed's edge.

"Just…I was on the ocean. I think I was like the Reverend Dimsworth, and I was drowning, and about to get smashed on the rocks—Aunt Sadie was watching me from the window. Then everything switched and I was standing at the window, as me, and I looked out and Kyle was the one drowning." Sean paused. "My God, look, I'm soaked with sweat."

"You okay?" Regina asked, smoothing Sean's mussed hair down. "What would Margaret do now to comfort you?"

"Oh, you better not touch me Regina, I might be contagious. Well… she'd probably get me a drink of water," Sean smiled.

"Timmy, go get Sean a drink of water," Regina commanded.

"Why do I…oh, never mind," Timmy sighed.

"I have a bad feeling," Sean said lowly to Regina.

Regina's left eyebrow went up.

"I do too," she said. "I think we should forget about it tonight. Can we still dress up though? The costumes are *awesome!*"

"No, I don't think we can forget it," Sean said. "I mean, the bad feeling I have—it's not like a premonition of…doom. For us, I mean. It's like… you know what? Maybe I'm being paranoid, but I think Kyle's in trouble. Right now, like. I think he…needs our help."

"Seriously?" Timmy scoffed, handing Sean his water. "Yeah, right! Like Invincible Kyle would take help from us."

"No, I mean it," Sean said, between gulps. "I snuck—I mean, I went up to his room a little while ago—he's not there. He must've gone out through the tunnel. But he locked the door."

"He *did*?" Timmy asked. "I was gonna say, we could take the tunnel when we leave here, and kill two birds with one stone."

"Not now we can't," Sean said.

"Oh, like Sherlock Holmes would let a locked door stop him! I bet all the bedroom door keys here work on all the doors!" Timmy answered. "Let's see if your key works! If it doesn't, Regina here is like quite the awesome lock-picker, aren't you Sis?"

"Nah, I don't want to get into that again," Sean said. "It was bad enough he caught us once. I don't want to violate his privacy again."

"But—"

"Sean's right," Regina offered. "Okay, but can we try on our costumes now?"

Sean and Timmy rolled their eyes at each other.

"What?" Regina protested. "This was your idea, Sean, you said we had to dress up like satyrs! C'mon!"

Regina jumped off the bed and lifted a mega-size plastic bag off the floor. A long white feather sifted out of the bag and sashayed down.

"Oh God help us," Sean murmured, falling back on one of Margaret's favorite expressions of dismay. Regina made a face but continued searching the bag for something. She finally pulled out a small make-up case.

"Okay, everyone into the bathroom. Makeup first."

"Why?" Timmy asked.

"That's how it's done, that's why."

She ushered them into the bathroom, directing Sean to sit on the toilet seat cover and Timmy to sit on the edge of the bathtub.

"Take your shirts off, please."

They grudgingly complied, Sean feeling very self-conscious as always. Regina first dampened their hair, then slicked it back with some gel. Next she got busy with this black stuff she carefully smeared beneath their eyes, and in a line down the middle of their foreheads.

"This doesn't hurt?" she asked Sean.

"Not...not too bad," Sean said, wondering if Sherlock Holmes had ever dressed up like a prancing swan/satyr to solve a case.

"There is the need," Timmy philosophized, "to dress up. Every primitive culture knew that to stay sane, you have to go a little crazy once in a while. That's why they had mad dress-up festivals, and Carnival, and rain dances, and what have you."

"I guess this would definitely fall under the category of 'what-have-you,'" Sean opined. "But it's funny you say that, Uncle Justin says that exact same thing. He's seen some really killer stuff from other cultures in his travels."

Lastly, Regina did something to their hair again, plastering down a front section of it onto their foreheads.

She smiled when she was done and began bouncing lightly on her toes. "So very cool!" she squealed. "Okay, now for the outfits. I'll be right back. AND NO PEEKING YET!"

She said this as Sean and Timmy bolted upright in an attempt to cram their faces into the mirror.

Regina returned in seconds—she clearly didn't trust them—and handed both young men a pair of—well, it was hard to say what they were. Ballet tights, apparently, that came down to their shins, and had dozens—no, hundreds—of white feathers glued to them.

"AWE-some!" Timmy shouted, holding his up. "Bravo, Sis!"

Regina, smiling ear-to-ear, took a bow.

"Alright, hurry up, put 'em on—I won't look," Regina commanded, whipping around the corner back into Sean's bedroom. Sean and Timmy removed their pants and pulled on the ballet tights. Sean somehow couldn't share Timmy's enthusiasm, and he secretly wondered what Sherlock Holmes would make of all this.

"Mine are too tight," Sean murmured. Timmy looked over.

"Oh dude, hello, you've got to lose the boxers. Dancers might wear like this funny little jock-type thing under the tights—but never big thick flannel boxers—especially green plaid ones that show through."

Sean felt himself coloring. "You mean we have to—"

"That's right, we gotta go commando style," Timmy said. "No undies. Lose the boxers, dude."

"Timothy Quinn, *what did I tell you?*"

"About what?" Timmy wondered. "Not wearing underwear?"

"More like the Hardy Boys! And avoiding certain words and phrases so I can write this all down, later. I can imagine no circumstances in which the H-B's would go 'commando-style,' or make mention of it in one of their books."

"You can't? Oh. Huh. Well, lemme see what I can do. Okay, right off the top of my head? Mrs. H is doing the boys' laundry, right? And she's just served a massive, fatty, cholesterol-laden 1950's lunch of dead cow buttock dripping in mayonnaise—and she finds a condom in the pocket of one of the boy's jeans—I'm not saying which of the two brothers it is. She gets so freaked out she gets sick, and pukes her guts out, all over the laundry. *Over* and *over* and *over*, with these big chunks of—"

"I catch your general drift," Sean interrupted.

"—and of course being a good Mom, she throws all that puke-covered laundry away and goes *right* out and gets the boys new clothes, including underwear. But this takes time, see, cuz she has a Tupperware Party to go to that night, so for two days the H-B's have no undies."

"Oh, right," Sean replied. "You got me on that one. Gee, why didn't I think of that?"

"Can I come in now?" Regina called.

"We're all set, Sis," Timmy answered.

Regina squealed with delight and exchanged a passionate high-five with her brother.

"You look awesome!" she cried. "Oh my God! Sean, stop, what are you doing? Don't pull so hard to get the pants lower, you're molting. And they're only supposed to go to the shins anyway. No really, you guys rock! Those professional guys at the ballet had nothing on you! Except their pecs were a little bigger maybe. Plus they had eight-packs, and you guys only have six—err, four…that is, two-packs."

"Uhm, easy to tell what you were looking at during that ballet show, Sis," Timmy commented.

"An artist's job is to notice everything. But really…awesome! Okay, we're almost done here."

Regina reached back into the make-up kit and pulled out what looked like a very thin tube of lipstick—except it was black.

Oh dear, it IS lipstick, Sean thought, as Regina applied it carefully all around Sean's mouth.

"Okay, now go like this, mmph, mmphh," Regina advised, clomping and puckering her lips.

A minute later, just as Sean and Timmy thought they were finally done, they realized that, no, they weren't done: Regina began writing things on Sean and Timmy's chests, stomachs, and backs.

"What are you doing now?" Sean wondered aloud, trying to hide the annoyance in his voice.

"I'm putting graffiti on you both," Regina answered. "I'm turning you both into walking subway walls. Real artists *never* copy, they take what's come before and morph it into something different. We can't do what's been done before!"

"God forbid," Sean murmured. Looking down, he could see that Regina had covered his exposed flesh with various sayings and symbols: the peace sign; a spider's web on his right shoulder; a scar across his belly, and several quotes: *Overthrow the Prevailing Paradigm*; *Question Authority*; *Where Have All the Flowers Gone*, and *If You're Not Outraged You're Not Paying Attention*.

By this time Regina had moved on to Timmy's fish-white flesh—was she writing a novel on his back for God's sakes? Sean squinted and read, *The law, in its majestic equality, forbids the rich as well as the poor to sleep under bridges, to beg in the streets, and to steal bread*, scrawled across Timmy's shoulders and back. Next, a bull's-eye was placed on the back of his neck; some funny Celtic symbol—it looked like three connected spirals—decorated each of his nipples; and then faux fishnet stockings were drawn onto both his shins.

Sean slipped over to the mirror and half-turned, craning his neck—my God! A *very* good caricature of Oscar Wilde covered all of his back! Underneath which was written—Sean had to squint again to read the words—*I have nothing to declare except for my genius.*

"Uhm, Regina, dear," Sean said, clearing his throat. "The idea to dress up like satyrs was so that we could *fit in*."

Regina turned swiftly away from her work and held Sean's eye for at least five seconds.

"Art must trump all other considerations," she said simply, then went back to Timmy's right arm, upon which she was writing, *Don't You Dare Legislate Desire.*

"How you feelin', dude?" Timmy asked Sean a minute later. They had been shooed out of the bathroom so Regina could get ready.

"Remember those old reruns of *Let's Make a Deal*, where people would dress up like carrots and stuff?"

"Oh dude, come on! Free your mind!" Timmy rejoined. "You look awesome!"

Regina exited the bathroom some minutes later, her arms out-stretched as she worked her imaginary catwalk, dressed somewhat like Sean and Timmy except that her ballet outfit was more tutu than leggings. Her red hair was nowhere to be seen: in its place was a shocking—no, *terrifying*—four foot high jet black Tina Turner wig that very nearly scraped the high ceiling. Sean thought it more than enough to scare animals and for the first time he was grateful that Little Biscuits the Dog was in Doggie Heaven, as otherwise all hell would have broken loose.

"Holy—" Timmy began.

"Don't say it, dude," Sean mumbled, but he was amazed he could even get words out of his mouth. To have said that Regina looked *entirely* different would have been the understatement of the century.

"Is that a dead Big Foot on your head or are you just glad to see me?" Sean asked.

"Do my back," Regina said to her brother, handing him the lipstick and ignoring Sean in her artistic frenzy. "Write, *To create is to sing with the voice of God.*"

"Cool," Timmy said, complying. "Who said that? Puccini?"

"No, I did," Regina answered. "Okay, picture time!"

Sean knew now what it meant to be in a police line-up, as he was shoved against the back wall of his bedroom while Regina and Timmy took turns snapping pictures from every imaginable angle.

"You should enter this in the state art fair, Sis," Timmy said admiringly at one point.

"Oh please," Regina answered. "They're far too bourgeois for this. Okay! Are we ready? It's almost dark out. I'm ready!"

"Oh, I was born ready," Sean groaned, looking at his friends. So much for the element of surprise. At least Margaret wasn't around to suffer forty coronaries at the sight of them. "Hey! There's no pockets!"

"I have my bag," Regina said.

"Alright then, here's our gear—flashlights, gloves, and…well, I guess we can forget about the ski masks."

"No ski masks," the Twins said, being sync-ish again.

"And put our phones in there too. We should probably put them on vibrate again."

"Done," Regina said, closing up her bag and slinging it over her shoulder. "Okay, it's exactly 6:30, and just getting dark out. Let's go! Sean, what do you think you're doing?"

"Uhmm, putting on my shirt?" Sean answered.

"No shirts!" the Twins commanded, again in unison.

"But—"

"Satyrs don't wear shirts!" Regina said vehemently. "I looked it up on the web! And besides, you'll ruin the art—and it's really warm out tonight, you won't need one!"

"I know, but what about the poison ivy? I don't want to get it all over the rest of my body. And it might get cold later. There's no telling how long we'll be out for."

They finally compromised by stuffing long-sleeved flannel shirts for all of them inside Regina's bag, just in case.

"I'm a swan, I'm a swan!" Timmy cried, flapping his arms as they moved down the main staircase. "And soon to be a very *rich* swan! Oh, wait—Margaret's not home, right?"

"Duh!" Sean observed. "Like we'd be winging down the front stairs looking like this if Margaret was home."

Once they got outside, Sean walked rapidly over to Timmy and Regina's Bug, assuming they'd be driving up to Mrs. Hutchinson's—

"Oh, Sean, hello, are you tripping?" Regina asked. "I can't fit in the car with this wig!"

"What, it doesn't come off?"

Regina folded her arms as one of her eyebrows arched.

"I've taken a vow," she announced. "A sacred, artistic vow. In the same way that lots of soldiers going into battle wouldn't put their swords back into their scabbards until their blades had tasted blood, I have vowed not to take this wig off *until we find that bell.*"

"*AWESOME!*" Timmy cried. "So if we don't find the bell, we won't be any richer—but at least we get to see Regina walking around for the rest of her life in a four-foot high wig! Yuck yuck yuck!"

"So you mean we're *walking* up there?" Sean asked.

"Unless you want to fly," Regina answered.

"Sure!" Timmy joked. "We could each take a feather from our outfits and shove it up our—"

"Don't say it," Regina and Sean said together.

"That's not really helpful now," Sean added.

"What's the matter with walking?" Regina asked. "Aren't you the nature boy who hasn't gotten a car yet? Even though you could afford ten of them? Because you love to walk so much and you want to protect the environment?"

"Fine, we'll walk," Sean answered. "I just wanted to be discreet."

"But this was all your idea, the costumes!" Regina protested.

Sean opened his mouth, then decided he'd be better off keeping it closed. Besides, he was distracted—he could no-way no-how shake the feeling that Kyle was in trouble, and needed their help.

It was true. All Sean's reason was against such a thing: Kyle was attitudinal, cocky, full of himself, and patronizing; and hadn't he dismissed Sean and the Twins as being "over their heads," and had stated that he himself could "handle" things on his own? Yes, he had. It was just a dream, that was all. Despite its vividness, there was no reason to believe it was some kind of sign, or omen—

And yet the feeling that Kyle was in trouble grew with every furtive step they took. Big trouble. It was like Sean was walking through invisible mud.

"This is like when Bilbo jumped over the hedge on his way out of the Shire, on the way to Smaug's mountain there," Timmy said, as they single-file swept through the back gardens of Greystones. "Just think what great adventures await us tonight!"

"I'm not jumping over hedges with this outfit," Regina replied.

"I never said you should, Sis!" Timmy said. "Why's everyone so touchy tonight?"

"Duh, take a guess!" Regina replied. "We go to our Waterloo!"

"What does Abba have to do with any of this?"

"Good grief, brother, what are they teaching you in that school?"

When they reached the tool shed, Sean stopped, went inside, then returned with two loppers.

"Room in your bag for these?" Sean asked.

"Just ask the forty clowns to move over," Timmy joked.

"Yes, but why?" Regina said.

"We might have to cut a trail, and your brother forget to get them on the way home. You'll thank me later, trust me."

They walked on again in silence.

"Hey, uhm, excuse me everyone," Sean mumbled, coming to a stop right before they reached the side of the Twins' house. "I…okay, this is weird, but I can't shake the feeling Kyle's in trouble."

No one answered.

"It's true," Sean said again.

Timmy just shrugged his shoulders, while Regina said, "Well, nothing we can do about that now, is there? Unless you want to drop the whole thing and go look for him in the car."

Sean thought for a moment.

"No. No, I don't know if that would…no, we better keep going."

They came to the Quinn's house and turned the corner.

Alas, Sean's fears of sticking out like a sore thumb proved all too true. They rounded the path to find, despite the darkness, a neighborhood kick-ball game in full progress under the streetlights. Becky Quinn, the youngest member of the Twins' family at age nine, was in fact rounding second after having walloped the ball over Robbie DeLisle's head, when the entire game came to a screeching halt.

"Oh my God, where are you going? Can we come? Is it a Halloween party?" came squealing from all over everywhere as a seemingly-multiplying group of local urchins clustered around them.

"You know what? You know what? You know what?" young Jamie Nichols was repeating *ad infinitum* to Regina, pulling on her feathered sleeve as his nose ran unchecked.

"*What?!!!*" she finally blurted.

"You look like…you look like…you know who you look like? You know who you look like? You look like…we went to…we went…a few summers ago, we went to…ahhh…"

"I was afraid of this," Sean mumbled, unable to move in any direction. "And you thought the paparazzi were bad."

"Death by a thousand rug rats!" Timmy cried.

"Money and candy!" Regina suddenly shouted, reaching into her overstuffed bag. "I have money and candy for everyone!" She took a handful of loose coins—along with some very old Sweet Tarts and salted peanuts mixed-up therein—from the bottom of her valise, and flung the whole lot into the street, behind them. The crowd dashed after the scattered goods. Sean and the Twins bolted in the other direction. They raced around the corner of Crow's Nest Lane and onto Ocean Road—and smack into a forty-something couple out for a jog. The man fell down, the woman screamed, and their large and rather ugly dog bared his teeth and lunged at them; yet, polite as they ordinarily were, and fearful of a regrouping of the urchins, they bellowed out, "Sorry!" and kept going.

"Who were they?" Sean panted, as they raced up Ocean Road.

"I think they're a new couple," Regina answered, running alongside Sean and keeping one hand on her voluminous wig. "We saw them in church a few Sundays ago."

"Talk about the welcome wagon," Timmy added.

A very large car approached. The nastiest part of the Thicket was just beside them, and they all three made the simultaneous decision that this part of the Thicket would have nothing to offer them but chaos, should they enter it now to avoid detection. The car slowed, the occupants gawked, and then nearly drove into the woods as they oozed by.

"Happy Halloween!" Regina shouted, smiling and waving.

"Who were they?" Timmy asked.

"A car full up with old ladies," Sean answered. "Don't know 'em."

"Me neither," Regina panted.

"Maybe they're on their way to Miss Sawyer's house for her dinner party," Timmy said. "She said she was having eight friends over."

"That's it, I bet you're right," Sean answered.

"Well, they won't be lacking in table conversation anyway," Timmy observed. "Not that there's ever any lack of that at Miss Sawyer's."

As Ocean Road climbed up to the heights of Nawshant, the three sleuths became aware of flashing lights and muffled chops of sound, skipping in from a few blocks over.

"Someone's house is on fire!" Regina gasped.

"I don't think so," Sean answered.

"Oh, you know what it is?" Timmy said. "There's like twenty cop cars up by the library. State Police, FBI, everyone except the KGB. I saw them on the way back from Miss Sawyer's. All…uhm…heck's breaking loose, because of the stolen painting."

"Right!" Regina hissed. "I'd forgotten about that. No wonder Kyle said they were after bigger fish than the $10 million painting." She gulped. "250 million, the man said."

They all fell quiet as they contemplated this astonishing figure.

They rounded another swooping curve on Ocean Road; there in the high distance, bathed in its own light, sat the regal *Linger Longer*, the jumping off point for tonight's fateful excursion.

"I guess we didn't do too badly," Sean said as they trotted up the seemingly endless driveway. "The only ones who saw us were the kids and that couple. Oh, and the ladies."

"The whole town will know in an hour," Timmy commented.

Sean took the lead. They veered off to the left and swept past the greenhouses, the ankle high fallen leaves muffling their footsteps. They came up to the beginnings of the south-sloping apple orchard, and halted beside a gnarled, massive trunk to catch their breaths. A tingle of fear jiggled down Sean's spine—this was where he had just barely evaded the maniacal *Three Spirits* last night.

"Okay, what now?" Regina asked.

"There's a bit of a trail that I made last night on the other side of the orchard," Sean said lowly. "We head for that. Listen you guys, we really need to be careful. That guy with the club last night looked like he meant business, and now…geez, I'm not so sure I should've told you guys about it after all. If anything happens—"

"Don't worry," Regina said. "I'm armed."

"You are?" Sean gasped. He couldn't believe it. My God, did Regina have a butcher knife? A gun? Nunchucks? But no, it was only a (seemingly) gallon-size can of *My Fair Lady* hairspray.

"Our grandmother gave me this for my sixteenth birthday," she shrugged, tossing it back into her bag. "I guess to signal my passage into womanhood. It's the heavy-duty stuff that the Blue Bubbles use before a wedding or an out-of-state trip. You could get sucked up by a tornado and still not a hair would fall out of place. I never thought I'd use it until I spotted it tonight on our way out. Every toxic chemical known to science is in this stuff. *I* wouldn't want to get sprayed with it."

"After only two applications, you walk around with your own personal ozone hole above you," Timmy commented.

"Well, alright then," Sean added, dubiously. "But seriously, don't take any chances, let's all stick together. Let me do the talking, and we'll tell them we're here for the ahhh…Satyr gathering. But if anyone starts shooting, hit the ground as fast as you can."

The Twins gulped at this sobering admonition.

"Or spray first, and ask questions later," Timmy mumbled, turning to a somber Regina.

They proceeded carefully, flitting trunk to trunk. Sean was barely able to hear Timmy behind him, mumbling, "Two hundred and fifty million dollars, two hundred and fifty million dollars…"

"That's where the Three Spirits dude picked up his box of groceries, and left another list," Sean said, pointing to the cider press. But it was pitch dark and they could barely make it out, the full moon thus far a no-show. "And that's the trail I made, where those broken branches are." He took a deep breath. "Regina, give us those loppers. Okay, thanks. Let's go."

They stole across the open area and ducked into the blackness of the Thicket. Sean's pulse was going so loudly and rapidly, he was sure the Twins could hear it. Sean and Timmy, each armed with a lopper, widened the trail as they progressed—and, of course, raised the clearance too as needed, so Regina and her wig could bring up the rear without having to stoop to the height of a worm.

The Thicket swallowed them up. Sean hated to do it, but it was necessary to break out one of the flashlights now. He partially covered the front of it with his hand, to dim the light a bit, while Timmy lopped with a vengeance.

"The coyotes were right here," Sean whispered a minute later.

"Coyotes!" Regina cried. "You never said—coyotes?"

"Sssssssshhh!" Sean hissed. "Not so loud! I guess I…forgot."

"Just use your hairspray, Sis," Timmy advised.

"Oh, like I'd spray one of God's beautiful creatures with that!"

They proceeded along without incident for the next few minutes, Regina only having to stop twice to unstick her wig from an errant briar. Sean was glad for the soothing clamor of the crickets—there were legions of them—as the sound also camouflaged the snipping noise as Timmy continued to lop away while Sean held the light. Sean was starting to get a little chilly in his shirtless state, even though the sweat of nervousness was oozing down his sides.

"Look!" Timmy hissed at one point.

They all turned to see. A massive orange full moon was rising through the scrub of the Thicket behind them, like some exotic bird lifting up from her nest.

"That's the Hunter's Moon," Regina murmured.

"Well, it'll be like daylight here in a few minutes," Sean said.

"I hope we're the hunters, not the hunted," Timmy said.

Alas, such was not the case—even now, their trackers were only several dozen yards behind them.

They forged ahead. They hadn't gone too far when Sean stopped short. "*Duck!*" he commanded. They all crouched to the ground.

"What is it?" Regina whispered into Sean's ear.

"There's someone just ahead," Sean whispered back. "Look carefully, just past that big rock! See his plaid shirt?"

Regina gasped and brought her hand to her mouth.

"I think he's dead!" Timmy announced in a low murmur.

"Careful, it might be a trap!" Regina cautioned.

"No, I don't think there's anyone else around," Sean said. "Haven't you noticed how the crickets always stop when we approach, then they start up again once we pass through? The crickets are going nuts just ahead. I think he's alone."

They approached cautiously, their senses on full alert. It was a large man, lying on his side in the grass, wearing a blue and red checkered long-sleeve shirt and dungarees. By his rising and falling chest they could see that he wasn't dead.

"Somebody whacked him with that club!" Regina gasped. "Sean, is this the Three Spirits guy you were talking about?"

"No! I don't know who it is!" Sean answered, bewildered.

"Well, his pulse is very strong anyway," Regina said. Like many of the young people in town, Regina was a certified Life Guard.

"We can't leave him like this," Timmy said.

"I know it, but something tells me we've got to move on, too," Sean said. "Let's call 911 and get someone to come up here."

Regina reached into her bag and pulled out one of their phones. But Sean raised a finger just as she was dialing.

"Wait," he said. "Call Doctor Hallissey instead. Something tells me… we need to keep this quiet, and not have 10,000 cops up here."

"I think you're right," Regina said. "Plus you know Dr. Hallissey, he'll come up right away. I'll call him now." Everyone in town knew Doctor

Hallissey's number—it was 555 (the town's exchange) S-I-C-K.

Regina gave Doctor Hallissey the directions three times over, just to be sure, and also advised him to bring someone along, or two someones, to help carry the man if he was still unconscious by then.

"But won't you be there?" the doctor asked.

"Oh no, we've got a party to go to!" Regina said. "Bye, Doctor!" Then she hung up quick before she could get a lecture.

"I'll tell him the truth tomorrow, so he doesn't think I'm a heartless loser," she added.

This done, they reluctantly left the wounded man and continued on their way, apprehension swelling with each step: there could be no doubt now: someone was out and about in the Thicket hurting people, and they could be next. It was discouraging, but not all that surprising, to see what some people would do for a river of money.

At one point they flushed three birds from an adjacent tangle—but clearly Sean and the Twins were more frightened than the birds.

"If we were ten years older, we'd be dead from coronaries by now," Timmy panted, when he could finally speak again. Then Timmy started chuckling. Regina was crouched in a *Charlie's Angels* position, both hands wrapped around the huge can of *My Fair Lady* like she was auditioning for an action-thriller.

"Sssshhh!" Sean cautioned again. "We're coming up to the clearing I was telling you about—careful! Let me go first!"

They slowed, and crouched down even further. A sudden silence seemed to blanket the night. The crickets had stopped.

"Let me go ahead and check it out," Sean whispered when they reached the edge of the strangely-open area.

"But—" the Twins protested simultaneously.

"No buts! Really, let me go first. I'll wave behind my back if the coast is clear."

"Oh, how about hooting three times like a screech owl, and twice like a barn owl," Timmy joked.

"Not so loud!"

Sean stole into the clearing, his ears pricked, his heart racing, and every sense on full alert.

It was still amazing that someone had done all this clearing, and fairly recently too. But why? Why cut down dozens of trees and uproot scores of bushes? It made no sense at all.

Despite Sean's distraction, the feeling that Kyle was in peril hadn't gone away—and now it was joined by a feeling of danger, coming closer, gathering all around him. The Doomsday feeling grew so strong that at one point Sean's neck rapidly twisted left, then right—but nothing could he see or hear. Still, the sense of danger was like an actual weight he could feel on his shoulders. He stopped, crouched lower to the ground, and proceeded, more or less crawling.

He could clearly see the path he had forged last night, dead ahead, as the Thicket continued again. But after a minute of excruciatingly-slow poking around, he found what he was looking for: a second path, this one obviously more used, wider, more open, easier, about twenty feet to the left of the path he had blazed last night, and veering off in more or less the same direction: into the heart of Thicket.

Yes! He had deduced this second path, and here it was! For the first time in this long and complicated case, he thought that, well, maybe he *really* did have some detective skills.

He looked all around again just to make sure—but still, the feeling of danger wouldn't leave him.

"Just your paranoia after you found that guy," he told himself.

Unfortunately, such was not the case.

Sean stopped and waved his hand behind his back, signaling the Twins that it was okay to advance. Not only was this "new" trail wider and easier to navigate—Sean felt strongly that it led directly to the bell. He was certain of it.

But what was keeping Timmy and Regina? He turned and squinted across the clearing, the moon still about five minutes away from rising out onto this part of the Thicket. He was surprised to see that they weren't dashing across the clearing. He waved again, this time *once more with FEELING*, as Ms. Jabowski was always saying in Music class. And then he waited, his eyes burning.

But no Twins.

And then he knew.

Throwing caution to the wind, he sprinted across the clearing and came to the space they had all occupied mere minutes ago. With a sickening feeling, Sean saw that the Twins were gone. His head, seemingly of its own volition, snapped right, then left. On the ground before him, he saw the huge can of hairspray, its cap off, the smiling, blue-haired old lady on its front label beaming, seemingly mocking him.

Lying next to it was Regina's wig and her bag.

The Twins had been taken.

CHAPTER TWENTY
A PRINCESS TO THE RESCUE

Hardly knowing what he was doing, Sean grabbed the hairspray and tore off, back in the direction of Linger Longer. Regina and Timmy—my God, if anything ever—he'd *never* forgive himself!

Heedless of the brush he was racing through—alas, much of it poisons ivy and sumac, *again*—he didn't realize he was crying until he felt tears flying off his cheeks.

God, there goes my makeup, he thought.

But he stopped on a dime, as it were, after half a minute of hard puffy racing—as if someone had yanked him.

This is all wrong—go back in the other direction.

He shoved this new thought away, continuing toward Linger Longer—but at a slower pace. His friends had been taken—by whom he could only surmise—and it was his first duty to see if he could rescue them, or prevent them from being hurt. That was more important than anything, certainly more important than finding the bell.

But every instinct Sean possessed told him he was needed elsewhere. For what, he couldn't say. Was he going nuts? It made no sense—and yet the feeling was so strong he could almost taste it.

He stopped short again, his fists clenched. He felt like howling, caught between fire and flood. As if to make up his mind, he heard a voice coming from the woods just in front of him. It was an unfamiliar voice, a man's, and gruff: "I'll go and get the other one," it growled.

That did it. He could be of more service to the Twins if he was free; captive, he'd be no good to anyone. He yanked around and dashed back toward the heart of the Thicket, at a speed he knew few could match. As he passed through the sheltering tangle where he and the Twins had paused at the edge of the clearing, he saw Regina's bag, and snatched it as he flew by, as well as her wig, which he stuffed into the bag. He pushed down a lump in his throat. He raced across the clearing—the edge of it now drenched in yellow moonlight and spreading like a tide—and tore down the other path he had discovered earlier.

Yes, people definitely had been using this path for a while. The tall, straw-like grass of summer was all trampled down, and totally erased in some areas. Grasshoppers, cicadas, crickets, and other nightlings sprang out of his way as he dashed along. Then he slowed, the cool hand of caution holding him back: it wouldn't do to go racing around here like an idiot. He must not be taken unawares, like the Twins.

He crouched down and slowly advanced, his breath coming in steamy bursts he could see: it was growing cooler and a little misty. The moon spilled onto the path, so bright it lit up the silvery, dew-drenched autumn cobwebs, spanning the spaces between the wild asters to the goldenrod to the milkweed. Yet the feeling of imminent terror had flown off as quickly as the quail Sean and the Twins had spooked earlier. Instead, it was replaced by the certainty that he was very close to the bell.

He rounded the next corner in the path. Uh-oh: someone, or something, had been digging here; the ground was all mucked and torn and muddy.

He spotted a smaller side path that penetrated into the very heart of a bewildering emerald tangle. Bittersweet, poison ivy, wild grapevines, briars, wild black raspberries, and sumac, none giving any quarter, had fought it out in this one fecund spot; the result was a veritable explosion of choking growth. Even the moon was useless here; Sean flicked on his flashlight. Thick, mechanical tracks—they looked like tractor marks—had chewed up the ground here. Sean followed them into the heart of the tangle, a feeling of foreboding flooding him. As his eyes adjusted he saw dozens of snapped briars, dangling like atrophied limbs from the archway of green above and beside him: someone had recently been here; they had not come in on little cat feet.

He pushed a few more dangling fronds out of his way and rounded another bend. The tall grass was sweet but a little fetid—the last breath of summer.

And then there it was, what he had been looking for, the thing that had fallen through a collective crack in the minds and tales of the people of Nawshant in general, and the Sutherland Family in particular: a dark-gray block of granite, thick with moss and lichen. It was altar-shaped, and about ten feet wide, eight feet thick, and four feet high.

But it was also freshly split in two, and one half lay half-tumbled on the ground. Sean squatted and pushed away more tangles and briars. The stone had been engraved with letters that were just barely legible:

What the sea has sundered, let God reunite in heaven.

Beneath were the initials:

S.D

S.S.

Samuel Dimsworth and Sadie Sutherland. Undoubtedly.

Sean had found their grave. The hints in Patrick's journal had been right—the star-crossed lovers were buried together—not in Mount Linden Cemetery on the other side of the Thicket as everyone thought, but here, in the heart of the Thicket, on what was once Sutherland land.

But even as Sean's heart overflowed with this discovery, frustration and rage bubbled up from his innards, nearly choking him. The top of the bisected memorial clearly showed rust and age marks, and these marks were circular: it was too clear: a very large bell had sat atop this memorial. But now someone had smashed the monument in two, had desecrated the final resting place of Sadie and Samuel, in their heartless attempt to snatch the bell at all costs.

And they had. He was too late. The bell was gone.

He heard a noise and didn't realize at first it was the wind gushing out of him, as if someone had struck a blow to his stomach. He found that he was squatting on the damp grass.

He began crying again, this time in frustration.

What else could go wrong tonight? Some poor guy had been whacked senseless over the head; the Twins had been captured; the bell was gone; all their work had been for nothing. He clenched his fists and opened his mouth to roar—he didn't care anymore if he was overheard—

—but even as he did, a winking green light beside him caught the corner of his eye.

Something was flashing in Regina's canvas bag.

The phones! He had forgotten! He could call the police and get help to the Twins!

He snatched at the bag and began rifling through it, and discovered it was the flashing of his own phone: well well well, he had a new text message—actually one an hour old. It took him three tries in the state he was in—all-thumbs—to retrieve it.

From Kyle, his screen read. My God, how did Kyle know Sean's number? But leave it to him...Sean's heart leapt up. But the next and only word of the message made his blood freeze:

Help

This one word made Sean's heart break. Big tough cocky Kyle needed him, had swallowed his pride, had called on one of the only family members he had left in the world, because he was in danger, maybe even—

Sean checked the time of the message. 7:17 pm.

Over an hour ago. A lot could happen in an hour. Sean hit redial.

The call wouldn't go through.

For the first time in this case, Sean grew terrified. What if his cousin should…well, die? And what if the Twins—

He couldn't even go there. My God, Kyle had been right—clearly they *were* over their heads. How could he have been so dumb? To so underestimate what some people would do for that much money?

He stared at the phone like an idiot, as if it should say something more, tell him what to do next. His fingers were trembling.

He dialed 911. He thought his thumbs were getting in the way again, as the first two times this call wouldn't go through either. When nothing happened the third time, he knew something else was up. He clicked his phone shut. He opened again and dialed Uncle Justin's number—Uncle Justin always knew what to do in any situation.

But that call wouldn't go through either. Then he tried using the Twins' phones, first Regina's, then Timmy's—nothing. Power must be out all over town.

Now what?

Yes, clearly he was over his head—no one could blame him now if he just went home, nursed his wounds, and called the authorities from the safety of his house's land-line—if that even still worked.

But somehow he couldn't do this. The conviction broke over him like a spring flood—it was up to him, and him alone. He had to act—now—there was something he had to do—

—and yet here he stood, shivering his head off, terrified, clueless, half-naked in a ridiculous outfit, and itchier than he could ever remember.

What happened next would be the most difficult part in all of this to explain, afterwards: it was as if a voice spoke to him then—*Go on!* it said. *Go on!* Aunt Sadie's mantra—but where to?

Before he was conscious of what he was doing, Sean found he was jogging back down the trail, following the fresh tractor ruts. They meandered a bit, at first, skirting a few errant boulders and a massive white pine, then cut due west.

My God, he thought in disgust, it was appalling the damage the thieves had done here with their tractor. Small trees were down, bushes pulverized, and, at one point, Sean saw something that wasn't moving, by the edge of the trail. It looked like either a rabbit or a possum—some poor thing unlucky enough to be in the way of the marauders. This seemed the greatest outrage of all. Sean was running at his top speed now, and after several minutes it was clear where the tractor's tracks were leading: to Nawshant's ancient burial ground, Mount Linden Cemetery, on the western border of the Thicket. On a bee line.

Of course. They knew what they were doing.

Just before reaching the cemetery, Sean could see by the freshly flattened grass that the thieves had placed the bell down for a moment, in order to smash through the old six-foot tall fieldstone wall that separated this part of the Thicket from the deep western end of Mount Linden Cemetery. Well of course no one would hear them way out here—it was probably at least a half-mile in every direction from anyone's home. The earth-scarring tracks continued into the cemetery, and here the blackguards had uncaringly bashed over half a dozen ancient slate tombstones on their way to one of the small roads that snaked through the centuries-old burial ground.

Sean kept running, passing through the wide gap in the tumbling stone wall, appalled at the thieves' arrogance.

Then he saw something. He froze, then ducked behind one of the ancient linden trees that gave this place its name: a large and vaguely mechanical-looking something lay just 50 yards ahead of him, under the black umbrella of a massive white oak older than the town itself. All seemed quiet, except for the thudding of pulse in his ears, and the profound chanting of crickets and cicadas.

He dodged from tree to tree until he was about twenty yards away, shoving recollections of Miss Sawyer's graveyard tale to the back of his mind. But Regina had undoubtedly been right: a cemetery was most definitely a different kind of place at night. Regina! What was happening to her now? Again he had to fight the temptation to run back and try to help the Twins.

He got closer to the object. Yes, there could be no doubt: the hulking machine was a medium-sized, fat-tired front loader, seemingly deserted. Sean hummed a flinty rock at it from behind the safety of his tree. When nothing happened after the sharp *clank*, he moved closer.

Undoubtedly it was the same machine which, only a short while ago, had carried the bell from its poignant resting place to here: the tracks ended right at this particular machine, and its engine was still warmly redolent with the smell of hot diesel. Emblazoned on the sides of the yellow loader was *Town of Nawshant*, wrapped around the town seal.

Talk about nerve—the thieves had taken the very machine that dug the graves and lifted the coffins here at the cemetery to do their dirty work, knowing the graveyard would be deserted at night, especially a Saturday night. *Aren't they the bold ones!* Sean could almost hear Margaret saying, in her accusatory facetiousness.

But then what? What had the thieves done after that? Obviously the bell had been transferred to some other vehicle. Errant strips of torn burlap littered the ground, amidst a stampede of footprints. Sean beamed the flashlight onto the ground: sure enough, the impressions of wide tires showed that a good-size truck had been here quite recently. Sean knew it was recent—tiny particles of dirt on the edges of the tire marks were still falling into the deeper ruts.

The road was still muddy and wet enough from the storm the other night to have left a bit of mud on the tires of the truck the thieves had used to take the bell away. Sean broke into a light jog, following the wide and muddy tire marks all the way up to the ornate traceries of the wrought-iron front gates of the cemetery.

Of course the gates were locked at this hour—or at least appeared to be; but on closer examination Sean observed that the padlock had been pried apart, and the gates were merely closed, not locked. But they were still too heavy and large for Sean to push open.

So he climbed up and sailed over them: but not without incident. One of the top spokes on the gate snatched at his ballet pants just as he was going over, and put a nice rip down one side of them. Good grief, whatever next? He clutched one hand to his waist to keep them from falling down, feathers and all.

Enough caked mud had remained on the truck's tires to leave a barely visible impression out on the road here. The moon was so bright now he didn't need his flashlight: the truck had turned left, westward, onto Ocean Road, upon leaving the cemetery. That made sense, as the Causeway, only half a mile down the street, was the only way in or out of town—at least by truck.

Sean jogged out onto the middle of the deserted road. From this height—the second highest point in Nawshant, after Linger Longer—he could see down to the Causeway itself.

My *God!* It looked like the authorities had taken Miss Sawyer's advice, and sealed off the town's border. All kinds of blue and red lights were flashing, and from here it almost looked like one of the town's two fire engines—Ladder One—was parked sideways across the road, partially blocking all entrance and egress.

It took Sean a moment to realize why the blaring, flashing lights stood out in such stark relief to the inky night sky: all other lights were out—streetlights, houselights, the works: the town was suffering a blackout. Coincidence? Sean doubted it. That explained why the phones were out as well—being a peninsula thrust out to sea, cell phones had seldom worked on the "island" until a tower had been erected up by Second Cliff eight years ago; it had already come down once in a blizzard— it wouldn't be hard for the thieves to disable it, thus rendering communication on Nawshant nearly impossible.

Go on! he heard again inside him, with more urgency. *Go on!*

Sean found next that he was trotting down Ocean Road, heading toward the Causeway, Regina's bag flapping lightly against the chilled bare skin of his back, and one hand still clutched at his waist where his ballet pants were torn. Although he was getting very anxious about the time—God knew where the thieves were now, and presumably Kyle with them—he didn't question his behavior—his instincts seemed to know what they were doing; or, at least, the voice did.

It wasn't until he was nearly at the beginning of the Causeway that his conscious mind understood why he had come here: if the thieves had left town, this is where they had done it, and someone here must have seen them. He hurried on.

What a scene met him—a blaring line of traffic trying to get out of town, a bigger line trying to get in, and at least seven police cruisers. *My God*, Sean wondered, *did they all just have new lights, bells, and whistles installed?* They were all flashing and chirping like a disco dance gone terribly wrong. Although Sean knew all the safety personnel in town, he didn't recognize anyone now— for here were State Police, Tactical Police, some kind of swat team complete with all the accoutrements, people from the FBI—

Some of the flashlight-wielding officers were occupied with those vehicles trying to get out, while others were questioning those trying to drive in. Other uniformed people stood in scattered groups, deep in conversation, their arms folded tightly and their legs spread wide. Sean approached the nearest of these.

"Excuse me," Sean began, tapping the shoulder of one of them, who was standing with one of his brethren. "I was wondering if you could tell me if a truck came through here a little while ago."

The man wheeled around, then jumped back.

"Get your hands up on your head! Do it now!" he barked.

"But I—there's some mistake, I'm just—"

"Do it now!" he echoed. He put his hand on his holster—my *God*, he was serious!

"Well see, officer, if I do, my pants will fall down and…well, I don't think either of us wants that," Sean dithered. "Now, if my father were a leading detective in Bayport, we wouldn't be having this misunderstanding." Sean smiled weakly, trying to crack a joke. But apparently the officer's youthful reading hadn't included the H-B's, as he didn't remove his hand from his holster—and he certainly wasn't laughing.

Then two flashlights blazed onto Sean's face. More police approached.

"Were you in a fire, sir?" one of the other officers asked.

Sir? "No, I—if you'd just let me explain, I'm Sean Sutherland. I live here in Nawshant, this is poison ivy, and—"

"Turn around," the first, humorless one barked, so quickly the words mushed together, and Sean didn't comprehend him.

"Excuse me?"

"Turn around!" he repeated.

This time Sean complied.

"*Question Authority. Overthrow the prevailing p—-paradigm*," the man read off of Sean's body—Regina's graffiti—though his pronunciation of the last word was, Sean thought, well…criminal.

"I told you terrorists were behind this," Sean heard the man mutter to his companion. "They steal art to finance their—"

"Look Jimmy, I don't think—" the other men began, but he was interrupted by the first one.

"I've got authority here, Ben, no offense. Or at least, the chief does. Let's see what he has to say."

The chief? Who the heck was the chief? Sean wondered.

Speaking into a walkie-talkie thingy that he unfastened from his belt, the first officer intoned, "Sir, we got a situation down here at Alpha Base One."

The Causeway was now Alpha Base One? Sean thought. And he himself was a situation? *Really?*

"*Go ahead, Base One,*" was the crackling response.

"We got...some kind of...weirdo, possibly a suspect. He's a radical anyway." The man paused, and looked at Sean with narrowed eyes. "He's got some fancy pants on, with feathers, and nothing else. And sayings written on his body about overthrowing *paradigums*."

"*I'll be right there. Detain for questioning.*"

Questioning! My *God! Quelle* nightmare—Sean didn't have time!

"Look officers, I'm really anxious now to find out if—"

But alas! Sean never finished his sentence; and what happened next seemed to happen in very slow motion. Something—or someone—grabbed Regina's over-the-shoulder bag from behind him, yanked on it with a gentle but insistent strength neither Sean nor gravity could resist, and the next thing he knew, the upper part of his body was executing a kind of backward somersault, the pivot point being his backside, which was suddenly pressed against something solid and metallic. The world turned upside down, the officers seemed to recede backward, and suddenly Sean found that he was on the pink-carpeted floor of the stadium-sized back seat of *Princess Margaret*—Miss Sarah Sawyer's block-long antique convertible.

"Gentlemen, this is Sean Sutherland. I know him well. He's done nothing wrong and is needed by Captain Smollett for questioning. I have special clearance from Captain Smollett! I have special clearance from Captain Smollett!"

Miss Sawyer kept braying this phrase over and over, her left hand on her fog-horn-like car horn, her elbow steering, and her other hand flapping an official-looking piece of paper as she dodged through and around the gathered crowd; then she raised choking clouds of dust and sand as she swept round the flashing *Engine One* blocking the entrance to the Causeway.

"H and B, Danny darling!" she waved, for finally here was a native manning Ladder One: Danny Munelly, twenty-year veteran of the Naw-shant Fire Department. "By which of course I mean, Hi and Bye!"

"Come back here!" Sean heard over a tinny bullhorn, as they raced away from the growing melee. He raised himself from the floor, his mouth open wide, and found Ms. Hortense Tremont, Miss Sawyer's sister-in-law and frequent guest at Lily Vale, smiling beside him. She was sitting primly, her hands folded on her lap, in the back seat on the other side of the car—as was her wont when riding with Miss Sawyer.

"Hello, Sean dear!" she smiled, with a little wave.

"Sean, climb up to the front, there's a good boy," Miss Sawyer commanded, brushing her hair out of her eyes as the car accelerated. "Horty had a chauffeur as a child and frequently likes to reenact the experience, so I indulge her, however specious. I say, Sean, your outfit seems to be a little worse for wear! What'd you do, fall down? And my! You weren't kidding about the poison ivy, were you dear?"

Miss Sawyer shouted out these words as she put pedal to metal and began racing down the two-mile-long causeway that linked Nawshant with the mainland.

Sean again reached behind him in vain for some kind of seat restraint, but no. He could hardly get a word out of his mouth.

"I…ahhh…" he stammered.

"Take your time, dear. It'll be several minutes until we come to our next….*contretemps*," Miss Sawyer smiled. Evidently she was enjoying this.

"Who's Captain Smollett?" Sean finally blurted, a question not quite at the top of the priority pile, but his mind was a reeling hot mess.

"Oh, *that*! I just flung out the first name that came to me," Miss Sawyer answered, with a careless wave of her hand. "Never doubt the long-term value of a liberal education, Sean Sutherland. In point of fact, Captain Smollett was the wonderfully commanding man who skippered *The Hispaniola*. In *Treasure Island*? You look at me as if I were speaking Greek! What are they teaching you in that school?"

Such a question seemed absurd at a time like this, so instead Sean asked, "Where are we going?"

"I don't know dear, you tell me," Miss Sawyer answered. "The thieves have left town—that much I can tell you. So, I suppose we're going after them, aren't we?" Miss Sawyer tossed the loose end of her flowery scarf back behind her neck. Then she turned to Sean. "Well?"

"What do you mean, the thieves?" Sean stalled.

"The bell thieves, of course!" Miss Sawyer blared.

"Holy—how do you know about the bell?" Sean stammered.

"My dear Sean! You simply *don't* allow for the inquisitiveness of people!" Miss Sawyer chuckled. "Of course, you know I'm good friends with Abby—Mrs. Hutchinson—and she mentioned to me some weeks ago that she was hearing a bell, tolling from the middle of the Thicket. I didn't pay too much attention to that until everyone started asking about Aunt Sadie and her bell—you, your cousin, that…odious real estate salesperson—inquiring at the library, digging up things at the Historical Society—so I assumed someone, at long last, had found Aunt Sadie's missing bell, and was ringing it in the Thicket."

"You should tell him about the Twins," Ms. Tremont interrupted loudly from the back seat. "And Sarah, do put the top up! My hair! This breeze!"

"Quiet, Horty, you're distracting me, and I can never drive when I'm distracted. Remember dear, we're just *pretending* I'm your chauffeur."

"But my hair!"

"What about the Twins?" Sean asked breathlessly.

"They're fine, dear. But all that must be later. Where to?"

"Just one more question," Sean persisted. "How do you know the bell thieves left town?"

"We've seen them!" Miss Sawyer announced dramatically. "Horty and I were coming down Ocean Road not so very long ago—I'm driving her home from my dinner party—and suddenly there was this large, boxy truck in front of us. It was that long stretch of the road that goes by the cemetery, and I knew they hadn't been in front of us before that. That raised my suspicions, for clearly they had come out of the cemetery. Well, then, I drove close enough to read the signage on the back of the truck—"

"We practically rammed them," Ms. Tremont called from the back. "I told her to—"

"I'm telling this, please," Miss Sawyer snapped, giving her sister-in-law a baleful look via the rear-view mirror, which was edged in rhinestones. "But when I read that the truck said *Museum of Fine Arts, Boston*, my suspicions were calmed. I assumed of course that the art theft had brought some experts up here. But the more I thought of it, the more it seemed the only place the truck *could* have come from was the graveyard. And so we turned round—"

"I can still smell the burning rubber!" Ms. Tremont shouted.

"—and drove back to the cemetery. I saw for myself the broken front gate and the truck's tire tracks, and knew something fishy was going on. It was just then that we saw the Twins. They were getting out of Doctor Hallissey's car, helping a wounded man into the Doctor's house—which as you know is right past the cemetery. They told us the painting theft wasn't the big deal—Aunt Sadie's bell was the big deal, and it was very close to being found, and it was somewhere in the heart of the Thicket, which was where you were, Sean, they said. They said they were going back to look for you in the Thicket, but we proceeded post-haste to the Causeway, as now my suspicions had been thoroughly aroused again. And then I remembered something else that my subconscious mind had observed, and I hadn't: the shock absorbers of the truck were pushed way down, as if the truck were carrying something *ponderously* heavy. And then I knew! The blackguards had the bell, and had plowed through the cemetery with it! But when we gave chase and came back to the Causeway, the prey had flown the coop. I don't know how they talked their way through, but they did. But, well, I suppose a *child* could do that!" Here Miss Sawyer laughed, and took a peek into the mirror.

"Anyway: we were waiting in queue with the other cars—you know how much I love that!—and then we saw you up the front of the line, being bothered by that rather obtuse and unevolved person with the shaved head. So we decided we had to come to your rescue. I believe you are now debriefed, Sean."

"My hair, Sarah!" Ms. Tremont wailed from the back seat. "I just had it done this morning!"

"One more word, Horty, and I put you out on the side of the road! You can walk home to Salem! But Sean, this brings us back to the original question—where shall we go? In other words, where have the thieves gone? How are we to know?"

Sean sighed. "I don't know. But if you think about it, the thieves have two choices: to put the bell into hiding for a while, somewhere local, or to get the heck out of Dodge."

"I would put my money on the latter, were I a betting woman," Miss Sawyer answered. "Which I'm not."

"Except for our monthly trip to Foxwoods," Ms. Tremont commented. *My God, she certainly had good hearing*, Sean thought, *to catch every word above the flood-rushing of the cool air.*

"I agree," Sean said. "So, if they're getting out of here, they'll definitely ditch the truck—which was stolen anyway of course. I doubt they'd take a chance driving somewhere far—besides, something this valuable will probably go out of the country. That means by boat, or air. So either the airport, or some close-by harbor."

"Very good, Sean!" Miss Sawyer beamed. "That's perfectly sound, and I note with pleasure that they *are* apparently teaching you something in that school!"

"But the biggest thing is—I think my cousin Kyle is with them. He's in danger anyway. He knew more about this all than we did somehow, and he sent me a text about an hour ago asking for help."

"*Did* he?" Miss Sawyer answered after a moment. Her tongue worked around the inside of her cheek thoughtfully. "Well then, I believe we're all set!"

"How do you mean?" Sean asked.

"I'll explain soon—get out. We must get you into the trunk."

Sean almost found himself on the hood of the boat-large vehicle, as Miss Sawyer slammed on Princess Margaret's brakes.

"But—"

"No buts!" Miss Sawyer commanded. "Just do it! There's another checkpoint ahead, or my name's Jackie Robinson. Get out, I say!"

Sean agreed this might be a wise thing to do under current conditions. He got out—being careful to keep one hand on his torn pants—then climbed into the trunk once Miss Sawyer opened it for him. As he did so, Ms. Tremont said, "Speaking of Robinsons, Sarah, did I tell you Alice Robinson's brother's uncle had his spleen removed last Wednesday? He's the one who owned that art gallery up in Ogunquit—"

"Hush, Horty dear, I'm trying to think of a good excuse," was the muffled response, as Miss Sawyer resumed her breakneck pace.

My God, Sean thought, it was vast as a living room here in the trunk; yet still he thanked saints that he wasn't claustrophobic, like the poor Twins. Well, at least they were safe—he couldn't wait to find out what had happened, and how they had gotten away from their assailants. Now his boat-load of grim worry shifted onto Kyle, and what might be happening to his cousin right now—

But these thoughts too were pushed away moments later as Miss Sawyer neared what must have been the end of the Causeway, where, apparently, more minions of the law were gathered. The car slowed. Sean heard muffled voices; then the car stopped, though Miss Sawyer did not turn off Princess Margaret's mighty engine.

I must ask you to pull over Ma'am, and turn off your vehicle while we search your vehicle. We've just had word you're harboring a fugitive.

"Fugitive? Nonsense! Horty here hasn't done anything illegal since Prohibition, have you dear?"

There was a young man in your car, ma'am, and I'm afraid—

"I'm afraid too, officer, and my fear is for your *job*, and any number of ugly suits-at-law, if I don't get Horty home to her medicine in a timely fashion. And if you're referring to the child we had in our car some moments ago, that was just a local urchin whom we dropped off at the beach a ways back."

What's wrong with your friend, Ma'am, that she needs medicine?

"Oh, well, uhm, where to begin? Let me see now…diabetes, glaucoma, beriberi, general malaise, ennui, rickets, cat-scratch fever, a persistent willfulness—you name it and she has it! It would be easier to tell you what the poor thing doesn't have. So, we must be moving on, you see, and—"

I'm sorry Ma'am, we'll at least have to search your trunk.

"Are you doubting my word, sir?"

Sean could almost feel the iron-gray bristling of Miss Sawyer from way back here.

No ma'am, but I have my orders, and those are to apprehend a car fitting this description that just left the other end of the Causeway against orders. So if you'll just—

But the rest of the officer's words were lost in a squealing of tires and the lashing of 402 horses, as Princess Margaret and its occupants departed the final checkpoint at what felt like the speed of sound. Sean, buffeted about in the trunk like a cork in a storm-tossed sea, didn't know whether to laugh or cry at this latest development.

"I'm not sure there was a need for that, Sarah," Sean heard through the back panels, Ms. Tremont commenting on their hasty departure. "You were going along quite nicely with all that lying about my medical conditions."

"Well, hardly," Miss Sawyer snuffed in return. "Your winsome smile at him when I was describing your alleged maladies hardly helped the cause,

I must say. Besides, don't you find, Horty, that a good old-fashioned car chase does wonders for the circulation? And we need to think about such things at our age."

"Car chase? Whatever can you mean, Sarah?"

"Turn round, dear."

"Oh my, you're right! Why, they're coming after us!"

"You have a flair for the obvious, Horty. Sean Sutherland! Sean Sutherland, can you hear me?"

"Yes, Miss Sawyer."

"There's a fat upholstered panel at the end of the trunk—push that and you'll come through into the back seat."

It was too dark to see in the trunk, so Sean had to feel his way around until he came to the object in question. With a good stiff bash, the panel popped out, and Sean squinted even in the night as he resumed his seat in the front, scrambling forward with a great deal of trepidation. In the far rear distance—but not far enough—he could see flashing blue lights in rapid pursuit. Whatever next?

"Now, Sean, show me that phone of yours for a moment. Ahhh! Wonderful! As good sense would dictate, you have laid in a newer version of these oft-times annoying but increasingly indispensable objects. Bring up your Recent Calls menu for me, if you would be so kind."

"It's freezing back here! Put on the heat, Sarah!"

"Sorry dear, will do. But if you really want to be helpful Horty, keep a weather eye on our pursuers and give me sporadic updates on their progress. Now Sean—watch this!"

Miss Sawyer snatched the phone from Sean, entered a few different numbers, (while still managing to keep half an eye on the swiftly passing road) then handed the phone back to Sean. To Sean's amazement, a screen he hadn't seen before materialized on his phone's display panel, ultimately showing what looked like a road map with a circled yellow object in its center.

Sean looked closer.

"This is…wait a minute, this is Salem, just a few miles north of here!" he gasped. "Lafayette Street, Canal Street—it's Salem!"

"Yes, the wonderful world of GPS!" Miss Sawyer chuckled. "Fortunately it seems your cousin left his GPS on, and—fortunately again!—we're on the road to Salem now, even as we speak. A quick drive through Swampscott and Marblehead, and *voila!* We'll be there! I *loathe* the technology—Big Brother, and eye in the sky and all that—surveillance is on the march, if not freedom—but I must admit it *does* come in handy from time to time."

"Like when one is chasing international art thieves, for example," Ms. Tremont commented, laughing. "By the by, they're gaining on us."

"Oh dear," Miss Sawyer answered, increasing the car's already reckless speed as she scanned the rear-view again. "Thank heavens today's Saturday! I always fill Princess Margaret up of a Saturday."

Sean was now shivering uncontrollably. He suddenly remembered his shirt in Regina's bag. He reached into the back seat, pulled the bag up front, and pulled out two of the flannel shirts.

"I say, what is that, in the bag?" Miss Sawyer commented, glancing to the floor beside her. "A family of beaver? You haven't turned into a poacher I hope, Sean?"

"Oh, no, that's ahhh…Regina's wig. It was part of our costume tonight, because…well, it's kind of a long story."

"The Twins told us all about it," Ms. Tremont yelled from the back seat. "By the way, Sarah, they're *still* gaining on us."

"May I see it, please?" Miss Sawyer asked, snatching at the wig. "Oh my! This wig is *fabulous!* I wonder from where she got it, did she say? No? Well, I've always believed there are certain activities that one performs better in costume. I think chasing art thieves and rescuing one's cousin would be two of these. Oh, look at *me!* I look simply *fabul—*"

To Sean's mingled surprise and horror, Miss Sawyer donned Regina's very large Tina Turner wig, and now resembled nothing more than—well, if not Big Foot, then perhaps Big Foot's mother-in-law. But alas! Miss Sawyer's sentence went unfinished; for she had forgotten—but the laws of physics had not—the rushing ocean of air pouring over and above and around Princess Margaret. The wig became instantly airborne.

What happened next, at the time, seemed the essence of divine intervention—so much so that Sean looked skyward to see if there might be any Moses' Horns or disembodied cherubs flying about. Later, Sean came to believe it was simply a matter of gravity, wind, and mass; at any rate, no matter the reason, the massive wig flew backyards, and came to an immediate halt against the first object it came into contact with: the windshield of the police car closing in behind them. The speed of the officers' car kept it lodged against their windshield like a splattered moth, splaying it out in fact so that navigation became guesswork at best—and hazardous at worst:

To wit: there was a squealing of brakes as the cruiser came to a somewhat sudden and careening stop. It bounced onto a deserted sidewalk, knocking over three newspaper vending machines as it did. Suddenly the air behind them was thick with penny-shopper tabloid periodicals, fluttering about like a thousand startled pigeons. As if in sympathy, the hood of the cruiser popped open, and steam—a sensitive car's tears—gushed forth hysterically.

"Oh dear!" Miss Sawyer commented blithely, as she scanned the rear-view mirror. "I believe they've come upon a lee shore!"

"It doesn't look like anyone's hurt," Mrs. Tremont reported a moment later. "In fact, one of the officers is shaking his fist at us."

"Well he might!" Miss Sawyer chuckled. "I've heard that song before! Resistance," she continued, "is *feudal*."

"Why, look, Sarah!" Ms. Tremont added. One of the loose newspapers had blown into the back seat and she was now perusing it. "*Priscilla of Marblehead* is having its annual autumn sale!"

Good grief! Sean thought. It was one thing for wealthy, mad-cap, politically-connected retirees to engage in car chases involving officers of the law; but he had a future to think about! Whatever next?

"Update me on the location of the thieves, if you please, Sean," Miss Sawyer commanded.

"They've turned onto Sea Street now," Sean answered, looking again at his phone. "They must have a ship waiting in Salem Harbor!"

"No doubt. But—I say—we're far too conspicuous in this vehicle," Miss Sawyer commented, as they crossed the town line from Swampscott into Marblehead. She pushed a button on her dashboard, and Princess Margaret's top began slowly, regally, rising.

"But you wouldn't raise it for me when I was cold, and concerned for my hair!" Ms. Tremont protested.

"Now if I had, dear, those fine young police officers would still be chasing us," Miss Sawyer soothed. She reduced her speed, obeyed all traffic lights, and even let a young family coming out of a frozen yogurt shop cross the street.

"It looks like the bad guys are headed onto Salem Neck," Sean reported a moment later. He looked up at the road before them, then craned his neck behind. There were no signs of pursuit.

"I just can't understand why they didn't radio ahead," Ms. Tremont commented, "and have other officers waiting for us, like they do in the movies. Oops! Oh dear! I've spoken too soon!"

"You've gone and jinxed us, Horty!" Miss Sawyer snapped.

Alas, it was true—three or four blocks ahead, where the main road split, two police cruisers, their lights ablaze, were partially blocking the intersection. Miss Sawyer responded by hanging a sudden right, which brought them down a quiet sylvan street of magnificent old Victorian-style homes.

"I don't think they saw us, but don't let's take any chances," she added, as she raced up the very long driveway of the fourth house down on the left. "Get down everybody!" she cried, as she shut off Princess Margaret and ditched the lights. They all scooted down. Less than a minute later, two patrol cars went whizzing down the street.

Everything was blissfully silent after that for a time.

My God, what a ruse, Sean thought. Either Miss Sawyer had watched too many detective movies, or perhaps had been a gun moll in a previous life.

"That was close, Sarah," Ms. Tremont commented. "But what are we to do now?"

"We do what all sensible people do in situations like these," Miss Sawyer answered, firing up the car again. "We *cause a diversion*." She squealed back down the driveway, then drove up to the corner, where she apparently found what she was looking for: a firebox. She trotted out, pulled the handle, then hopped back into the car.

"I've never done that in my life before!" she giggled, almost deliriously. "And don't either of you tell me that, like me, you haven't always longed to!" Then she turned the car around, headed back down the side street, and, after a myriad of twistings and turnings, came out on the other side of the police blockade, close to the Salem line. When they turned around, they saw that the blockade had been abandoned in the thought that a fire was taking place round the corner—or perhaps they had joined in the pursuit.

Sean inwardly groaned—between the occasional expletives, and Miss Sawyer's less than upstanding behavior—however necessary—he didn't see how he could ever chronicle the Mystery of the Tolling Bells.

They crossed over the bridge into Salem, and then Miss Sawyer took an abrupt right, which quickly brought them into a waterside industrial neighborhood of old factories, rotting warehouses, and fish processing plants. A clammy, oily smell stained the air. Wraith-like strands of fog spun up from the water, draping things in a surreal melancholy. Sean was feeling both hyper and depressed.

"Now, this is the very oldest part of Salem," Miss Sawyer briskly commented, unaffected by the surroundings. Unbelievably she pulled over and, reverting to her Head Librarian tone, turned to Sean and said, her eyes half closed, "It is thought that it was somewhere round here Roger Conant first landed, almost four hundred years ago. And *don't* dare ask me who Roger Conant was, Sean Sutherland! We're also quite close to where the Great Salem Fire of 1914 began."

"Oh, that's…interesting, Miss Sawyer! But maybe we should—"

"Move on? Yes. Where are the thieves now, Sean?"

"They're out on Salem Neck," Sean answered, keeping one eye on the phone. "It looks like they're heading to the eastern end of it."

"Winter Island! Or Halftide Rock, then," she murmured. "No, it wouldn't be Winter Island, that's too residential. Far too many prying eyes—Halftide Rock, I'll bet. Fort Avenue, then!"

She increased her speed and navigated the labyrinthine neighborhood as if she had grown up here—she hadn't, she mentioned this several times. There was some difference of opinion at one point, where a new development was about to go up, and Ms. Tremont insisted that they go left. They did, and it turned out to be the right move. They came onto Fort Avenue, the long straight road that ran out to Salem Neck, an oblong chunk of land bravely thrusting its rocky head out into the Atlantic.

"They've turned left at Columbus Square," Sean reported.

"What?" Miss Sawyer gasped. "Hmmm. That can only mean one thing—they're making for Salem Willows Park. Very interesting."

"Why?" Sean asked.

"Well, for the simple reason that there are arcades there, and an amusement park of sorts, rather old fashioned. And centuries old white willows. Don't tell me you've never been there?"

"Uncle Justin brought me there when I was little, and we'd ride the merry-go-round," Sean answered. "But I don't remember much of it."

"I would think it would be quite crowded on a Saturday night. But perhaps they think they'll attract less notice as a result."

"There was such a case in a Sherlock Holmes adventure," Sean re-called. "The murderers shot someone next to a shooting arcade, and went thoroughly unnoticed."

"Hmmm," Miss Sawyer answered. "I must have missed that one—but perhaps our thieves did not."

They turned left at Columbus Square, and within seconds came up to the entrance of the old amusement part. A gate across the road said that the park was closed for the season, for renovations.

"They went around, look at the tracks!" Sean cried. "And the signal's gone now from the phone!"

It was true. The display panel on Sean's cell now read, *Signal Lost.* He wondered what that meant— probably nothing good.

"Hurry, Miss Sawyer," Sean mumbled. "I have a bad feeling!"

Miss Sawyer hit the gas as she, too, wheeled around the gate. They turned onto Restaurant Row, a willow-shaded by-way that took them past the various boarded-up eateries here, keeping an eye to the left, where the rock-bound ocean lay. Miss Sawyer dimmed, then finally cut, her lights. In a moment their eyes adjusted—the full moon lit up the land like a weak sun. But beneath and beside the rows of ancient willows, all was impen-etrable. Where was Kyle? Had they discovered his phone?

"Under that tree right there was the very first place a man kissed me," Ms. Tremont reminisced from the back, rearranging with one hand her navy blue pill-box hat. The interjection seemed to come at Sean from another realm he was so anxious, his pulse hammering in his ears again. A sense of urgency was rising around him like a flood—

"And not for the last time either, eh dear?" Miss Sawyer answered. They turned a bend. The road became a cement walkway through the grounds, but it was easy to see where the truck had gone, for the divots in the grass were plain as day. They followed along. They came to a bit of a rise and could see in the short distance a wharf stretching out into the foggy water; the white metal gate to the dock had been knocked down, and a boxy white truck, its back door thrown up and open, sat at the end of the pier, the fog wraiths streaming loosely all around it. Next to the truck was a now-abandoned small tractor, a large-ish Bobcat by the look of it. The scene had a general air of abandonment about it. The *glug-glug* of the sea went on unperturbed. "There they are!" Miss Sawyer hissed, as a vague outline of a large boat materialized through the fog.

"We're too late!" Sean cried at the same time. He vaulted out of the car, not bothering with the heavy door. "Call the Coast Guard if they take off!"

"Sean! Get back here!" Miss Sawyer cried.

But Sean was already racing across the grassy slope leading to the dock, one hand on his pants. He cut left, diving into the deep shade of the willows that gave this park its name, then bounded from tree to tree. The fog around the end of the dock spun and drifted nightmarishly—yes, definitely something large and seaworthy was alongside the dock. His pulse pounding louder in his ears, Sean slipped over the broken dock-gate; then, half-crouched, cautiously made his way down the long wooden dock.

A large, sleek, exotic-looking white ship—not quite a yacht but near enough—was tied up at the dock's end. Her bow was heading into the open seas. She had no name, but a long series of numbers; it was registered, Sean noted, under the Panamanian flag—which, like Biblical charity, he knew, covered a multitude of sins. He could see no one, nor could he hear any voices. She was big—a fifty-five footer at least. He crouched down, then sidled out of the blobs of moonlight illuminating most of the dock. With a deep bass throb the ship suddenly roared up, with cloggy rumbles. Sean thought he might pass out, so startled did this make him— whatever she was, she was packing lots of firepower. He trotted back down the dock, toward the ship's stern, utterly bewildered and powerless, yet still almost immobilized by the sense of urgency he felt. What should he do? And why had they ever ditched the police? They needed them now!

He heard a voice, echo-ish and blunt; then the unmistakable sound of heavy rope being chucked ashore—she was casting off!

Sean took a deep breath, kicked off his sneakers, and without thinking sailed over the dock's railing and landed with what he hoped was a quiet, all-fours plop onto the starboard deck. At the same time the ship throttled down, then began slowly chugging backward; then she came astern and began heading out.

Breathless, hardly believing what he had just done, Sean waited for his rib-banging pulse to slow before trying to figure out what his next move should be. There was no turning back now! There were a series of cabinets lining the lower part of the deck; some opened from the front, others from above. The fourth one of these latter was open; Sean scrambled inside. The storage box was empty except for a vast length of blue fiberglass rope, neatly coiled in one corner, and a life-preserver of sorts in the shape of a seat cushion. The compartment stank of rotten shrimp or something. The box was almost tall enough for him to stand up in; he lowered its top almost all the way, leaving about an inch from which he could peek out.

He took stock. They had left the dock behind and were chugging around the northeastern edge of Salem Head, the boulder-strewn shore fifty yards or so off the starboard side. Past the southern edge of Salem Head lay the mouth into Salem Harbor; they certainly wouldn't be headed into port at this point. Once around the Head, they had two choices: they could pick up Salem Channel to the northeast; or Marblehead Channel to the east. In either case caution was vital: the waters here were studded with treacherous rocks, complicated ledges, and almost-hidden islands that were tricky enough by day—but could be deadly at night, especially in fog. While Sean and his friends may not have known the various chants that described the diverse buoys around Nawshant, as past generations had, they did know, from years of sailing and cruising up and down this coast, the maritime hazards that were scattered just offshore: Ram's Head Rock, Abbot Rock, Little Haste and Great Haste Islands, the Egg, Pope Head, Satan Rock, Finn's Ledge, the Great Ledge, and dozens of other disasters-waiting-to-happen.

He calmed himself enough to realize his phone was still clutched in the tight red fist of his left hand. Somehow this comforted him, this link to the outside world. He lowered the cover of the storage bin all the way and dialed the Twins, first Regina, then Timmy—but nothing went through. Whether service had been restored on Nawshant he wasn't sure—because he checked his signal and saw that, like most places along the coast, the reception was spotty at best, nonexistent at worst.

He opened the hatch again and resumed his careful watch. They were rounding the southern edge now of Salem Neck; the fog was growing thicker, and they were leaving the shore behind now, though still heading south. Sean knew the captain would soon have to decide which of the two channels to choose. *My God*, Sean thought—what in the world was he to do? What if they were heading to South America, Europe—Asia even? A ship like this certainly had it in her—and he knew he couldn't stay in here forever. Sooner or later he would have to get out and…do something…

But what? How many people were aboard? Was his cousin one of them? He must be—but what if the thieves had already…already done something to Kyle, and left him—or his remains—behind? Had Sean willingly climbed aboard his own final voyage, to no avail?

A wave of anxiety assailed him. His mouth went bone dry, and for a moment he almost panicked inside his dark hiding place.

"I'll be gibbering like an idiot soon if I don't get a hold of myself," he mumbled. He did some deep breathing and tried to calm down.

No no, Sean was certain of it—his cousin was somewhere aboard this ship. He knew it, like he knew his own name. His only hope was that he might be able to find Kyle, and that he was alone. Maybe together they could do something.

He lifted the cover a little higher—yes, undoubtedly they were heading south—they had passed by Salem Channel and were now along Marblehead Channel, and would need to pass to the eastward, then southward, to avoid the huge chunk of town jutting out into the Atlantic. South America then?

Sean felt his panic galloping again, but forced it down.

It was time to do something. He knew it.

He took a deep breath.

It was the hardest thing he had ever done, what he did next: raising the cover just enough for him to slip out of his hiding place, he climbed out, and took stock.

They were coming up to Pittman Rock as they slowly cruised to the eastward, about to swing around Marblehead. Sean knew sound carried clearly over the fog-draped water, and now and then he could hear—though not see—other vessels passing them on the port side. But how could he signal to anyone through the fog? He walked a little further, his sides quivering. He came amidships and could now see the stern. In between where he stood and the stern, there were two steps going down to a cabin door. A weak light was seeping out of an open porthole window between him and the door. He crouched down and ducked underneath it. There was a sound; he froze, and his heart lurched; then he realized it was some kind of radio or television. He didn't dare look in the open window. He crawled past, then came finally to the door, after what seemed the most frightening trip of his life.

His hands and face were drenched with sweat and condensed fog. The ship slowed; something vague and ominous materialized on the starboard side; the foggy vapor drifted away a bit as they neared the object, and Sean recognized it as Cormorant Rock.

It would be relatively easy now to redeem his fool-hardy capriciousness of twenty minutes ago—he could slip over the gunwales and swim to the rock, for the ocean was calm tonight; a passing boat would see him eventually. What possible good could he do here?

And yet he couldn't leave, not until he knew whether Kyle was on board or not. He would not desert his cousin. He would answer the pathetic call for *Help*. He turned the handle of the door. It was locked.

At the same moment he heard a voice—this time unmistakably live, and human—and footsteps approaching from the bow. He froze in panic. At the last possible second he did the only thing he could do. He grabbed onto the edge of the open porthole window and lifted himself up. He saw a room inside, appointed with a white sectional sofa and blue carpeting. In the middle of the open space there was a large object, swathed in burlap and tightly bound with cables and hooks.

Aunt Sadie's bell.

Sean pulled himself through the window. He got stuck at his hips. With one last terrific yank he popped through, but his feathered ballet tights didn't quite make it. He reached behind him and pulled them through, then scrambled onto the floor, crouching beneath the window. The room was empty. He knew he had made noise when landing. He waited. The footsteps were right outside the window now. They stopped.

So, the person *had* heard him. Sean looked around frantically for somewhere to hide: nothing. He tried to make himself as two-dimensional as possible, and pulled his body into the wall, his head craned upward at the window four feet above him. A shadow passed across the opening, then a head materialized. Sean closed his eyes after he saw a black goatee poke through first. A childish part of him thought that if he shut his eyes, the man wouldn't see him. He held his breath. He knew all the man had to do was look down, and he would be discovered. The boat increased its speed with a low snarl.

A glugging wave slapped against the hull, making a light *smack*. A second later, Sean heard the footsteps again, moving off. Perhaps thinking this is what he had heard—a wave and not a stowaway—the man proceeded toward the stern.

Sean dared to breathe. He half-stood to a crouching position and put his torn tights back on. His teeth were chattering, but not from cold. He carefully approached the bell. He put one hand on the burlap, then took a few pictures of the wrapped bell with his phone.

"Help, Aunt Sadie," he murmured.

He took stock of the room. It was fairly large. One door was to his left; this turned out to be a small bathroom, as Sean had anticipated. The other portal was a door-less passage, and led to a bedroom: this was some kind of suite. A large bedspread in the pattern of leopard skin was the only remarkable feature here. A musty smell rose up around him. His eyes adjusted from the fluorescent glare of the room and he gave a little lurch backward when he saw a gun on the night stand beside the rather opulent bed. He moved closer, lest this be some kind of (tasteless, Sean thought) ornament, like a cigarette lighter or something.

No, it was a gun, and there was something sinister about such a casual display of the object: it might have been a throw pillow. His hand instinctively reached for it—this could be his ticket out of here, or certainly a defense should things get ugly—as they soon, of course, must.

But he couldn't do it. He had been brought up a Quaker. Although he was still trying to figure out the whole religion thing, one thing he did embrace: the unwavering nonviolence that was at the heart of the faith that had been in his family for centuries. *What you take into your hand, you take into your heart*, he remembered Uncle Justin telling him, when he had been talking to Sean about violence and weapons.

He didn't want to touch such a thing.

He turned and went on.

One door led from the bedroom. The sound of human voices came to him again, from the other side of the door, but not immediately against it.

Sean turned the handle. This one was unlocked. It took him three minutes to crack open the door, so slowly did he pull it back. There was a dark galley here. The human voices grew louder, though still choppy and indistinct. They were coming from the right. Sean got down on his knees. He turned around to make sure no one was sneaking up behind him—his paranoia was running at high tide now. He stuck his head out into the galley, as slowly as the rising of the moon. The dark hall was about twenty-five feet long, ending in the glassed-in bridge. There were at least two and possibly three people there, one seated at the helm.

It was undoubtedly the fanciest ship he had ever been on, and a part of him longed to trot up front to check out the gadgetry—as well as the awe-inspiring view from the deck, as the boat cut through the fog-draped water. But then his eyes riveted onto a supine lump halfway between him and the bridge: my God! It was Kyle, and he was bound and gagged, the hands tied behind his back, his feet bound at the ankles with bungee cords, and a ugly patch of duct tape smeared across his mouth. He was shoeless for some reason, and wearing the checkered shirt and tan chinos he had had on earlier, with a thin, dark-colored zip-up jacket, half open. And he seemed—unconscious. My God, he wasn't…?

Sean's heart rushed out to the lifeless form, while at the same time a sizzle of rage flared up—who were these people to do such things? He felt his eyes burning, so intently was he watching his cousin's chest, looking for some sign of life. But it was so dark in the galley—but there—yes! *Yes!* A little movement, the rise and fall of breath—and then the big toe on Kyle's right foot twitched. Thank God, he was alive!

But now what?

Sean's wondering came to a premature end. What happened next happened quickly, though later it would seem dream-like, nightmarish, and torturously long in its duration. The boat's communication system crackled to life. It was a Coast Guard vessel, making routine inquiries—or so it sounded. Sean didn't catch all of the exchange, but enough to hear that the boat was making for Grand Bahama Island. The shadowy figures in the bridge exchanged looks. The communication ended.

"All right, let's do it now then, in case they board us," the captain—or at least, the man navigating—said. He picked up a square walkie-talk-ie thing and called over the ship's public address system, "Miles, Miles. Come up to the bridge. Let's get him overboard." The man had sandy-colored hair, glasses, and spoke so casually that he might have been giving the weather report. He put the boat into neutral, got up, and walked back to Kyle. His easy manner seemed the height of monstrosity. Sean lowered himself to the shadowy floor. Thank God it was so dark where he was.

"Neil, no!" someone said, rising from where they had been sitting. It was a woman's voice. Dottie LaFrance! The rasp was still there, but gone now was all the exaggerated affectation.

"Dottie, look—we had this all out before. He's seen us all, most of all you. Take a walk. We have orders. This has to be."

The first man—the one Sean had seen first, with the bushy black goa-tee, evidently Miles—walked onto the bridge, put his hands on his hips, and watched stoically as the man Neil grabbed Kyle's ankles and roughly dragged him onto the bridge. Sean dared not move. He hoped the hallway was dark enough so they wouldn't see him, his head crouched around the corner, watching in horror.

When the man dragging Kyle passed from the galley to the bridge, the passageway was raised two inches, and Kyle's head banged as his body was pulled over the edge. Not that Sean expected gentleness from the man—after all, he was about to murder his cousin—but this small gesture spoke more about the man's monstrosity than anything else. And yet Sean pitied the man at the same time—

Goatee-man joined the first man. He yanked up the back of his slip-ping jeans, rubbed his nose, then came around to Kyle's head, grabbing him up by the shoulders. Dottie folded her arms tightly and turned away, keeping her eyes peeled out the front windows, watching the fog wraiths dance and curl across the water as the ship idled. An odd tincture of com-passion went out to her, from Sean—as if her very soul were at stake here. The first man dropped Kyle's feet, then leaned over to the control board and snapped off the ship's outer lights. This done, he grabbed Kyle's ankles again, lifted him up, and continued with the grisly chore.

They passed through the portal that led from the bridge to the deck. *Now!* a voice seemed to shout in Sean's ear, finally freeing him from his moribund inertia. He found that he was standing. He walked down the hall, as if in slow motion. Dottie heard him, and turned. Her eyes enlarged when she saw him. She backed further into her chair beside the controls.

"You!" she hissed. She looked entirely different.

Strangely, Sean nodded. Dottie seemed paralyzed—at any rate she didn't move. Sean turned from her to see the men out on the deck swinging Kyle's body back, once, twice; then they heaved him into the black water. Sean waited to hear the ugly splash. Then he burst through the open door onto the deck, as if in a dream. Keeping his eyes riveted onto the fog-draped water, he drew his hands together and took a breath. He stepped up onto the deck's railing. As if his costume was coming to his aid, he executed a perfect swan dive. One of the men grabbed for him— Sean felt the brush of his hand on his ankles—but missed.

The water, when he hit it, was cold, but not breathtakingly so. He had to find Kyle. He had to find Kyle. He surfaced, gulped air, and craned his neck wildly about. There was shouting and confusion behind him, the running of feet. He paid it no mind. Already the boat had drifted past him and was half-vanishing into the fog, like a ghastly nightmare fading to black. But where was Kyle? *Where?*

Sean dashed the water from his eyes, took another deep breath, then re-submerged. He clamped his mouth shut to stop the chattering of his teeth. The water was ink, he could see nothing.

He resurfaced again. A darker bobbing object that he mistook at first for a wave was twenty feet before him. He heard a noise and didn't realize at first it was his own frantic whimpering. He sucked another desperate breath and made for the object with all the power he had. His two flannel shirts were weighing him down. He tore them off, popping the buttons.

Oddly, the ballet tights were sticking to him now like a second skin. The silly jingle Mrs. Murphy—his first swim teacher—had taught them all popped into his mind—*Talk to the fishies, listen to the fishies.* Breathe in, turn the head, breathe out. It comforted him somehow. He reached the bobbing object. It was Kyle's jacket, puckering and buffing in the ocean. Sean clawed at it in desperation, but it was empty.

That was his worst moment. He struck out wildly for a time, then stopped, panting, gasping. He mustn't panic. He hadn't thought about his own drowning until just now. He shoved the thought back down as if it were a poison rising within. Something told him to look behind him and he saw Kyle then, bobbing, floating face down in the water. He raced for him as Kyle began submerging again. He lifted Kyle's head from the water when he reached him and ripped the soggy duct tape from his mouth. He opened one eyelid. There was life in him yet. Was he super-drugged up, or half-drowned? Sean kicked his own legs frantically, treading water, as he pinched Kyle's nose closed with his thumb and forefinger, then pushed his lips against Kyle's mouth, and blew in fiercely. Once, twice, three times. Nothing. He placed his head against Kyle's chest. There was a still a heart-beat, though it was weak and rapid.

He slung Kyle over his shoulder. But where to go? None of this would do them any good if they couldn't find land soon. But where was land? Where was west? Where was anything? Sean was fully disoriented, nor were there any moon or stars to guide him. He finally struck out in one direction, choosing. He had chosen correctly, he hoped, or they would both be dead soon. He knew this, and committed to it.

Then the ship materialized fifty yards in front of him, knifing out of the fog like a monster in a child's dull-delirium of a fever-dream. Two frantic spot-lights knifed the fog-draped water. She had come about and was hunting them down, making right for them. Sean took a deep breath, coughed, took another, then placed his hand over Kyle's mouth and nose. He dove back down, yanking Kyle with him. The searchlight danced over his head. They were just beneath the surface, it was impossible to get down deeper. His opened eyes showed Sean a large black object, blacker against the inky ocean, making for them. Streams of bubbled water clove at her approach. He kicked off frantically to the left, but they were moving in slow motion. The smooth white keel passed ten feet beside them. Sean doubled his efforts, knowing the mighty propellers would suck them in if he didn't get away. He didn't look, but swam with all the strength he had. He felt the pull as the propellers passed behind them. The hair on his head, and his right foot, were yanked back as if by a tractor beam. He heaved Kyle's body before him in one last desperate gesture. Unexpectedly, Kyle kicked him then. They broke free of the pull, then bobbed to the surface again, just in time to hear gunshots.

The scene was beyond surreal. The ship's two spotlights, coming from the bow, seemed like frantic spider legs, dashing across the water. Bright white fog wraiths glowed when the lights hit them. Thus far they hadn't been seen, due to the fog. The ship slowed, then looked as if she might be coming around again. Human voices chopped over the water, then more gunshots. Once again the ship vanished into the fog, beyond them. But Sean's hope left him. He was already exhausted.

It was then that he heard it. He shook his head, flinging the water from his ears to make sure: bells; or, rather, a bell. The soft clanging sound of a buoy bell, tolling sporadically in the night—an ominous sound on most occasions, but now music to Sean's ears. But where was it?

Clearly from this direction. He repositioned Kyle across his shoulder, swimming with one hand while his other hand held tightly to Kyle's belt at the back of his cousin's waist. Then the roar of the boat's engine, as she leapt into full throttle, passed through the water like the rumble of underground thunder. Something must have happened. Or maybe they had given up, and were now thinking only of escape.

Sean felt his face tighten in determination. They had escaped the boat and these killing people—he would not, he would *not*, let this be the end of them. He had only one enemy to contend with now—not the ocean, but his own fatigue—his dizzying head and bursting lungs. He knew he could have made the buoy ten times over by himself—he wasn't as good a swimmer as Matt, but he could hold his own with almost anyone else in Nawshant. But with Kyle, it was taking forever.

The minutes passed, and seemed to become hours. Sean stopped once to catch his breath, but when he did Kyle slid off the bare slicked skin of his shoulders, and he almost lost him to the depths. He wouldn't try that again.

His breath was coming in loud jagged gasps. His legs were starting to go numb as hypothermia set in. He closed his eyes and shoved down the thought that it would be such a comfort to stop now, just stop and sleep. *To sleep, to sleep*—where was that from? He couldn't remember. The idea of sleep seemed to take physical form inside him, a thick, comforting ooze that was slowly spilling into his limbs and heart and mind. He shook his head, and resumed his one-armed swimming.

Finally Sean's body just stopped, exhausted. He pulled Kyle's body tighter into him. What a warm comfort it was. He couldn't see the buoy, nor hear it anymore. Probably he had come in the wrong direction. He was totally disoriented again. The fog was thicker.

This was the end.

He didn't want to die—he was too young, there was too much he wanted to accomplish—but he was simply at the end of his strength. There was nothing left inside. He would've panicked if he had the energy.

Oddly, a strange peace came at him, now that he had—well, not given up, but accepted his fate. He held Kyle tighter. He supposed there were worse ways to go. He studied his cousin's face. How beautiful he was. How peaceful he looked! He was sorry he hadn't gotten to know Kyle better. He came in close, and kissed him on the forehead.

Then he let himself relax, even as his two arms encircled Kyle more tightly. His legs stopped kicking. They hovered for a moment at the water's surface, then began to submerge.

It was as they were going under that it happened. The grey swirls parted, a blur of blue–gray moonlight leaked through the fog, growing in strength like a sound—and an object took vague shape to the left of them. It was the buoy, not fifty yards away, bobbing gently back and forth, and shining in the wet moon-glow.

It was the most beautiful thing Sean had ever seen. He burst out crying as he vaulted himself upward again. A seemingly extinct volcano of strength roared up from his soul. His arms and legs were numb, but seemed to move of their own volition. He dipped Kyle under the water, then came up with him half on top of his shoulders. His right hand grabbed onto Kyle's belt again, while his left began paddling frantically. He told himself he had made it, they had made it, and rushing panic now would kill them—but he knew too that he only had this one last burst left inside him. It was now or never.

It seemed every time Sean raised his head to look, the buoy was getting further from them, rather than closer; but then quickly his frantic arm found its barnacled, rusted underpart. Half the skin on his wrist came off as he grasped onto it. He didn't care.

It would have been wiser to wait a few minutes, until he gathered his breath; but a part of Sean knew he was suffering from hypothermia already—and that went double for Kyle, no doubt—if Kyle was still alive.

Sean heaved his cousin up onto the wooden-planked platform, barely four feet across. Kyle fell back onto him, submerging them both. Sean tried it again, his mind and arms going numb. Finally Sean climbed up himself with the bloody hand, then hauled Kyle up after him, heave by heave. Kyle was nothing but dead wet weight.

Sean's entire body was shaking violently. He laid his cousin flat on his back, then placed Kyle's arms behind his head. He blocked Kyle's nose again, then blew with all his last strength into his cousin's mouth. Once, twice, thrice. The fourth time he did this, a warm spew of swallowed seawater came flying up from Kyle's lungs, into Sean's mouth. Kyle began coughing, and he drew up one leg from where it was dangling in the water. Kyle's wrists were still tied together, but somehow his ankles had loosed themselves from their bungee-cord restraints.

"Yes! *Yes!*" Sean sobbed, pumping his weary fist weakly into the air. He grew faint, and passed out, falling flat against his cousin's chest. The last thing he was conscious of was the continued coughing and retching of Kyle—and a little plaque on the inside of the buoy's iron legs. Sean read the words by the moonlight just as his body shut down:

Third Cliff Light. May, 1867

Well—my God—who would ever believe it? And yet, why not? This was Aunt Sadie's repositioned buoy that had saved their lives.

CHAPTER TWENTY-ONE
THE NO-BELL PRIZE

In Sean's dream he was swimming in deep water, rising up, up, shooting toward the surface like a slow but determined arrow. The water was icy cold; but as he drifted upward, the warmth of the sun, spangling through the water, oozed into his body like warming honey.

At the same instant that he cut through the surface of the water in his dream, he burst through the membrane between dreamers and the conscious—he woke.

Funny. He wasn't home in his bed at Greystones. Where was he anyway? There were faces around him, contorted with concern—Timmy and Regina, dressed ridiculously; Miss Sawyer and her friend Mrs. Tremont; a hovering Uncle Justin and a frantic, owl-eyed Margaret; others too, whom he didn't immediately recognize—

An easy rocking motion told Sean they were still at sea. He was lying on a stretcher in some kind of berth. Ian Munelly, one of the younger members of the Nawshant Fire Department, was rubbing Sean's arms vigorously, while Margaret was fussing and clucking beside him, crying openly, applying layer after layer of scratchy but heavenly blue Coast Guard issue woolen blankets and trying to hip-check Ian out of her way.

"He's awake, look he's awake!" someone shouted.

He stirred, turned his head to the left. Ten feet away, his cousin Kyle, bleary-eyed and pale-looking, was sitting up on his own stretcher, a blue blanket around him. He was sipping something steamy from a mug—and sobbing openly while he pointed at Sean. Kyle! Sobbing!

He must be dreaming still. Sean closed his eyes and slid back down into the delicious warmth—for now the ocean in his dream had turned tropical.

Margaret bustled out to the front hall for the fifteenth time in fifteen minutes, and peeped through the thick leaded window on the side of the front door.

"Any sign yet?" Miss Sawyer called, from the kitchen.

"No!" Margaret cried, smashing her closed fist into the palm of her other hand. "For once I wish *you* were driving them home from the hospital, Sarah, and not Justin. Can that one drive at any more of a glacial pace? I think not! *I think not!*"

Margaret and Miss Sawyer had buried (probably only temporarily) their ice-cold hatchet in light of recent circumstances. After all it was Miss Sawyer who, like a manic, convertible-driving Paul Revere, had raised the alarm along seven miles of the North Shore that Sean and Kyle were in trouble at sea with art thieves; and today was the day that Sean and Kyle were coming home from the hospital, where they had been recovering from hypothermia for the past thirty six hours.

It was a Monday, just before noon, the first day of October, and as fine a day as anyone could ask for: blue skies, a few lazy, puffy white clouds, temperatures in the low 70s, and a sweet breeze from the northwest that carried with it the scent of ripe apples and fallen leaves.

Dubiously Miss Sawyer asked, when Margaret returned to the kitchen, "Did those meringues hold, Margaret?"

"Ouf, of course they did!" Margaret snapped back. "Don't be absurd, Sarah! I don't know what happens in your own kitchen, but all cookery here in *this* house is done with scheming and perseverance—nothing is left to chance! Tell that lot out back to be quiet!"

This being Nawshant, the members of the senior class had been given a few hours off to attend the surprise welcome home party for the Sutherland cousins. Sean's landscaping clients, neighbors, police and fire people—in all more than one hundred souls—were gathered just outside the Snuggery's French doors, *most* of them invited. Long banqueting tables had been taken down from the attic, white linen table cloths starched and ironed, balloons blown up, vases stuffed with asters and chrysanthemums, and a celebratory luncheon for some 120 guests prepared by Margaret, with the assistance of Miss Sawyer, Mrs. Tremont, the Twins and their parents, most of the lacrosse and football teams, and anyone else Margaret could shanghai into stepping and fetching, pulling and hauling, or slicing and dicing. In fact it had been Miss Sawyer's suggestion that, with the crowd expected, and the sublime weather forecast, they have their luncheon *al fresco*; Margaret had dismissed this idea at first, as she said she wanted nothing in the way of Italian cookery for her lambs, as it might be too spicy for the boys in their current state. When she had been bluntly made to understand that this meant lunching outside, she agreed. "Less of a disaster for me to clean up afterwards," she had pronounced.

"*SSSSSSSSSHHHHHHHHHHHHHHHHHHHHHHHHH!!!!*" Miss Sawyer hissed, popping her head through the French doors into the back gardens. Then just to make sure—or perhaps (more likely) because it felt so good to do it—she did it again, *once more with feeling*.

"My God, that was a *tsunami* of a shush!" Regina said, daring to be the first to break the silence. No one, of course, could shush like a head librarian with several decades experience. Coupled with the audio was the added talent Miss Sawyer brought to this skill: the ability to screw up her face until it resembled something deeply unpleasant from Greek mythology, then glare around, daring anyone to defy her.

"HERE THEY COME!" Margaret suddenly roared from the front

hall. "Take your places everyone, OR YOU'LL ALL COME TO GRIEF!"

With squeals of excitement, people scattered throughout the garden. Some hid behind the 10′ x 50′ banner that proclaimed, WELCOME HOME SEAN AND KYLE—in Bookman Old Style, of course. Others ducked under the tables or hid behind the rose bushes. Regina and Timmy, with their usual flair for the dramatic, were dressed all in white, and stood in the basin of a large stone fountain, hand-in-hand, miming classical garden statuary: water nymphs, of course.

"Should I pee, to make it more authentic?" Timmy whispered.

"Don't make me laugh!" Regina hissed.

Margaret, unable to restrain herself, bolted from the front hall and raced across the front lawn like a dog after a car, Miss Sawyer gamboling right behind her. Miss Sawyer had assisted a reluctant Margaret in her dress, and both women looked like they were escapees from a *Gone With the Wind* tea party, right down to the flouncy, yard-wide hats and billowy, watered-silk gowns. Uncle Justin, with Professor Singleton in the front passenger seat, brought his car to a premature halt so as not to run over the enthusiastic, tear-splotched women.

"My lambs!" Margaret sobbed, wrenching open the back-seat door and hauling Kyle out, where he was instantly subjected to the biggest attack of gestures futile and otherwise (hugs) he'd probably received in years. Sean was getting the same treatment on the other side of the car, from Miss Sawyer and her fuchsia-colored lipstick; then everyone exchanged places. Moments later, all six of them, arm-in-arm, made their chattering way up to the house.

"Into the dining room now with the lot of you, and we'll have a fine lunch," Margaret ordered. "It looks like the both of you have been wasting away on that hospital food! And then it's upstairs with yez for a good rest!"

In truth both young men looked the picture of health, and had rebounded quickly from their ordeal at sea. There were few extra beds in

Lynn General Hospital, and so both of them had been placed in the pediatric ward, in separate rooms.

Just as everyone got seated comfortably in the dining room, Margaret called from the kitchen, "Sean! Kyle! Run out to the garden, can't you, and pick me a fresh mess of chives! A big mess, now!"

"So much for the rest," Sean chuckled, as he and Kyle exchanged looks, slouched up, and made their way to the other end of the room. They opened the French doors and stepped outside. They froze when they saw the banner—then over a hundred voices shouted out, *WELCOME HOME!* as people—scores of them—seemed to pop out of the very ground. Uncle Justin then began a rousing chorus of *For They're the Jolly Good Fellows*, which at least half of those gathered seemed to have heard before. Miss Sawyer was *not* singing: one eyebrow raised, she was checking to make sure no one was texting at this supreme moment: they had been forewarned.

Kyle jumped back, startled and scarlet-faced. Soon they were engulfed in a mass hug-in, as the Twins, Mrs. Hutchinson, many of their teachers, the lacrosse and football teams, members of the fire and rescue squads, parents of their friends, and staff members and volunteers of the library and historical society all pressed in to welcome them home. Two members of the press were there, snapping away with their cameras and jotting down comments, and Miss Sawyer was now entertaining one of these over by the punch bowl with a dramatic recounting of the car chase. Scene stealer that she was, she had just exchanged her flouncy Scarlett O'Hara hat for—a four-foot-high Tina Turner wig, which had arrived just that morning via overnight express. The original hadn't been released yet by the police. Several calls had been made over the last 24 hours (of course) from Miss Sawyer's cousin, the (ex) Governor, to the Nawshant Police; at a press conference earlier that morning, Captain Curry had announced that no charges would be filed against Miss Sawyer, "Due to extenuating circumstances."

Sean's arm grew sore from all the hand wringing, but the smile on his face never dimmed. While it could be a challenge at times to live in a small town, where else could one find this kind of loving community?

At one point Mr. Dockney, their very large Math teacher, put Sean down after lifting him up with the power of his hug, and when the former walked away to find Kyle, there was Matt standing in the recently vacated space in front of Sean. Sean tensed and felt his heart lurch, even as his smile grew wider still.

"Hey," Sean said.

"Hey yourself. How...how's it going?"

"Okay. Quite the homecoming."

"I know."

They took a step closer to each other. Matt had his hands jammed in his pockets, and now he took them out.

"I was waiting in the lobby of the hospital for like four hours last night," Matt explained, "but you had so many visitors they wouldn't let me in to see you, like."

"Oh. That was Miss Sawyer, and most of the members of the Nawshant Garden Club," Sean laughed. "They all took the freight elevator up to avoid detection. Oh, and Uncle Justin and Margaret too, going back and forth between me and Kyle."

"Only family, they kept telling me," Matt added.

"Well...in that case then, they...they should've let you go right up," Sean answered. "At least, as far as I'm concerned."

Something at the back of Matt's eyes lit up then.

"They say...everyone's saying you saved your cousin's life," Matt said, running a hand through his hair. "Good...great job, there!"

Sean was finding it hard to concentrate, so beautiful did Matt look with the sun in his hazel eyes.

"Oh, uhm, I dunno," Sean stammered. "Anybody would have."

"There was a rumor around late Saturday night that you guys had drowned," Matt added.

"Matt," Sean asked seriously, taking another step closer. "How come… are you crying?"

Matt flushed up, then set his mouth, and turned away.

"It's good to see you again," Sean said, pulling Matt back. He couldn't believe the feeling of warmth pulsing through him. And then Sean leaned in, and kissed Matt lightly on his lips.

They stepped back and looked at each other. Sean had never seen this look on Matt's face before, like he'd been whacked on the back of the head with a two-by-four. Then Ms. Clark, their school's vice-principal, suddenly cut in between them, to congratulate Sean. Matt turned and left.

"Alright everybody! Sit down! Sit down, I say! SIT DOWN!!!"

It was Margaret, standing on a chair, and it took even her two minutes to break up the throng and get everyone seated at their tables. Once at table, a fine luncheon of wild green salad, with cherry tomatoes, goat cheese, and grilled chicken, was set before them, washed down with gallons of Miss Sawyer's extra-special homemade Lavender-Mint-Lemonade. The dessert that followed, thrown together by Margaret just the night before, was a very large cake—in the shape of a bell. The Twins had frosted it this morning, and *Proclaim Liberty Throughout the Land, To All the Inhabitants Thereof* was written on its side; Regina said later that she had tried to write something about "overthrowing para-diggums" on the top of the cake—but Margaret wouldn't hear of it.

Sean and Kyle sat at the head table, with Justin (Margaret was too busy and excited to eat, she said) Professor Singleton, Miss Sawyer, Mrs. Hutchinson, Regina and Timmy, and a red-faced Matt. As the meal went on, Sean was filled in on the last missing details of the case.

"So, tell me more!" Sean said to the Twins, as he finished his first course. "You started telling me last night at the hospital before they kicked you out. What happened to you guys?"

"You won't believe this," Regina said, putting down her fork and plopping her hands in her lap. "Okay. Well, you know the whole *Satyr City* thing, and dressing up in costumes?"

"Yeah?" Sean asked.

"Well. What you really heard the man say was *Sadr City. SADR.*"

Sean made a face.

"Ahhh…what's that mean?"

"It's a city in Iraq, where there was a lot of fighting during the Iraq War," Timmy explained. "There are, as a matter of fact, three guys living in the Thicket—or they were, anyway. You were right about that much. They're soldiers, veterans from the Iraq and Afghanistan Wars. Remember Jimmy Earl?"

"Sure, God rest him," Sean answered. Sean hadn't known him well, but Jimmy was a young man from Nawshant a few years older than themselves, who had died in the wars three years earlier.

"Well, these guys served with him, and were his best friends," Regina said. "Jimmy was always telling them how beautiful Nawshant was, especially up by Linger Longer, where he used to help out with the apple picking every fall. When his three friends were discharged, they came back up here to see it, and scatter Jimmy's ashes, which is what Jimmy wanted. They didn't have any family of their own, and they thought it was so beautiful they just stayed up there, and Mrs. Hutchinson started bringing them food, without really knowing who they were."

"The one you met is still a little freaked out—Post Traumatic Stress Disorder and all that," Timmy jumped in. "That's why he shouted out *Sadr City* when you two bumped into each other that first night in the Thicket. Turns out he was as scared as you were, probably more, and he had like a…like a flashback or something. Anyway, they were the ones who first found the bell, underneath years and years of brambles. Smitty—that's the one you called *Three Spirits*, because that's what they called themselves collectively when they signed their notes to Mrs. Hutchinson—loved to ring it, in Jimmy's honor. And so that's what Mrs. Hutchinson was hearing."

"Wow!" Sean said, slowly. "And—what about when you guys vanished? I was so worried—"

"Oh, yeah," Regina continued, "right, when you cut across the clearing Saturday night, and told us to wait you mean? Right before we vanished? Two of them grabbed us—they thought we were the ones who had knocked out their friend, when all along it was Dottie's Gang. Once we explained everything, we all helped carry their friend to Linger Longer, where Doctor Hallissey was waiting. He took us all back to his house to fix him up."

"With twenty miles of bandages," Timmy laughed.

"So where are they now?" Sean asked. "You said they had been living in the Thicket—where'd they go?"

"They're ten tables down, over there," Regina said, craning her neck. "But they're all working for Mrs. Hutchinson now. And living inside in the beautiful old gate house. Linger Longer's a big old place, and needs a lot of looking after. Plus Mrs. Hutchinson doesn't like to drive anymore, so one of them is going to be her chauffeur now. I guess they didn't have much family to go home too, and they really like it up here, so they're going to stick around. They're really nice guys, and everyone loves them."

"Oh my God, so cool! That's one happy ending anyway! Kyle, you should hear this," Sean said, turning around to where his cousin was seated. But to Sean's surprise, his cousin's chair was empty.

Sean looked around and caught Uncle Justin's eye across the table. "Where'd Kyle go?" he mouthed above the hubbub.

"He just asked to be excused a minute ago, dear boy," Uncle Justin answered, leaning toward Sean. "You know how…uhm…*reticent* he is. I think this is all a trifle overwhelming for him."

Sean nodded his head. He was beginning to realize that a lot of what he thought was his cousin's attitude was just intense shyness.

"So did you get the dirt out of Kyle? Like how he knew so much?" Timmy asked. "Speaking of Kyle?"

"We talked a little last night, when he visited my room," Sean answered. "Well, you know how he first heard about the bells ringing, through the grate in his room when Professor Singleton was telling the story at dinner Thursday night. And then I guess later that night, Kyle was putting his stuff away, and when he heaved his suitcase onto the closet floor he heard how hollow it was underneath. That's when he discovered the tunnel, and snuck out that night to go up to the Thicket and check it out, at the same time I did. And though my side of the family seems to have forgotten about the bell, Kyle's side never did. I guess his grandmother on his father's side—like Uncle Justin's second cousin or something—was a real family history nut, and they knew all about the missing bell. Kyle said he grew up hearing that story, so he figured it was all true, and that the ringing bell really was Aunt Sadie's bell."

"What about the flashing lights from his room, when he was signaling with his flashlight?" Regina asked. "What was that all about?"

The light faded from Sean's eyes.

"Kyle was really close to his Mom," he explained. "I guess he just felt really lost and alone his first night up here, and he was…like signaling to her, up in…up in heaven or something. Like Morse Code. She told him when she was dying to do that, and she'd know it was him. He was like a thousand shades of red when he told me that last night, he was so embarrassed I'd seen him."

"Oh my God, that is *so sad*," Regina gushed after a moment. "I don't hate him anymore, by the way."

"That's a bummer," Timmy agreed. "Poor dude. Even a worse bummer than us losing out on the two hundred and fifty mil."

"Oh, not that again," Regina chortled, throwing her arm around her brother's shoulder.

"A man can dream, can't he?" Timmy answered wistfully. "But I guess my Maserati can wait. We'd rather have you back safe and sound anyway dude, than all the money in the world."

"That goes without saying!" Regina cried, hugging Sean for probably the twentieth time.

"So…still no word on their whereabouts?" Sean asked.

"The bad guys? No, nothing," Regina answered. "All anyone knows is that someone picked them up on a cigarette boat, and they vanished. They found the cigarette boat later, off of Georges Island, and they figure a seaplane picked them up after that."

"Who blew up their ship, the big yacht?" Sean asked.

"The paper this morning said they did it themselves, shortly after they abandoned it," Timmy sighed. "I just don't understand why they had to destroy the bell, once they knew the Coast Guard was after them and the gig was up."

"Destroy the evidence," Sean and Regina said at the same time.

"And the tunnel?" Timmy asked. "Do we know where it goes?"

"I found that out too," Sean answered. "One trail dead-ends up under Linger Longer, Mrs. Hutchinson's house, which I guess was on the Underground Railroad too. There's an old door there but it's barred and padlocked, and probably comes out in one of the old cellars up there. The other one comes out by Swallow Cave, but you'd never see it from the other end, it's hidden so well by bushes and brambles and stuff, and you can only get out when the tide's low."

"Cool!" the Twins said.

"Yeah, let's check it out this weekend," Sean agreed.

"Oh, and the painting of Aunt Sadie," Regina murmured, lowering her voice to a whisper. "Rumor has it, it showed up on the front steps of the library."

"Oh," Sean said. He looked around. "Uncle Justin and Miss Sawyer returned it late last night, around midnight. On the sly, after me and Kyle told them about it. Hopefully that will be the end of that. But keep that between us."

"Do I look like the type of guy who spreads gossip?" Timmy asked, feigning shock and touching his fingers to his chest.

"Let's not get into that now, dude!" Sean laughed.

"Well, what about you, Mister Hero?" Regina asked. "Miss Sawyer told us how she and her sister-in-law rescued you and everything, and you tracked the thieves up to Salem Neck—and then you jumped out of the car and onto the boat, just as it was pulling out. What happened?"

Her eyes—Timmy's as well—were full of admiration.

"I just...something told me Kyle was on the boat. He'd sent me a text message earlier, asking for help, right after we all got separated up in the Thicket. They...they threw him overboard, then I jumped in and we swam to the buoy. That's all. No biggie really."

"No biggie!" Timmy chortled. "Dude, you're a hero! You saved his life!"

"Anyone would've," Sean stammered.

"And kind of ironic, isn't it, that you should swim all the way to Aunt Sadie's buoy out in the Sound, no?" Regina wondered.

"You can call it ironic," Sean said, after a pause. "I really think...I think it was something else." Sean fell silent, knowing he never would have pursued the thieves, and his cousin, were it not for that strange inner voice, urging him on, telling him that Kyle was in trouble. "Oh, and check this out," he added. "Uncle Justin's already commissioned a new bell to be made, and the grave stone restored and everything, the way it was for so many years. He's already worked it out with the conservation people. There's going to be a little ceremony next spring, when the bell's done."

"Nice!" Regina said.

"We'll want you guys there, as representatives of Patrick, your great whatever grandfather," Sean added.

"Of course," Timmy said. He paused. "I'm ahhh...saving my satyr costume just for the occasion."

"Oh Timmy, give it a rest! Stop teasing Sean about that, will you?" Regina said. But she pursed her lips after she said the words. Then they all looked at each other and then burst out laughing.

God, Sean thought, *it was so good to be home.* His eyes caught Matt's across the table, and lingered there. Then he had to look away—and then look back because, of course, he was still a little OCD....

Sean woke about five, from a luxurious nap Margaret had ordered, once she'd chased everyone out of the garden at exactly 2:30. He got up, took a long shower, then dressed and went upstairs to Kyle's room. Already Sean's poison ivy was clearing up— because of his long immersion in the salt water, Margaret insisted.

Kyle had said that he wanted to speak with Sean, once things settled down a little. Oddly, Kyle's door was wide open—but his cousin wasn't here. The late afternoon sun was flooding the room in rich golden shafts. Sean walked over to the window facing eastwards, and looked out. Third Cliff was lit like a diamond, the brilliant October sun illuminating the rich rusts and browns and grays of its rock. The sea at its foot was like shimmering glass.

"I'm sorry, Aunt Sadie," Seam murmured aloud, putting his hands on the old wooden sill. "I failed you. I didn't save your bell."

At the same moment, Sean heard something in his heart—that was the only way he could explain it. A gentle, refined, but persistent voice: *You saved something much more important—our cousin.*

So vivid was this...well, message—Sean actually turned to see if someone else was there. But there was nothing. Just a sweet breeze, dancing through the curtains as it swept out of the room.

Suddenly Sean had to be up there, in person, up at Third Cliff. Margaret was still busy cleaning up the back gardens, and Uncle Justin was on the phone with more reporters, so Sean slipped out, unannounced and unnoticed.

A vermilion and purple sunset was beginning to flaunt itself across the vast, ocean-girt sky when he pushed through the last of the sumac and bayberry bushes, and walked out onto the rocks of Third Cliff, seventy feet above the ocean. The view was startling, still: panoramic, limitless, and enough to take the breath away, no matter how many times one had seen it. Like the face of a beloved, it was always different, yet always the same. But Sean froze and came up short: someone was sitting near the edge of the cliff, one knee drawn up contemplatively.

Kyle.

Sean was thinking about slipping back into the bushes and leaving Kyle with his privacy. His cousin must have sensed him though, for Kyle turned abruptly. It still came as a shock, how closely they resembled each other. With the brilliant, gathering light behind Kyle, and he in a bursting silhouette, Sean for an instant felt as if he was staring at himself. Kyle's eyes were moist with emotion.

"Oh, well, hey," he said, awkwardly but not uncivilly.

"Hi," Sean answered, walking forward. "Ahhh...I didn't mean to startle you or anything, I didn't know you were up here."

"Oh. S'no problem."

Kyle turned back around, and quickly blew his nose with a bright white handkerchief he took out of the front pocket of his red and tan flannel shirt.

Sean stood there for a moment, his hands jammed into his back pockets, not knowing what he should do.

"Room enough for two," his cousin finally called, rising up. He had been writing in a little notebook, and this he put away into the back pocket of his tan khakis.

Sean smiled, nodded, and walked over. His cousin regarded him for a moment, then folded his arms across his chest and turned back to look at the sunset. Then they both sat.

"If this isn't the most beautiful place on earth," Kyle said after a bit, "I'd sure like to see what is."

"Mmmmm," Sean agreed, so happy to hear this. He let out a deep breath. "I'm...so glad you...I'm glad you're seeing that, how beautiful it is. Up here, I mean."

They sat in a contented silence for a bit, looking out.

"Our school was up in the foothills of the Blue Ridge Mountains," Kyle finally murmured in a soft half-drawl. "And whenever we could, we'd light out for camping trips, sunset hikes, any kind of lark. One time we found this little hidey-place like this, on the edge of a cliff that just dropped down into eternity, and there laid out before your eyes was ridge after ridge after ridge, marching off to the horizon, each one a lighter blue."

"Sounds beautiful," Sean encouraged. "Ahhh…who's we?"

"Oh, me and Eric, my best friend Eric from school."

Sean was almost sorry he asked, as the topic seemed to sadden his cousin.

"Anyway," Kyle said a moment later. "I thought that was the prettiest spot on earth, till I seen this place. The ocean and all. A body could do a powerful lot of thinking up here. Or no thinking at all."

"Right," Sean agreed. "Something about it."

"You know," Kyle continued, "the ocean is so strange and new to me. But it's funny, at the same time it feels like coming home when I see it. Like I've always known it."

"It's really nice," Sean agreed. "But wait till you see the backside of those far cliffs over there. There's all grottoes and caves and what we call chimney stacks—just tall piles of rock that have separated from the mainland. I think you'll like it. I'll…take you up there sometime."

"Good deal," Kyle said. "I'd like that."

They fell silent again. A flock of terns raced the sunset west. Closer at hand, a dozen swallows, the sky's acrobats, tumbled through the velvet air, which was turning a throbbing crimson now. It was the most intense sunset Sean had seen in a long time.

"You…said you wanted to talk," Sean said. "Is now good?"

His cousin shrugged his shoulders and grimaced.

"Ahhh…sure. As good a time as any, I guess."

They were quiet for a while. Sean didn't push it. For the first time, it felt comfortable to be with Kyle—no doubt because of the cathartic experience of the other night.

"Anyways, what I got to say? I might as well say it," his cousin finally blurted, his blue eyes averting Sean's.

"I…the thing is, I…I didn't want to come up here. No way. Way up north, I mean. I guess that's no secret. And when I did, I was sure I didn't need anybody. I guess…I guess life proved otherwise."

He turned to Sean.

"Well, like I started telling you last night, you can probably figure out what happened Saturday night. I had this here feeling they'd try to take the bell that night, so I snuck up to the Thicket in the afternoon, after we-all parted. I didn't know exactly where the bell was, but I had a pretty good idea. Well, before long I heard someone ahead of me, and started following him. Problem was, it was one of those other fellows that are living up there. And he was just ahead of me when he come upon the bad guys in their front-loader. He asked them what they were doing up there, and while they were giving him the royal run-around, another one of 'em snuck around and whacked him on the back of the head with a two-by-four. Just like that. I jumped into the fray, cuz I was sure they was going to kill him. It was a hell of a fight—but there were three of them, and finally one of them stuck me with a needle when the other two got me down.

"Almost right away everything went kind of queer and far-away; and the next thing I knew, I was being lifted onto this big ol' truck. That's when I signaled you with my phone. After that I got really loopy, and then they tied me up at some point and took my phone and wallet. Oh, Uncle Justin had given me his number, and your number, and Margaret's number when I first met him down in Georgia the day I came up, and I'd entered them into my phone, that's how I was able to text you. I tried to keep awake, but I couldn't—it was like every time I tried to wake myself up, there was this big weight pushing me down back into sleep. But I woke up again when they lifted me up and carried me into their ship there."

Kyle closed his eyes and shook his head.

"It was some horrible—I was aware of everything that was happening, but I couldn't move. Not a finger."

"What a nightmare," Sean said.

"I passed out again on the boat. I knew I was in trouble, deep trouble. I kept thinking…I kept thinking how I could've used a friend right about then, and what a mistake I'd made thinkin' I could handle it all on my own. Just plain dumb and cocky. I came to a bit again later, when they dragged me out onto the deck and my head whacked on the floor there. Just when I realized that was what they were gonna do, they hurled me overboard.

"And then I…" Kyle fell silent. He turned away, and looked back at the sunset. Out of the corner of his eye, Sean could see Kyle's lip trembling. Kyle heaved a deep breath, then began again, in a voice cracked with emotion.

"The thing was, I…I knew my life was over. I couldn't hardly believe it. Even if I wasn't all drugged up, I couldn't move anyway, with my hands and feet tied. And I…well, the truth is, I ain't never learned to swim yet."

Kyle winced as he relived the memory.

"I heard you saying later the water weren't all that cold, but you Yankees sure got peculiar notions of what's warm water and what isn't. I went down some, then came up, then went down again. The water was going up my nose, and I was coughing, even though my mouth was taped. Then I guess I passed out of it again, or maybe…dunno, it was almost like I—died. Everything slowed down, like. And then it stopped. I didn't see no bright lights, or go down any tunnels like you sometimes read about, but…well, it was pretty bad."

Kyle fell silent. Before Sean knew what he was doing, he found that his arm had come up and laid itself upon Kyle's shoulder. Kyle flinched but didn't pull away. Their eyes met, and Kyle's were liquidy again, and large.

"Then…then it was like…all of a sudden it was like I was rushing through cold water, like being hauled upwards by some…some force outside myself. And though I felt I would die all over again from how cold I was, I could breathe again, really breathe, even though I was coughing plenty as I did it. I had this image of…well, this'll sound weird-o, but like a…an angel, hovering over me, holding me up, and dragging me to safety. It's no word of a lie! At first…at first…like I say this'll sound mighty peculiar, but I thought at first that maybe it was Aunt Sadie. I guess I never mentioned it, but I got this…" Kyle paused, looked away again.

"Go on," Sean encouraged, as gently as he could.

"Well, this…thing, like…like ESP or something. Where sometimes I just get these visions? Like a trance or something?"

"I figured," Sean answered. "That happened when you first looked out the window at Greystones, right? Your first night here?"

"It sure did," Kyle answered immediately. "And lemme tell you, it freaked me some. It was like I could see the wreck of the *Southern Cross* taking place—right here." Kyle tossed his head to the waters below them. "And then when I read at the library about the wreck of the *Southern Cross*, that freaked me out even more. I'd hoped I'd left all that behind me when I come up here. But it was almost the first thing that greeted me."

"So this is something you've had all your life?" Sean asked.

Kyle nodded. "Off and on. We went camping one time, the summer I turned ten, my folks and me. We picked up Gran in Tennessee, then headed west, back to where Gran's side of the family had come from. We spent the night in this old wooden cabin, and I woke up halfway through, screaming bloody murder, for I'd seen a thing in my head. This…massacre, like. All these Indians getting killed by white soldiers. Men, women, children…and a tall white soldier man on horseback watching it all, with a rifle in his hand, and long gray side-whiskers." Kyle shook his head as if trying to rid himself of the memory. "It was like I was right there, seeing it all. My parents kept telling me it was only a dream—but Gran was quiet. She knew the history of those hills like the back of her hand, for that's where all her kin were from, and it turns out I described something that had actually happened—right down to the last detail. Wasn't till I was fourteen she told me that, and told me she had it too. Second Sight, she said. She called it The Gift. But I called it a curse."

Kyle shook his head again.

"I wish a pile o' things, but I sure wish I didn't have that."

A seagull squawked as it flew over their heads.

"Well—maybe…maybe someday it will help you, somehow. And I think I have it a little too—I mean, that's how I knew you were on the boat and everything, and that you were in trouble. I guess it's a family thing."

"Like the OCD?" Kyle asked, smiling a little.

"You know—how do you know about that?" Sean asked, a little outraged.

"Of course I know! I knew about it the first night I came, when you did that…thing you do with your ball cap, three times in a row!"

"And I saw you touching the wall once we reached the top of the stairs," Sean laughed. "Because you had touched the other wall by accident with your other hand." They stared at each other, smiling, both feeling the family connection more deeply.

"It is what it is," Kyle shrugged.

"Right," Sean agreed. They fell silent again. Kyle looked away first. "So…ahhh…what else do you wish?" Sean asked after a bit.

Kyle turned and eyed his cousin. He shrugged again.

"A heap of things. I wish I didn't have this gift, like I say. I wish I didn't have the OCD thing, drives me nuts sometimes. I wish my Daddy were still alive, and that my Momma never died. I wish I could see her smiling face one last time, or hear her leading us in night prayers. I wish…uhm… I sure do wish I knew how to be friendlier, and let people in a little more. It seems… it seems there's something raw to the touch on the inside o' me, and the rough ways of the world and its people don't agree with me at all.

So I pretend to be cocky, a know-it-all—and sometimes I can't tell who's the real me when I do that all the time, you know? I...I wish I were a different person in that regard. But I'm not. And mostly I wish—"

"Yeah?"

"Well I...never mind."

Again, Sean didn't push it.

They both looked out. Now the mighty cumulus clouds, stacked in rows stretching out to the far horizon on the North Atlantic, were a deep purple, with golden light leaking out from beneath them, like gilded water spilling from behind a door. Gulls called raucously as they raced the wind home. Kyle unclenched his fists, and sighed deeply.

"Anyways, like I was saying," Kyle went on. "I got this here thing to say to you. When I started to come-to Saturday night, it was like being yanked back into the world again, and I was some glad. I guess by then you had hauled us up onto that buoy. It seemed to me like...like I say, it seemed like it were an angel that brought me back to life, because...it was like an angel was hovering over me, breathing life back into me. I...I could feel the warmth of its body on top of mine. My eyes half-opened and I...I seen its feathers. Then I *knew* it was an angel."

Under other circumstances, Sean would have laughed at this allusion to his swan costume. But someone being snatched back from death was hardly humorous; and his cousin seemed to be choking up with emotion again. Sean got the sense Kyle seldom bared his heart.

"I guess you know they found us not long after that. You were out cold by then, and I was still a little drugged up, and not sure if I were dreaming or not. I barely remember them pulling us onto the big rescue boat, and by and by they gave me some kind of other shot, and I started snapping out of it then, my head clearing and what-all. Uncle Justin was there, and Margaret too, and them friends of yours, the Twins. And a couple of fellas from the rescue squad. And I was telling anyone and everyone..."

Kyle was speaking with more difficulty now, and his breath was coming in pants. "I was …I kept telling everyone it was an *angel* brought me back to life. And, and, then I looked over, and saw you on the stretcher. You was out cold, and fish belly white, and they were working on you. And then I seen what you were wearing—I seen your feathered pants, that funny costume the Twins was wearing too. And then I knew everything that had happened. And they told me how you'd jumped onto the boat right before it took off. And it…it hit me powerful that *you* were that angel. You were the one who somehow found me in the water, and hauled me to the buoy, and breathed the breath of life back into me when I was more dead than alive."

Kyle took a jagged breath, looked away, and swallowed. He stood up, and looked down at Sean. Sean stood up to face his cousin.

Kyle turned to look at the ocean again, then he looked back at Sean and blurted, "You saved my life. You did, no question! You s-saved my life. I'd said you were over your head, and I could handle things on my own. But it was *you* saved my life. I don't know how you found me in that dark water, and hauled me up, and carried me, and swum so far with me being out like that. They was showing me on the map yesterday morning." The tears were racing down Kyle's face, and he dashed them away with his closed fist. "I jes' don't know how you did it, I know I couldn't have. But you did, and I owe my life to you." He took a snatch of breath and went on.

"I been thinking about that strange thing you said, at the breakfast table t'other morning, about what we would…proclaim to the world, if we had the chance. And this is what *I* want to proclaim now to the world: every single thing I do from now on with the rest of my life, it'll be because you saved me, and gave me my life back. Every breath I take, I'll take it because you put the breath of life back into me. If I ever have children, it'll be because of you. If I ever do any good in this world, I'll…I'll have you to thank. I don't mean to forget that. Ever. And I…I need to tell you… and I'll tell the world…that I'm *proud* you're my cousin. I'm proud and honored to belong to the same family you do."

Suddenly they were in each other's arms, there at the edge of the cliff, the day smudging into night, and Kyle holding onto Sean as if for dear life. Sean held his cousin tightly, until Kyle's sobs finally subsided, with several mighty sighs. And still they held each other, and the day left, heading off to the west with the last of the terns.

Finally they pulled back. There was nothing left of the light—just an ephemeral radiance which, if one tried to pinpoint it with the eyes, vanished. The wind had swung around to the east; and from a half-mile offshore, the faint but unmistakable clanging of a buoy bell sounded.

Sean strained to listen.

Yes! Undoubtedly it was Aunt Sadie's buoy bell, the replacement one she had put further out—the one Sean had miraculously found the other night, the one that had saved their lives.

Sean laughed.

"Do you hear bells?" he asked his cousin.

The End